Soldier of the Republic

Ben Slythe

This edition first published 2015, first edition.

Published by Yellow Plank
www.yellowplank.com

ISBN-13: 978-0956999054
ISBN-10: 0956999050

www.benslythe.com

For Mel

Part 1 - Redemption is a dish best served cold

Education Facility 7

Taeris woke suddenly. Something was different this time. He looked around his cell briefly, but even as he did so he knew such an examination was futile. His cell was one of a number of essentially identical ones cut into the rock of the asteroid. It contained nothing but Taeris. Electrically controlled cage doors blocked each cell from the corridor, but inside the cell itself there was nothing. Literally nothing. Taeris was naked, like all those sent for education, the almost perfect absence of gravity made such things as furniture pointless. Students floated in their cells, naked, until they were permitted out. Flat grey light seemed reluctant to creep into the cells from the sealed lighting units in the corridor outside, the translucent panels smeared with grime, sweat, blood, other things. Could it be a new lecture?

Opposite the entrance to his cell was a screen, mounted onto the corridor wall. This showed the lectures while the students were awake. At first Taeris, like all students, had resolutely refused to pay attention but it was the only stimulus in his entire existence and within days he had memorised all the lectures. Not many days later he would have begged for different lectures to replace the ones he already knew by heart. People went mad in their cells, quite often. Some tried to scratch their way through the solid rock of the asteroid, most of the cells had old bloodstains from such attempts. Madness was seen as a setback in the education facility but the mostly

3

automated systems still operated; routine instructions to leave the cell, attend the refectory, wash, return to the cells. Every day, or not day, the facility might operate on the day-length that Taeris remembered from his youth or it might not. Who could tell?

No, the lecture cycle on the screen, timed to wake the students at the proper time for their daily schedule, hadn't started yet. Maybe it was only imagination? As senses slowly came into sharp focus, Taeris realised he wasn't the only person to be awake. This was extremely unusual, human bodies were extremely obedient to routine and once they'd adjusted to the schedule they slept when they were supposed to; woke when that was expected of them. Whatever it was, it must have roused a number of students. There was a slight vibration in the rock walls. Taeris touched one of the bars of the door and it, too, was vibrating to his touch. Someone a way further down the corridor stifled a terrified yell. Taeris had also wondered if the block was to be vented, but it didn't feel like that. In fact it felt like the sensation of docking when a ship came to deliver students or supplies. Of course it couldn't be that. The last ship had come only seventeen sleeps ago, the next wasn't due for another thirteen.

A whimper escaped someone in a nearby cell. What did he know? Had he been here longer than Taeris? Taeris wanted to call out to him to ask what it meant. He didn't. He didn't want the answer. Everyone knew the entire cell-block could be opened to the sharp, warm vacuum of space at the touch of a button. The whimperer couldn't have ever lived through that, of course, but he could, perhaps, have lived through it happening to one of the other seven corridor-blocks that made up the facility. Taeris had never met any of the students in the other corridors, their schedules for the communal facilities were

4

different. Only, occasionally, the groaning of the recycling processor in the lobby as it had to process a whole dead person gave testimony to the fact that another block had been through recently.

Oh no. Yesterday. Was it yesterday? Maybe it was three days ago? One of Taeris' fellow students had refused to eat. Started screaming incoherently. Block-madness, they called it. The students of his corridor had been on their way back to the cells. Nobody had noticed he hadn't eaten. Then he began the screaming and the wailing. Everyone had gone back into their cells except the wild-eyed screamer. The cell doors stayed open. Taeris drifted back into the corridor. He tried to speak to the man. Just screaming, screaming. Broken. Another student drifted into the corridor, then another. Taeris and another exchanged a look. Gently they had flown over to the screamer. Taken firm hold. Spoken quietly to him. Throttled him. He must have had a name once. Now he was 'that screamer'. When it was done, hard but kind, the students returned to their cells. For the night the corpse floated in the corridor, in the morning two students towed him to the recycling unit. It groaned quietly with the effort, digesting a person. Recycling the remains into useful material. Water. Food.

Had they done it wrong? Hadn't they killed him quickly enough?

The vibration suddenly stopped. Even in the quiet of the block Taeris could sense a collective lessening of the tension among the students. Some were already making the sounds of falling asleep, passing gasses from each end as their muscles relaxed. It must be an unscheduled delivery, maybe someone so desperately in need of education that a fortnight could not be allowed to pass before he was delivered.

Taeris closed his eyes and tried to recover his rhythm but

5

no sooner had he done so than the main door at the end of the cell-block opened, a noise he'd heard thousands of times and could not mistake. Some, half fallen asleep, let out cries or whimpers, sure they were to be purged, but in a second or two everyone had realised that the air wasn't screaming from their lungs and instead they were waking up to see what was going on, a rare moment of novelty in their otherwise endless routine.

Three men entered, two armed and in the armoured uniform of the 1st Guards Regiment, one dressed smartly in civilian clothing. It was absolutely preposterous that anyone in the cell block could offer a threat that only two fully equipped guards could repel, their powered armour, lethal weaponry and enhanced senses made them more than a match for an essentially infinite number of naked men.

Taeris, along with everyone else, stared at the newcomers in disbelief. None of them had seen anyone wearing clothes since the day they arrived, it almost seemed that this experience must be pure hallucination.

Slowly the three men drifted down the corridor and, astonishingly, came to a stop directly opposite Taeris' cell. For a long moment they paused, while the civilian looked carefully at Taeris, as if confirming his identity. Large beads of sweat were stuck to the forehead and temples of the visitor, with no gravity to pull them away they stuck there like tiny marbles.

"Taeris?" He said.

Taeris looked at him blankly, talking among students was discouraged by the monotony of the routine, there was generally nothing new to be said, he hadn't been asked a question for a very long time. "Yes." He finally said.

The civilian nodded and must have done something more as the door to the cell slid open. He impatiently gestured for Taeris to follow him and he turned and made his way back down the corridor. The other students watched in amazement as he passed. Nobody could remember the last time someone had been released from EF7 and surely that must be what was happening here, surely? One or two of the students began to cry as he passed. This event would be interpreted by many of the students as hope, the possibility of redemption. In the years to come, under the bland brutality of education, that hope would slowly fade for those poor men locked away here and as it faded it would leave a deeper, darker emptiness in the hearts of every one of them. Taeris' removal, whatever the reason, was utterly cruel to those left behind.

Taeris followed his three visitors into the lobby and they all turned into the communal space. Taeris was perfectly smooth and graceful in his flowing movement, effortless movement in freefall was a legacy of his time in the asteroid. The soldiers were smooth enough, but the massively overpowered suits inevitably made it hard to avoid a slightly jerky, point-to-point style. The civilian, in contrast, seemed to have little experience of freefall. As he moved he seemed to flutter his hands and arms as if trying to flap like a bird to change direction. It was subtle, but it was obvious to people who knew how to handle themselves in space. In the communal space the civilian stopped and the other took their cue from this and brought themselves to a stop too. There they drifted, silently regarding each other. Eventually the civilian spoke. "I'm Narantael, Under-Governor of Earth. You are Taeris, formerly Legate Taeris of the Third Guards Legion."

Taeris couldn't believe that such a man was here. An Under-Governor was extremely high ranking in the hierarchy of the entire planet. Taeris had never heard of him, but Earth hadn't been much in his experience during his former career and his promotion could have been fairly recent, within the time Taeris had been incarcerated. He nodded silently, not sure what was expected of him.

One of the soldiers floated a parcel of clothing through the air towards Taeris, he caught it automatically and then looked at Narantael, waiting for some indication of what to do. In EF7 you didn't do anything that wasn't ordered. Narantael said, "Put them on."

It took Taeris a minute to get dressed, the feeling of clothing unfamiliar after so long without them, they had probably been selected based upon his size when he had last been a soldier, because they hung loosely on his wasted frame. When he finished dressing he looked to Narantael questioningly.

Narantael nodded briskly in response. "You will come with me." The two guards took hold of Taeris and pulled him along as they effortlessly made their way back out to the air-lock and through it into a small, but very well appointed cutter, fitted out for executive use. Taeris heard the lock close and detach from the asteroid and then the unmistakable lurch of his stomach that told him the jump-mass in the ship had been engaged. After that momentary feeling the ship and everything inside it would have reduced inertia or weight so acceleration felt enormously less powerful once the jump-mass was enabled. This effect happened at the atomic level, so the entire ship's effective mass was now a tiny fraction of normal and the required engine power to make it accelerate was also vastly reduced.

Taeris looked across at Narantael and finally asked, "Under-Governor, have I been educated? Have I graduated?" The question seemed the obvious one to ask but Narantael looked at him in complete surprise. He just shook his head and started working on a small data-tablet he pulled out.

Of course, the question must have seemed foolish, even

insane, in the seven years that Taeris had been in Education Facility 7 not a single person had graduated; in his experience education ended with the student's death, usually at the hard but not unkind hands of his block-mates. Whatever reason the Republic had for ending his education it could hardly be because they felt he had assimilated all they could impart. Taeris looked out of the small viewing window as the asteroid receded behind him, evidence on its surface of the facility contained within and the damage caused during its former role as a mining installation, then vanished as the engines, now clear of the immediate area around the facility with it attendant dangers, fired and the almost inertialess ship shot forward at a vast acceleration. Within minutes it would be travelling at a substantial proportion of the speed of light, flying out of the solar system perpendicular to the ecliptic, straining to reach a place where space was very, very dark. Taeris remained silent, he had no idea what was going on and any thought or hope that this might mean a return to his old life, to Laesa, to home, was something he would not let himself think. If that hope was dashed then it would be a cruelty beyond any inflicted upon him these last seven years. He must not hope. Taeris occupied himself with examining the cutter. He hadn't seen it from outside, of course, nobody would ever suggest putting windows in an education facility, but there were clues in the curves and shapes of the cabin that suggested the cutter was designed for atmosphere. Likely Narantael had walked aboard on the surface of Earth and flown out of the gravity well in this same ship. Powerful people travelled like that, something big was going on. It was a few hours of travel that was fast, but perhaps only enough so to raise a single one of Einstein's eyebrows, before the ship made ready to leap through the light-barrier and into a space of physics that would make any great 20th Century mind

9

choke on his tea. In a carefully orchestrated manoeuvre the inertial compensation was increased towards the point where the ship would have no inertia at all, simultaneously the CONAN drive reduced power, but not quite so quickly, engaging the less powerful, but fully reverse-massed of its two engines. Now, courtesy of a small jump-mass made of ionic particles being fired from the rear of the ship, those tiny pieces of matter became millions of times, then trillions of times and eventually infinitely more heavy than the entire ship and its contents. All the sensors and screens on the ship faded as the cutter powered on to many times the speed of light; no sensor designed to work on electromagnetic radiation would provide useful data at this speed. The remaining part of the 'jump' would take place at a precise, computer selected, moment. The ship would turn, its engine would fire, as the ship fell back through the light barrier the inertial compensation provided by the jump mass would be gradually disengaged as the cutter slowed. The smoothness of this technique meant that Taeris only saw the instruments drop; felt nothing of the astonishing speed as the cutter now travelled towards some unknown destination.

The Praesidium

The cutter slowed back through the light barrier after less than an hour. Since a ship could, for all intents and purposes, travel infinitely fast with a jump-mass on board the travel-time suggested that absolute haste wasn't entirely necessary, a measure of safety was included in the flight-plan.

Taeris was astonished that he could still remember such things, but remember them he could; perhaps his former life hadn't been wiped from him entirely. Nobody had spoken to him during the journey and he was far too disoriented to initiate a conversation himself. It was another five hours of rapid but sublight travel before, out of the viewing window, Taeris began to see the ruddy glow of atmosphere flowing past the hull of the cutter. Very gradually the sensation of weight began to return, as the inertial compensation was reduced. There was no sound and little vibration, of course, inertial damping reduces such physical sensations. After less than half an hour the ship began to manoeuvre for a landing and eventually came to a stop with the pads of its undercarriage just touching the ground of the landing pad.

Taeris braced himself, automatically, years of experience reasserting themselves.

There was a violent lurch and the cutter suddenly dropped onto its suspension, sinking quite discernibly as the jump mass was entirely disengaged. For Taeris that was the least of his problems. For the first time in seven years he was feeling the weight of a full planetary gravitational field act upon his body and he screamed in pain as his own flesh, now heavy, tore at his wasted bones and muscles. At first he was sure something had broken, but the pain did subside after a few moments and though it hurt to do so he was able to wiggle his fingers and toes. The pain was confusing, agony like giant claws tearing at his flesh but coupled with strange numbness in the extremities. The numb, disconnected feeling was awful but, Taeris thought, if there was going to be numbness then why couldn't it do something to ease the pain?

The guards returned and roughly dragged him onto a board-like stretcher. As Narantael calmly descended the ramp, as if walking was not that impressive a trick, the guards carried Taeris down onto the landing field and walked him towards a large building. It was impossible to see where they were going because Taeris couldn't lift his head, but as the passed through a large white pleochroic stone arch, dazzling in its beauty, he could make out the writing above it. In letters, carved into the stone above the door was the motto, 'Vox populi, vox dei'. The voice of the people is the voice of God. Only one building in the entire republic would bear such an inscription. Taeris was being carried into the Praesidium itself.

Immediately inside there was the dry, brisk sense of artificially circulated air. The Praesidium was the palace of the President. In Taeris' bewildered mind he wondered if the President himself might be waiting to meet him; if so, Taeris didn't even know if the current incumbent was the one he'd met before his education.

Many different thoughts crossed his mind. Surely they wouldn't have brought him to the centre of government for the entire Republic if their only purpose was to kill him; such a task could be carried out anywhere and even if it had been decided to kill him away from the Education Facility then he could have been thrown into space from the cutter. Perhaps he had been pardoned? Perhaps he was to be interrogated? These thoughts offered him nothing but false hope, or false fear. He forced himself to calm and await his fate.

He was carried through the impressive arched halls of the Praesidium building, he had been through many times before but his current prostrate position afforded him a stunning view of the mosaics that adorned the ceilings of every corridor and room. Every doorway was perfectly cut from dark grey granite, every room's ceiling tiled with the same sparkling white stone as the main arch, expertly inlaid with brightly coloured stone chips forming abstract but wondrous patterns.

Eventually the two guards stopped, and his stretcher was propped at an angle so he could, to some extent, see ahead of him by staring down his nose. In front of him stood a tall, thin man. On Esperia being tall and thin was hardly unusual, those born here generally were, courtesy of the relatively light gravity, not that Taeris was feeling it to be all that light at the moment. The man was also wearing an elaborate military uniform; one that would identify his rank as a Legate, the commander of a legion. These clues were not needed on this occasion, because Taeris knew him, or had known him, before his denouncement and discharge from the guards. Taeris was far too confused to make sensible conversation but the Legate, Caeranion, was more than happy to lead.

"Taeris," he said, "it's very good to see you."

Taeris knew that was a lie but he squinted at the Legate. "Caeranion? It's been a long time."

Caeranion seemed to pull himself up even higher as he surveyed the pitiful man in front of him; his patrician looks emphasised by a haughty, almost expressionless face. He took in the slender, wasted figure in front of his eyes and replied, "Too long." It was undeniably true. Taeris had been a tall, fit, muscular man, with thick black hair and a strikingly angular face. Now he was no more than half his fit weight, his hair had turned grey in the absence of fresh air and fresh food. His face now stretched across the bones of his skull like taught yellowish leather. Only someone who had been told who he was, or knew him extremely well, would have recognised him.

Taeris' mind had filled with a thousand questions, a thousand hopes. He couldn't remember the correct forms for addressing a Legate, he couldn't remember whether he was allowed to refer to himself as 'I'.

Caeranion's gaze was unwavering. "I imagine you have questions."

Taeris almost cried. Yes, he had questions, but which of them were permitted? Nobody had told him which one to ask. Taeris ventured a question that couldn't be taken as disloyal. "Could you tell me how I may serve the Republic?"

Caeranion nodded and sat in a comfortable-looking chair. No part of Taeris would be comfortable until he could get back into freefall. "The Republic faces a threat; a military threat."

The very thought of it was shocking to Taeris. Every human that lived was a Republic citizen, whether they wanted to be or not. Could this mean that some alien presence had been encountered?

Caeranion continued without pause. "The threat is from a number of traitors. Our beloved President has come to feel that our normal responses to such things will not suffice on this occasion. He feels, in fact, that someone such as yourself might offer the best way to put down this treachery."

For a moment Taeris wondered which of the two of them had completely lost his mind. Obviously Caeranion couldn't

14

mean that he would resume his role in the Guards legions. Briefly he fled to the refuge of solipsism, pretending that the entire situation was his imagination, but Caeranion was still looking at him, waiting for a response.

Taeris gritted his teeth against the pain and forced a question from his lips, "Me?"

Caeranion's face hardened. "It is not for us to question the decisions of the President."

Taeris found in the recesses of his mind a long remembered response to that prompt. "His wisdom inspires us all." How many times had he said that phrase? Had he actually understood it, or merely repeated it, like a prayer to democracy.

Caeranion looked delighted that his old friend had not forgotten everything from his former life. "As you may know, our armed forces are much smaller than they were, say, seven years ago." Someone not familiar with the histories of the two men might have thought that the span of time chosen was entirely arbitrary, but Taeris was exactly seven years out of date with his knowledge of the Republic armed forces, naturally.

Closing his eyes, casting back his mind, Taeris tried to regain any information that he might be able to use for comparison. Most of those things he'd known were no longer there, pushed into oblivion by the patriotic songs, economic lectures and inspirational speeches repeated endlessly on the screens in Education Facility 7. One thing, perhaps he could offer. "The Third Guards Legion?"

Caeranion shook his head suddenly. "No such formation exists. I believe, if memory serves, that such a unit did once appear on the order of battle, but I think it was purged after its commander was found to be sowing seeds of sedition within the legion."

Taeris was stunned, but kept his face as impassive as

possible, easier than it might have been as unaccustomed gravity was forcing a rictus to remain his only expression. His mind raced. He thought through all the implications. When the legion was purged, they surely hadn't executed the entire formation? A fully-staffed legion fielded some 31,000 troops, could the Republic have eliminated them all because of him? "Legate, do you happen to recall the form the purging took?"

Caeranion studied the taut face before him. "If I remember correctly the President ordered the legion decimated."

Decimated. So one tenth of those men had been executed after Taeris was denounced. 3,000 soldiers who had served alongside him had lost their lives because of his carelessness. "Merciful, indeed, is the President, as the entire legion was at risk of corruption."

Caeranion smiled broadly as it became clear that Taeris had learnt to follow the conventions properly. "I am humbled and enlightened by the President's generosity on a daily basis." How clever was Caeranion to be able to express so eloquently and in his own words the bald phrase 'His mercy inspires us all.'

Taeris felt he was still no closer to finding out the specifics of his job following his retrieval from the education facility. "Please, Legate, tell me what I must do." Even to his own ears, the voice Taeris used seemed weak and plaintive.

The Legate looked down at the small data screen in the table in front of him. "Our Republic needs you to be a soldier once again."

If the pain, the shock and the racing mind behind his eyes hadn't made it impossible Taeris might have laughed out loud. How could he be a soldier when he couldn't even stand? Didn't a soldier also need to be self-possessed and confident? He gathered his thoughts before responding. Obedience was the only acceptable course for anyone in the Republic, especially

16

those serving in the military. "I serve at the pleasure of the President."

It was only a moment before Caeranion nodded and spoke. "Are you familiar with the planet 'Prosperity'? In any case, there is a group of anarchists that has found a home there and they are causing the President much concern."

Taeris said, "The President must be worried for all the planet's citizens." Surely this was true? Had Taeris accidentally overstepped an invisible line?

The Legate carefully responded, "He is deeply concerned for them all."

Of course, Taeris thought, concerned was the correct word, the President must be above such human frailties as 'worry'. "The Guards must be eager to intervene?" Surely that must be true; seven years ago a Guards legion would have been sent at once to deal with the matter. After a few explicit demonstrations of the risks inherent in turning from the Republic the most despicable traitor might think again. Assuming there was enough left of his head to do any thinking.

This time there was a long pause, perhaps Caeranion was replaying Taeris' words to see if he could detect any trace of sarcasm or rebellion. "Of course the Guards leapt at the chance to serve, as would be expected, however there was something of a difficulty with the Legion in question. It seems the Legion may have been disloyal."

Disloyal? A Guards Legion disloyal? Such a thing should have been unthinkable, though Taeris had first hand experience telling him that it could happen. "What happened?" He was so shocked he didn't find a way to express it in the meandering way that citizens favoured.

Caeranion shook his head slowly in deep sadness. "The Second Guards Legion was sent to deal with the problem but they failed."

Taeris tried to frown, but it was too painful. "The Second Guards, that's your legion."

Caeranion froze and spoke very stiffly. "It was not. I was promoted to full-time staff of the Legacy five years ago."

Taeris fought an urge to blurt out something stupid. So Caeranion had been promoted, at least he saw it as a promotion. Taeris was never sure if those Legates assigned to the headquarters on Esperia were there because of exemplary service, or because they were conveniently close to the Praesidium and easy to watch for any unrepublican activities. It also stripped them of their legion, of course. "So the new Legate of the Second, perhaps, failed in his duty to inspire true devotion to the Republic?"

Caeranion still looked stone-faced. "Wishing to give them every benefit of the doubt, our President asked for a full investigation, but it appears they failed even to secure a proper landing on the surface of Prosperity. As the orders were framed by The President there is only one permissible conclusion."

Of course, only one conclusion was permissible. The decision to send them was made by The President. The orders were framed by The President. If the orders were not carried out as intended then the loyalty or competence of the legion must be the culprit, as the only other possibility was that the orders were flawed and this was unthinkable. "Did the investigation reveal the nature of the disloyalty?" This was not a trivial question. When the 3rd Guards were decimated after Taeris' denouncement their disloyalty was obvious; they had followed the orders of their commander rather than the standard, approved, general orders of the armed forces. Surely this hadn't happened again?

Caeranion studied Taeris' face, as if to see if there was any artifice in the question, but he responded after a moment, "The orders were simple. Board the Second Guards Legion on the Second Fleet. Transit to Prosperity, land and secure the entire planet, eliminating any resistance. Find and destroy any ringleaders, bring any captured back to Esperia. In general, ensure that The Republic's justice, order and protection is extended to include all of her citizens once more."

Taeris certainly had to agree the orders were simple. Much, however, had been left unsaid. Standing orders for Guards Legions included the instruction that a soldier must never retreat, not even a single step, and must advance as far as logistics permit. Seven years ago, just a little more than seven, Taeris had led his legion down onto the surface of Citaeron, flushed with the honour of taking part in the President's annual war-game. Yes, it was a large simulated battle, but it also showcased the skills of the soldiers in front of their commander in chief. For the first day Taeris had watched with pride as his men scored higher than their 2nd Legion opponents at the shooting range, over the orienteering course, repairing damaged equipment and completing hard physical tasks while in full kit. The second day was given over to the huge main event; a giant battle with training weapons. That day had been Taeris' last as a Legate.

Caeranion interrupted this recollection, "So the President has asked that you be tasked with taking command of a Regiment and settling the problem on Prosperity. He asked for you by name."

A regiment? Just one? The Second Legion would have been five times that size. "It is my duty and honour to serve." Taeris knew he couldn't ask the important questions here, not of Caeranion either. At the back of his mind something was vying for attention. Why would the President choose him for

19

this; and by name. "I assume the Second Fleet has returned and we can embark on their ships for the journey?"

The Legate didn't answer for a very long time. So long that a dark and frightening suspicion began to form in Taeris' mind. Finally the Legate spoke. "It appears that the Second Fleet may also have been..."

"Disloyal." Taeris finished the sentence himself. This was not some local problem that needed to be squashed. This was a rebellion that had eliminated one of the famed guards legions and destroyed an entire fleet. Aside from the simple loss of life, easily 30,000 must have been killed or captured, there was a more sobering thought. The armed forces of the Republic, under the President's command, had never been defeated in their entire history. Until now. No, wait. There hadn't been a defeat. The legion had become disloyal, the combat record remained intact. Well, if disloyalty was the problem then that would not be repeated. If education had managed but a single one of its goals then it had ensured that Taeris would be the most loyal soldier it was in his power to be. What remained undecided was one, tiny detail. Taeris had yet to decide whether his loyalty would be given to the Republic, the President, Caeranion or another party entirely. His loyalty was absolute, his master yet to be determined. EF7 had left him a blank slate. A robot to be commanded. He would, in time, select a commander.

"Precisely," Caeranion replied, "Now you will be eager to undertake your mission, and I suspect there is some personal work to recover your physical capabilities. Your forces are at Pandemos and I've arranged a ship to take you there, with a short stop on Citaeron to collect your chief of staff."

"Thank you. I will succeed." At the back of his mind Taeris was trying to force down any visible sign of the secret he bore. Caeranion didn't notice.

"Naturally," said Caeranion. He was right of course, success was the only possible result, the only result allowed in the Republic.

The two power-suited troops stepped forwards to take hold of the stretcher once more. As they lifted him a thought crossed his mind. "Caeranion? What happened to Laesa?"

There was a moment of hesitation before Caeranion answered. "She was reassigned, as you had no need of a woman and she is an exceptional one." There was another pause. "She was, as is not uncommon, reassigned to the person who denounced you to the President."

Laesa was indeed exceptional. A woman ideally suited to be the companion of a Legate and far too lovely and brilliant to remain unassigned once that Legate had been sent for education. The image of her had never drifted far from Taeris' mind during his stay at EF7. Sometimes he thought his fantasies of her were the only thing keeping him sane; sometimes he thought those fantasies of the woman he had lost would be the thing that would drive him block-mad. Again the soldiers carried the stretcher towards the door, as they walked through Taeris called out to Caeranion. "Now that she is yours, Caeranion, please treat her kindly." From his position on the stretcher he couldn't see if Caeranion's expression changed.

Citaeron

The wonders of medical science. Taeris had spent only two days on the small private ship that carried him to Citaeron, but in that time the medical facilities had forced calcium back into his bones, in fact toughening them beyond his old self. Muscles still took a while to regain their strength, but a course of corticosteroids and synthetic hormones had given the process a fast start. By the time the ship touched the dirt and the efficient pilot had disengaged the jump mass Taeris was able to shakily stand and walk, though with considerable discomfort. Taeris had only a short walk across the landing pad to the imposing arch that covered the entrance to the headquarters of the Second Fleet. Former Second Fleet, perhaps. Citaeron was bathed by light much softer than the sun of Esperia, perfectly white but shedding less warmth onto the surface of the rocky world. The atmosphere felt thin and sounds were tinny and high-pitched, there was also a subtle taste of something metallic in the air. The sky was very pale in colour, and with a distinctly blue tinge close to the sun, fading rapidly to colourless further away.

The walk was short and the gravity relatively low, but even so it was with great relief that Taeris found his way into the large entryway of the building and sank into a comfortable chair. The building, as was common for military establishments, was made of prefabricated carbon fibre structures formed into a skeleton, then filled with poured concrete. A dark doping agent added to the mix made the finished walls appear almost black in colour, but there was still enough texture visible to give an impression of immovable solidity. Floors were also poured, but then textured by dropping a carbon mesh into the surface to provide grip. As a building method it was extremely fast and made for sturdy buildings, but a trivial amount of time spent inside them could deliver an oppressive sense of monotony. It was his plan to walk further in search of his appointment after a short rest but he was still recovering when two men approached him. One was wearing the uniform of the Republic Security organisation, with the small badge indicating he worked for the 11th Division of that apparatus. Anyone who served in uniform knew the 11th Division well, it was responsible for military security; essentially for ensuring that the military was acting in the best interests of the Republic, or of the President, should that take precedence. These political officers had no loyalty to the military hierarchy and they sent secret reports back to the Praesidium. In the days when Taeris had been a Legate in the Guards his loyalty was assumed to be flawless and so he rarely had dealings with these people directly. This time things were obviously going to be different. Taeris felt a shiver of fear run through him as he observed this man.

The other man was a well-dressed civilian who stepped forward to shake Taeris' hand warmly. "Good morning, welcome to Citaeron."

As soon as he spoke Taeris detected the deep, slow accent of a man who not only was local to Citaeron but for whom English might be a second language. It seemed likely that the man wasn't originally from the city of Tyrenia, where they now stood, but from the smaller, remote areas around the city of Aepolia, far away on the other side of the planet. Speaking Aepolian was technically illegal, but it had never been seriously prosecuted; the scowl that crossed the Security Officer's face when he heard the voice suggested that he would be sending in a report on the matter when he had a convenient moment. "Thank you, my name is Taeris."

The Citaeronian smiled broadly and said, "Of course, we've been expecting you. I'm Salfa, one of the Governor's staff here."

The Security Officer finally spoke, but offered no hand in greeting. "I'm Adrael, your chief of staff." He almost spat out the description, clearly he was not pleased to find himself junior to a denounced guardsman, even one back in service to the Republic.

Salfa said, "What service can we provide you?"

Adrael immediately interrupted, "We will be leaving immediately, this was simply a suitable location for Taeris to join me." So it wasn't their respective ranks that was irritating Adrael, he didn't see himself as junior.

Taeris sighed inwardly, this was going to be a difficult relationship if he began it by pulling rank over Adrael, but it had to be done. "Actually, if you don't mind, I will need to visit the barracks of the Second Guards Legion before we depart. It shouldn't delay us by much." Taeris felt a look of abject pleading come across his face as he spoke. That must be new. In his former life he surely didn't beg for things?

Salfa bowed and led the way, Taeris slowly following as best he could. Adrael hung back still further giving Taeris the strong impression that his new subordinate was studying his back looking for the perfect place to stick a knife. Taeris was already berating himself for the weak and plaintive request he'd made to delay their departure. He was an officer again; if he wanted something he should demand it, not beg like a child.

It was several minutes before the three entered the

barracks, mostly because Taeris was moving so slowly. The building was low and heavy, with thick walls and few windows. Constructed around a large central courtyard it faintly resembled an ancient castle, except that the main wall was actually the outer side of a huge single building. The barracks was square, with four entrances; one in the middle of each side of the building. These would continue directly into the courtyard, with all of the entrances into the building itself coming from that central space. It caused Taeris a moment of surprise that the entire barracks seemed to be deserted, but of course a Guards Legion had no non-combatant staff and every single soldier would have been shipped off when the orders came. Was that also true of the infantry units? Taeris couldn't remember any more. Perhaps the infantry did have support units, technicians, medics, and administrators. In the Guards those functions existed but they were carried out by guardsmen themselves, as an adjunct responsibility. It led to the common phrase that 'a soldier's home is under his foot', after all, the unit moved as a complete entity, not a single component of its fighting strength was left behind. What was abandoned could be rebuilt, if needed, so Legions left basic logistics behind, things too heavy to move. One of these things was the reason for Taeris' visit to the facility.

Taeris was unfamiliar with this barracks but there was a standard way these places were laid out and he moved confidently towards the middle of the facility until he found himself at the large door securing the armoury. This space was constructed inside a structure known as the keep, a massively fortified building in the centre of the courtyard, taller and vastly more solid than the surrounding building. The keep held the combat centre, communications array, computer room and on its flat roof, defensive artillery. If the system hadn't been updated to accept his biometrics this could have been a pointless journey, but when he twisted the heavy handle the door slid open without complaint.

Inside the armoury was a treasure of military equipment, weapons of many types, tools for maintenance and communication, the engineering and electronics of war; but the real reason Taeris had put his aching muscles through the torment of the walk into the barracks was a huge piece of equipment on the far wall. In essence the device was an automated tailor, but one that only offered one outfit, the powered battle-armour of the modern infantryman. Taeris stepped into the familiar spot on the measuring platform and in seconds the system had identified the required pieces to assemble his perfectly fitted suit. Quiet and smooth machinery at the back of the armoury collected the prefabricated pieces and deposited them on a rack alongside the machine, now all Taeris had to do was to assemble the armour on his body. Seven years ago he would have managed this task in less than a minute, in fact there were often competitions in training camp to find who could set the record time. Anything under 30 seconds was outstanding, anything under a minute was good enough that the soldier wouldn't be holding up his unit. Anything over 90 seconds could earn you a great deal more practice, under the supervision of a superior soldier with impressive lung capacity and sturdy vocal cords. On this occasion he managed in a little under 10 minutes; acutely embarrassing as this agonised fumbling was in front of a civilian and a Security Officer. Adrael had probably never had to assemble such a suit against the clock but he must have seen it done frequently. If he was unimpressed with Taeris' efforts, though, he didn't reveal the fact.

Finally the suit was assembled, the seals complete.

Immediately Taeris felt like a soldier. The armour was air-tight, proof against hard vacuum, toxins, fire, water, temperature ranges of well over a thousand degrees. The powerful capacitors built into the interstitial layers and the fine, almost invisible, mesh sunk into the outer layer could absorb a great deal of energy, enough to make him proof against most small arms. The power also meant he could leap over 50 metres straight up on a planet with standard gravity; he'd manage more than 60 metres on Citaeron. Wearing such a suit a soldier could carry vast loads, over tough terrain, mile after mile, almost forever. Even if that terrain was the surface of a moon with no atmosphere, or a knee-deep pool of lava.

As Taeris stood up, he felt no strain on his muscles. The suit identified the tiniest of movements and took all the strain. Quickly bringing up the configuration options for the suit Taeris adjusted the power assistance so that the suit would not help him as much as it could. A few movements demonstrated that he had found the right balance; the suit would make him work his muscles somewhat before it took over and helped. This was an old trick, used by soldiers to help them build their own muscles, forcing them to work harder; something very useful if one day you found yourself without the aid of the powered equipment. This time Taeris was using the same technique to help him recover his strength while reclaiming the ability to move quickly and with little pain. Two strides carried him to the weapons rack and he pulled a heavy longarm from the rack, in one smooth movement reaching back over his shoulder to lock it into the retaining clips on the back of the suit. Another smooth movement and an officer's sidearm was clipped to his hip. The larger weapon would have been useless to an unarmoured soldier, at least on a planet surface. On Citaeron it weighed a little over 1000 newtons, its listed mass

27

rated at 120kg.

Salfa looked a little intimidated by the man who now stood before him, presumably the troops stationed here had rarely worn their armour when on the planet's surface. Taeris turned his gaze upon Adrael. "Do you need armour?"

Adrael scowled back but responded, "Of course not, I have armour of my own, it should be aboard our ship now."

Taeris noted that Adrael had already decided this ship was partly his, even though he'd never even set foot upon it. "Then we should go. Thank you, Salfa, you have served the Republic." Of course Salfa had done nothing, certainly nothing that required any unusual offer of thanks, but formally offering these thanks were one of the mechanisms by which the Republic pretended that its people had free will. Had Salfa refused to help, or been unable to, he might have found himself being educated inside an asteroid within hours.

The journey back to the landing pad was wonderful for Taeris. Finally he was free of severe pain, leaving just the dull ache of muscles working hard. In the Education Facility it had been impossible to work muscles properly and he found he'd missed that feeling. He was also able to easily keep up with the others; in fact he could have set a pace that would have left both of them far behind him, had he wanted to. As he walked he also modified the external appearance of his suit, usually in battle the colour was set to a matte black so unreflective that the wearer looked like a shadow rather than something three-dimensional. Out of combat each Republic unit had its own colour scheme, often of vibrant hues, and at the moment the suit was displaying the bright yellow of the Second Guards Legion. The colours of the Sixth Infantry Legion were cornflower blue with black stripes in a pattern still referred to as 'tiger stripe' despite the fact that tigers had been extinct for centuries. Regimental colours were usually displayed on the left shoulder, while battalion colours covered the right shoulder. As Taeris was the commander of the Regiment he set both shoulders of the suit to the burgundy of the 23rd Regiment and his helmet to the bright reflective silver of a senior commander.

Just a few minutes and he stood at the foot of the ramp into the spacecraft. Adrael strode confidently aboard without a backwards glance, but Taeris stopped to thank Salfa before he turned and climbed aboard. The pilot must have been aware of the importance of urgency, because the entryway had barely closed when the jump mass was engaged and the gravity fell to almost nothing. Had Taeris not been wearing the armour he would now be able to move freely with almost no exertion, but the armour had its orders and it would continue to gently resist every muscle movement Taeris undertook; he would get his strength back as soon as possible.

Pandemos

The small craft was buffeted as it fell through the windy atmosphere of Pandemos towards a landing field invisible in the white blizzard that surrounded the ship. On planets with relatively calm atmospheres the jump mass could be gently reduced in power on such a descent but here the ship fell through the atmosphere with inertia at close to normal because the vicious winds would throw the ship in random directions if the inertia was too low. Adrael looked decidedly uncomfortable as he was thrown around, something that made Taeris smile. Once you'd spent a long time in free-fall there was little your body couldn't accept in terms of movement.

Adrael stared at Taeris angrily and said, "Did you put him up to this?"

Taeris had no response. If Adrael didn't understand the way spaceflight worked then that was his problem. The descent was quite long, because the atmosphere was thick and the planet large, but that was all as expected. Adrael put his head back and began breathing deeply, trying to restrain the contents of his stomach. Taeris privately hoped that it would be a losing battle, and sure enough the ship dropped into a relatively sheltered valley at the perfect moment. The pilot instantly increased inertial compensation and the passengers suddenly felt much lighter. Adrael's tortured stomach was not happy with this sudden change, equivalent to a lift car dropping at a pretty high speed. At once Taeris was extremely grateful that the compensation was relatively low, otherwise the cabin would be filled with floating vomit. Adrael wiped his mouth and looked thoroughly miserable. Taeris ignored him.

In fact Taeris was more buffeted internally than he was by the wind. He had made a decision, one that would either prove to bring him the strength he needed or, alternatively, might have him back in EF7 before he'd even taken command of his troops. His simpering weakness in front of Adrael was in the past now, and couldn't be repaired, but he would not repeat that performance in front of his soldiers. He would act as a leader should, even though his stomach churned at the thought. He would command and be obeyed. Either he would emerge as the officer his men needed and deserved or he would be denounced for his arrogance, Adrael fearing that his lessons had not been learnt in EF7. If Adrael harboured that concern then it was baseless. Taeris had learnt a great deal from EF7 and now he had the time and space to run it all through his mind he had become, perhaps, that which Adrael should legitimately fear. Taeris now knew exactly what was expected of him and he could recite those words, bow to those individuals, obey those orders and all the time, his mind would still be working away. Adrael might not know the great secret of EF7, the one that nobody discussed. Taeris knew it well, and it was the stuff of his private terrors. He would do his duty, but not for love of the Republic. He would do his duty for hatred of it.

Moments later the ship touched down, compensation was switched off and the full effects of gravity could be felt. Pandemos was larger than Earth and its gravity was somewhat higher. Not enough to be a serious problem but enough to make everything seem heavier than it should be until you adjusted. This was one of the reasons it had become a useful training facility for the military. The ramp opened and the blizzard was allowed to gain access. Taeris bounded out in his powered armour, Adrael must have been regretting his choice to remain in normal clothing for the arrival.

Taeris turned at the foot of the ramp to look up at the pale-looking Adrael who had his arms wrapped tightly around himself. "Cold?"

"Of course I'm cold!" Adrael snapped, "I didn't know it would be this bad."

"It wasn't in the brochure?" Taeris responded as he led the way to the entrance hall for the terminal building. Immediately he regretted his flippancy. Was that the first time he had said something mocking in seven years? If so then trying out his humour on Adrael was a ridiculously poor choice.

As was generally the case when arriving on a world in the grip of terrible weather the greeting party was waiting inside the building rather than braving the weather outside. After the large steel doors had closed, shutting out the cold and the noise, Taeris saw a group of about fifteen people, most of them in armour much like his own, some in the lighter, closer-fitting pressure suits of naval personnel. One of the armoured men stepped forward and extended a hand in greeting. "Welcome to Pandemos, I'm Doloras, Adjutant of the Twenty-third Regiment, these are my senior staff and representatives of the Third Fleet, in orbit around the planet."

Taeris nodded in response, "Thank you, I'm Taeris, newly appointed Colonel of the Twenty-third Regiment, this is Adrael." Taeris didn't need to explain who Adrael was, it was only the pride of a Security man that could make someone leave his armour aboard ship on such an occasion and the officers in the room could read insignia for themselves. The group moved off slowly deeper into the complex. At first they passed the huge steel doors of maintenance bays, hangars and armouries, but as the corridor continued the environment seemed to become more conventional. Now the doors were mere person-sized, the corridors narrower and the lighting more effective. Adrael, unarmoured and unfamiliar with the local gravity, had become a little flushed in the face when the group finally turned into a large lounge and made for a central table containing food and drink. It was a tradition that might have dated back for thousands of years; share food before the serious business gets underway. In this case the food was decidedly military in that it definitely emphasised quantity over quality, however it was vastly better than anything Taeris had eaten at the Education Facility or on his recent journeys and he fell onto a plateful with great enthusiasm. Adrael, by contrast, seemed unimpressed. Perhaps the Security man had enjoyed finer foods as a matter of course, if so that was nothing that hadn't fuelled the rumour-mill forever. It was a common complaint, in fact, that soldiers uttered as they ate. All soldiers seemed to believe that their own food, while edible, clean, healthy and nutritious was still utterly disgusting and that somewhere there were people who ate much finer foods. Taeris had broadly subscribed to this theory before EF7. Now every packet of food tasted like a banquet to him.

Doloras clearly couldn't wait for information, so he was the first to break the silence. "Do you have a mission for us, Taeris?"

Taeris looked around the faces, all now staring at him. "Before we get to that there's something I must explain. Something you should all know. For the last seven years I have been subject to education, because I was denounced for unrepublican activities. Thanks to this education programme and the limitless trust placed upon us all by the President I have now been redeemed. It is my privilege to have been permitted to lead this regiment and I shall do so for as long as the

President asks it of me. I hope I can still count upon your support." A quick scan of the faces in front of him made it clear that this wasn't news to anyone in the room. There seemed to be a wide variety of conflicting emotions displayed as well. Some seemed thrilled that he had been redeemed, after all that was the stated goal of the education programme, but nobody would have been able to easily recall another case in which education had actually led to true redemption and a return to the status or rank previously held. Even the most successful students tended to be reassigned to sort vegetables for Agricorp or sweep debris clear of Transcorp's landing fields. Returning from education even to some minor technical role within public service was very rare, as citizenship was normally out of the question once a person had been denounced. Some in the room might have doubted his loyalty, others might be afraid for their own skins if his loyalty faltered once again. Adrael was studying him intently as if looking for some visual clue that the redemption was false. Security men always looked like that, though, so it was important, thought Taeris, not to let paranoia creep up on him. "My time at EF-Seven has given me a new perspective on my life and the contribution I can make to our great Republic." This time he saw his words had hit home. Education Facility 7 was one of those dark secrets that was so fascinating that everyone knew about it, even if they spoke of it only in whispers. That barren asteroid was where the irredeemable were sent; the thought of a student returning was baffling. One returning after seven years seemed miraculous, practically resurrection.

"I also have a mission, yes. The Twenty-third Regiment has been tasked with resolving the civil crisis on Prosperity. If you are not familiar with this problem, it is my understanding that a small group of dissident individuals have begun a small-scale civil war, wittering on about freedom, the way such people always do. We will attend, intervene and resolve this matter with as little actual fighting as possible, returning Prosperity to the embrace of the Republic and offering such education or reallocation as is necessary for the instigators of this little problem."

All of the assembled officers seemed to sag a little at hearing this news, which baffled Taeris, since they had to know the appointment of a new Colonel had to be presaging some form of action.

Doloras was the one to speak again. "We are familiar with this local matter, as you suggest. It is, however, possible that we are more familiar with it than you seem to be, if you'll forgive the suggestion." He threw a glance at Adrael in case he was exceeding his authority. "Might I begin by asking how the Twenty-third will reach the surface of Prosperity to enact the just resolution of the vile rebellion?"

Taeris looked around the room, confused. "We have at our disposal the Third Fleet. This will convey us to Prosperity."

Oddly this didn't seem to answer the question, but it was another who spoke up. "My name is Raephus, Captain of the battlecruiser Spica, flagship of the Third Fleet. I must first convey my apologies that the Admiral isn't here to greet you in person, he was called away on urgent business and hopes you will understand."

Taeris understood only too well. Someone wouldn't have risen to the rank of Admiral without having a clear understanding of which people he should, and shouldn't, associate with. "A pleasure, Raephus, I'm sure your fleet will provide us excellent conveyance and substantial combat support as needed."

Raephus looked uncomfortable. "Of course, Sir, that will

be our intention, and for as long as this course is ordered by the President we shall bend our every effort to it." With that Raephus had completed the necessary preamble. "My concern is simply that we avoid the same outcome as that experienced by the Second Fleet. I was merely asking if you had yet formulated a strategy for us to begin disseminating and practising so we can serve the Republic to our best ability."

Taeris felt the ground under his feet become a little less solid and chose his words carefully, what was this man talking about? Surely the details of the naval operations could be safely left up to the fleet personnel? "Thank you Raephus, for your wisdom. I confess I have yet to be apprised of the contact reports from the intervention by the Second Guards Legion and it would be premature to plan until this information is at my disposal." He threw a piercing look at Adrael. Why hadn't the Security man yet provided him with the information he needed?

Doloras spoke up at once. "Perhaps I can help here. There is no contact report for the activities of the Second Guards Legion as they never made contact. The Second Fleet was attacked and destroyed in orbit, while still carrying the legion, before a single soldier had reached the surface of Prosperity."

Taeris was now staring only at Adrael, his natural sanguine demeanour being sorely tested for the first time since redemption. "This is information of which I had not been made aware."

"So you perhaps see the wisdom of my question? Is there a strategy to protect the fleet for long enough to effect a landing?" Raephus repeated.

Taeris kept his stare firmly fixed on Adrael as he responded, "It seems I will need access to much more information before a decision can be made, but trust this:

them."

Adrael stared Taeris down as he said, "No mistakes were made. The loyalty of the personnel failed at the critical moment. They were unable to remain firm to their task. I trust this will not be a problem on this occasion?"

Taeris instantly replied, "My apologies, Adrael. You're right, of course. We will not falter."

Now everyone was staring at Adrael. Nobody voiced the obvious comment. Nobody dared. For Taeris it was clear; the 2nd Guards had died before having any opportunity to demonstrate their loyalty and as for the 2nd Fleet it had stood and fought, literally to the last man. The failure was one of strategy, not of loyalty. Of course this thought was supposed to be unthinkable. The President had established the rules of this engagement and it was his leadership that led to this disaster. Taeris pushed that thought back in his mind. Dangerous thoughts were breeding grounds for disloyalty; education had drummed that into him. He silently repeated in his mind one of the educational slogans he remembered, 'I obey the President for he is wise. I obey the orders for they bring success. I obey the Republic for it is everything. I obey.'

Taeris finally nodded. "First I must look at the readiness of the Twenty-third, then I shall visit the Third Fleet. In the meantime, I'm sure Adrael will provide me with all the information I require about the loss of the disloyal forces that were sent to deal with this problem earlier." He continued to stare at Adrael, wondering if the man would at least have the good grace to feel ashamed of his pointless secrecy. Not a sign of contrition crossed Adrael's face; he was a Republican through and through.

Adrael's face was stiffer than if it had been carved in stone.

He waited a few seconds before answering, "Any assistance I can provide to enable the Colonel to avoid the failures of previous operations will be given, of course."

Taeris was actually extremely angry that his first conflict with Adrael had been in front of a large group of men, especially those that would fall under his command, but he said, "You are gracious, Adrael."

I obey.

The 23rd Regiment

Understanding the structure of the 23rd Infantry Regiment could have been handled extremely quickly, but there was a prescribed way of doing these things and so that was how it must be done. While the exact details of which officer commanded which battalion had not yet sunk into Taeris' mind he was nonetheless able to understand the unit as a whole very easily. The 23rd, like all the front line units in Republic service, was entirely homogeneous; five identical battalions each with a Major commanding. The battalions each comprised 1,000 armoured infantry and personnel to operate the armoured landing craft and weapons attached to them. In total there should be 1,250 troops in the battalion and 125 landing craft. As the unit had been on a peace-time footing the entire unit was essentially fully staffed. Battalions in the Republic were individually numbered, and the five that made up the 23rd Regiment were the 111th, 112th, 116th, 117th and 120th. The armoured vehicles attached to the formation acted not only as craft for the last few thousand metres of the landing but also operated as armoured support and transport vehicles on the ground. These vehicles were what made the unit a fully mechanised formation and they were recent versions of a multi-role type known as the 'Tyrant'. Tyrants were a very impressive piece of military engineering. In addition to transporting eight fully equipped and armoured soldiers, their supplies, their communications devices and modest repair and maintenance facilities, these vehicles could land and lift the force from a planet, resist substantial attacks with their armoured protection and move very quickly when needed. Each was equipped with a heavy weapon in a powered turret, massively increasing the firepower of the force as a whole and, similar to the personal armour, the vehicles were camouflaged with the ability to adjust their appearance to any imaginable shade or hue and in any pattern. Environments so hostile that they could overcome the remarkable toughness of the infantry armour might still be endured if the soldiers remained inside their Tyrants. It was sometimes said that in a Tyrant the army could fight a battle across the surface of a sun; factually untrue, but not due to any weakness in the vehicle. Generations earlier an army would have deployed a range of vehicles, each with its own distinct function. In the Republic, now and for many more years than Taeris could remember, the design of modern infantry armour and the Tyrant vehicle was seen as infinitely flexible; no other equipment would or could be needed. Doctrine was firm on this point. Over the last few decades this philosophy had been extended to every unit in the military so now even the conventional infantry forces used Tyrants and Tyrants alone as their combat vehicles. Only in the Guardians could you still find a variety of equipment, and even there the range was now limited, principally to vehicles for defence or low-intensity conflict.

The parade gave Taeris ample opportunity to examine the vehicles and the armour of the men as they smartly marched past. Tyrants loomed above the tall armoured infantry, looking reminiscent of armoured vehicles of the past. The front armour, sharply sloped backwards to deflect enemy fire, the rear armour, sloped backwards as well, with a ramp door that fitted into a pressure-head almost seamlessly. From the side the Tyrant looked a little like a parallelogram in shape, except that the angle at the front was notably more acute than the one at the rear. On both sides there were infantry doors, in the middle of the vehicle, armoured and powered. They would fold open forwards on hinges to widen the protective area when infantry were leaving the vehicle. The real secret of the Tyrant's potential was contained in the four corners of the vehicle, its simple lines broken by the rounded housings of the lift engines. There was no sign externally of the power-source, the sealed lithium fusion engine mounted under the driver's seat at the front of the vehicle. No ports or hatches adorn the front of a Tyrant, the driver and gunner live by data-feeds from cameras and computers, a deliberate decision to ensure they don't place undue weight on the information from their own physical location.

Slouching atop the middle of the vehicle was a flat, powered turret. The mounting for the Viking cannon was deliberately fixed far above the head of any passing infantryman, the turret could turn a full rotation, locate its next target and engage it in a fraction of a second, while the gunner picked out the next sequence of targets inside the vehicle. It could also be programmed to over-ride and engage other threats, incoming missiles, rockets, enemies that were firing at it or its fellows. Watching the Viking swing back and forth, engaging dozens of discrete targets in a few seconds, was a sight that was memorable indeed. No enemy could ignore its potency.

While a Tyrant might look a little like any other armoured vehicle, at least in silhouette, the powered armour of the marching troops was a very different sight. The armour was tight-fitting, made of solid pieces connected at the joints, the bulk of it came from the strange assortment of lumps and shapes that defined the additional modules: the power cell, the capacitance unit, the bulky helm with its enhanced senses and the launchers for the two aerial recon drones. The additional strength enhancements were all but invisible, hidden in the slim, contoured, armour plates. An infantryman looked more like a beetle than a man, bulbous at the joints, covered in contoured bumps.

Despite the homogeneity of the force it was policy that every unit be paraded, inspected, evaluated and noted; a process that took an entire day. Everyone involved would have good reason to thank their armour as the parade and inspection was carried out in the large central square, open to the sniping wind of the hemisphere's alleged summer. After the formalities were complete Taeris asked for a private word with the Adjutant, Doloras. An office had been set aside for Taeris and it was here that the two met.

The two men were almost identical in height, but while Taeris was stringy and thin as a consequence of his long time in freefall, Doloras shared the build for more natural reasons. His light frame seemed fit enough, though, and his powered armour made him the physical equal of any soldier under his command.

Taeris looked at his officer for a moment. He hoped he appeared to be confident, but internally he was trying to remember how to sound like a soldier. Mentally he thrashed around for something positive, something he could hold in his mind that would allow him to command with fortitude. After a moment it struck him. Something Caeranion had said. The President had requested him by name. Requested him despite his status. Requested him because of his status.

Taeris spoke as soon as the door was closed, "You must lack confidence in me."

"No," Doloras replied, "The President chose you for this command and he knows far more than I ever could."

Taeris said, "Ah. I see. You are confident in me because the President is confident in me. Do you imagine the President was confident in the commanders of the Second Fleet? The Second Guards?"

Doloras frowned. His entire background was telling him that this was a trick question, one which any answer could lead to purging. "Their loyalty was insufficient, I imagine."

"Possibly," Taeris said. In that moment he decided to be entirely frank with Doloras, partly because they would necessarily work closely together but also because even in the back-stabbing Republic it was rare and suspicious for a person to denounce his own superior. "I suspect their loyalty was not the crucial element that led to their failure. In fact I suspect it was their over-confidence, their lack of proper reconnaissance and their determination to stand and fight in a losing battle, rather than adapt their plan or retreat to launch another attack in a more imaginative way."

In his entire life Doloras had never heard so many unrepublican concepts expressed in a single sentence. The military of the Republic did not retreat, did not reconnoitre and certainly did nothing in a way that might be mistaken for imagination. All this smacked of initiative, something that was drummed out of citizens throughout their lives. What he said, however, was, "Naturally I don't know what actually went through their minds, but I do know that this was one of the best legions and one of the best fleets in the Republic. Nothing they faced could have overwhelmed them if they had remained true to their oaths and orders." He paused briefly and a sly smirk crossed his face, "I believe, in fact, that seven years ago they defeated the old Third Legion in the annual war-game; is that not so?"

Taeris nodded firmly. Clearly Doloras had done his

research and had found out how Taeris had been denounced. Of course he recalled the events of that day quite differently. "There it is. Overconfidence and inflexibility." He poured them a pair of drinks, so as to make the meeting a little less formal. "I shall be doing things differently. In part this is so I can prove to the President that I have learnt my lesson, in part it is so I can hope to achieve my objectives without catastrophic losses. I need something from you, Doloras. It is possible, merely possible, that some of the orders I give may not be enshrined in the standard rules for military engagement as we all studied them. If that comes to pass I need you to carry them out anyway."

"My troops have all studied the rules as well. They won't know how to act unless they have training in this new conduct." Doloras wasn't going to allow this newcomer to corrupt him from the true course of the good Republican.

"These are not complicated orders, nor do they represent a doctrinal shift away from the standard orders and the philosophy of the Republic. It is merely the case that I might, for example, order the forces to be deployed in more than one line of defence, rather than forming them into a single block."

"But that means they couldn't all concentrate the fire of every weapon on the attack!" Doloras was stunned by this thought.

"True," said Taeris, "I had thought of that. More to the point it was my intention. As a consequence it means that the entire infantry line cannot be broken with a single movement forward. Instead an enemy would lose some of its attack on the first line, some more on the second, eventually the complexity would confuse and stop it."

Doloras stared at Taeris, a dark suspicion beginning to form in his mind. "You never said what it was that led to your denunciation."

Taeris sighed, if Doloras wanted the full story then he could have it. "Ah, yes. My former unit was chosen for a very public exercise and I won that exercise. The manner of my victory was denounced by the then Legate of the losing formation."

"This 'manner' was the decision to carry out an attack in a way not established in the standard rules?"

"Yes," Taeris said, sadly.

Doloras was now staring in open horror. "And this is the way you intend to use the Twenty-third Regiment even though the last time it was tried it led to the denunciation of you as commanding officer?"

"Again, yes."

"And what happened to the troops under your command, once you were denounced?"

"They were decimated, for failing to disobey my orders."

This time Doloras laughed aloud. "So you now offer this again as an exciting opportunity to face denunciation, decimation or worse? As a loyal soldier of the Republic I need no inducement to make me obey the standing orders, but if I needed such a prompt then the rewards awaiting those who follow your lead might well encourage me to denounce you myself, and right now."

"Clearly you have this option. Despite the unfortunate lack of successful precedent of officers denouncing their own superiors." Taeris was trying hard not to look too frightened at the thought of what might happen to him after another denouncement.

Doloras stood. "It's not an option, Colonel, it's the only proper response to your words." He strode towards the door, clearly he had assessed the danger of denouncing his new superior somewhat differently to the way Taeris' calculations had suggested.

Taeris realised he had just one chance to stop Doloras from leaving and carrying out his threat. "Of course, knowing this was my approach is the reason I was placed in command of this regiment. So clearly if someone were to denounce me then that person would be questioning the orders of the President himself."

Had the door been welded shut it could not more effectively have prevented Doloras from leaving at that moment. The Adjutant turned and stared at Taeris with a frown of concentration on his face. "I understand, I think."

That was good enough for Taeris, at least for the moment. "Following the exact standing orders was how the last attack on Prosperity was carried out. A fleet bigger than the one above our heads now, soldiers outnumbering us five-to-one and all of them absolutely devoted to the Republic, the President and the standing orders. Now let us briefly analyse the outcome of this attack. Prosperity remains outside the lawful grasp of the Republic, the mighty forces sent to liberate it were annihilated, and it was then that the President sent for me. He has implicitly asked me for my best and while the orders might be unorthodox they will also be given in the best interests of the Republic. They will undoubtedly prevail over these anarchist terrorists. I will absolutely not change my approach if the only reason to do so is the standing orders and I am confident that the President chose me for this assignment specifically because of my unorthodoxy in this regard."

Doloras didn't nod but he said, "Perhaps, sometimes, unorthodoxy may be desirable. Temporarily."

Taeris waited for a further response but it became clear after a moment that Doloras had nothing to add. "Now,

Doloras, I shall go and visit the Third Fleet. It is possible they will have questions about my leadership as well."

"Yes, Sir, they will, if for no other reason that you are not in command of them at all."

"I'm sorry?" Taeris was truly confused.

"In your former career in the Guards you may have become used to the concept that the other branches of the military fell under your command. Now you are Infantry. Nobody else has to take your orders at all."

Taeris thought for a moment. This could be a problem. Even if, like most soldiers, he generally thought of the fleet as a glorified taxi service, with the additional function of keeping the enemy away from the space directly above his head, he still needed to be able to rely on them following the same plan that he was. "So how do I issue instructions to the Third Fleet? Without them we can't even get off Pandemos."

Doloras couldn't resist a smile, "I think you'll find the fleet will follow instructions from Adrael, your security aide."

This, thought Taeris, was a definite problem. "Oh," he said.

The 3rd Fleet

Taeris was this time the one dressed strangely as the small craft carried Adrael and he up to the battlecruiser. The Spica wasn't the newest type of battlecruiser in the fleet but a mere seven years earlier, as Taeris was denounced, she was undergoing her first cruise. Taeris drank in the sight of the mighty Spica as the naval pinnace carried him along its entire length, something that Taeris thought was strictly unnecessary and he ascribed to the pride their skipper felt in the ship he served. Pride in the best of the fleet was something of which Taeris heartily approved, as his experience told him that there was a direct correlation between the operational performance of a ship and the enthusiasm of the crew. Spica was much longer than she was broad, with partially streamlined forms on the forward-facing elements of her capacitance armour. Large flat panels of steerable tmetics were spaced periodically in their toughened housings, fixed in position with no moving parts at all, and her main turrets were sunk into their barbettes and only briefly visible as each was passed. Not far away he could make out the shapes of other ships in the fleet. Long, slender, destroyers and elegantly proportioned cruisers. Mentally he compared them to the ships he remembered and he approved. The heavy-set battleships and troop ships were much less attractive than these warships with their relatively light armour. Destroyers, in fact, were almost entirely unarmoured, their speed and defences being their only protection. In the distance was the unmistakable outline of a large fleet carrier, smooth, compared to the rest of the ships, and beyond that, just visible, a battlecarrier, a hybrid of hangar bays and large tmetics with the bulky housings along its length. While the naval personnel on the ship would be wearing powered suits they would be a great deal less bulky than the armour Taeris wore. Adrael was still in normal civilian clothing and his comfort was assured in the super-light gravity on board the Spica. Everything about Adrael annoyed Taeris. The man's blithe refusal to wear powered suits except when absolutely necessary shouldn't have been one of them, but in fact it was. Was there some training course the men of the 11th directorate undertook entitled 'Irritating your fellow man'?

The pinnace came to a stop, relative to the battlecruiser, next to a large opening to the hangar bay. Taeris exchanged a glance with Adrael. This was unusual, surely? The landing slot should have been cleared during the flight so the pinnace could smoothly slide in on schedule with no delays. Adrael glared at the pilot but the wait dragged on and on. After several minutes of waiting The Pinnace began to slide into the bay and moments later was docked on one of the pressure-structures inside.

Adrael threw an angry glance at Taeris. Did he blame him for the wait? Perhaps so; the reason for the delay might have been to remind Taeris of his status on this ship, in this fleet.

The two disembarked and found Raephus waiting for them in the main dorsal corridor. There was a small amount of gravity, maintained by increasing the power of the jump mass a little at the rear of the ship. Effectively this made it easier to keep the ship free of debris, as anything would naturally float slowly aft until it encountered a bulkhead or partition. To humans, this gentle pull was almost undetectable, but it was easy enough to test experimentally. Only the larger vessels in the fleet could feather the jump mass this way so it had become shorthand among naval personnel to refer to the battleships, battlecruisers and larger carriers as 'top' ships, since they effectively did usually have an 'up' and therefore there was a top, at the bow of the ship. Naval personnel on the smaller vessels tended to use different words than 'top' to describe the top ships, often these were not particularly complimentary; among the most polite in common usage was 'sinkers'. Decades earlier the Republic had made an attempt to stop naval personnel from enjoying their habit of belittling any ship that they, personally, hadn't served within; the fleet had gently resisted such efforts. Competition between ratings, officers, entire ships, was a good way to keep everything running smoothly.

Raephus led the way, easily manoeuvring his way through the corridors. Taeris had seven years of experience in full-time freefall and was every bit as graceful. In comparison Adrael was competent but little more; moving in a series of staccato jumps and landings, never having learnt the efficient, smooth movement that came eventually to everyone who lived without gravity. Something so trivial shouldn't have made Taeris as happy as it did, but immediately he thought that if Adrael noticed and felt inferior even in so unimportant a skill then it might be yet another thing that made it harder for the two of them to work together.

It was a very short trip to the wardroom behind the bridge and the room was empty, perhaps Raephus intended the first serious discussion to be one without much input from the fleet staff.

After the three entered the room, the door soundlessly closed and Raephus spun so his back was to the main aft bulkhead and he was facing into the room. "Welcome to the

Spica, honoured guests. I trust you find her to your liking?"

Taeris was about to offer the usual platitudes but Adrael got in first, "She is impressive, Captain. I assume you've received orders to make the fleet available to me as needed?" So there it was, completely unmasked and as blunt as it was simple. When it came to the fleet, at least, Adrael was in charge.

Raephus nodded calmly, but Taeris thought there was a slight tension about the temples of the grey-haired officer. "Of course, we are happy to offer any help we can to the loyal Security Officers of the Republic."

Adrael smiled, the smile of someone holding a very good hand of cards and knowing it's too late for his opponent to do anything about it. "Please describe the Third Fleet in more detail, so I can make suitable demands on its capabilities." Adrael was starting, very slowly, to drift away from the forward bulkhead into the no-man's-land of the middle of the cabin, Taeris thought briefly about mentioning this but decided against it.

"Of course," Raephus answered. Whatever else he might be he was a military commander and he knew his order of battle as well as he knew his birthday. "You are currently aboard the battlecruiser Spica. She is the effective flagship of the Third Fleet. I am her Captain and she carries the flag of Admiral Tynaesi, who commands the fleet as a whole."

"And who is still unaccountably detained." Adrael spoke dryly.

"Who sends his apologies," Raephus continued smoothly. "Our main strike capability is provided by the fleet carrier Sextans, and we have recently added the battlecarrier Vega to our strength. We have a total of three cruisers in the fleet, two of the older Aurora Class and one of the new Leopards. We have three frigates for independent operations and on our list there appear six destroyers for defence, additionally we have been assigned three of the littoral ships for landing operations and that is how we can serve the needs of the Sixth Legion in low orbit." Taeris remembered that these littoral vessels were known as '5V' ships, but he couldn't remember why.

Adrael nodded once at the end of the description, "Excellent, Captain. Could you remind me of the distinction between a battleship and a battlecruiser?"

Raephus nodded at once. "Yes Sir. A battleship is very heavily armed and armoured, essentially a ship designed to offer the greatest individual potential in both attack and defence, to engage and destroy other large ships. A battlecruiser is generally somewhat less capable in main tmetics and less well protected. On the other hand it tends to be a more agile platform in terms of both role and movement, faster and equipped with a small fighter complement, numerous missile batteries and usually more light tmetics for fleet defence. The new battlecarriers essentially extend this model further, removing even more of the main battery for a substantial fighter complement and even more active defences. A battleship is broadly a massively larger heavy cruiser, a battlecruiser is a massively larger light cruiser and a battlecarrier is a massively larger escort carrier. This is because an escort carrier is a more balanced ship than a light carrier, intended to operate as a gunnery platform as well as a hangar. Is that explanation sufficient, Sir?"

Adrael nodded sullenly. Taeris was however curious about one piece of artful phrasing he'd detected. "Captain, why did you say that six destroyers appeared on your list?"

For a moment Raephus looked conflicted, but he finally decided how to answer, "Colonel, the six destroyers are not all effectively functional. In practice, age and a lack of maintenance parts has left three of them with much reduced capacity."

Adrael snorted, "I'm sure whatever limitations they have will be overcome by the devotion of their crews."

"In some respects you may be right, Sir." Raephus paused for a moment before continuing, "These three destroyers are no longer able to achieve mass compensation in excess of unity."

This was not something that could be cured by enthusiasm after all, if the compensation was less than unity then these ships could not jump, however loyal the crews; they were deployable only in the orbit of Pandemos. Clearly Raephus felt guilty that he had been unable to keep these ships useful and it was something that Adrael was happy to discuss as well. "How did this state of affairs come about, Captain?" Adrael chose this moment to shift his position and discovered that he was drifting helplessly in the middle of the cabin, out of reach of the wall. Taeris fought the Herculean battle of suppressing a smile.

Raephus held his tongue for a moment before replying, "Four of our destroyers are of the D-Nineteen class. All these ships are essentially obsolescent, more than ninety years old in service. No provision has been made for their overhaul in my time in the navy and eventually I was forced to borrow working components from some ships to keep the others operational. Sadly we've now reached the point where we have but one in useful condition and that is somewhat deceptive as she, D-Twenty-seven, is well below optimum."

"The other two destroyers?" Taeris asked at once, faintly hoping they might be from the E55 class.

"D-Thirty-six and D-Thirty-seven, of the D-Thirty-three class. Both are elderly but are well maintained and have experienced crews. Our frigates are newer than even our best destroyers, all three are of the F-Fifty class."

"Still," Taeris offered, "the F-Fifties were hardly the latest type seven years ago; could I ask how the Third Fleet, overall, compares with the former Second Fleet?"

Adrael opened his mouth as if to point out that it was not appropriate to discuss a unit that did not currently appear on the lists of the Republic; except to describe its part in a stupendous historical victory. He stopped himself before speaking, though. He too, perhaps, wanted to understand the differences.

Raephus thought for a moment. "The Second Fleet had two battleships, we have none, it also had one of the new Lyra class carriers, much more modern than our own. On the other hand it had no battlecruiser, no battlecarrier. As for the lighter vessels, the second was equipped with more cruisers, destroyers, frigates and littoral ships than we have, and for the most part they were newer. More importantly they had a number of light carriers, a type we lack entirely." He brought up a fleet overview on one of the active cabin walls and as they turned to see it he, very subtly, touched Adrael's elbow and steered him back to the bulkhead.

Taeris constructed the fleet in his head. He hadn't really understood how powerful the 2nd Fleet had been. Filled with new ships, configured for any conceivable type of encounter, a little local difficulty on Prosperity should have been ground into a paste beneath it with no trouble at all. In particular, the presence of battleships, heavy cruisers and frigates in quantity implied a role that was much more powerful in attack and bombardment, the lack of a battlecruiser easily balanced with light cruisers.

Adrael seemed to ignore Raephus' subtle assistance along with anything he didn't want to hear and said, "Fine, I will consider the disposition of the fleet accordingly, more importantly I believe the time has come for me to meet with the Admiral. When can I see him?"

"At once, Sir." Raephus responded to nobody's surprise; the Admiral wasn't avoiding Adrael, after all, so there would be no difficulty locating him. Raephus and Adrael immediately left the wardroom. After a moment of wondering if he was expected to wait, Taeris decided that he would head back down to the surface of Pandemos and take on his own responsibilities. Once out into the corridors he immediately became lost, something that is very easy to do in freefall, even for those familiar with it. After several minutes of aimless floating up and down companionways he found the main dorsal corridor again and followed it aft, assuming he'd recognise the hangar when he reached it. He had just located it when a young junior officer flew against the bulkhead alongside him and looked carefully at him to confirm his identification, though who else would have been wearing the full powered armour of the 6th Legion on board this ship?

"Sorry, Sir, message for you."

Taeris nodded to encourage the youngster to continue.

"Admiral Tynaesi requests that you report immediately to the bridge."

Well the good news was that the bridge would be easy to find, it lay at the other end of the dorsal corridor. Taeris nodded and pushed off from the bulkhead, noting as he flew down the corridor that the young officer was obviously impressed with his grace. He'd be much less impressed if he knew how the skills had been acquired.

The ship was not at action stations so the simple act of approaching the doors to the bridge was sufficient to make them part automatically. Taeris drifted smoothly through, hoping the designers had thought to put a suitable grab bar inside. He needn't have worried, the ship was expected to spend most of its time under effectively no gravity and there was an abundance of useful handles to bring someone to a stop. Once inside Taeris rapidly took in the scale of the bridge. Even for someone used to military technology this was an impressive environment, busy and full of equipment. Towards the rear of the room he saw Adrael, Raephus and a fat, bald man who could only be Admiral Tynaesi.

The Admiral spoke first, "Delighted you could join us," he spat.

Taeris smiled and answered, "Pleased you invited me, at last." In his mind Taeris was becoming accustomed to that lovely thought that he, personally, was the President's chosen man. He wouldn't accept anything less than the appropriate deference, even from an Admiral.

Tynaesi looked furious at that, "On board my ship you will show me respect, or I will have you removed." Adrael seemed to take a slight pleasure in this, as much pleasure as he took in anything, at least.

Taeris ignored the Admiral's comment. "What brings me here?"

Tynaesi seemed even more infuriated that he was being ignored, so it fell to Adrael to pass on the essential information. "It appears that the local rebellion is becoming somewhat less local. We have received reports that an invading force has arrived on Citaeron and is currently trying to wrest control of the planet from the local Guardians."

Taeris thought for a few moments, then he nodded emphatically. "It seems we have a war to win, gentlemen."

Return to Citaeron

Taeris hadn't been offered a cabin aboard Spica for the journey to Citaeron. Some might have felt bitter at this deliberate insult, especially since Tynaesi had been so gracious in extending an invitation to Adrael, but Taeris was entirely happy with his bunk on Littoral Ship 7. His memories of time spent on similar vessels in the past flooded back and they were good times for the most part. The troops of the 111th and 112th battalions seemed to be excited at the thought of action and even more pleased that their new Colonel had 'chosen' to accompany them for the trip.

The route out of Pandemos space took the fleet past the jump relay for Citaeron, something that was not accidental, so the very latest local information was received just before the fleet moved into jump itself. This jump was a military jump, however, and as soon as the fleet dropped back into manoeuvre speeds the inertial compensation was slashed to a fraction of its maximum. Had he been on Spica Taeris was confident he'd have been able to enjoy the discomfort this would cause to Adrael, but he was imagining it in any case.

LS7 was configured for landing operations in many ways and one of them was the provision of an extensive command suite. Taeris was there with Doloras as they jumped into the Citaeron system and they carefully studied the information pouring in to see what had changed in the brief period of communications darkness. Immediately it was obvious that what new information there was left something to be desired. The traitors had landed a substantial force around the city of Aepolia and were in the process of completing its capture. The Citaeron Guardians, the local militia, were outclassed and outnumbered; fielding a single infantry regiment against two infantry divisions. The remainder of the Guardians were concentrating on fortifying Tyrenia on the assumption that it would come under attack soon.

Doloras frowned slightly as he worked, "Why attack Aepolia first? I'd have gone for the barracks in Tyrenia."

Taeris smiled. "It's caution, on their part. See here and here? They had pockets of treason in Aepolia and these rebelled at the same time as the landing, giving the defenders too much to do at once." As he spoke Taeris pointed to the colourful complexities of the display and assuming, correctly, that Doloras would be able to keep up without difficulty.

"Ah," Doloras nodded, "My mistake, it was a good strategy."

"Oh no," Taeris smiled at him broadly, "It was a poor strategy. Those little rebellions could have tied up half the Guardians while the other half were crushed by the main attack. If they'd been bolder then both cities would be theirs already but for a few pockets of resistance."

"So we can land and protect Tyrenia ourselves."

"Yes," said Taeris, thoughtfully, "But I will not make the same mistake and be too cautious. You will lead the One-eleventh down to secure Tyrenia, along with the three battalions from the other ships. I will take the One-twelfth to Aepolia and see if I can make this caution very expensive for them."

Doloras frowned at his commander, "But one battalion? Against such a force?"

Taeris grinned carnivorously. "One battalion and the element of surprise is better than a legion that they know is coming." Doloras nodded but clearly uncertainly.

He opened the communications bubble to include the bridge crew on Spica and explained his plan. LS7 would drop off the 111th and then appear to retreat towards orbit, the other two littorals would then follow the same path. While the opposition was concerning themselves with the new arrivals, LS7 would suddenly turn into a polar approach and release the 112th a way north of Aepolia.

Adrael, naturally, hated the plan. He had been opposed to coming to Citaeron at all, given that their orders required them to liberate Prosperity, but even he had to concede that Citaeron was a more important target and that the President had no way of knowing it would come under attack when he'd given Taeris the commission. Now Taeris was suggesting dividing their forces, a concept directly opposed to the standing orders. Even worse, it seemed that behind Taeris' plan was a desire to launch a sudden attack, cause maximum damage and then withdraw. No matter if you described it as a 'withdrawal', a 'manoeuvre' or a 'tactic', this was clearly a retreat. No combat force in Republic history had ever moved away from the enemy when the option existed to move towards it. Despite this, Adrael was forced to accept the simple fact that when it came to ground operations, he was not in charge so he fumed and grumbled but changed nothing. Taeris, for his part, was finding it intensely frustrating that his plans seemed to need Adrael's tacit approval before his own troops would follow them. He was eager to get down to the surface of the planet and into action that would be too rapid and flowing to allow Adrael any time to intervene.

Taeris watched his screens in the suite alone, as the 111th dropped out into low atmosphere and began the plunge to the surface, he then had to hurry to jump into his command vehicle for the drop of the 112th, just minutes later. He was waiting all the time for the dread news that a huge traitor fleet had appeared and was going to destroy the 3rd fleet and all its vessels just as it had with the 2nd, however this news didn't come. Had the traitors failed to prepare their fleet for another large action? His Tyrant vehicle sat at the front of the drop bay, essentially the same as all the other 125 Tyrants that made up the fighting force of the 112th Battalion, though with the space for infantry replaced with a command space and somewhat enhanced protection. These Tyrants were of a later model than the ones he'd used before his denunciation but they were functionally identical, merely more powerful.

He listened as eagerly as any first-dropper for the countdown from the bridge of LS7 and as it reached zero he clenched his teeth and closed his eyes. Immediately he was thrown against his restraining straps as the powerful rams in the drop bay shot his Tyrant out into the atmosphere. In a ripple, behind him, the other Tyrants were being ejected in turn. The shaking from the wind was intense, even in the atmosphere of a planet like Citaeron, which was less dense than most. Vision became a useless blur as the vibration shook the craft, the occasional communications from other Tyrants were barely comprehensible, the speakers were being shaken so hard. In the chaos and the noise, Taeris heard that one of the Tyrants of C Company had been destroyed by fire from the surface and he immediately wondered if he'd made the drop too close. After a few minutes the vibrations eased and the craft became stable, his screens showed only one Tyrant destroyed, so clearly his judgement hadn't been too far off. Finally the formation settled into its low altitude pattern and flew, mere metres from the surface, towards Aepolia.

Contact with the enemy on the surface was not expected for some minutes so Taeris quickly scanned the status of the other four battalions. As expected there had been next to no resistance in Tyrenia and the city was simply being reinforced. Doloras was already setting up his command centre inside the old barracks. Once assured that the initial objective was well underway, Taeris turned his attention back to the attack on Aepolia.

The city was constructed in a rare piece of relatively flat terrain at the bottom of a deep, twisting canyon. The digitally plotted maps were based, in fact, on historical data as fear of heavy weapons sited in the city had deterred any of the fleet vessels from flying directly overhead. In this part of the planet the complex marbled patterns of the rocks were mostly of a reddish hue, because of the rich iron content. Taeris had plotted the assault to take place along these red canyons, to keep his forces from being vulnerable to long-range direct fire. If the rebels had expected a counter-attack they would have tried to protect these canyons but they might not have had time or the mass of weaponry necessary to defend them properly. This, at least, was Taeris' hope.

The 112th was still several kilometres from the near edge of the city when it began to come under sustained fire. Immediately the Tyrants stopped and disgorged their infantry, eight soldiers per Tyrant. This was standard doctrine, practised and perfected in countless training sessions. The Tyrants each had a heavy weapon mounted in a turret, this would provide protective fire for the infantry, but it was the infantry that would lead every attack. This approach was how the Republic fought every battle, using the infantry as skirmishers, observers, a swarm of interlocking sets of eyes and sensors, exposing little of the fighting power of the legion to danger in any single discharge of a weapon.

Almost 1,000 armoured infantry advanced in a bewildering dance of speed and power. In their armour these soldiers were hard to kill, carried weaponry far too heavy for an unaided human to lift, moved faster and further, were essentially invulnerable to environmental factors, had camouflage that made them more shadow than man and had senses that were vastly enhanced over human norms and shared their every image and datum with their comrades. Such was the Republic at war. Every infantryman and every vehicle was pouring information from its sensors into a central system, complemented by similar streams of data flowing in from the fleet above. In his command Tyrant, Taeris was seeing tight-beam feeds from over a thousand different sources, feeding information about every threat and every weakness as it appeared. Rapidly it became obvious that the defenders had found a sheltered cave-mouth, probably a mine entrance, on the outside of one of the canyon's turns and had filled it with heavy weaponry. Taeris cursed under his breath, such a trivial position shouldn't have delayed his attack this much. Doctrine would call for the mass assault of the infantry, a strategy guaranteed to overwhelm the defenders by sheer numbers; offering simply too many targets moving too quickly for heavy weapons to significantly harm, but speed was critical and Taeris could see a way of bringing the Tyrants' heavy weapons to bear without exposing them to return fire from the mine. Quickly he relayed orders to every Tyrant with a line of sight to the cave and the quick-firing Viking cannon in their turrets opened up almost together. The target wasn't the cave itself, but the cliff-face above it, and in a few seconds gigajoules of energy had poured into the rock. Because they were aiming above the enemy position, the Tyrants could stay hidden behind rocky cover, unable to see the cave mouth, but perfectly invulnerable to fire from the defenders' position. Their target was the sheer rock-face fifty metres above the entrance to the mine, the tmetic beams stitching a jagged horizontal scratch through the dense ores of the canyon. In addition to lacing the rock with cracks and holes, the energy had to escape somewhere and the super-heated iron ores exploded, tearing a huge slice of the cliff away from the canyon-side in a ragged mess of boulders and slabs. In almost no time, the cave entrance was buried and the weapons inside silenced, at least until the trapped enemy could carefully use their own equipment to dig their way out.

Rapidly the infantry climbed back into their Tyrants, but it seemed horribly slow to Taeris. Every second gave the enemy more time to prepare another line of defence and he couldn't afford to get bogged down in a dozen small wasteful encounters like this first one. As soon as possible he got the formation moving again, but this time gave orders that the entire force should not stop as soon as they started receiving fire. It turned out to be a wise precaution, within a few hundred metres the battalion passed another prepared position but this time swept past it, accepting the risk of losing a few Tyrants if the weapons were well used. In fact the position barely got the firing underway and only marginally troubled the capacitors in a couple of vehicles before the 112th made it past the next twist of canyon and was out of their range again. Twice more the battalion passed defenders in concealed positions but on both occasions the defences were ignored and caused no appreciable problems. Speed was armour, speed was surprise. Finally with one last tight twist of canyon the 112th poured out into a rapidly widening plateau over 600 metres across; in front of it lay the city of Aepolia.

As a city Aepolia was far from picturesque. Surrounded

by a fracture-pattern of straight-edged fields for grazing animals on the valley floor the city was mostly a dull sandy colour that was horribly drab compared to the amazing swirls of coloured ore that made up the beautiful patterns of the canyon walls. Aepolia was essentially constructed of concrete poured into moulds to form the shapes of repetitive buildings and narrow lanes bounded by low, thick walls. Nothing in the outskirts of the city was more than three stories in height and it all looked similar enough that it might pose real navigation problems to the pedestrian visitor. Towards the middle of the city there were a few more imposing structures, but these hardly seemed more diverse than the smaller buildings and with their height came even greater solidity, which made them seem chunky, like upscaled models rather than architecture to inspire and invite. On the far side of the city there was a shallow lake, fed by a few streams and a tall waterfall, an artifact, that flowed out of a disused mine entrance 500 metres up the cliff wall. This single piece of real beauty only highlighted the stolid ugliness of the city itself more clearly.

While it may have lacked much to attract a visitor, the architecture did make for an effective series of challenges for an invading army to overcome. The solid concrete structures and labyrinthine lanes of the city would be a hard place to take by force. Taeris had already issued his orders and he was delighted to see that the battalion was carrying them out flawlessly. Tyrants would normally have paused to drop off their infantry and then the force would have moved deliberately towards the city, engaging each enemy position as it was revealed, the infantry screening the vehicles. Taeris had ordered a different approach. Not slowing, but spreading out across the valley floor, the Tyrants charged at full speed towards the city. In just seconds the plan would either work or it wouldn't, Taeris stared at his information screen as if he could will it to change by force of mind alone.

Whoever was commanding the enemy had made the standard doctrinal decision to put huge numbers of lightly armed infantry in the outer layer of the defences, they should have been able to cost Taeris' skirmishing soldiers dearly before they were forced to retreat inside the city and begin the vicious butchery of a close-quarters battle. Had they been perfectly disciplined these defenders would have held their fire, knowing that the Tyrants couldn't simply keep charging into the city. At some point they would have to drop their infantry and if they did it too close to the city then these troops would be briefly in small groups, close together, vulnerable to area weapons and effective infantry engagement at close range. Of course it's one thing to issue orders that the thin line of defenders should hold their fire; it's quite another for a soldier to maintain that discipline as a powerful armoured vehicle bears down on him at full speed. The defenders began to open fire, first just a few of them and then, jumpy rebels feeding off their neighbours' actions, rapidly swelling until hundreds of lighter weapons were pouring fire into the Tyrants. It was useless. The Tyrants were much too well protected to run any real risk of damage but all the time their sensors were carefully identifying every window, every doorway, every loophole, every rooftop from where the fire was emanating. One heavy beam fired at close range slammed into a Tyrant, punching through its capacitance and splitting it open, destroying it. Other Tyrants returned fire automatically at that position, their computers reacting to a threat without human intervention.

Exactly as demanded by Taeris' plan the Tyrants slowed just before they reached the city, turned as a single unit and flew back down the canyon the way they had come. It was possible that among the defenders there were some who might have thought, just for a moment, that they had driven the Tyrants away. If such a notion did cross their minds then they didn't have long to enjoy their moment. The retreating Tyrants had turned their turrets back to face behind them and now the battle computers had been given enough time to carefully and automatically assign targets to each. All in a single heartbeat the massive Viking cannon on every Tyrant fired and each had its own building or window or roof to strike. Faster than the human brain could function each Tyrant then engaged its second, third and fourth targets. Every vehicle had multiple targets, ordered by the number of weapons that had been detected in each hiding place. Everywhere a Rebel had positioned himself, and foolishly fired at a Tyrant, was on the target list and the concrete walls, possibly capable of shielding a defender from infantry weapons, was overwhelmed by the power of the heavy tmetics on the Tyrants. A Viking cannon could smash an unarmoured building to powder with a single shot. Even as the 112th bunched up to disappear back into the canyon the outer edges of the city had been punctured in a thousand small surgical strikes, it took longer for the damage to fully tell, as buildings collapsed and the smoke and dust cleared; the dying would take even longer to be finished, but the screaming had begun already.

After the Battle

Taeris waited until all of the Tyrants of the 112th had made their landing in Tyrenia before he dismounted from his own craft and strode into the barracks building. In total only two Tyrants had failed to return and one of those had managed to get most of its infantry clear, they were being collected by a pair of the Tyrants of the 111th Battalion and were expected back in Tyrenia soon.

Entering the barracks this time was a much more familiar sensation; the complex was filled with soldiers, the noises of preparation, of laughter, of equipment being racked, slotted and occasionally dropped. Lounging in the main areas of the barracks were hundreds of armoured troops, none of them bothering to remove the armour as it was both comfortable and tedious to replace. Where the last visit to this barracks had been eerie, quiet, like an ancient tomb, this time it was 'military' with the appropriate noisy brashness that such places inevitably exhibit. Soldiers jumped to attention, or saluted, or at least looked guilty if they failed to do so in time as he passed, but on Taeris' face was a beaming smile and nothing sets an infantryman's mind at ease faster. One or two called out comments to him, something that was technically a breach of discipline but not something Taeris was worried about; not today.

The command centre was constructed, as was normal, on one side of the main square. Predictably Taeris guessed wrong when he entered the square and so had to walk three sides of it before he reached the suite where Doloras had made his base of operations.

Doloras immediately jumped to attention and saluted. "Lap of honour, Sir?" He said with the slightest of smiles. Obviously he'd noted Taeris' route all around the courtyard.

Taeris returned the salute as he laughed. "Doloras, may I just say, that is a fine battalion you've given me. Good work."

Doloras smiled, but replied, "I cannot take the credit. The regiment is made of good Republicans, their devotion to our President is as we would expect."

Taeris wiped the smile from his face. This was exactly the sort of thing that had got him into trouble seven years ago. Even in moments of thrill he must concentrate on showing the proper deference to the President. Silently he thanked Doloras for reminding him of this reality with a slight inclination of the head. Truthfully Taeris didn't know if Doloras was so devoted to the Republic that he might denounce Taeris for such slips, but whether the reminder was intended as a friendly gesture or as a warning it was received loud and clear. The moment might have been awkward after a few seconds, but it was at that moment that the communications channel opened up with the bridge of Spica, orbiting far overhead. Adrael, Raephus and a somewhat flustered Tynaesi sternly viewed the two officers for several seconds before Tynaesi spoke. "Taeris. Explain yourself."

Taeris frowned slightly as he tried to guess what had raised the Admiral's hackles. Nothing obvious sprang to mind. Eventually he decided he had to say something. "Admiral, I'm sorry, could you perhaps be a little more specific?"

Adrael interrupted. "The Admiral and I are both curious as to why your battalion fled the battlefield at Aepolia. Aside from the obvious fact that it is expressly against standing orders for the Republic military it is also something that will raise the morale of the treasonous enemy."

Ah, thought Taeris, Adrael had obviously described the plan to the fat Admiral and not in glowing terms. Taeris tried again to deflate the red faced Tynaesi. "Are you under the impression that we were defeated at Aepolia?"

"Worse!" Tynaesi spluttered, "Routed. Scared away from the fight. How can we win this if we let the enemy sweep us before them?"

Taeris took a moment to compose his thoughts. "With respect, we did not flee, we were not defeated and we did not fail. My mission for this particular day was to cause them a wound and retreat in good order rather than let my regiment get destroyed in endless close-quarter fighting. We inflicted a serious blow on them today."

Tynaesi was not placated. "So you say! We smacked them like a child and then ran away. What kind of battle is this for a warrior?"

Taeris nodded. "Perhaps it is not the ideal battle for a warrior, but I, Sir, am a soldier. I don't fight to prove myself brave, I fight to win objectives. Today's objective was completed, almost without loss. Naturally I'm going to have to rely on information from your fleet to tell me what damage we are estimated to have caused."

Tynaesi almost spat. "The damage you have caused is damage to the morale of the entire regiment. Such other damage as may have been involved is incidental."

Raephus mildly spoke up, "Approximately 1,500 enemy combatants dead or seriously wounded."

"What?" Tynaesi turned on him, "What does that mean?"

"You said that the damage caused to the enemy was

incidental, perhaps so. I felt we should all be acquainted with the numbers so we can see just how incidental." Somehow the almost complete lack of emotion from the quiet Captain made his pronouncement more telling.

Tynaesi clearly felt his teeth had been pulled somewhat. "In any event I imagine you'll be tendering your resignation from command, eh?"

Taeris shook his head slowly and deliberately. "Our President in his extraordinary wisdom and foresight placed this responsibility upon me and I will not relinquish it until he places it upon worthier shoulders. Or would you rather I disobey the President?"

There was a shocked silence. The Admiral carefully considered the words for a moment. Like most senior officers he had been promoted under a system overseen by the President; he had clearly not offended the President or he would not have reached his current rank; or reached his current age, come to that. He spoke the right words, understood the right responses, had denounced enough people to show he was enthusiastic about the Republic, but not so many as to irritate his superiors. What he couldn't in all conscience say was that he'd actually been personally chosen for his role by the President, not really. It was more that the President had allowed alternative candidates to fall by the wayside; and yes, some of those that wouldn't fall were pushed. Tynaesi began to think about the problem from a different perspective. If Taeris had been personally selected then perhaps he was intended to take that mandate forward as he, himself, saw fit. Admiral Tynaesi was, in fact, perfectly poised on the horns of a dilemma. Strict observance of the protocols pointed his actions in one direction; strict obedience to the President pointed him in another.

It actually fell to Raephus to break the silence. "Admiral, I have a large number of new contacts on the screen. This could be the traitor fleet."

On this occasion Tynaesi felt he knew what was expected of him. He would show a proper example to his fleet, the enemy and not least to Taeris. "Attack at once!"

In the few seconds that followed it slowly dawned upon everyone that this was the entire extent of the orders the Admiral would issue. He offered no instructions on disposition, formation, target selection. In fact he had yet to even examine the display in front of him to learn enough about the enemy fleet that he might even begin to construct a plan of action.

Taeris desperately hoped he had the Admiral enough on the back foot to press home an advantage, though it was insanely risky to try to debate someone of such rank and generally foolish to debate someone of such stubbornness. "Admiral, this seems likely to be the enemy formation responsible for the loss of the Second Fleet."

The Admiral ignored him but Adrael responded, "Assume it is, for the time being."

"In that case," Taeris said, "These enemies may be extremely dangerous."

This time the Admiral did respond, "And we shall engage and defeat them. Our mission is on behalf of the Republic."

Once again there was a quiet intervention by Captain Raephus, "Admiral, the enemy formation consists of a large number of ships, many more than our own fleet. None of them is larger than our lightest cruiser, however."

Tynaesi folded his arms with satisfaction, a broad smile on his face.

"How modern are they? How new?" Taeris asked, playing his only card and hoping the answer might sway the Admiral.

71

Unruffled, Raephus took his time. "Hmm," he eventually said, "They are all very recent vessels; much more modern, in fact, than our own, as far as I can tell"

Taeris looked at the information on his screen. He was no expert, but these vessels didn't look like warships. They looked like fast, modern merchant vessels. Varying in size from perhaps a hundred tonnes to a few thousand they had independent jump capabilities and the larger examples might carry fighters, but not in the numbers that a fleet carrier could manage. As information poured in it became apparent that they had been armed and shielded with a wide variety of equipment, no two vessels seemed identical. While larger in number and newer in construction, these vessels were reminiscent of the independent corsair fleets that had proved so difficult to find and crush across Republic space. This was how the 2nd Fleet had met its end. Not through a secret weapon, not through treason, not through disloyalty. A fleet of gunboats, sufficiently numerous, could destroy even the mightiest of battleships. Taeris grimaced to himself. He was sure he'd now understood the traitor fleet but such an attack with many small ships must have led to horrifying casualties among the rebels. Each major combatant in Republic formation must have destroyed dozens of these small vessels before falling to their attacks. How big must this fleet have been before that great battle over Prosperity? Twice the size? How could the traitors possibly command such numbers of people?

Adrael looked sharply across at the others on the bridge. "Captain, can we defeat this enemy force?"

Raephus kept his expression carefully neutral. "Those of us filled with love for our Republic, devotion to our President and staying true to his teachings are capable of extraordinary things."

Tynaesi smiled the smile of a satisfied man however Adrael could read between the lines as well as anyone and it was he who raised the question. "And if we were to prevail today; would that be an extraordinary thing?"

Raephus, this time, nodded as he replied, "Yes. Yes it would."

The Admiral had taken a little longer to catch up with the conversation. "Doctrine calls for attack." He seemed concerned that Adrael might intervene over his command, with some justification.

Adrael spoke immediately, "It does. But doctrine always calls for attack. I am wondering if there isn't a theoretically possible set of circumstances in which attack is not the best choice." To express such a thought out loud Adrael must be incredibly sure of his position. Immediately Taeris was convinced that Adrael, too, had been personally appointed by the President.

Tynaesi looked lost. "What? What kind of doctrinal classroom are you running here?"

Raephus, however, had picked up the ball and was running with it. "Perhaps there is more than one avenue of attack?" He paused and looked out of the screen at Taeris. "Colonel, do you feel that the forces you have on Citaeron are sufficient for you to complete the successful destruction of all enemy forces on the surface?"

Taeris was stunned for a moment but he felt he had to answer honestly. "No, Captain. We can probably prevent any further loss of territory, at least for the moment, but we do not have the necessary forces to launch a full-scale assault on Aepolia."

Raephus nodded carefully. "Our first duty is to provide

the Twenty-third Regiment with the support it needs, Admiral. We must at once leave this system and return with additional ground forces."

The Admiral looked around the group, confused as to what to say next. He needn't have worried, Adrael spoke up, "Captain, please arrange for the entire fleet to jump at its first available convenience." Next to him, Tynaesi looked bewildered. Hadn't his orders to his fleet just been completely ignored? How could his fleet be taken from him without even a word of protest?

Adrael had barely finished issuing his command when the communications channel dropped away. Raephus must have been quietly preparing for that exact order for some time. Taeris looked at Doloras with wide eyes. They were now alone; no fleet to protect them and an enemy fleet above. Doloras clenched his teeth thoughtfully and finally said, "So, we should probably begin putting a plan together."

Taeris nodded. "We attack," he said without a hint of irony.

Doloras looked at him, expressionless. "Naturally, Sir."

The Guardians

Taeris stared calmly at the officer before him. Brigadier Chasfaen certainly wore the uniform of a soldier, he clearly believed himself to be a soldier, he stuck his chin out as if to demand the respect due a soldier. There was something missing, however, in his constitution that made Taeris think he wasn't really a soldier at all.

"We've been somewhat depleted by the cowardice or disloyalty of the Second Guardian Regiment but we retain one full infantry regiment and a battalion of mechanised troops." This was, it seemed, what Chasfaen felt was a complete accounting of the state of his brigade. "Now, Colonel, if you would give me the current situations and dispositions the troops you have brought us?"

Taeris swallowed an exclamation of surprise. Of course, Chasfaen was the ranking officer. Because the Guardians were an irregular formation and often perceived as little more than a joke by the professional soldiery Taeris hadn't even considered the thought that he might fall under the command of such a person. Life in the Guards had certainly been a different experience. Putting the thought behind him, for the moment, Taeris forced his face into the blank expression soldiers learnt in basic training. "Yes Sir. The Twenty-third Infantry Regiment has five, fully equipped, mechanised battalions. After the One-twelfth scored a victory at Aepolia I've put them on rest, the other four are on standby in the barracks."

"Victory, eh?" Chasfaen chortled, "I dare say if we have a few more 'victories' like that we might lose the entire planet, no?"

"Yes Sir." Taeris knew when an officer just wanted his opinion validated.

Chasfaen dropped his cheerful affect. "Well we can't have the troops just laying about the barracks making it look untidy, can we? I'm going to inspect the troops and while I do, you can work out where to send each battalion to engage the enemy where he is most intractable."

Taeris' face remained perfectly still. If there was one, single, absolute rule of successful strategy it was to engage the enemy where he was the least intractable; asleep if you could possibly arrange it. Even the optimistic doctrines of the Republic permitted a commander to attack where the enemy was at his weakest; Chasfaen was clearly an idiot. He said, "Yes Sir."

Chasfaen strolled off with a genial expression, followed by Doloras; already tapping on his communicator to ready the regiment for this unannounced inspection. This was, ultimately, the result of the indoctrination of the military in the Republic. Men like Chasfaen wanted to find where the enemy was strongest and fight them there, proving courage, loyalty and supremacy. In Chasfaen's mind an enemy could be shattered in such an attack, their morale crushed. Obviously history had countless examples where that strategy had been successful, most of them were on the curriculum in the officer training courses, but the reason they were so successful and so notable was their rarity. History also recounted the grinding trench-warfare and endless, pointless sieges that cost thousands of lives and eventually led to the downfall of empires.

Taeris turned his attention to the alleged brigade he could

now count as allied. The single infantry regiment was far from fully staffed; even though the unit was supposed to be somewhat smaller than the 23rd, lacking the latter's vehicles and crew, it should still have carried approximately 5,000 infantry. In fact the most recent muster showed only a little over 2,000 had reported for duty. In the mechanised battalion the news was even worse. In the regular army a unit counted as 'mechanised' if it had armoured its infantry, equipped them with fully integrated landing and support vehicles and those vehicles carried heavy support weapons. A Republic mechanised battalion was arguably more heavily equipped than an armoured battalion would have been during the time of the heavy tank. This battalion only fielded three companies, all were comprised of armoured troops but none had more than 180 of the 200 they were intended to field; worse, they relied exclusively upon their powered armour for their mobility. The only vehicles were five obsolescent Vulture armoured fighting vehicles, all in working order and all nominally attached to 'A' Company for the fire support role. The Vulture had been a useful piece of equipment thirty years ago, perhaps forty; its protection scheme was far too heavily skewed to resisting explosive damage for a modern battlefield and as a consequence it was too heavy, too slow and carried a large but slow-firing weapon that was essentially useless against aerial targets and armoured infantry. The five of them together might have matched the fighting power of a single Tyrant commanded by a good pilot, and these days Tyrants were kept safe behind skirmish lines of infantry because they were too vulnerable, imagine the vulnerability of these obsolescent Vultures. One mechanised battalion, when marked as such on a map, implied a fighting force of 1,000 armoured troops supported by 125 armoured vehicles each with two fighting crew. Instead the formation the Guardians fielded was 500 strong, of unknown quality, supported by five old battlewagons. As he was now alone Taeris allowed a soft sigh to escape his lips and he then turned and strode outside to see the waiting brigade and identify for what, if anything, it could be profitably employed.

In fairness the troops, once they dropped their mugs and formed themselves into a semblance of order, looked like a reasonably fit and competent group. It appeared that they'd taken the time to spray slogans of loyalty to the President on the sides of the Vultures in black and a quick check of the vehicles showed they were in good working order. Even better news was that some enterprising engineer had managed to find two newer chain-cannon to replace the main weapons on two of the vehicles. Taeris noticed a few mounting points added to the outside of the Vultures implying that they'd used the vehicles, at least in exercises, and had modified them to transport soldiers, wounded, additional equipment or weapons. Such a sign was always encouraging. The powered armour they wore looked very new; suspiciously new, in fact. Taeris assumed they'd made use of the equipment in the barracks just as he had.

After a few minutes checking the readiness of the unit and exchanging salutes with the battalion Taeris moved back inside to the command centre to await the arrival of Chasfaen. The wait was somewhat longer than expected; clearly the brigadier was enjoying strutting his way around the inspection of the 23rd. Taeris sat down to study the terrain of Citaeron and to check all the information he could find on the enemy's strength and he had nearly an hour of research completed before the door opened and Chasfaen entered, followed by Doloras. Chasfaen was beaming, but that seemed to be his normal expression, Doloras looked somewhat less excited.

The Brigadier threw himself into one of the large chairs

that dotted the room, a useful thing about these control centres is that they were designed for the use of people who might, from time to time, wear bulky armour; something that was very useful for the armoured Taeris but also suited the rather overweight Chasfaen. "So, Colonel, what do you have for me?"

Taeris nodded in and said, "I have the makings of a plan."

"Excellent," responded Chasfaen and beamed, it it were possible, even more widely, "Show me the plan."

Taeris began by pulling up the information he'd been working with and highlighted some crucial pieces of information. "Let's begin with the orbiting fleet. The enemy has absolute superiority above the surface, but the fleet consists of mostly merchant ships, largely unsuited to atmospheric operations, with relatively few atmosphere-capable fighter-craft, we think. So far they seem to want to hold such vessels in reserve, so we have yet to be attacked here in Tyrenia." He stopped to look at Chasfaen, who was studying Taeris curiously, as if he was a strange puzzle, but he was smiling. "Their troops at Aepolia are numerous and we have some useful information. Unlike our mechanised forces, the traitors have chosen a non-homogeneous order of battle." He paused for a moment to see if Chasfaen was following, he was still smiling but the smile had become fixed, the eyes glassy. "I mean that they have distinct units of artillery, of aerial support, of anti-armour troops, of air defence and area denial." Still there seemed little change in the brigadier's expression. "What this means is that if we use our vehicles to attack their anti-armour units then we cede to them a huge advantage; however if we can arrange to force the enemy to use their specialised units in a manner for which they are poorly trained and equipped then we could overwhelm them quickly and for little loss." Chasfaen's face was now a frown. Taeris continued, "So we can try to control the perception of the battlefield in such a way that we encourage them to deploy their troops in a predictable manner, then the actual battlefield operation will be quite different; one for which their deployment is poorly suited." Taeris waited for some response.

Eventually the corpulent brigadier exhaled loudly and spoke, "This is simply no good at all, Colonel. When I asked you to come up with a plan what I wanted was a plan of action, not a plan of inaction." He stopped to have a chuckle at his own joke. "I want you to tell me where the enemy is, how we get there and when we can attack. All this fiddling around with details is beneath people of our rank, leave that up to the noncoms, we must set an example of leadership. We stand at the front, order the men to follow us and sweep down on these traitors with the President's heart beating alongside our own."

"You know," he lowered his voice somewhat, "I was worried when I heard you'd had to be educated that you might not have the proper spirit of a Republican. Never thought I'd see it for myself; someone who used to be a ranking member of the Legacy talking like a manipulative, treasonous enemy of the people. You're a disgrace, Colonel." This was literally the first time Taeris hadn't seen a smile on the man's face. "Now I know the President sees something in you, so I'll hold off on denouncing you for cowardice this time, but I shall be taking personal command of the attack and you will be denied the place of honour at the vanguard of the force."

Taeris felt that if this fool was setting the strategy then the vanguard would not so much be a place of honour; more a place of suicide. He said, "Yes, Sir." Deep within him there was that tiny element of doubt. Was he foolish to so often be at odds with those around him? Could the entire hierarchy of the Republic be simply wrong and he the lone voice of reason? Laughable though it sounded he couldn't dismiss his instincts.

80

What was worse, he'd nurtured a compact, dense hatred for the political officers of the Security divisions but Adrael, a Security man through and through, had been far from the most troublesome person to deal with since he left Education Facility 7. Seven years ago Taeris would have said that the senior officers in the Guards varied in ability somewhat, but he hadn't encountered such stubborn idiocy in the past, or had he? Was it possible that he, Taeris, had been the stubborn idiot seven years ago? Casting his mind back, he recalled the times his officers had asked him to adapt his strategy, most memorably during that last war-game. He had resisted all such suggestions. Yes, he had been stubborn. Foolish and stubborn. Taeris considered the past and he regretted his overwhelming self-confidence but he couldn't entirely believe that he was wrong, even on that day seven years ago.

After a moment of sneering disdain had been allowed to pass from Chasfaen to Taeris the brigadier spoke in more measured tones. "The centre of the enemy formations is doubtless still at the city of Aepolia. We mount up at once and all fighting forces will launch a full assault. This time tomorrow the treason will be nothing but a bad memory."

Privately Taeris thought it was more likely that the forces under his command would be a memory, but in the Republic there was no such thing as a bad memory. Failures were ruthlessly expunged from history so the progress of the Republic could be seen a a shining path with not a single mis-step.

Doloras said, "I assume, Sir, you don't mean that all of our forces should be sent to Aepolia."

Chasfaen snapped at him, "Of course that's what I mean!"

Doloras remained immaculately calm as he continued, "Excluding the unarmoured infantry, of course."

"What? Yes, obviously excluding those."

It was a measure of the esteem in which Taeris had held Chasfaen that his opinion of the brigadier actually improved slightly as it became clear that the man wasn't going to order a unit of unarmoured infantry to march 10,000 kilometres across bare mountainous rock to engage the enemy.

Doloras left the room at once to get the attack underway and Taeris followed him out, all the time feeling the glare of the brigadier on him. The benefit of having just inspected the troops was that they were still in full uniform, vehicles readied, there was little delay as the combined formation set off for its first battle under the command of Chasfaen. Within an hour the troops were on the move.

Chasfaen had spoken briefly to a few of his officers and they had chosen a path to Aepolia that appeared to offer the easiest terrain. His plan essentially consisted of following that route and then attacking, other details were beneath his rank, seemingly. Among the smaller details, ones that Chasfaen had chosen to ignore, was one fact in particular. During the previous attack on Aepolia the Republic had absolute superiority in space and the atmosphere. The nature of the attack meant that the only practical result of this superiority was the ability to incorporate additional layers of information into the computers, but still that superiority was there. Now the Republic advanced under a hostile sky; orbit was dominated by the traitor fleet and its capabilities were unknown and untested. Based on the information gathered about the traitor fleet it seemed unlikely that they had huge numbers of atmosphere-capable fighters, but even a handful could be a very dangerous force if they had no need to worry about their dominance of the air being challenged. Even had the ground troops been able to move at the pace of a Tyrant vehicle this would have been a problem, but the pace was limited by the speed of the infantry in their armoured suits. They moved at a pace unthinkable for an unaided man but much slower than the vehicles and they had to pick carefully their route through the precipices and crevasses of the terrain, where vehicles could simply have flown above them. While the armour was an enormous help, over such a surface an unaided man would have had to resort to ropes and climbing equipment every few metres, they were still painfully slow and the time would sap the energy and alertness of the troops. Doloras made a few cautious attempts to encourage Chasfaen to change his mind and allow the 23rd to go ahead alone to carry out the attack but the brigadier was immovable. Perhaps his opinion might have been different if he wasn't riding in one of the command Tyrants himself.

Taeris fumed silently to himself. He couldn't even vent his frustrations on the pilot of his own Tyrant as it was never clear which of his staff were actually secretly placed in the unit by the Security men. In little more than half a local day the force had covered almost 2,000 kilometres and only his anger was keeping Taeris awake when an alert came over the computer. The enemy had been spotted.

The Canyons

Taeris had no idea how the enemy forces had managed to get so close to Tyrenia. He had, at best, a limited idea of their strength and disposition but he was sure most of them were unarmoured infantry forces, well suited only to defence and with little ability to manoeuvre on a planetary scale; even a small one such as Citaeron. His mind worked rapidly through the possibilities; only a few seemed plausible. These troops could have been broken into large numbers of small groups and scattered by flight-craft across the planet to interfere with Republican movement in any direction, or they could be marines, dropped by the orbiting fleet, also in small groups and therefore troops that were new to the battle, or they could be a large and powerful force placed here on the assumption of the Republic's likely approach route. Within seconds it was clear that it had to be the last of these choices, the enemy force was powerful and well prepared. As the Guardians were moving in skirmish formation as a matter of necessity the 23rd had taken the decision to use them as their line of skirmishers, so Taeris was fully aware that he should expect disproportionately high casualty figures among those armoured infantry, however he anticipated being able to throw the power of the Tyrants into the attack rapidly to give the infantry the support they needed.

In fact the updates pouring across the screens showed utterly illogical results. It appeared that the traitors were already mixed in with the line of skirmishers, without the infantry having noticed their presence at all. Even more strangely there had been a number of losses already among the Tyrants, but not a single casualty among the Guardian infantry.

Over the communications system Taeris heard the voice of Chasfaen screaming at him, "They must have known we'd come this way! Don't you know anything about warfare?"

Taeris swallowed the obvious retort; Chasfaen had wanted to throw his forces at the enemy where they were strongest and this, it seemed, was what had happened. No, there was something else to this. However two-dimensional the brigadier's mind might be, and allowing it the second dimension might be considered charitable, Citaeron was essentially a globe. Tyrenia and Aepolia, the two cities, were almost on opposite sides of that globe. While, for various reasons, some routes were shorter, or easier, or better suited to infantry than others the reality was that the Republic forces could have essentially left Tyrenia in any direction at all and ended up at Aepolia. It was simply impossible for the enemy to have been so confident that this would be their route that they could put a substantial force to interdict; unless their forces were orders of magnitude larger than had been previously seen.

There was a much simpler explanation. The rebels had been told where to lay this trap, told by someone who knew the details, someone in the Republic forces. In fact, given the haste with which this operation had been assembled it seemed more likely that the enemy had been placed here for some time and Chasfaen's attack was then manipulated to use this route. Taeris tried to remember the names of those officers Chasfaen had asked for advice on his plan, fruitlessly. Had someone in the Brigadier's inner circle been disloyal? As more information flooded in it became obvious to Taeris that it wasn't 'someone' at all. The explanation for the losses among the Tyrants but the lack of any among the Guardians was simplicity itself: The rebels weren't firing at the Guardians. The entire Guardian formation was traitor.

Taeris took but a few seconds to go through all this in his head, but even that seemed far too slow as his troops were dying out there in front of him. He started issuing orders as fast as he could. Disengage the enemy, use the flight ability of the Tyrants to climb out of the canyon and away from this rebel threat and the turncoat Guardians. He'd just finished issuing these orders when his mind caught up with his decision. No! What a fool! Remember the air-superiority held by the rebels. Tyrants flying high above the landscape would be cannon-fodder for fighters and as soon as this thought crossed his mind he understood that it, too, must have been part of the trap. No wonder the advance had been uninterrupted by enemy fighters, they had been held back waiting for this moment to inflict heavy casualties.

He was just in time. New orders flashed across the screens of his troops and their Tyrants dived into a different canyon that would offer shelter from above and protection from the infantry, now on the far side of a canyon wall. They had barely made it when a formation of more than 100 fighters swept past overhead. Some few of them did manage to hit a tyrant or two but the wholesale slaughter the enemy had planned was largely avoided.

New orders to stay low, to fly fast and scatter through the complex maze of interlocking valleys, were issued. The nature of the terrain meant that the command Tyrant couldn't directly contact every other vehicle, but the way the computers worked was that they relayed instructions on to each other, bouncing the new instructions rapidly from point to point. In practice even the tight beams did run the risk of allowing some EM scatter from the metallic canyon walls but orders had to be issued and the risk of revealing the position of a handful of the Tyrants was the price that had to be paid. Occasionally a Tyrant flew up to crest the canyon walls to pass on information to those in other valleys, mostly their exposure was short enough to avoid the fighters, but not always.

Brigadier Chasfaen had been carried along with the Tyrants as they fled the scene, as he had taken a seat in one of the Tyrants of the 23rd as his command position. Briefly Taeris wondered if the man was chastened at his own unit's desertion or enraged at the 23rd Infantry's flight from the battle; it was a concern that faded neatly from consideration as the escape became more certain and the enemy was left further behind them. Instead a more pressing concern began to assert itself: What sort of reception would the Regiment receive from the infantry elements of the Guardians of Citaeron that had been left behind? Was it possible that the treason had been confined to a single battalion of mechanised forces? How hard, Taeris wondered, had the other regiment of Guardians, those stationed in Aepolia, fought to defend Citaeron? Had they also simply thrown their weapons down and joined the enemy? Clearly this was a question that could be answered only by approaching the city and discovering if they were met with weaponry.

It would have been foolishly confident for Taeris to have assumed that there were no other traps waiting for the 23rd Regiment as they made their way, in scattered groups, back to Tyrenia. In fact several small groups of rebels did make life difficult and given that the Tyrants had to hug the floor of the canyons to evade attack from the fighters above these little obstacles were more dangerous than might have been the case. They also offered a chance for the deeply resentful 23rd to take out its anger on an enemy that they had yet to engage in proper battle. A little over half way back to Tyrenia one such group had laid a trap for the small group of Tyrants that, by chance, contained Taeris' own command vehicle.

The first indication of this was a solid hit on the lead Tyrant; not enough to cripple it, but its pilot wisely sought shelter in the rocky formations at the foot of the valley. Other Tyrants gathered in the same area and rapid exchanges of tight-beam described the enemy position as the computers had identified it. The rebels had placed their position in a small cleft on top of one of the high ridges. While this position was very exposed to any attackers overhead it was a commanding position for engaging an enemy forced by circumstance to remain deep in the valley. Obviously the traitors had assumed the skies would be friendly to them when selecting such a position. At least two heavy weapons had been mounted there and sited to threaten the Tyrants for a good length of the valley as the ridge was on the inside of a long, sweeping bend in the canyon. As a position it was extremely well chosen and getting past it at full speed would likely cost a number of armoured vehicles along with their crews.

Taeris found he was actually smiling as he issued orders for the armoured infantry to deal with this threat. His smile may even have broadened as he joined in the attack himself. With the EM absorption turned to maximum the armour of the troops as they picked their way up the canyon wall seemed to have no depth at all. The troops appeared to be shadows cast on the rock with no shine or glint of reflection possible. If human eyeballs were the most dangerous sensing apparatus the enemy could field then a sympathetic colour scheme of camouflage could be automatically applied to the armour, but Taeris didn't know if there were EM sensors in the enemy camp and it was therefore safer to permit no radiation to leak out at all.

The rock face was almost a kilometre in height and had a human being had to ascend it with rope and pick then it would have taken days of hard and dangerous work; the armoured infantry climbed it at almost a dead run, using gloves and boots augmented with devices that could make their own cracks and pits in the rock for traction, cresting the top in just a few minutes. As Taeris rolled over the top of the ridge he lay flat, taking his heavy rifle from his back and taking careful aim on the enemy. In fact the position was not visible from here; a spire of rock stuck up from the ridge-line and blocked the direct view. Silently Taeris waited the moments for his fellow troops to join him and then stood to sprint to the spire. Enemy troops opened fire from two flanking positions, both on neighbouring ridges, as the Republic forces were perfectly outlined against the skyline, a foolish mistake that Taeris vowed not to repeat. It wasn't only Taeris who had made a mistake, however, as the rebels had occupied flanking positions quite far away and the unarmoured infantry couldn't wield the kind of heavy infantry weapon that armoured infantry took for granted. Even Citaeron's relatively thin atmosphere attenuated the shots significantly and no damage was caused. The same could not be said of the return fire. The carefully sited flank positions each concealed but a few soldiers and no heavy weapons; their task was to protect the central position from infantry attack. The one to Taeris' right suddenly exploded in a noisy blast of rainbow energy as several of the Tyrants on the floor of the valley below found that they had a direct line of sight to it. Five of the armoured infantry had begun returning fire at the other infantry position and immediately it was silenced as its troops were either incapacitated or taking cover and unable to return fire. Taeris continued on his dead run towards the main position and chose to scale the spire rather than work his way around it. The choice was wise. As he crested the top he could look down into the enemy position, three heavy weapons sited in a row with more than a dozen unarmoured infantry in partially covered positions around it. He could have chosen any target he wanted for himself as none of the traitors seemed to be looking upwards but he was part of a mechanised infantry formation and such selfishness was entirely counter-productive. In less than a second he had assigned targets to each of his troops and then he waited for the computer to tell him that everyone was in position. Seconds later the attack began as nine battlesuited soldiers each leapt in a perfectly choreographed movement from behind cover to draw a line of sight on the enemy. Each of his troops was already in possession of the precise location and nature of his primary and secondary target and was able to fire to exactly hit that position even though they had, up until that second, had no visual reference for themselves at all.

From the perspective of the rebels they would have gone from a state of tensely waiting for sight of the enemy to all being dead at the hands of that enemy in just a second or two. Powered armour definitely gave a significant tactical advantage in combat.

Taeris foolishly gave himself a moment to smile at his success and during that time his armour began warning him of incoming threats. While the armour had managed to remain perfectly stealthy throughout the attack, the large splashes of EM radiation released as the weapons struck troops, weapons and the surrounding landscape had obviously been enough to attract the attention of a fighter above them. Taeris, especially, was horribly exposed on top of the highest point of the nearby landscape and he threw himself off the top of the spire, hoping he had given himself enough sideways momentum to clear the sides of the ridge below and fall down into the valley. He was only just in time as it seemed gravity was agonisingly slow at pulling him down. The powerful weapons on the fighter poured gigajoules of energy into the spire, just below his former position, enough to cut the spire in half, and even after that the remnants of the energy couldn't escape fast enough and the solid rock exploded along whatever were its weakest points in a blast of light and heat. Taeris fell, and as he did, superheated fragments of metals and ores splattered against his armour. Taeris fell and his computer briefly froze with the speed at which its information was changing. Taeris fell and fell and fell.

Handover

It's all very well for the designers of an armoured suit to affirm that their creation can easily withstand a kilometre fall; it's quite another to watch the jagged rocks of a deep-red canyon approach at hundreds of kilometres per hour and place your trust in the equipment. When the impact came it was punishing. The deceleration felt like all the flesh was torn from his bones and in the agony of the moment Taeris lost consciousness.

He woke just seconds later, partly because his injuries were relatively minor, partly because he was in too much pain to lose focus, partly because the armour, carefully examining him for systemic problems, had poured adrenaline into him.

He awoke screaming. He tried to rise and find a more comfortable position but the effort was largely futile. A brief scan of the armour's readouts explained why: The suit had held up admirably, but there was little it could do to ease the damage caused by so massive a deceleration. While the bulky protective helmet and the carefully stiffened spine and organ shields had done their jobs perfectly, Taeris had broken his left tibia and right femur in the fall. So competent was the suit that even with such damage he could stand and walk, but the pain was intense and the subtleties of controlling his legs had gone with the bones. Even the powerful analgesics the armour could dispense offered little ease from the pain.

A moment later one of his troops landed beside him,

picked him up as if he was a child's toy and ran him back to his command Tyrant. The little detachment got underway soon after.

Despite the pain, Taeris stayed awake, watching the information screens as his Tyrant made its way down the canyons. Separated from almost all of his troops by the massive rock walls he had no idea of how many of his troops were facing attacks from the air, or from ambush. Still he watched the useless screens. Immobility robbed the pain of its sting and left a dull, hollow ache that was being dealt with efficiently by the synthetic opioids coursing through him, but those same drugs made it hard to focus.

Hours later Taeris' Tyrant joined with the others of his regiment in the last twisting canyons before they were to spill out onto the small elevated plain where the city of Tyrenia stood. This was as far as his orders had taken them because they now faced the dual dangers that the enemy fighters might cause immense damage once they moved into the open and their alleged allies in the city might open fire on them as they neared it. Information was now beginning to flood into his computer, as each Tyrant came to rest in the open gullet of the last canyon. Fully a third of his force was now in reach of communications, hopefully the remainder were approaching similar positions in nearby canyons.

Taeris grunted as he turned his head to review the screens in front of him. The 23rd was largely intact and in pretty good order, at least those parts of it he could see. That might be enough to make the gamble of a dash to the city worthwhile. He was weighing up the options when the communications channel opened and the voice of Captain Raephus cut across his thoughts. "Taeris, this is Raephus, we are holding orbit above Citaeron, give me your situation."

It was a measure of Taeris' character that this good news was immediately tempered, for him, by the worry that the fleet might be placing itself in severe danger. "Raephus, good to hear your voice. We're safe for the moment, can you hold position or is there an immediate threat?"

Raephus responded, "We brought some friends with us this time and it seems the fighter complement of the rebel fleet has been called away to deal with some other matters on the surface of the planet. We're looking at a victory up here."

Taeris was staring at the information flooding in from the ships above. He now had a good view of the movements of enemy fighters and the disposition of their fleet. Raephus was right. The rebel fleet was smaller than before, perhaps half the size it had been when it first appeared, and it had sent its fighters down to annihilate the Republic troops on the ground. There was a strong numerical advantage with the lumbering, elderly ships of the Republic. As the data updated he saw several of the rebel ships jump away from the battle, not in a coordinated withdrawal but just a ship here and there. Some of the rebel ships might be waiting for their fighters to return but given the rate at which they were being torn apart by Republic forces it seemed unlikely that would happen. More and more rebel ships were destroyed, more and more jumped to safety. Raephus was unable to prevent the traitors from fleeing, but those that stayed were being crushed. As the situation shifted the remnants of the traitors finally decided to abandon Citaeron and their fighters, jumping out to save their own skins. In orbit the enemy was routed. Taeris' computers were also now receiving updates from Republic fighters, pouring into the atmosphere to hunt the rebel ships. That, too, would be a very asymmetric battle and, once completed, those fighters would be free to directly support Taeris on the ground. The same line-of-sight communication was now filling in the missing information about the remainder of the 23rd, Taeris breathed deeply and thankfully as the data began to show an almost complete regiment.

The danger from the sky eliminated; Taeris ordered his troops forward to reclaim Tyrenia immediately. His haste was an attempt to further divide enemy forces. Possibly some of their fighters might not have yet begun their climb to fight the new aerial threat, if so then offering them a new target on the ground might entice some to stay deep in the atmosphere. As he wasn't sure if the troops in the city were allies or enemies he was unable to issue the kind of aggressive orders that would have suited the situation; instead he sent the Tyrants forward quickly and gave them a suitable distance from the city to release their infantry. This was a cautious approach, not entirely Taeris' favourite kind of plan, but it had the virtue of permitting the forces to prepare for any kind of reception.

The Guardians of Citaeron inside the city started firing on the 23rd as soon as they got within range of the walls, and Taeris swore loudly at the betrayal, but the battle was tremendously one-sided. The 23rd had the advantage of numbers, equipment, heavy weapons, vehicles, training and leadership. As the engagement distance closed Raephus was even able to send a few smaller craft down to provide Taeris with aerial reconnaissance as the defenders fled deeper and deeper into the city. Had the Guardians been determined to hold the city they could have hidden traps and soldiers throughout to make the process of capturing Tyrenia, if not ultimately more challenging, much more expensive and time-consuming. Determined they were not. Before the close-quarter fighting had even begun in earnest the Guardians were surrendering in large numbers. The battle in the skies was, arguably, even more successful. Rebel fighters were either shot down or made emergency landings close to the rebel stronghold of Aepolia. While these landings may have saved the lives of a handful of the pilots, their fighters were destroyed on the ground and any attempt at air defence from within Aepolia punished with heavy strikes from orbit.

Raephus had landed and was already in the command centre in the Tyrenian barracks before Taeris had made his slow, uncomfortable, way into the room. Adrael stood calmly alongside the Captain and it was he who spoke first, "Colonel, welcome back. I'd like to introduce you to Admiral Raephus, the commanding officer of the Third Fleet."

Taeris blinked briefly; so that was why Adrael had spoken first, it was to let him know of Raephus' promotion. In the Republic this sort of thing happened quite frequently and Taeris knew to not ask about the whereabouts of Admiral Tynaesi, if for no other reason that both Adrael and Raephus would probably pretend they'd never heard of him. Once a man was denounced it was improper to speak of him ever again. Casually Taeris wondered why the former admiral had been denounced. It could be some overheard remark, some trivial act of disloyalty or, as Taeris suspected, Adrael might have denounced him simply to remove an incompetent man from command. If that was true then Adrael was a force to be reckoned with indeed, not every man could denounce an admiral and make the charge stick.

Before Taeris could begin to discuss the next steps in the campaign the door opened and Chasfaen bustled in, looking slightly wide-eyed but well enough. "Colonel!" He shouted across the command centre, "I hold you responsible for this desertion."

Taeris was, perhaps, in too much pain to muster much

enthusiasm for another argument so he simply responded, "Desertion?"

"Yes man, desertion. Your Twenty-third fled the scene of a battle with hardly a shot being fired! As there are senior officers present I am now denouncing you to them for disloyalty, cowardice and unrepublican conduct."

For a moment there was no sound in the room, as everyone waited to see how Taeris might react. Eventually, picking his words carefully, he said, "Brigadier. My forces did not flee the battle they, in fact, engaged enemy troops on the ground, an action that I participated in personally and which led to several injuries being sustained. Did you assume that I had accidentally broken both of my legs while shaving?"

Chasfaen took in a deep breath as if to respond but Taeris continued, "As for the troops under your own command, one formation deserted to the treasonous enemy without a single shot being exchanged, the other chose to welcome my troops back to our own barracks by entertaining us with a spectacular laser show. One intended to kill us all. While this was going on I note that you had placed yourself in a vehicle belonging to the Twenty-third, rather than one of the vehicles of your own unit, thus meaning that as the battle developed you became nothing more than malodorous ballast in the back of one of my Tyrants. I have decided to overlook all of these shortcomings and pardon you for them, as they are actions of pomposity, not disloyalty. I am unable to forgive, however, this transparent attempt to evade responsibility for your incompetence. I believe it implies that you are incapable of learning from your mistakes. As our great President has stated, 'wilful ignorance is a crime against the Republic', and I denounce you for being useless for any imaginable duty within this, the greatest and most humane nation ever to exist. On a related note I have decided that your ignorance is such that education cannot, by definition, make you productive and accordingly I offer you the mercy of a quick death at my hand."

In the back of Taeris' brain the old joke, based upon ancient jurisprudence, floated to mind, 'you have the right to a swift execution, if you cannot afford a swift execution then one will be provided for you.' He forced the thought down, such references were not permitted in the Republic, uttering such a thing out loud could be grounds for denunciation.

The brigadier had gone very pale, not a good look on a man of his girth. "I, I, I'm a senior officer of the Republic, the President himself has to..." It was the last thing he ever said as his head suddenly twitched violently and sprays of blood and brain came out through his nose, mouth, ears, eyes. Taeris started in surprise and turned his head to see Adrael calmly returning his side-arm to a concealed holster.

After he'd readjusted his clothing Adrael looked at Taeris and, seeing the look of surprise on his face, said, "I'm sorry if I startled you. He was starting to become irritating."

Taeris flicked a small piece of brain from the chest of his armour and turned to the newly promoted admiral. "Raephus. You seem to have brought a substantial fleet to Citaeron."

Raephus nodded slowly. "Technically not just one fleet. Essentially I have the Third and Fourth Fleets here along with the littoral complement that brought the Eighth Guards Legion."

"The whole legion?"

Adrael and Raephus both nodded, Raephus smiling broadly. Taeris was frankly surprised and, again, had to reassess Adrael's power in the Republic; he'd have been pleased if the fleet had returned with one or two of the other regiments that comprised the 6th Legion but it had returned with another fleet and a full legion of guards; more than 30,000 highly-trained soldiers. "I'm a little rusty on the Fourth Fleet."

Raephus' grin widened. "It's rather larger than the Third Fleet, partly due to its three battleships."

In response Taeris could only shake his head in wonder. "Am I right in assuming that the legion isn't here on a sightseeing tour?"

Adrael had returned to a businesslike expression. "You are," he said, "They are here to crush enemy forces on Citaeron and they will keep the Fourth Fleet for their use. The Third will be tasked with transporting the Twenty-third to Prosperity as was originally intended."

Taeris said, "Understood. If the legate wants our assistance here before we leave for Prosperity then I'm happy to oblige, of course."

Adrael didn't believe in pulling punches, something to which the leaking corpse of Chasfaen mutely attested. "He wants you off his planet as soon as possible. He is, perhaps, unconvinced that a man with your past makes a good colleague."

If Taeris had been asked ten years ago if he would want to work with a man just released after being sent for education he would probably have had just as many reservations. He nodded his understanding and sank into a chair.

Assembling the 23rd Regiment for lift was not an enormous task, given that the unit was mobile and carried all its personnel with it, as was always the case for Republic mechanised units. Taeris was not looking forward to the process himself because of his broken bones, but the armour immobilised them well enough to permit healing and once he was certain that he could leave the remainder of the lift to his subordinates he took the stronger of the offered drugs and became quite blissfully unconcerned with such trivialities. As the littoral ship gently lifted from Citaeron Taeris had a tremendous view of the 8th Guards Legion landing in force. No matter how much experience of military operations a man could have it is doubtful that he would ever become immune to the sense of wonder associated with a sky full of thousands of armoured vehicles overflown by hundreds of sleek fighters. The legion landed in immaculate order, as expected, with their equipment. Adrael was being lifted in a shuttle to the battlecruiser Spica and Taeris opened a channel to him just as the littoral ship left atmosphere. "Adrael. I forgot to leave instructions about what to do with the captured Guardians."

Adrael's voice came back immediately, "I ordered them all executed. The Eighth will take care of that."

Taeris signed off and closed his eyes, letting the drugs flow through him. He idly wondered if he, too, would have ordered the unit annihilated. Probably, was his conclusion, as there was now overwhelming force to deal with the remainder of the rebels on the planet. As if to act as a punctuation mark for the visit to Citaeron there was a sudden hollow bang as a small piece of debris left from the space battle bounced off the port and span away into the upper reaches of the atmosphere where it would form part of the spectacular display of meteors that always followed a battle in low orbit.

Prosperity

Bones healed very quickly indeed under the influence of modern medical technology. Of course there were some things that were still generally fatal, including most of the severe bacterial infections, but physical medicine was almost always fast and perfect, whether it was to deal with breaks, tears, cuts, ruptures or surgery. Taeris needed just a handful of hours for the bones to be mended and a few more hours for the pain to largely disappear. He spent this time in his cabin on LS7 while the fleet made its stately progress to Prosperity and he studied everything he could about the planet.

By the time the fleet arrived in orbit the entire formation was at action stations, not knowing what kind of a reception might be waiting for them. In fact the only warships in place around the planet were three large trading vessels, all new and all in the range of 2,000 tonnes. Taeris had made his way to the bridge of LS7 to make use of its communications and its displays of the external sensors fitted to the fleet as a whole and he was not particularly worried by the tiny force. "Presumably they'll flee or die."

The young captain looked a little less certain. "We've seen those before, the traitors use them like frigates."

Taeris snorted, "You sound too nervous for this job, Captain."

In fact there was one other obvious fact that had escaped Taeris momentarily. There were no jump relays in the

Prosperity system, either they'd been destroyed by the traitors or by the Republic, but either way it meant that normal communications were limited to light-speed, unless ships sent their own jump probes out to move the messages faster. Sure enough one of the rebel frigates launched a missile off away from the orbit of Prosperity, possibly containing a message identifying the arrival of the Republic fleet and asking for reinforcements. If so that message was destined never to reach its target. Destroyer D36 opened fire with a volley of most of its available beam weapons and in just seconds the missile was disincorporated. The frigates might attack or they might jump away from Prosperity but they had little time to decide either way as the 3rd Fleet aligned itself for a battle. Before even the first engagement orders had been properly issued two of the frigates vanished as they flicked their jump masses on to full and set off at speeds that mere laser could never reach, but the third didn't make it in time. Powerful beams from several ships struck it as it began to reduce its mass compensation and in such a state it could absorb a great deal less energy into its hull before catastrophe. One entire flank of the ship simply exploded outward and behind it the contents of the vessel were coughed into the vacuum. While the vessel hadn't approached the speeds necessary to qualify as a jump it was still travelling very quickly and the remnants of the craft sped out of sight in seconds. Taeris turned his attention to the planet.

Prosperity was an extremely distinctive planet. Of all the worlds settled by humans it was the most recent but its climate, its geography and its relatively low population made it top of many people's list for an ideal holiday or retirement destination. Less than a century before the planet had been a bare, rocky world, with no atmosphere and little to commend it. At first the reason humans had been drawn to it was the simple opportunity it offered as a place of expansion. Prosperity had familiar gravity, radiation levels, would, on average, be warmer than Earth and had the right size to hold a good atmosphere. It turned out to have some useful minerals, including a substantial quantity of pitchblende, and the decision to turn it into a human-inhabited world was unanimous. As it had cooled more gently than Earth and had much lower tectonic activity the world appeared almost strangely smooth, the fairly even surface only being seriously affected by the huge number of meteor craters that covered it. Once the atmosphere, the plants and the water was in place on the surface these craters became countless thousands of roughly circular freshwater lakes. In essence, therefore, Prosperity consisted of only one continent and that continent covered the entire planet, but despite this the surface was almost 75% water; mostly warm, shallow, fresh pools, some very large, some tiny. Coupled with the oddly shaped 'streaky' clouds that formed the principal weather system and the deep green foliage that grew everywhere the water left uncovered Prosperity looked unlike any other world. Prosperity had almost no tilt with respect to the angle of its sun, so it was seasonless. The poles were always very cold, the equator always very warm. A steady variation of temperature and humidity from the equator to the poles meant that almost any kind of agriculture could be sustained and, in particular, farming the lakes was the major industry. Even the polar regions were green, courtesy of the careful engineering of plant species that thrived in temperatures below freezing and the frozen lakes in those regions made for a very useful resource for lifting water into orbit, where it wouldn't melt, so it could be shipped to planets that were drier or had large and thirsty populations.

In addition to providing accommodation for the relatively small number of residents, Prosperity was a major agricultural contributor to the Republic, with the surface covered in small farms, and many of the lakes used to rear fish. This existence needed no cities or major population centres of any kind. The population spread to where it was needed and where it was needed was where the food was being grown. It was an old joke, but largely appropriate, to say that the capital city of Prosperity used to be Tomaech's Farm but now it's Franker's Farm, because Franker put in an extra bedroom. Coming up with a sensible strategy for taking such a world by force might mean taking each and every property by force, one after another. Taeris wasn't looking forward to the task.

As he assembled his men for the drop he at least was now free of pain, that alone was enough to improve his temperament significantly. In fact there was no work for him to do, the troops knew their vehicles and equipment as well as anyone could and they'd practised the process of getting ready for deployment hundreds of times until the whole operation became almost automatic.

The drop was routine, as expected, because the site Taeris had chosen for the landing was almost uninhabited. Despite this there was always the threat that the enemy might have laid traps for the unwary. As the last attempt to retake the world had got no further than orbit there was no prior intelligence that Taeris could use to give him an insight into the defenders' preparations.

As soon as the Tyrant made it to ground, Taeris opened the top hatch to take a deep breath of the sweet and fragrant air of Prosperity. It was hard to imagine this idyll as a place of unrest against the lawful Republic. Now the broken bones had healed Taeris was able to properly enjoy the sensation of weight again and he enthusiastically pushed himself out of the hatch to stand on top of the Tyrant itself. Inside his helm the information flowing in showed a completely peaceful and easy landing, perhaps if he'd been less intoxicated by the sheer joy of arriving on the planet he would have thought about this more carefully. He let the warm, humid air flow into his lungs, savouring the taste of the fresh scent of trees and grasses. There was a gentle, but steady, breeze.

Luck favoured Taeris on this occasion. The sniper's first shot missed him by inches, but hit the turret of the Tyrant, causing a little puff of steam to come off as the capacitors absorbed the energy and bled it back out to the atmosphere. It was the only warning Taeris got but it was the only one he needed. Most sniping weapons needed several seconds between shots and he had the time needed to hurl himself in a rather undignified head-first scramble back into the Tyrant. While Taeris was still trying to right himself the gunner of his vehicle had identified the origin point of the shot and returned fire with the might of the Viking cannon. After a moment he confirmed the kill. Taeris was rapidly warning his troops on the ground about snipers, but already the troops had discovered such enemies for themselves. Worse, several of the 23rd's Tyrants had set off land mines and at least one had come under fire from a concealed heavy weapon that had torn through its armour and killed its crew. Across the regiment, thousands of armoured troops were jumping clear of their Tyrants and methodically hunting their surrounds for any sign of enemy positions, by doing so they relinquished the protection of the Tyrants but in exchange massively multiplied the number of information sources and weapons deployed by the regiment while also providing the enemy with many more targets to engage and defeat. For Taeris the major problem was that the sheer number of firefights and their scattered nature made controlling the deployment effectively impossible; he would have to rely on the troops making good choices and clearing their immediate areas of threats with little help from their commanders. Fortunately the rebels had taken what weaponry they could find and hidden as individuals and small groups in forests and makeshift shelters. Most of their equipment was incapable of harming a Tyrant and some of it would barely scratch the armour of an infantryman. If this kind of force was the worst that the enemy could muster on Prosperity's surface then the battle could have only one outcome, though it might take painstaking effort for a long time to clear the planet of all such opposition.

Within an hour the 23rd had cleared the landing area of enemy forces, or at least of those enemy forces foolish enough to reveal their position by opening fire. Some casualties had fallen to heavy weapons but the majority of losses the Republic had suffered were caused by mines and traps. Taeris carefully examined his position to see what major threats remained. The regiment was essentially spread over a relatively small area along a peninsula caused by the overlapping edges of two of the giant circular crater lakes. On one side of the rough triangle was dense forest, on the other two sides were water, and thanks to the size of the craters it was fairly deep. Taeris thought this was a fairly good place to form a lager for the first day and issued orders to begin the standard watch procedures. He was a little cautious at the thought of boats, as he had little experience with them as weapons of war. He knew a fishing community had to have many such vessels and, as every child learnt in school, a boat could carry a lot of weight very efficiently. Tyrants could travel over water as efficiently as land, naturally, but the flat surface would leave them vulnerable to direct fire.

That night the boats came. Four of them, not large or powerful, low in the water with weight of weaponry. They were issuing no radiation so their approach was unheralded, but in the night, without infra-red to guide their attacks, they failed to achieve hits with their opening shots. Thanks to the watch being kept by the 23rd their opening shots would also prove to be their last. Taeris was comfortable with the defence he'd established, and perhaps failed to appreciate the real purpose of the enemy attack. By the morning it would be clear that those boats had been meant to prevent the Tyrants turning on their active sensors for fear of enemy weapons silently and passively guided towards them.

The geography of the area implied that there should be a similar peninsula on the other side of the water and indeed there was. By the morning this ground had been carefully dug and covered into a series of protected positions by a large concentration of enemy forces. Taeris, even as he cursed his arrogance, calculated that this was a dangerous force and one that could absolutely prevent the Tyrants from crossing the water, even at speed. This left him with much slower or more meandering approaches, something he hated.

Doloras joined him in his command Tyrant for a mutual venting of frustration.

"We were thinking they'd always fight in small groups, Colonel."

"Speak for yourself," Taeris responded, "I wasn't thinking at all. I've barely done any thinking since I arrived on Prosperity." He sighed and began looking for a swift and sure way to defeat this enemy concentration but he was interrupted by a call from orbit.

"Taeris, this is Spica."

A sinking feeling filled Taeris as he responded, "Taeris. Are you about to tell me you're abandoning me on another rock?"

"Actually I was wondering if you'd like some friends. We've got the rest of the Sixth Legion up here and they seem to fancy stretching their legs on the prettiest planet around."

Doloras started to smile. "I'll direct them to the other side of the lake."

"Not too close to the water," Taeris warned, "I assume the traitors have set traps on their positions."

Doloras nodded and strode off to his own Tyrant to start making the necessary plans.

The 6th Legion was low on personnel, having only four of the five regiments that should have been its complement; three fresh regiments, however, would bring more than 18,000 more troops to the fight. Taeris allowed himself a little smile.

The sheer size of the force meant that it would have to be landed in stages, the 24th Regiment would come down first and the Legate himself had chosen to ride with the first group. Taeris slipped out of his Tyrant and gathered together the infantry commanders of the 112th, his most hardened battalion. As the landings progressed he would personally lead the battalion on the attack.

Tyrants poured out of the littoral ships, twisting and turning to make a hard target as they dropped towards the planet. Some didn't survive but overwhelmingly they did and as they reached the surface they spat out their infantry, all at once, like silent, matte-black explosions. The enemy had set traps and left small numbers of troops to protect their escape routes from the peninsula, but these were swiftly overwhelmed by the vast numbers of armoured infantry that were now landing. As soon as it was practical the 24th started its manoeuvres, exerting inexorable pressure, forcing the enemy forces along the peninsula towards the lake shore. Behind them the Tyrants of the 27th Regiment were beginning their landings onto areas already cleared and vacated by the 24th. Step by step the traitors were forced backwards, the lake at their backs and the Republic fiercely attacking their every position. It was only a couple of hours before the rebel forces were pushed back into a tiny area of the tip of the peninsula and they were still resisting desperately, still causing casualties, still not giving in to the inevitable. Warfare was in some ways a very different thing than it had been before modern technology. Soldiers were faster, tougher, better equipped and vastly better informed than a Greek Hoplite could have imagined. Even so, a force of stubborn soldiers, backs to a wall, or a lake, hiding in holes, fighting to the end; this was still a battle the ancients would have understood. No matter the power of the orbiting fleet, there was no way to be certain that you had cleared the enemy from their tiny hidden positions until a soldier had walked over the area and confirmed it.

It was Taeris and the 112th that finally broke all resistance. He had taken the battalion through the lake, walking their armour along the bottom, away from enemy detection. At the crucial moment he detonated a small explosive charge underwater to act as a signal and almost 1,000 armoured infantry leapt as one from the calm waters of the lake to land, seconds later, on the shore amid the carefully prepared positions of the rebels. The effect on morale alone might have ended the battle at that point, but this coupled with the blizzard of firepower that the 112th unleashed upon the rebels finally saw resistance end.

Taeris surveyed the scene before him. He had finally won a victory and he could scarcely comprehend the distance he'd covered from hopeless prisoner to victorious commander. He opened a channel to the fleet officers and the infantry commanders. "The Republic has added another glorious victory to its storied rolls of history."

On the ground before him was a leg, still wrapped in a green scrap of camouflaged trouser, blasted and cauterised free from the man it once served. Victory might be less glorious than he'd imagined, but it was clearly preferable to the alternative.

Part 2 - Redemption's Legacy

Legate

Adrael took his time visiting the forces on the surface. Possibly he had matters of far greater importance to occupy him in orbit. Taeris, perhaps uncharitably, decided that the most likely reason was the fear that the area hadn't been completely cleared of rebels. While it might be a fear that could be mocked by the soldiers it was a legitimate fear; the reality was that despite enormous efforts and continuing vigilance there were still snipers and traps being uncovered by the 6th Legion. Some of the snipers were wielding weapons that were not up to the task of overwhelming the capacitance of the armour worn by the troops, making their effort utterly pointless. The stupidity they showed in carefully approaching the 23rd and opening fire with a weapon no more useful than had they merely shouted an insult in an aggressive tone was taken by members of Taeris' unit as indicating how foolish people became once they rejected the order and sense of the President's law. Taeris privately wondered if it might indicate something else.

Doloras was seemingly appeased regarding his previous concerns over the conduct of his new commanding officer. Possibly a first true victory had helped, or maybe it was the way that Taeris seemed to never find his way back to the doctrinal approach and yet the Republic seemed to permit him all his freedoms, a concept lost on Doloras.

When Adrael finally came to visit Taeris in the makeshift camp on the edge of the forest he seemed thoughtful. For the first time Taeris saw the man in full armour, a wise precaution given the unsure environment on Prosperity. "We must talk privately," Was all that Taeris could get from him until they were safely ensconced in the command Tyrant, away from any possibility of being overheard. Once there Adrael still seemed unforthcoming.

"This is as private as I can arrange," Taeris approached the topic.

Adrael nodded and began, "A few notes for general updates. Of course these will all be passed to you in time in the proper manner, but the Republic has begun the recruitment of a new fighting formation, the Fifth Guards Legion. It will probably be coupled with the new warships currently under construction. The President has personally overseen the selection and training of this new legion and it will therefore be the finest fighting force in the Republic."

"Naturally," Taeris responded.

Adrael continued. "I have been handed a prisoner, Faeral, who was the commander of the forces at this recent battle." The way Adrael said 'battle' made the engagement sound like a matter of curing a fungal infection rather than an act of war.

Taeris nodded. "Do you wish my help in framing suitable questions for the prisoner?"

Adrael looked affronted as if he would never have come here on such a trivial matter. "Of course not. He must speak English but he refuses. He will only communicate in this illicit dialect from Citaeron."

"Aepolian," Taeris supplied helpfully.

"Whatever," Adrael responded. "In any event there is little or no point in our people speaking with him, as none of our men can understand this rancid tongue. In absence of any use for him, it is felt that he should be handed across to the Legate of the Sixth Legion, for him to administer such inducements, such coercions and ultimately such justice as he feels this man deserves."

Taeris nodded as he replied, "Reasonable and just. If the man cannot act as a useful resource then perhaps he can serve as a terrible warning of what happens to traitors."

Adrael almost smiled, "I knew you would understand. Now on to the other matter. Despite our best efforts it appears the current Legate of the Sixth Infantry Legion will not be able to continue in that capacity."

Taeris frowned. "I had not heard that he received an injury during the battle."

"No," replied Adrael, "he has contracted cholera."

In such a moment the normally laconic attitude of military commanders was expected to falter and Taeris looked truly shocked. "So there is no hope?"

Adrael looked like a man without confidence. "Of course his immune system might overcome the disease but it is a bad one. Nothing can be done other than limiting his symptoms and his pain until he either recovers or dies."

Cholera, even by the standards of fatal diseases, was extremely unpleasant. While it gripped a victim there was little chance of remaining hydrated and even if fluids were introduced directly into the veins the infection might not be halted by the victim's immune system quickly enough for the patient to recover. Taeris feared it as all men did. "I understand."

"So," continued Adrael, "The Sixth needs a new Legate. I have sent a relay to Esperia for the President's approval of you as the new Legate for the time being. He responded recently. Congratulations Legate Taeris."

Taeris stared in undisguised shock at Adrael. His mind

was racing and his heart trying to keep up with it. "Thank you, Adrael. I did not expect this. I did not expect that you, of all people, would suggest me for this honour."

Adrael smirked back, "And your expectations would normally have been fulfilled. On this occasion, however, there was a dearth of candidates with experience of fighting these rebels. I cannot assure you that your promotion to the Legacy will be permanent, but for the moment you are the man for the job."

"Again, thank you."

As if moving on to less important matters Adrael shrugged and then began rapidly describing the duties of a Legate. Not only had Taeris known them since childhood but he had acted as a Legate in the past and lived by those codes as if they were commandments from a god. Taeris ignored most of the formulaic information but towards the end of the speech he did catch one thing. "I'm sorry, could you go into a little more detail about that?"

Adrael sighed as if he was unused to being interrupted for foolish questions. "The rights, titles, possessions, duties, goods, wages and chattels will be returned to the Legate as befits his complete redemption and welcome back into the embrace of the Republic."

Taeris thought for a second before asking, "And when you say goods and chattels?"

Comprehension finally dawned on Adrael's face. "Of course your former paramour will be reassigned to you once more as you would expect."

Taeris couldn't keep the smile off his face. He would see Laesa again. Not just that, she would be his once again.

Adrael scowled at him. "I see you've lost all sense for the moment. I'll have the prisoner transferred to your custody. He is of no use to me, so you can do whatever amuses you. I could recommend that you make his death painful, prolonged and salutary but I suspect you'll make such decisions without my aid. In case they didn't cover the matter in your former military career I might point out that drowning is both the most frightening and painful death." He stood and stalked out of the Tyrant. He had travelled less than a metre before a puff of steam on the back of his black and white Republic Security armour indicated that a sniper had, once more, scored a perfect hit on a high-value target for no actual practical purpose at all. Turning, he glared at Taeris. "Also, when you have a moment, stop the bloody rebels shooting at me." In the background the cracks and pops indicated that beams of tmetic energy were responding to the rebel's effort.

With that, he was gone. Taeris took a moment to consider all that had changed in the last few minutes. Perhaps a sober analysis of the meeting would point to his promotion, the final redemption implied by his return to his former rank, the job of overseeing four regiments where before he had only one to ponder. In his mind he could only think of Laesa. He had won her back, somehow, and this time he would keep her.

In the distance there was the sound of energetic explosions as a Viking cannon carried out the necessary reactions to turn a nearby sniper into a sticky piece of forest fertiliser wrapped in strips and fragments of green cloth.

Taeris stepped out of his Tyrant and walked slowly down the ramp. He was not fired upon, or at least not by a sniper with the aim of the one who had scored a hit on Adrael. As the Republic forces had recycled that marksman into heat, light and scattered molecules he had one less rebel to worry about anyway. Above him he saw the reassuring shape of the Viking cannon and scattered around the beach, where the warm lake lapped against the shore, were hundreds more in individual protective lagers. Approaching 25,000 troops now fell under Taeris' direct command. Something, deep at the back of his mind, was screaming at him but he couldn't hear it. He walked to the beach and sat, surveying the calm waters and tried to clear his mind. At the core of his being there was one question that demanded an answer. Seven years ago, back when he had been denounced, it had been for a crime of disloyalty. It must have been for that crime. Surely. However hard Taeris thought about the decision that had cost him everything, he couldn't really understand why it had been so terrible. Of course disloyalty was unforgivable, that was accepted, that was obvious, but were all disloyalties equal? It was certainly something to consider. In the immediate future he had to deal with this traitor, this Faeral, a man who had raised arms against lawful authority. That was a form of disloyalty that should command the most severe of punishments. Taeris gave that a moment's thought and decided that perhaps flaying was the correct punishment for such a treasonous act. Not only was it immensely painful and could be made to last for hours if the man with the knife had skill, it was also a very gripping spectacle and could possibly encourage loyal behaviour from a large number of people who witnessed it. Drowning was obviously more painful and a wise man feared that death above all others, but it was less compelling or instructional for the witnesses. Finally he made a decision as to how the traitor should be treated and gave the orders accordingly, Faeral wouldn't die at once, some attempt would first be made to wrest information from his stubborn body. With that decision made, Taeris strode back to his command Tyrant and began the arduous process of issuing orders for the establishment of a large lager dispersed among the entire legion. In an environment surrounded by dangerous enemies this process was far from trivial and might require alertness and care from every unit as it took its turn on watch; not all snipers fielded weapons that were useless against powered armour, some even had heavy weapons that could make a Tyrant pay for arrogance. Periodically there would be the deep rushing sound of a Tyrant lifting off or landing, the vehicles made excellent platforms for reconnaissance of the surrounding forest, though a tree still made for useful cover for an infantryman if he took care to disguise his heat and shape.

Laesa, he thought. He remembered her beauty. He remembered her laugh, her poise. How many of those memories were real? How many were visions dreamt up by his unconscious to keep him sane in EF7?

Finally the orders were issued. Taeris closed his eyes and imagined Laesa's face.

Language and Barrier

Faeral was not expecting mercy from his captors. In fact it was the Republic's inflexible adherence to unmerciful and draconian punishment for the slightest of infractions that had led him to being nominated first as a representative of Prosperity's agricultural workers and later their leader in a rebellion that would now cost him his life; as it had so many others. When he was placed into a small holding pen attached to one side of the main camp of the enemy he quickly looked around to see if there was useful intelligence that could be gleaned from his surroundings. Arrogant as the Republic was, they made no attempt to hide their strength, their ranks, their deployment. The stripy armour showed immediately that the unit here was the 6th Legion and a rapid assessment of other markings showed that the lager was used by all four regiments that made up the legion's strength. His information on this unit was relatively sparse, though he knew it had been involved in the battle on Citaeron and had since been the major force he faced on Prosperity. He turned his attention to the small cage, finding to his surprise that he wasn't alone. On the opposite side of the pen was a skinny and bedraggled-looking wretch. The first thing that could be spotted about the man was his strikingly grey hair, not merely grey but white, almost transparent. His ribs and spinal processes were clearly visible under taut skin and he was so thin under the ribcage that subtle bumps and curves might actually reveal the topology of the underlying organs. Faeral's cellmate had been a prisoner for a long time. Of course that didn't imply that he could be trusted, but fortunately Faeral had a perfect test for that. "Fipeya yesta?" He asked.

"Mipeya Kitelya."

So the stranger's name was Kitelya, positive in more than one way. First he clearly spoke Aepolian and secondly he understood it natively enough to modify the consonant sounds properly, a typical Republican would have pronounced this very well-known name 'Gidelya' without a moment's thought. While this couldn't rule out the possibility that Kitelya was not an ally of Faeral, it at least made it clear that he was not a loyal citizen of the Republic; no loyal Republican would have broken the law by speaking an illegal language, the nature of the Republic meant that even its secret agents had to be good Republicans. Especially its secret agents, in fact. "Mipeya Faeral."

Announcing his name seemed to cause real surprise to Kitelya. He reacted as if he had been shot and rapidly began speaking in Aepolian asking if it was true, if the war was being won, if Faeral had news from Citaeron.

Faeral held up his hands as if to stem the sudden flow of questions; obviously the Republic hadn't quite broken this man yet, though they'd clearly tried. As Kitelya moved across the pen there were weals visible on his legs where both had been broken. Of course that was possibly a consequence of fighting or of fleeing but in Faeral's mind it took on the dark shadow of torture.

It rapidly became clear that Kitelya was from Aepolia on Citaeron. He wasn't exactly sure of the timings involved but he'd been captured in the battle of the canyons and ever since had been questioned about the rebellion. Faeral's name meant to him as much as it did because so many of the questions that the Republic had asked were about Faeral. This was fame, of a sort, when people Faeral had never met were being beaten and tortured for not being able to answer questions about him. Faeral apologised, feeling some responsibility for the pain this man had undergone. He also told Kitelya that his own approach was to speak only Aepolian and suggested that it might be a useful trick for any prisoner in their position. Kitelya tried to smile, but it rapidly shifted to a grimace of pain; he had tried the same approach.

It wasn't long before the soldiers came. Two of them in full armour. They opened the door and strode into the small pen, taking Kitelya and dragging him out. Faeral watched them leave with anger shaking him to his core. Now they had the rebel leader why would they keep tormenting this poor captive. He almost called the soldiers back, but immediately stopped himself. He was, perhaps, not known to the Republic as the overall leader of the rebellion and if so he couldn't give them that information.

It was more than a day and a night before Kitelya was returned to the pen. He had been horribly mistreated, his left arm shattered, and he was covered in bruises. More worryingly the soldiers had been careful not to break his skin or cut him, something that might lead to an incurable bacterial infection and end his suffering in days. It seemed they had no intention of permitting him to die until they'd finished with him. Food was thrown into the pen a little later and Faeral collected a portion and took it to his cellmate. Kitelya was essentially unresponsive, pain had turned him white and he was trembling. Faeral made him sit up to take some food and water, even though he was aware that he was hurting the man by doing so. If Faeral hadn't been there, he suspected Kitelya would have just lain in pain and waited for death. After a while Faeral heard Kitelya ask a question, one that he would probably have asked as well.

"Tisitroskeysa miti yesta?"

Are they going to kill us? Yes, probably, thought Faeral, but he responded, "Tisitroskeyfonsa miti." Maybe. Kitelya seemed to deflate, Faeral asked him why he wasn't looking forward to death; after what had been done to him. In fact it was a simpler answer than he expected. At his core, Kitelya was a believer. He wanted to see the Republic crushed, he wasn't worried about his own life as he'd long since decided to sacrifice that as necessary, the thing that had finally broken him was the capture of Faeral.

The injured man finished with one thought, "Mipeya anusti; fipeya elanusti", I am nothing; you are everything.

Faeral wished he could reassure the suffering man. In truth it was going to be a serious blow to the rebellion if Faeral was unable to continue but there were other commanders, in fact he had left strict instructions not to waste time and resources on attempting to rescue him; instead there was a skilled deputy who had his own units and weapons. He could also frame attacks of his own, one in particular that he'd been talking about for a while. In fact, with the Republic currently limited to a small area such as this there was every chance it could be carried off. If Faeral could judge the moment correctly it might even cause enough chaos to permit him to escape during the battle; though a glance at Kitelya suggested that there was no way they could both escape. As he started to plan he told Kitelya of his purpose and apologised again, this time for having to leave him. Kitelya seemed to immediately lose some of the air of doom that had surrounded him. He said that should Faeral make his escape as planned then he would happily wait in the pen to laugh in the faces of the soldiers.

The door to the pen was made of stiff mesh netting; essentially a structural material that military units had in abundance. While it was almost impossible to tear or break it was possible, if enough effort was applied, to twist and bend it, possibly enough to make a gap for a man to wriggle through. Tonight would be the night, any earlier and the rebels wouldn't have been able to get into position, any later and the 6th Legion might begin to move outward from the lager they still occupied and disperse more widely over the region. As night fell Faeral began working the mesh with all his might knowing that if the attack didn't come then he would never be able to evade the alert soldiers and in the morning the twisted mesh would alert them to his escape attempt. Still, it was worth doing because if the rebels attacked tonight then in the chaos he might escape and there was no other time he thought it even a remote possibility.

After two hours he paused and crept across to Kitelya. Pain was keeping him awake so Faeral made him take some food and water, if the plan worked it might be the last chance to help him. Kitelya looked at the sad little gap that Faeral had managed to open and his eyes told the obvious truth; so far the gap was too small to fit a person. Faeral rested a little longer and began to explain the plan to Kitelya. Possibly the reason he felt obliged to do this was that the plan would possibly kill Kitelya directly, and if it didn't the aftermath of it might lead to his execution. Faeral told him that, one way or another, Kitelya's suffering wouldn't last much longer. He told him of the other commander of the rebel forces. In a low whisper he described the plan, the batteries of home-made rockets that had been prepared, the carefully sited launch trenches, the movement training the rebels had received. Kitelya closed his eyes as he was told what the future might be, but a subtle smile seemed to play at the corners of his mouth. After a while Kitelya finally dropped off to sleep and Faeral went back to his work at the fence, now feeling he had an ally, a friend, even if he was a friend who was too crippled to assist.

After a few seconds there was a loud shout from behind Faeral in English, "Action stations! Rockets! Mount up and get airborne!" Faeral turned and looked for the source of the shout, but he could see nothing outside the dark pen. It was then that he realised the shouts had come from Kitelya.

It took a few seconds for Faeral to understand what had happened. In those seconds the lager came alive with activity. Soldiers ran over to the gate to the pen and pulled it open, they had a stretcher with them, and barely taking note of Faeral at all, they placed Kitelya upon it. By the time they'd bustled out again dozens of Tyrants were beginning to launch into the sky; within moments it was hundreds. Faeral let out an animal cry of anguish. Assuming he was right about the planned attack it was now doomed to be a costly failure and that was his fault, his mistake. In a few minutes it became clear that Faeral had been quite correct in his assumptions. Tyrants were striking down into the forest all around the lager, infantry weapons firing as the troops deployed. Despite this, some rockets did launch and flew into the camp, but instead of a massive and destructive bombardment these attacks were sporadic and small. Worse, their intended targets were mostly no longer in the lager and so those that did land did little damage. Faeral found himself wishing that he could be lucky and a rocket might land on the pen, but even here he was to be cheated.

In reality battles don't end; they peter out. Eventually there were no more rockets, then there were no more energy discharges out in the forest, then there was the gradual and uneven return of the Tyrants and their troops to the lager. Seeing these enemies relaxed and celebrating their crushing of another rebel force was bringing tears to Faeral's eyes. He was imagining the dead out there, the comrades slaughtered from the skies, his fellows butchered because of his stupidity. A few prisoners had been taken and were being brought through the camp. One of them saw Faeral and shouted an apology to him for having failed. Faeral dug his fingers into the earth and dropped his head in dismay.

It was only a matter of seconds before the pen door banged open again and two soldiers came and dragged him to his feet. They said nothing to him and didn't hurt him but they pulled him firmly along the ground towards the back of a Tyrant vehicle, where the main door was open.

Inside was Kitelya. He was sitting up on a stretcher while two men worked on setting his broken arm. While he was a bit pale he wasn't making much noise, tribute to the pain-killers he must have been given. Faeral stared at him in incomprehension. "Yesta?"

Kitelya focused on Faeral. "We both speak both languages fluently. Stop being so irritating. My name is Taeris, Legate of the Sixth Legion."

Faeral

Taeris was carefully dressed back in his armour; once the injuries were stabilised he was better off in the suit than out of it. He got to his feet as soon as he was able, a wince of pain crossing his face briefly, then stepped down from the back of the Tyrant to stand in front of Faeral. "Your rebellion is over," he said, "Give us a complete accounting of the traitors and in exchange we will offer them fair treatment and spare their worthless lives."

Faeral looked like a man with little left to give him care but he said, "And what of me?"

Taeris showed no emotion at all. "You will be executed, naturally."

Faeral almost managed a smile. "Naturally. I will not help you bring down the rebellion. It is a just cause. I know you can't see that."

Taeris shook his head firmly. "Whatever the rebellion was it is now finished. Save as many of your fellow traitors as you can, if you retain any honour."

"Honour?" Faeral looked upwards and shouted into the sky, "What does the Republic know of honour?"

The thought crossed Taeris' mind briefly that this rebel might be insane but then he rejected such a possibility. "The Republic is founded on honour. We act in accordance with the will of the people, the whole people, not just some tiny faction of anarchists."

Faeral smirked back and said, "You are the right arm of a malevolent dictator. Arguing with you about freedom is like trying to discuss space-travel with a fish. You are hopelessly lost to the propaganda of the Republic. Kill me as you will, but you are wrong and one day I hope you will realise that."

Taeris was about to stalk off but something in Faeral's words stopped him. "Well then. I am here, tell me your cause. I will listen to you."

Faeral was stony faced. "No you won't. You are incapable of even thinking a thought that has yet to be approved by the Legacy."

"You might be surprised. I was denounced by the Legacy for unrepublican activities. I was educated back into the mould of a proper citizen, regained the trust of my President, the faith of my military. I have recently been returned to my former rank. Your suggestion that I am incapable of thinking independently stands false. Would you test the remainder of your theories against me so I can show them all as lies?"

Faeral frowned at Taeris, obviously he believed him, why would someone invent such a story, but this was the first time he'd ever heard of someone going through the education process and being restored to a former rank, just coming out of education alive was a challenge. "You were educated?"

"Yes," Taeris said impatiently, "Education Facility Seven, for seven years. I learnt my duty and incidentally your language. I was returned to the Republic only recently."

For a moment Faeral gathered his thoughts. EF7? This man went through EF7? "My own past is less illustrious. I am an agricultural worker, I've lived on Prosperity for my entire life. As I have a facility with languages I began to be approached by fellow workers to represent them in legal proceedings, financial negotiations, that sort of thing. About two years ago I represented a group of farmers when they wanted to negotiate a raise of their fees for providing food to the Republic. I was arrested."

For Taeris this was the natural consequence of such treasonous behaviour. "Obviously. Almost every word you've said is the very definition of treachery."

Faeral continued, "Agricorp decided that my behaviour was treason and sentenced me to death. I demanded a trial as is my right as a citizen and I was refused."

For Taeris the story was becoming hard to follow. "You had no right to a trial, your treachery was against Agricorp, not the government, and you are an employee, not a citizen. Only the Republic conducts trials and only for citizens. Why do you claim a right where no such right exists?"

Faeral approached from another direction. "Agricorp works within the Republic. It must be subject to the same laws as the citizens, yes?"

Taeris concentrated for a moment then asked, "Why?"

So this was the gulf between them. Faeral looked out at the forest. "The Republic has these enormous corporations and they are effectively above the law."

Taeris shook his head sadly and said, "All the corporations have their own laws and they enforce them and abide by them, all you have to do is obey the law and everything works. Why must you belittle a system that has kept stability and order in the Republic for thousands of years?"

To Faeral it was clear that this soldier couldn't understand him at all, even when they spoke the same language they spoke different languages. "I pity you," was all he could eventually say.

Taeris smiled. "I rather admire you. The rocket barrage was a very clever idea, very clever. Modern armies aren't used to weapons that are indirect, so usually if your weapon can see me then I can see your weapon, but these rockets, although primitive, were to be fired from deep in the forest. We would have had no chance of returning fire immediately."

"Until I gave the plan away."

Taeris laughed. "Yes. Until then. Of course the rockets were fairly primitive and would have needed a direct hit to damage one of my vehicles, but they were concentrated in number. Your betrayal of your allies might have saved me a few dozen casualties but it had no bearing on the outcome. You know the progress of the Republic is inevitable, if history has taught us nothing else it is that absolute fact."

Faeral closed his eyes and took a moment before responding. "The Republic ruthlessly eliminates anything it doesn't want in its history. That's why the march of history looks to be inevitable. Let me ask you something. What happened to the Third Guards Legion?"

The words stunned Taeris and it showed in his face. "What do you mean?"

"What do you think I mean, Legate?"

"There is no Third Guards Legion."

Faeral nodded, again more with sadness than triumph. "It was destroyed in battle, here on Prosperity. This information is not included in the Republic histories, in fact it is a crime to speak of it."

The Legate stood, too quickly, pain shot through his arm. "You lie!"

The captive before him just kept speaking quietly, "It was sent here three years ago under the command of a Legate Caeranion. I assume it was sent to put down our rebellion."

"Don't lie to me, traitor, the rebellion is only just starting."

"No, Legate, the rebellion has been underway for nearly five years and, whatever your history might tell you, we have

130

won more battles than we have lost."

Taeris reached out an armoured hand and slapped Faeral with it, knocking the prisoner to the ground. "Do you think you can intimidate me with lies?"

Faeral wiped a small trickle of blood from the corner of his mouth. "What happened to the Eighth Guards Legion, then? What is happening right now on Citaeron? The Republic is founded on lies so pervasive that even its own commanders know nothing of it."

Taeris waved over two soldiers. "Take him back to his cage. Make sure he can't get out this time." The soldiers picked up Faeral and started to move off. "And break his right arm for me will you?"

The armoured men didn't even break stride as one of them slightly changed his grip, the sound of snapping bone and the sudden cry of pain lifted Taeris' mood somewhat, but not enough. He couldn't completely dismiss the feeling that the traitor had, in some way, emerged from their private battle victorious.

Doloras answered his summons immediately, a smile on his face. "Yes, Legate, how may I help?"

Taeris rested a friendly armoured gauntlet on the shoulder of his subordinate. "It seems the Twenty-third Infantry Regiment needs a new Colonel."

Doloras nodded, trying not to be too eager. "Yes, Legate."

"You have been invaluable, discreet, loyal and skilled. Your allegiance to the chain of command and to the principles of the Republic is unequalled and you have shown a willingness to fight courageously and stand up for your beliefs, even when they disagree with my own. More importantly you have come to be my most valued counsellor on matters both military and not."

Doloras tried to keep his face impassive but he was smiling a little.

"So," Taeris concluded, "I was wondering if you had any suggestions as to whom I should appoint Colonel of the Twenty-third?" Doloras' face must have fallen a little at least, because Taeris reacted to it and laughed heartily. "Congratulations Colonel Doloras. Take good care of my former regiment."

The smile returned. "Thank you Legate."

Taeris grimaced a little as he shifted his weight. "Now we need to plan on the systematic elimination of the rebel threat from Prosperity. I also require an update on the progress of the Eighth Guards on Citaeron."

Doloras looked sharply towards his superior. "Why, Sir?"

Taeris was wondering if this would be likely to make a man like Doloras suspicious, clearly it had. "It appears that the traitor Faeral may be the overall leader of the entire rebellion. I was thinking we could execute him and announce the rebellion to be over, but tonight's little attack proved that his fellows will continue even without his supervision. Accordingly I need to shut down the treason with words as well as deeds. Let me know when I can announce to the traitors here that the invasion of Citaeron has been crushed by the Guards."

Doloras frowned slightly. "So announce the victory of the Guards."

Taeris thought for a moment. "Do you mean the Guards have been victorious? Already?"

Doloras was now looking very confused. "I don't understand the question, Sir. You want to tell the rebels here that the Guards have crushed their brother-infestation on Citaeron. Why not announce it?"

Taeris now understood exactly how much of a Republic

man Doloras was. Words and deeds need have no correlation at all, of course. One could say one thing and do another, announce a truth that was a lie. Actions were that which needed to be done in the service of the Republic, words were things that needed to be said in service of the Republic. Sometimes these two things might be perfectly opposed to each other, but it mattered not at all. "I'm sorry, you're right of course. I shall wait on the announcement however until it will cause the greatest harm to the psychology of the enemy."

Doloras nodded and left the Tyrant but there was a flicker of concern, perhaps, on his face. Taeris suddenly felt oddly vulnerable despite his mighty legion surrounding him, he wondered if it might be that Faeral, alone in a cage, nursing a painful injury, surrounded by enemies, might nonetheless feel less unsure.

Taeris gathered himself and strolled out of the Tyrant into the bustle of the lager. Around him were groups of soldiers singing the standard, approved, victory songs. Some of them were preparing for the slaughter of their prisoners, but as was tradition they would all be executed at once in a blaze of ferocity. All but one, of course. Faeral might yet prove a valuable resource.

A group of junior officers from the 23rd beckoned Taeris to join them. Naturally they didn't really want him there, but it was not wise to offend a superior. He walked over to join them and to participate in the synchronised mass execution, maybe once he'd ripped the limbs off a screaming traitor he'd feel a little better. Somehow he doubted that was the solution to his ennui.

Franker's Farm

The nominal capital city of Prosperity was optimistically named Pinnacle City. Since the entire planet was essentially flat, with little more than ridges around the edges of the craters and some splash-spires in the centre of some of the lakes, it seemed the word 'pinnacle' was intended to be figurative. The soldiers of the 6th Legion had taken one look at it and elected to refer to it, as in the old joke, as Franker's Farm. Its environment was lacking in the picturesque subtlety of much of the planet as it was buried in the centre of industrial farming and fishing units. Worse was the fact that the city was essentially one large factory for processing food and getting it onto ships for the lift to orbit; meaning that the entire place consisted of single-story prefabricated units placed for functionality rather than with any aesthetic in mind. People who lived here tended to live in small buildings wedged out of the way of the robots and automated systems and the population was only a few thousand strong.

Taeris took in the view through the powerful cameras on his Tyrant and turned to look with a sour expression at his driver. "This can't be a real capital city."

The driver shrugged. "It's the largest population centre, Legate."

Taeris humphed and turned back to his screens. "Pinnacle City. You think one of those buildings is the highest point on the planet?"

"Legate, I think the highest point on the planet is probably wherever the tallest man on the planet is standing."

Taeris chuckled in appreciation at the man's joke and opening a communications channel, Taeris spoke to his commanders. "Begin assault now. Try to preserve, as much as possible, the Agricorp infrastructure." This was something Agricorp was very exercised about. People could be easily replaced but some of the farming equipment was expensive and complex.

Within a few seconds the attack was in motion. The entire 6th Legion flew into action from all sides, dropping infantry near the edges of the city and then covering them with the cannon on the Tyrants as they seized the city, one building at a time. It took only a few minutes and there was not a single shot fired.

In the middle of the city was a large square that served as a main landing pad for the shuttles. Today the captive population of Pinnacle City was gathered in a large group in the middle as Taeris strode towards them. He glared at them for a few seconds, wondering how he could tell if any of them were traitors. "I am Legate Taeris," he bellowed, making use of the suit's microphone and speakers to ensure he could be heard by everyone assembled. "Who is in charge here?"

There was a pause for a few seconds and then an elderly man at the front of the group called out, "You are, Legate."

Taeris stared helplessly at the civilians in front of him. "Identify which of your fellow citizens are supporters of the traitor rebels. Bring them forward to face legal process."

The entire group seemed to look at each other in complete bafflement.

Taeris had a limited patience for such things. "Identify the guilty individuals or I will order this city decimated. I will then ask the question again and if there is no answer I will

135

decimate again. You will run out of ignorant people before I run out of weapons, I promise."

The elderly man shouted out, "Legate, I don't believe anyone here is a traitor. I think the traitors live in the forests."

Taeris considered this for a moment. It was possible, he had to concede. Maybe the planet still had loyal citizens and if so they might remain in the cities while the traitors ran off to live in the forests. After a moment he nodded and stalked off. Passing his honour guard on the way out he waved a negligent finger back the way he'd come. "Put them all back to work, except that old man. Bring him to me, and Faeral as well."

He made it back to his Tyrant just a few minutes before the two prisoners were pulled up to the rear hatch and stood, waiting. Faeral was cradling his broken arm. After taking a large drink of fresh water he turned to look at the men. He started with the old man. "What is your name?"

"Kranet, Legate."

"Kranet, do you know this man?"

Kranet looked at Faeral. "Not personally, Legate, but I could guess his identity I think."

Taeris nodded. "Then by all means, guess."

"I think he might be Faeral."

Taeris smiled. "You are an excellent guesser. He is Faeral. Now tell me what you know of Faeral."

Kranet blinked a few times. "Legate, I know only that which others have told me."

"Then relate for me these stories and legends, Kranet."

"Yes, Legate," Kranet said, "I have heard that Faeral was a troublesome worker in the food factories who was scheduled for execution by Agricorp. I have been told that he escaped death and fled to the forest. I have also heard that in the forest he has been associated with a band of traitors that have tried to stop lawful order on Prosperity. This is the substance of that which I have heard."

Taeris nodded indulgently. "Did you hear what his position might be within the traitor band?"

Kranet looked straight ahead. "Sir, I heard that Faeral might be the leader of the traitors."

Taeris turned his attention to Faeral. "And you, Faeral, what can you tell me of Kranet?"

Faeral clenched his teeth briefly and then said, "Anusti."

Instantly Taeris slapped Faeral to the ground. "I thought we were past that little charade. If you know nothing of this man then say 'Nothing'."

Faeral picked himself up, slowly because of the way he was trying to protect his arm. "Nothing. I know nothing of Kranet."

As Taeris turned his eyes back to Kranet he could see that the man was trembling a little. "Kranet, what is your job in Pinnacle City?"

Kranet had a tremor in his voice. "I am... Legate... I am the shuttle coordinator. It is my responsibility to, to..."

"To coordinate the shuttle flights, yes, I'm not a complete idiot." Taeris glared at Faeral. "So you, a leader of rebels, trying to infect the remainder of the Republic with your little disease, do not know the identity of the man in the best position to help you smuggle people or messages off the planet? Is this what you continue to insist?"

Faeral tried his best. "I lied, Legate. I am familiar with Kranet and his job. I had hoped to recruit him in the future."

Taeris nodded. "You lied. Yes, I believe you did. I believe the reason you lied was to convince me that this man, Kranet, is unimportant to your treason. In fact, I suspect he is a part of your treason; perhaps an important part."

Faeral said, "No, Legate, that isn't true."

Taeris looked back at Kranet. "Nobility is a rare commodity, Kranet. When I asked for answers from the employees in the square you spoke up, and only you. This is because you hold, in your mind, some authority or responsibility here. You couldn't be stupid enough to believe that any job assignment could make you an authority in a city under my guns, therefore it must be that you are a traitor rebel and you feel responsible for those in the square who are also traitors. As it happens we were able to secure the city without any damage being done to its infrastructure and so Agricorp will be satisfied with the outcome. It seems, however, unfortunately, that a large number of employees were lost during the capture of the city. Roughly half of them, in fact."

Kranet yelled, "No! Legate, please, they are innocent!"

Taeris ignored him and raised his eyes to two of the soldiers standing at flawless, powered attention behind the captives. "Men, take this Kranet away to the centre of the city and dismember him. Please ensure it is done very, very slowly." The two soldiers reacted instantly.

As he was dragged away Kranet screamed out, "Please! Legate! I can tell you about the rebels!"

Taeris turned to a sickened-looking Faeral. "Can he?"

Faeral nodded miserably. "He can."

"Soldiers! Bring back Kranet! I have need of him yet."

As Kranet was dropped at Taeris' feet he was a pale, shaking, sobbing wretch of a man. "So. Tell me your role in the treason."

Kranet looked ashamed as he glanced across at Faeral, but the rebel leader was staring at the ground and didn't acknowledge him. "I helped with moving rebels, traitors, from here. I helped disguise the conversion of civilian ships to combat vessels. I oversaw the calibration of CONAN drives on those ships. I stopped reports on rebel activities being sent to the Republic. I used the jump relays to send messages for the rebels. I can tell you everything you need to know."

Taeris was expressionless. "I think you already have, unless there's something else that is yet to happen."

"Yes! Please! If you don't kill me I can tell you about the next attack."

Taeris was pleased to see Faeral's head snap up at that. "I can promise you a better death, at least. If the information is really good it might even be worth your life or the lives of others."

Kranet closed his eyes, as if to distance himself from the betrayal he was about to commit. "The rebel fleet is preparing an assault on Esperia."

Taeris suddenly laughed. "You expect me to believe that? The attack on Citaeron has been crushed, the remnants of the rebels here on Prosperity are scattered and yet, you claim, the next attack is at Esperia?"

Kranet nodded vigorously. "Yes, Legate, you have to believe me!" The attack on Citaeron has been mostly successful, at least the last I heard. Most of the rebel fleet was withdrawn back to a staging location, to re-equip with the main military force. They will attack Esperia while your forces remain stuck at Citaeron and here."

"This staging location, where is it?"

"I don't know, Legate, I swear!"

Taeris looked at Faeral. "You will confirm his story and tell me this staging location, no doubt?" Faeral made no sound or movement; if not for the gentle motion of his ribs as he breathed he might be dead. "Kranet. I will confirm your story. Until then you live. Soldiers! Take them to separate pens."

Turning back into his Tyrant, Taeris opened up a channel to the battlecruiser in orbit. "Adrael, Taeris."

It took a few minutes for Adrael to respond. "Adrael."

Taeris said, "Adrael, I have been given some information that might be true. If it is then it is serious indeed. I need you to send requests for information through the jump-relays."

Adrael responded at once. "Information is my area of responsibility, Legate. You do your own job."

Taeris hardened his face. "Then I have information for you. A captured rebel broke down in front of me and he told me a few things. He told me that the battle on Citaeron is not proceeding as we would hope. He told me also that the reason for our victory in orbit above Citaeron was that the rebel fleet had been withdrawn for other duties. He didn't admit to knowing where they were now. He finally admitted that the fleet, with new rebel troops, will be launching an attack on Esperia."

Adrael took a moment to respond. "Clearly he was so terrified that he made up outrageous lies."

Taeris was tempted to agree but he couldn't ignore the possibility. "I suspect you are right, Adrael. I wouldn't feel I had served my duty if I did not bring this matter to your attention, however."

Adrael's voice responded at once. "Your loyalty does you credit, Legate. I am now apprised of the information and you may leave the matter to me."

If Taeris could have been certain that Adrael would investigate he would have signed off at that point, but he simply didn't know the Security man well enough. "Will you investigate this matter, Adrael?"

Adrael disconnected communications without responding. Taeris thought about that for a moment. He couldn't decide if that was a good or a bad sign. He was certain less than an hour later.

A channel beeped open in the Tyrant. It was from the Spica, Adrael was calling him. "Taeris here."

Adrael's voice seemed subtly different somehow. "I have news for you, Legate. It appears that the suppression of the rebellion on Citaeron is progressing towards its inevitable conclusion in the Republic's favour. It is, it seems, taking a little longer than first seemed likely and it might require the deployment of a few additional units to finish off the last few pockets of resistance. Raephus has been making enquiries as to the likely whereabouts of the balance of the traitor fleet and he has not found any useful information. It is the considered opinion of the Republic that this means the fleet has either been disbanded or has fallen into disunity as is inevitable when anarchists try to form organisations that need coherence. My researches are completed and I will have no more of this matter. Raephus has indicated that he would listen to any suggestions you might have as regards the disposition or deployment of the Third Fleet."

The channel dropped immediately. Taeris stared in astonishment at the place the light had been blinking until a few seconds earlier. So it was all true. The 8th Guards were losing on Citaeron, new units would have to be sent to avert disaster. The rebel fleet was somewhere unknown and nobody other than Raephus was even looking for it. He summoned Doloras immediately.

Doloras arrived after some ten minutes. He had been inspecting the 23rd Regiment several kilometres from Taeris' command vehicle. "Legate, you called me?"

Taeris nodded and decided to explain as clearly as possible, so he invited Doloras into the Tyrant and closed the hatch.

"It appears we may have a problem. The battle on Citaeron is not going well. It seems the bulk of the rebel fleet is preparing a new attack even now and this attack is aimed at Esperia."

Doloras looked stunned. "The Praesidium? Impossible."

"Let me ask you this, then. How long will it take us to eliminate rebellion here on Prosperity?"

Doloras immediately responded, "The rebels will fall before us in no time at all."

Taeris nodded. "A loyal answer. Now, try the truth. How long do you think it will take us to round up the entire population of Prosperity, interrogate them all, find all of their caches of weapons and supplies, find all their hidden bases and bolt-holes. How long will we be here if our goal is to leave not a single rebel on Prosperity."

Doloras looked confused. "As I say..."

"Truth." Taeris interrupted, quietly.

Doloras looked as if he as being led into an elaborate trap but finally he said, "If we have to completely eliminate all rebel activity on Prosperity, such a task might consume the remainder of our lives."

Taeris nodded, satisfied. "On Citaeron the rebels were able to exploit a landing rapidly because of a powerful fleet and sympathetic traitors on the planet surface. Is it possible these same conditions might prevail on Esperia?"

Doloras shook his head emphatically. "No, Legate. On Esperia there are two Legions of Guards, a large contingent of Guardians and the First Fleet is stationed there."

Taeris thought for a moment. "Making an easy attack unlikely. But is it possible?"

Doloras turned the idea in his head a few times. "I admit to possibilities, only."

"Possibilities are enough. Prosperity could take many years to purge of rebel activity, but it is not a great danger to the Republic at this moment. I have decided we are to prepare to leave this planet at a moment's notice. Whether we fly to the aid of the Guards on Citaeron or to protect Esperia, I don't yet know, but one of those worlds is likely to be in far greater need of us than this overinflated fishing village."

Doloras nodded at once, obedience to authority was perfectly ingrained. As Doloras left through the rear hatch of the Tyrant, Taeris touched the contact that would open a channel to one of the junior officers in the lager. He was a man of his word so he had to reward Kranet for his information. "This is Taeris. Take that old man, Kranet, to the town square. Randomly select one twentieth of the local employees and shoot them, while he watches, and then dismember him. Do it slowly, but not very slowly. This is an important distinction, I promised him it would not be done very slowly."

Taeris turned back to his Tyrant's console and opened a channel to the Spica. "Raephus. Taeris."

The 4th Fleet

Taeris travelled to Citaeron in the Spica. In fact the quarters were probably less impressive than the ones he'd had on LS7, but Raephus had made the offer and Taeris was pleased to accept. The only potential problem was the fact that he was now in physical reach of Adrael, whose power in the Republic seemed almost limitless. For all his dangers Adrael was clearly very competent, skilled even, which made him both a very useful man to know and a stunningly dangerous man to cross. Taeris had always preferred competent allies and incompetent enemies; the danger represented by Adrael if the two fell out was ever-present.

Raephus also impressed the Legate. He seemed to be one of those cool and confident people who diligently carried out their role in a manner for which the only suitable adjective was 'classy'. In this case, however, Taeris was also coming to have a genuine fondness for the aristocratic Admiral.

Faeral had been kept alive, for the time being at least. He was enjoying the hospitality of the 136th Battalion, part of the 27th Regiment. Betrayal by his fellow rebel on Prosperity seemed to have taken some of the fight out of him; he was quiet and brooding and only by grabbing his broken arm were his guards able to make him utter any sounds at all. When he had learnt of Kranet's fate he had glared at Taeris with such venom in his eyes that it seemed he would want to throw himself at his captor and claw at the powered armour with his very fingernails.

Taeris wondered about the devotion that the rebels demonstrated for Faeral and wondered if it was, in some way, related to the devotion that Faeral seemed to exhibit towards the rebels and employees. Definitely something to ponder.

Taeris was invited to join Raephus on the bridge for the jump manoeuvre, and he did so, mostly to spend more time with Raephus, but also because in the absence of any infantrymen to command he literally had nothing else to do. A jump was pretty unremarkable, wherever you stood to watch it, but the preparations and orders on the bridge before the jump took place were an interesting diversion. At exactly the proper moment the sensation of inertia, almost the sense of self, fell away and the smaller of the two nuclear engine sets in the CONAN drive fired a tiny impulse of energy. Transit was almost two hours, something Taeris thought unacceptably long, but the reason for it was sensible, moving more slowly allowed for greater accuracy in identifying exactly where the ship would fall back through the light barrier, permitting a close, almost stealthy, approach to a system.

The 3rd Fleet fell out of its jump in the middle of a battle.

Had Taeris been relying on his eyes to tell him that battle was joined he'd have had a hard time confirming it. Battles in space, even in orbit, involve ships that may be thousands of kilometres apart, their weapons often move faster than any eye can see and in the case of tmetic beams generally show no evidence of their passage. The process of slowing the ship and gently disengaging inertial compensation gave a brief impression of the planet Citaeron charging towards the ship at an impossible, terrifying speed. A more significant effect, however, was the immediate impact of the Spica throwing all compensation away and the sudden lurch that caused in the bellies of the men on board.

For a brief instant the 3rd Fleet would have an advantage, conferred by physics, as they could instantly perceive the other ships in system, but those ships that had already been in the area would have to wait for light to reach them from the new arrivals before they could tell that the 3rd Fleet had arrived. Mere humans couldn't have reacted close to quickly enough to take advantage, but the fighting systems on a modern ship were overwhelmingly controlled by computer and only the management of their behaviour was established by a human operator. In general the warships had access to two distinct types of weapon, missiles that caused damage through kinetic energy and tmetic beams that battered an enemy with intense electromagnetic radiation. Missiles could move at roughly the speed of light, or even faster, but their launch procedures would take too long to capitalise on the brief light-sphere window of advantage for the 3rd Fleet. As the computers began their calculations before the fleet even slowed below the threshold of light-speed it was possible for the beam weapons to hit their targets at almost exactly the same instant as the light from the fleet reached them. This form of attack was known, for historical reasons, as a lightning strike.

On the bridge, countless displays flashed a myriad of coloured indicators to show the current status of the fight. While the specific and subtle details of the conflict would be beyond Taeris' immediate understanding he could see an overview of the battle and the ships serving on each side.

In fact the traitor fleet had arrived in the orbit of Citaeron only a matter of seconds before the 3rd Fleet. By using information provided from the ground, and smuggled out of Citaeron they had identified the approximate location of their main target for the attack, the battleship Hydra. A jump-relay update had fired out to their location a matter of less than a minute ago and its information had given them a path for the ideal attack, straight down the Hydra's throat. The attack force wasn't anywhere near as large as the mighty 4th Fleet, but to a great extent this didn't matter. The attack was to be launched, the fleet engaged and then the raiding rebels could flee back to wherever they'd come from. As a plan it wasn't bad, though the sheer quantity of weaponry on the large warships fielded by the Republic was a serious threat to any such raiding force. As a plan, however, it relied heavily on the 3rd Fleet not randomly turning up in system at the worst possible moment and this was essentially what had happened.

The rebels had sent a force of six ships to carry out their raid. One was a substantial merchant cruiser massing in excess of 5,000 tonnes. All the other five were of a size, roughly 400 tonnes each, and though no two were exactly alike, having been converted from a variety of civilian ships, they had all been converted for the same mission, that of striking hard against much bigger ships. Almost all of their disposable tonnage had been given over to the task of carrying missiles, weapons that could certainly cause a vast amount of damage for the size of the launching craft.

It was, certainly, possible to produce a missile that was not equipped with a jump mass. In fact such weapons were often deployed against targets on a planetary surface and therefore shielded by an atmosphere. In space such things were a waste of time, as the automated beams, operating at the speed of light, could easily pour into such a relatively slow device a terminally destructive amount of energy. Capacitance shielding or ablation protection could provide a measure of defence, but in practice a missile had to be small to be portable and if it were small then its protection must necessarily be light. No, in deep space the ideal arrangement was to use an invertable jump mass.

147

Such a mass could be engaged at launch, reducing the missile's inertia to a tiny fraction of normal, then a modest burst of power from an engine could throw the missile up to a sizable proportion of the speed of light. Of course in the EM-rich environment of a battle, reducing inertia to absolutely nothing could be extremely dangerous, in particular because the ability of any object to withstand damage from tmetics was directly proportional to its structural capacitance, a function of its operating mass. Because of this, missile designs rarely carried enough compensation to drop inertia to zero and reach through the light barrier. Instead the cruise speed of the anti-ship missile was usually a leisurely 0.95C. As the target ship was approached the inertial compensation would be thrown into reverse, increasing the mass of the missile by roughly three orders of magnitude above its uncompensated 'dead' mass. Though the missile would immediately start to lose speed it would have not much further to go before it hit its target. Each kilogramme of missile would hit with the force of a tonne, a tonne travelling at perhaps eighty per cent of the speed of light. In theory these weapons made a small ship into a giant-killer. In practice there were a few drawbacks. One of these drawbacks was about to become all too apparent to the traitors in Citaeron orbit. In order to allow for the fact that the target ship is also likely to be able to compensate for inertia and then go through a very rapid manoeuvre missiles were typically launched in large numbers and in a spreading pattern, making the effect not unlike a giant shotgun. For the target ship the sheer speed with which the missiles approached made destroying them extremely difficult, but for a ship that was not in the direct line of flight of the missiles these same projectiles might be fast but they were also predictable and most light beams could steer onto a target at the speed of light, it being a function of their electronic steering, a matter of diffraction, and therefore not requiring a physical turret to turn. On board the ships of the 3rd Fleet computers handled the destruction of the swarms of missiles before the humans on board had even registered that their arrival was compromised by enemy action.

There was then a brief lull in the fighting as the purely automated anti-missile systems fell quiet and the humans on board made their decisions about the enemy ships. Raephus' crew reacted before the traitors, probably because the traitors had been shocked by the misfortune of the sudden appearance of the 3rd Fleet. On board the Spica and the other ships of the fleet there were large beam weapons mounted in fast-tracking turrets and these weapons now flicked around to engage the enemy vessels. The frigates and destroyers engaged the small missile-boats, while the heavier ships opened fire on the cruiser. As a consequence of the fact that all the enemy ships had selected the Hydra as their target for every heavy weapon they had to scramble to try selecting more appropriate targets. They were too late. Massive pulses of radiation tore into the rebel ships, turning solid hulls into clouds of cooling vapour. Before the final destruction of the rebels a new battery of beams sliced into them from the 4th Fleet. In such a mass explosion of energy there would be no need to look for survivors.

The entire battle had been fought and won in just under three seconds, fast even for a naval battle, impossibly outside Taeris' previous experience of warfare. As the screens started showing calming blue and green patterns and the complete absence of any damage on the Republic side became clear Raephus opened a channel to the 4th Fleet.

"Fourth Fleet from Admiral Raephus."

"Admiral Distrapis, Fourth Fleet commanding."

Raephus nodded as he went on, "Greetings from the

Third Fleet, confirming complete destruction of the enemy force."

Distrapis' voice came back at once. "Enemy destruction confirmed, your assistance is appreciated."

Raephus smiled at that. "No problem, Admiral, happy to serve the Republic."

The Hydra was now being depicted on many of the screens on Spica's bridge. She was noticeably more solid, more armoured, than Spica. She also carried more main weapons and larger ones. Taeris thought she was impressive, but not as pretty as the battlecruiser; assuming those who served aboard cared about such things.

Adrael had been on the bridge for the jump as well, and he spoke up, "Admiral Distrapis, this is Adrael. I will come aboard your flagship immediately."

Taeris noticed that Adrael seemed to treat everyone the same, as if they were his personal servants. Well, at least he treated everyone like that and not just Taeris. Adrael drifted out of the bridge to head to the hangar, not inviting anyone else to join him.

Taeris turned to Raephus and said, "Admiral, is it possible to connect with the current military situation on the surface?"

Raephus simply touched a control and the screen in front of Taeris changed to an overview of the planet.

It was sobering viewing. The 8th Guards Legion was fighting its way through the maze of canyons that Taeris remembered so well, but not affectionately. It had made progress steadily towards the traitor stronghold of Aepolia but at a terrible cost; two of its five regiments were essentially units in name only and of the other three only the 40th Guards Regiment had more than half its full complement of troops remaining. By checking through the battle reports now being saved and catalogued on the Spica it was clear how the fighting on Citaeron had become such a slow and costly business. Every few kilometres in every individual canyon the 8th Guards had faced an ambush. Their tactics when coming under attack were the ones ingrained into their commanders as those that showed the most Republican of behaviour. The Guards simply charged at each ambush, weapons blazing. It didn't take long for the traitors to set up ambushes behind minefields so the charging Guards would take brutal losses in their approach. It also didn't take long for the enemy to site a series of ambushes around a single location, so as the Guards charged towards one group of rebels they would come under attack from a second or a third group placed to maximum effect. The 8th hadn't changed its tactics one iota since their first battle. Screen after screen told the same story; the rebels were constantly improving, refining, modifying their tactics to increase their success. Simply, the 8th Legion had only one manoeuvre and they always executed it in exactly the prescribed manner. Since their commanding Legate seemed to think that as long as they were advancing they were, by definition, winning and therefore there was no problem with the strategy, this could prove a costly campaign indeed. Despite his optimism it had cost him more than 20,000 soldiers to advance just a fraction of the distance towards Aepolia. If his rate of loss remained the same he would need roughly 150,000 troops to complete the mission. At their peak, before the loss of the 2nd Guards Legion, the Guards had numbered about 120,000 troops.

As this information slowly sank in Taeris began to feel physically nauseated. The loss of lives was inevitable in warfare, as the traitors on those modified merchant ships had learnt, but to lose people for no productive reason seemed more than simply inefficient; to Taeris it felt wrong.

He tried to crush the feeling. He thought back to his education. There were no moral questions, no right or wrong, something either served the needs of the Republic or it did not. The battle on the planet below advanced the Republic and therefore it was to be applauded. The problem was that Taeris could see that this battle only appeared to serve the Republic, in fact it could be a giant grave for the Guards Legions and with them the government. No. This must not be. Obviously the Legate had passed his reports back to the Legacy and from there to the President. The President was obviously satisfied or he would have ordered something changed. If Taeris couldn't trust the President he could trust nothing at all. Then he felt a tingling in his spine. He could trust nothing at all. He closed his eyes and remembered his education. EF7 had filled him with the slogans and rituals of the Republic, but it had also stripped from him all his previous individuality. He had become, under the pitiless regime of that blasted asteroid, a blank slate. Now he tried to recapture that feeling. Strip away everything he had been told, right back to his childhood. He snapped his eyes open. From this moment he would evaluate that which he saw and heard without applying the complex filters of Republicanism to every experience. He would start his re-education once more, this time learning from everything about him. For good or ill, he would begin again. He desperately hoped that this process would reignite his devotion to the Republic, not as a slave, but as a free and thinking man.

It was less than an hour before Adrael returned. He announced that the 3rd Fleet would be receiving some reinforcements from the 4th. One of the new arrivals would be a very new light cruiser that would significantly improve the defence of the fleet. Additionally two littoral ships and the two old battleships of the Majoris class would be joining them.

While the battleships were far too old to be capable of holding their own against modern capital ships, their old heavy beams could be a powerful addition to the bombardment capabilities of any fleet and they had been fitted with a few new light beam arrays to give them a fighting chance against fast missiles. Sadly the 4th Fleet could spare no carrier tonnage and was only willing to surrender the oldest of their capital ships.

Raephus had a certain amount of planning to undertake so that he could incorporate the new ships directly into the 3rd Fleet. As this planning would involve the movement of quite a large number of personnel, not least the redistribution of thousands of infantry onto new littorals, there was going to be a day or two's delay in Citaeron orbit. As the Admiral got started on this work Taeris was summoned to Adrael's cabin.

The 8th Legion

Taeris was truly starting to dislike Citaeron. He was here for the third time and every single visit had been disheartening in one way or another. Adrael had sent him down to Tyrenia to discuss the progress of the battle with the Legate of the 8th Guards Legion and this was a prospect that clearly failed to draw much enthusiasm from that august individual either. The metallic scent in the air now felt less like a break from the dry, windless environment on a ship and more like the taste of blood in the mouth.

At least this time he knew his way around the barracks that had been the home base for the 2nd Guards Legion and now served as the operational headquarters for the Republic forces on the planet. Once he arrived he made his way quickly to the command centre, hoping to deal with this unpleasant duty as quickly as possible. Unfortunately the Legate, a man of Taeris' prior acquaintance, had decided to be absent from the building when he arrived.

When Taeris entered the command centre he found himself in the presence of two middle-ranking officers. "Where's Legate Graelen?"

One of the officers responded, "He's busy with important matters." The line was delivered by a smirk, matched only in its humour by the one plastered on the other officer's face.

Taeris noted they didn't address him by his rank, but he expected that, Guards officers always felt themselves superior to mere infantry. The clear implication that any business that could exist between the two legates must be unimportant did irritate him a little, however. "Then fetch him here. I'm only on the planet for a few hours."

The other officer spoke this time. "We do not 'fetch' our Legate. He comes and goes as he pleases."

"In that case," Taeris responded, "How do you get him here in case of an attack or loss of life in his Legion?"

Smoothly the officer continued. "Procedures are in place to be used if the Legion is in immediate danger of taking casualties, of course."

Taeris nodded and sat in one of the chairs. "Then initiate these procedures at once."

A slight chuckle escaped the lips of the other officer. "Do you think the Legion is in danger?"

"Well," Taeris said with a level stare, "I think it might be about to suffer one or two casualties, yes."

The smirks dropped from their faces at once. Of course they couldn't know for sure whereof this Legate before them derived his confidence. A moment of thought was all it took for them to decide that the risk was far too high if the only reward was to save Graelen from an unfortunate discussion.

Graelen entered the room ten minutes later, deliberately affecting an easy and slow walk. He certainly tried to give the impression that he was calm and relaxed, something most Guards officers tried to manage even when bleeding to death. "Taeris. I thought I'd seen the last of you seven years ago."

Taeris nodded. "I thought you had too. Sometimes the personal magnanimity of the President awes and humbles even the most embittered of his servants."

Graelen frowned as if trying to detect any sarcasm in Taeris' voice. "What do you want? I'm a busy man."

Taeris nodded genially. "I know as well as anyone that commanding more than 30,000 troops is a full time job. However you seem to have exceeded everyone's expectations by finding an entirely new way to lighten that onerous burden."

Graelen took a second to catch up. "What are you talking about?"

Taeris kept the tone of his voice light as he went on. "I merely stand in awe at your uncanny ability to take a full legion and tame its daunting complexity by reducing its number of troops to little more than a reinforced regiment. It won't be long before you can abandon even the need for modern technology and simply raise your voice to communicate with your entire command."

Graelen glowered and began to redden. "You will show me the respect my position demands or I will denounce you!"

Taeris kept his voice calm. "I will show you all the respect you have earned. Right now that's less than I extend to the ship's cat aboard the Spica. In fairness, though, that is an unusually charming cat."

The Guardsman was clearly so filled with rage that he was finding it hard to even construct a sentence in response. Taeris thought that an invitation to continue. "At your current rate of progress you will run out of troops long before you capture Aepolia. I know you have been out of school for a few years now but this simple mathematical truth can't have escaped you, surely?"

Graelen finally caught his breath. "I note that in your two recent battles on this planet you fled the enemy, both times. I considered the wisdom of following your example and simply running away at the first sign of the traitors but discarded it as a plan. I felt it might not achieve my objectives. I'm sure this simple truth did not escape you. Do not think to presume that you know my plans or how this war will be fought. I am preparing an attack that will end resistance on Citaeron for good."

Taeris shook his head sadly. "The only action you could take to end this war quickly is if you were to surrender to the rebels. I do not advocate this as a stratagem."

"No!" Graelen thundered. "There is a way to end this war, you unrepublican bastard. You want to see? I will show you and then you can leave with your band of worthless militia on your pointless duties. It may take me a year yet, but I will see you denounced again and when I do there will be no comfortable education programme for you. It will mean your death!"

Taeris privately wondered how long the bellicose Graelen would have survived in 'comfortable education', but he was more interested in how the man planned to emerge victorious from the canyons of Citaeron. "Very well, Legate, show me your strategy."

Graelen turned to the computer in front of him and rapidly authenticated himself. Once he could see the relevant files he opened up a dossier called 'Justinian'. In seconds it became clear what the strategy would be.

Taeris was truly stunned. "You can't mean to do this! The repercussions will be unimaginable!"

Graelen smiled a grim smile, clearly he enjoyed shocking Taeris. "I can and will. Justinian goes into action in two days and the traitors will die. All of them."

"And the innocent?" Taeris was still having difficulty believing that anyone could consider such action.

Graelen laughed a humourless laugh. "What makes the innocent 'innocent' is the fact that they are loyal republicans. It will be their pleasure to lay down their lives in the republican cause. Any who are not thrilled at the opportunity must have been disloyal to begin with. In any event I have shown you what is to come and why I am confident. Now scuttle back under the protection of Adrael and get off my planet."

Taeris had no idea what he could do. Probably nothing he said or did could divert Graelen from his plan and it was strategically sound. Justinian would almost certainly end rebel resistance on Citaeron but Taeris could see that it might also lead to fresh rebellions all across the Republic. Graelen was the perfect product of the officer training that had made him. He could only see the outcome in a narrow sense that related to his own theatre of responsibility. He would carry out his mission without thought of the wider effects and of course he had no morality but the one that had been imposed upon him by the religion of republicanism. In that moment Taeris realised that Graelen could be replaced with an automaton without losing any command abilities, or actually that an automaton would be indistinguishable from Graelen.

Graelen locked the console and stormed out. Taeris helplessly watched him go. After a minute to gather his thoughts he returned to the small shuttle that waited to transport him back to the fleet.

He found Adrael in the bridge, and immediately asked to speak to him privately. Behind the bridge was a conference room that was empty so the two men floated inside and closed the door.

Adrael was his normal composed self. "I expected your survey to take longer than this."

Taeris was grim-faced. "The Legate was less than pleased by my arrival."

"So you failed to get any view of the operation?"

"Oh I got a view," Taeris said. "I got a full view. Graelen

is aware that his strategy will lead to running out of men before he captures Aepolia. He has simply been using the lives of his troops to shrink the geographical area that the rebels can claim to control. He then intends to use a bombardment by the Fourth Fleet to eliminate all resistance in that area."

Adrael shook his head. "Ridiculous. He can't destroy a third of the planet's infrastructure."

Taeris answered, "He doesn't intend to. He's been breeding fleas with Yersinia up in orbit. He'll bomb the traitor city and all the area around it."

There was a long pause before Adrael spoke. "Then it seems my concern was misplaced. Clearly Graelen will wipe out the rebels rapidly. Thank you, Taeris."

Taeris fought to keep his voice calm. "And once the plague is released on Citaeron, what if it spreads to Tyrenia? What if it gets off world?"

Adrael smiled his thin smile. "It can't. Not through the vacuum of space."

"And what if the news that the Republic unleashed plague on Citaeron makes other worlds rebel?"

Adrael thought about it for a moment. "I suggest we don't allow that news to spread until after the plague has subsided. Once it has we can simply explain that the plague was being grown by the traitors and it escaped their control."

Taeris was silenced. Of course that was what the Republic would do. It always blamed others for anything that couldn't simply be written out of the historical narrative. He tried to think of a way to make Adrael use his power to stop this monstrous act of war but he could think of nothing and Adrael was already opening the door to leave the room, seemingly happy with the way things were progressing. Taeris was very glad that he would be leaving in less than a day with the 3rd

Fleet. He didn't want to be an eyewitness to such wanton slaughter. A measure of how desperate this news made him was that he actually considered trying to tell the rebels about the plan, tell them to seal themselves in protective suits. He couldn't even do that, so he returned to his quarters and hung in the dark, thinking about all the things the Republic had told him in the past. How many of those were true?

He had a further matter to consider. Using his new approach of taking nothing at face value, he thought on the plan Graelen had constructed. It had caused an almost visceral reaction inside Taeris' mind, but that had to be discounted. It would end rebellion on Citaeron and do so without destroying the precious mining infrastructure. It would free the remainder of the 8th Guards to move on to other areas of concern. It would raise the spirits of the loyal republicans and, as news spread, confirm the dastardly conduct of the perfidious rebels. Could all those outcomes be so easily dismissed? Yes, Taeris thought. It relied upon the slaughter of millions of innocent people in the name of an ideal and that ideal was already planning to lie to the survivors about the nature of the sacrifice. Taeris brought that one fact into the fore and placed his trust upon it. If the Republic was planning to blame the traitors for an act then that act must be something in which it couldn't take pride. By definition that was something dishonourable or criminal. That alone proved the act was unacceptable.

After a few hours he was summoned to the bridge by Raephus. The tall man drifted smoothly inside the huge room, his grace coming from years of experience of free fall. He smiled warmly when he saw Taeris. "Welcome, Legate. I have some news and I thought we should discuss it."

Taeris felt the colour drain from his face. "We're not leaving orbit soon."

Raephus nodded. "Exactly. We've been asked to hold here for two days to assist with a strike mission on the surface of Citaeron."

"Justinian."

Raephus looked a little confused. "You are remarkably well informed."

Taeris closed his eyes. "Graelen boasted about it to me."

"Ah," said the admiral, "I see."

Taeris said, "I assume you've been told the details of the plan?"

"Yes," said Raephus, "I always require a full accounting of any missions that require my assets."

For a moment Taeris thought about asking Raephus if he had any moral indignation over the plan but he dismissed it from his mind. He honestly didn't want to hear a man like Raephus, someone who embodied the best that the Republic could be, confirm that he had been made so republican that he had lost all sense of right and wrong. In the Republic these concepts had been replaced by twisted and stunted versions of themselves. Taeris sadly left the bridge. Was it possible that the only man in orbit who shared Taeris' values might be the condemned traitor Faeral?

Faeral was awake when Taeris entered his small room. He cradled his injured arm and sullenly glared in silence at the legate before him.

Taeris drifted across from him, also silent for a time. Eventually he asked the prisoner, "Do you think there is such a thing as evil?"

Faeral ignored him.

Taeris tried again, "If I kill someone, is that evil?"

This time Faeral couldn't resist. "No. Killing is an act. Evil is a religion. What allows us to commit acts of immorality is our own susceptibility and because of that it is our own responsibility."

Taeris snorted, "Evil made me do it?"

Faeral shook his head slowly. "No. Listen carefully. Morality is in all of us but so is immorality; in our greed and lust for power. Lack of moral understanding doesn't make us commit vile acts, it simply gets in the way of the better parts of us. Immorality permits the act, it doesn't drive it."

Taeris thought for a moment. "Do you believe the Republic is evil?"

Faeral closed his eyes and seemed to relax. "The Republic isn't an actor in its own right, it is amoral. It is the sum total of the actions carried out with its authority and in its name. It is not immoral, but it provides tools for immoral men to do horrible things. It also creates a twisted form of ethics that makes it immoral, but that is generally true of all things other than individual men. It is also a religion, with its own rituals, and adherence to this religion requires, like all religions, that the congregant believe things that are impossible or stupid."

Taeris said, "So, if murder is the worst of crimes, in general, you think the Republic allows us, encourages us, to murder in its name."

"Not at all," Faeral said, "Murder isn't the worst of crimes. The worst of crimes is neglect. Allowing people to suffer, toil, die, without caring or even noticing. That is the crime that leads to rebellion. It is also the function of the Republic, denying any humanity to most of those within it. It is a core tenet of the religion."

Taeris turned to the door and opened it with his suit controls. "I think you may soon come to revise your definition of what might be the worst crime."

Faeral's eyes snapped open, they were hard and staring.

He must have realised that Taeris was talking, if obliquely, of something monstrous. "Oh no, Taeris. I think whatever crime you are describing will be carried out by people who have had their decency scrubbed from them in their training. I think I will believe that it is you, Taeris, who is guilty of the worse crime. I think you know it should be stopped and yet I think you will do nothing to stop it. I think you are the closest to evil that I have ever met."

Taeris felt anger swell in him. For an instant he thought of turning back and hurting Faeral. Then he left and closed the door behind him. That rage wasn't aimed at Faeral. He was enraged with himself; how did Faeral get to understand him so well?

Justinian

Taeris had debated with himself whether or not to watch the unfolding action. He was sickened at the thought of it and yet he couldn't avoid visiting the bridge on the Spica and be the only senior commander to be absent. He had already finished any involvement he had in preparing his infantry for the jump to Esperia, since he had planned on being there by now. He floated numbly down the corridor to the bridge, hoping he would see some indication of concern on the faces of the men assembled there. He didn't. Even Raephus looked sanguine, the origin of that term seeming more appropriate than ever.

The information flowing across the screens was not easy to decipher. What was harder, though, was the routine and impersonal nature of the data. It turned mass murder into numbers, graphs, tables and blinking indicators.

Below, in the atmosphere, fighters from both fleets were spreading out across the rebel-held areas of Citaeron. Each fighter was carrying a cannister of live fleas, millions in each streamlined device, and those fleas were all infected with the Yersinia Pestis bacteria. The fighters each slotted onto their carefully-planned attack routes and they opened the backs of the cannisters precisely on schedule. Millions of fleas poured out of the back of each cannister at a carefully calculated rate, ensuring that each fighter sowed a long, broad furrow of devastation on the ground. Fighters that had routes crossing over Aepolia took some fire from the ground and a few were lost, but the majority were bombing canyons and the enemies there were hiding in caves with no view of the sky, fearing the direct-fire weapons that a fighter could carry. Fearing the wrong thing. Taeris wondered if the rebels were confused by the flights. Were they wondering why no rockets or bombs had been dropped? Had they simply counted themselves lucky that the fighters seemed to simply fly overhead and cause no damage? Had they examined the wreckage of a downed fighter and started to spread the alarm? None of the displays could answer these questions and they were questions just as important as the information on whether the fighters had delivered their loads and made it back into orbit intact. Justinian had taken time to prepare, breeding the fleas and infecting them, designing the delivery mechanism and making the devices, planning and briefing the pilots. However once it was underway the mission lasted little more than half an hour. For most of the people under the fighters the day continued after a brief interruption, the dying wouldn't start for a day or so, by which time it would be too late to help the infected. Each fighter jettisoned the empty cannisters in the upper atmosphere before returning to the fleet, in case a few fleas or a smear of infected fluid remained inside. The vacuum of space could be expected to disinfect the outer surfaces of the fighters themselves but even so there were special procedures for handling them on their return. These procedures would also apply to military facilities on the surface, of course, because disease was something everyone feared.

Taeris waited the absolute minimum time before leaving the bridge. He had been upset by the bombing but more horrified by the smug and satisfied reaction from the commanders on the bridge. He had barely started on his way down the corridor before he heard a voice behind him.

165

"Taeris!" The shout came from Adrael, who had quietly followed him.

Taeris turned and glared at the Security man. "I have nothing to contribute on the bridge."

Adrael drifted closer to him and lowered his voice to barely a whisper. "I have developed a belief that your objections to Justinian were based, in part, on personal qualms of conscience."

Taeris also whispered. "Not so, Adrael. My reservations were strategic, not moral."

Adrael stared at the Legate intently for a few seconds. "Very well. I will take you at your word for now." He turned and floated back toward the bridge.

Taeris let out a little breath that he couldn't remember taking. If he was going to remain alive, let alone a Legate, then he had to hide his morals better. Possession of a conscience was a capital crime in the Republic. Graelen wouldn't spot a conscience in another, he was too stupid, but Adrael was quite clever enough to spot the signs even though he had presumably not experienced the feeling of one for years, if ever. Taeris turned and made his way back to his quarters. He decided not to emerge until the fleet was ready for the jump, which would give him a few hours as the fighters were recovered and prepared for action again.

Raephus actually decided on a longer delay to allow his crews to sleep and recover their alertness before the jump to Esperia. Taeris would normally have been irritated by delays that were of another's making, but this time too much was on his mind for him to worry about relatively trivial problems. He toyed with the idea of visiting Faeral again. Now Justinian was complete it was possible to relate the tale, and even Adrael wouldn't have objected as long as he thought the reason for the visit was to gloat. Eventually he decided against it, not for security reasons, because he was literally ashamed he had been unable to prevent the plague from being launched. Actually that wasn't true. He'd barely even tried to prevent it; he hadn't found a way of convincing the Republic officers that the plague was a bad idea from a tactical perspective, the only perspective that an officer could safely hold.

When the command crew gathered on the bridge of Spica for the jump Taeris had recovered some of his calm and most of his purpose. Raephus had decided to keep his flag on the battlecruiser rather than move it to one of the battleships that temporarily formed part of his command. This was, arguably, against Republic protocol as battleships were ranked higher in the order of battle but as the ships were only a temporary attachment and the Spica was significantly larger than the old Majoris battleships, Ursa and Canis, there wouldn't be any criticism of the Admiral's decision.

Before departure Graelen opened up a channel for communications and the entire bridge was treated to his opening statement. "It seems some nasty rumours have started on Citaeron about an outbreak of plague." He was almost chortling with glee as he spoke. Taeris threw a glance at Raephus and was pleased to see the Admiral looked a little unhappy with the joy that mass slaughter seemed to have provided to the giggling Legate. Everyone else seemed to be enjoying making sounds of shock, exaggerated for comic effect.

Adrael, of course, remained impassive and it was he who spoke, "Do you have an assessment of the extent of the casualties yet?"

"Not yet," Graelen continued. "I'm told there will be a significant delay before the bulk of the traitors become symptomatic. At the moment there are just a few people becoming sick."

Taeris knew this was accurate. Bacterial infections spread quickly and killed quickly too. Even back when antibiotics had worked the plague had been a difficult disease to fight, now there was almost no hope. Some forms of the disease were almost always fatal and even the least virulent forms killed two-thirds of their sufferers. This was the disease that the happy Legate had unleashed and he, safe within his armour, must have seen only benefits to the attack. Was it possible that Graelen literally had no concept of morality, or was it more likely that his native conscience had been drummed out of him by the Republic? Taeris cast his mind back seven years. Had he, also, been entirely sociopathic before his fall from grace? He found it hard to imagine that was the case, whatever conscience he now possessed, it must have been present before the brutalities of education; after all education was supposed to exorcise the student of any unrepublican inclinations. He thought for a moment of Laesa, and the moment he would see her again. He ran a hand through his white hair, wishing he looked younger, stronger, more like the man she had been given to years ago. How would he explain Justinian to her? Would she agree with him or might she look at him in confusion, as a loyal citizen of the Republic would. Justinian's full horror would take a long time to be revealed but the deed itself was already done and could not be undone.

Adrael must have known this as well. "Send more information through the relay to Esperia as you have it. We will be leaving Citaeron orbit soon." He closed the channel without waiting for a response, such was his confidence that his orders would be carried out, but he saved a sly, dirty glance for Taeris. Either he didn't trust the redeemed legate or he still objected to the plan to move the fleet to Esperia. Or it could be both.

Taeris was thinking, once more, about Faeral. The traitor languished in his cell and would be making the jump to Esperia along with the ship. What would a man like Faeral think of unleashing the plague? Taeris was filled with cold dismay as he thought it was likely that Faeral would not only hate the idea of such an attack, but would have laid down his life to prevent it. Taeris felt guilty and ashamed once more. How many lives would have been saved had he told the rebels about the plague?

His thoughts were interrupted by the lurch as his inertia disappeared and the Spica leapt through space toward Esperia.

Esperia, the capital of the Republic, the home of the Praesidium, the Praetorium and the Legacy. For Taeris it was also home. Only once had he been onto its surface since his redemption and that was as a bed-ridden cripple. This time he would be walking under his own power, and he would find Laesa waiting for him; if Adrael had been telling the truth.

Immediately he turned his thoughts to Laesa. He missed her terribly and thinking of her was certainly less troubling than thinking of the plague. Then his conscience growled once more. What would he tell Laesa of Justinian? Would he try to defend his part in it? This was an increasing worry. Why couldn't he put this matter behind him for ever? Adrael and Graelen didn't seem to feel guilty, why did Taeris? Was it, as so many seemed to believe, that he was unrepublican in nature? Why was he so tempted to talk to Faeral? To Taeris, it felt as if he wanted to speak to Faeral to clear his conscience. He would speak of his crimes and he would unburden himself of them. The ancient Catholic church had developed a process called confession, which every Republican child learnt about and was instructed to mock fiercely as it was a consequence of the concept of 'sin'. The Republic had abandoned religion centuries earlier. No, that wasn't true. The Republic had abandoned supernatural religion, replacing it with the religions of capitalism and presidency. That last thought was so completely unrepublican that Taeris was convinced he must be utterly aberrant. For a moment he thought of telling Adrael of his thoughts and letting the security man end his suffering in the surest way imaginable. It was Laesa that stopped him. He literally couldn't face not seeing her again, now he was so close. Redeemed, restored, on the way to Esperia at the head of a legion once more. He could speak to her and she, not being a man, would not be a danger to him. Women had no status in the Republic, no rights, no authority. Two roles remained to them, that of being a trophy for a man who had aided the Republic and that of being a mother to the next generation of children. Women were placed into groups and shipped from one planet to another to keep the gene-pool as diverse as possible. According to the Praesidium it was possible for isolated communities to rapidly 'speciate', becoming non-human, something that must be resisted. How quickly could that happen? Taeris wondered about the Aepolian community on Citaeron. Had they isolated themselves? Begun to speciate? Was Faeral actually human at all? If only the Republic taught science to general students he might know the answers, but once Taeris had been identified as a soldier he was taught nothing more than war; as was proper. He had been seven, maybe eight? Then, again, thoughts of Laesa forced themselves across his mind and he calmed.

Esperia

The 3rd Fleet arrived in Esperian orbit in perfect formation. Countless fingers hovered over controls in many ships, ready to launch fighters, target weapons, communicate with friendly vessels. In fact there was a sensation of relaxation almost as powerful as the lurch back to inertia when it became clear that the fleet had jumped into calm space. Adrael immediately went to his cabin to begin communication with the planet surface, presumably his superiors in the Magisterium, not that Taeris knew their names or ranks.

The first channel to be opened was from the battleship Scorpius, flagship of the 1st Fleet. "Raephus from Kreltaen. Scorpius calling."

Raephus smartly responded, "Raephus. Spica here."

"Congratulations on your promotion old friend. Well earned."

Raephus smiled warmly as he answered, "Thank you, Admiral, I would like to buy you a drink to celebrate once we're squared away."

Kreltaen's laugh was distinctly audible, "And I would like to let you buy the drinks. What brings your fleet to Esperia?"

Raephus responded with alacrity, "Sorry, Admiral, I have to keep counsel on that for the moment."

Kreltaen didn't seem offended. "Splendid news, sounds important. I was worried they might be using you to ferry traitors around the Republic."

Raephus winced slightly on hearing those words. "Well, now that you mention it, it's a part of the job."

There was a noticeable pause before Kreltaen came back. "Well you are the most junior Admiral in the Republic. Too much to hope you'd get a good solid duty like mine at first."

Taeris was wondering why Kreltaen would consider a job of war less impressive than one of simple protection, but of course the answer was obvious: The armed forces of the Republic were almost exclusively used for ensuring the government retained control over its citizens. If your job was to be stepping on sedition then you might as well do it in orbit around the capital.

Raephus spoke up again, "Admiral, it would be wise, I think, to prevent any ships from Citaeron from landing on Esperia. There's been an outbreak of plague."

"Plague?" Kreltaen was clearly horrified. "I will see to it, of course. How did plague get loose again?"

Raephus answered as if he was reading from a script, perhaps he was, "Rebels released it in and around Aepolia, presumably by accident."

The pause was long enough this time to allow for some looks to be exchanged among the officers on the bridge. "Rebels released plague accidentally you say? Well that is a grave matter indeed."

Raephus seemed to put much more emotion into his answer. "Yes. Grave."

Taeris couldn't shake the thought that some hidden message was being passed between the two admirals.

Kreltaen said, "And the gravity of the situation is understood by the commanding officer, I assume?"

Raephus spoke with precision and some emphasis. "Graelen, Legate of the Eighth Guards Legion, seemed not to

172

appreciate the gravity of the situation."

"And Admiral Skaertil?"

"I'm not sure, I didn't discuss it with him in detail." Raephus was slightly more relaxed this time.

Taeris was convinced some secret information had been passed. Skaertil was Admiral of the 4th Fleet, there's no way Justinian could have been coordinated without his involvement; something Raephus as the junior admiral in the area would have discussed in detail anyway. Was it really possible that the nature of the attack hadn't been discussed in terms of how serious it might be?

Replaying the conversation in his mind he began to think that the word 'grave' carried special meaning for these two admirals. Did all the senior officers have such jargon-codes? Of course the question answered itself. The 2nd Guards Legion had been 'disloyal' as they were defeated. The fact that they'd been annihilated in orbit without even a chance to draw a weapon mattered not at all.

Taeris got a message that his shuttle was ready for departure and he hurled himself quickly down the companionway. He was increasingly confused by Raephus. The man seemed intelligent, capable and rational but his words and deeds showed nothing but blind obedience to the will of the Republic. Taeris was saddened that he could no longer be such a man; it was a simple way to live.

Adrael was already in the shuttle when Taeris arrived. He looked up. "Legate. I appreciate your speed. Did Raephus enjoy catching up with his childhood friend?"

Taeris knew this was far from an idle question. "He seemed to. He also asked that ships from Citaeron be prevented from landing on Esperia, because of an outbreak of plague."

Adrael smiled as he answered, "And did he describe how the outbreak occurred?"

"Indeed he did. He was succinct and accurate. I'm sure you'd have approved."

The shuttle moved smoothly free of the battlecruiser as Adrael said, "Accuracy is very important, I think."

Taeris nodded. "You don't have to convince an infantryman of that." The viewing windows gave the passengers an excellent look at Esperia as the shuttle descended through the atmosphere. It was a world of wealth and it looked it. The only city, also called Esperia, appeared to sit at the centre of a giant orb-web, the network of fixed infrastructure that formed the backbone of the planet's economy. The city itself was huge, easily the biggest in the Republic if you excluded the teeming pits of humanity that concentrated in one metropolis or another across the wasted planet Earth. Esperia city had almost three million residents and this amounted to a relatively small fraction of the sixty-million that called the planet home. Again, excluding Earth, almost half of the Republic's population lived on Esperia.

As the city grew before his eyes, Taeris could make out the distinctive hexagonal shape of the administrative centre of the Republic. Six buildings surrounding a large central space, Republic Plaza, for shuttles and acting as open spaces for the modern Princes who worked in this most influential of square kilometres. From each corner of this hexagon stretched the six major transport and infrastructure spokes that continued, in essentially straight lines, for thousands of miles across the surface. Within the city boundaries the larger and larger hexagons that connected these spokes together were not too far apart, but once leaving the city they became erratic, inconsistent and infrequent though a keen eye could still pick out the attempt to match the city's layout. In the first sector behind the Praesidium were the giant blocks of the corporations, far larger than the government buildings. For most visitors to the capital their mental or actual image of the centre of government would be taken from the middle of the Republic Plaza, the Praesidium in the foreground and looming behind it, occupying almost all the sky from that angle, the giant corporate towers.

The shuttle dropped into the plaza itself, something that was a carefully guarded prestige location, and as it settled onto its landing-gear, a ground car rolled to a silent stop alongside. Under the plaza, in fact under all major roads on Esperia, was a complicated series of magnetic coils powered from the main power grid for the planet. Vehicles driving along the surface could be powered by a process of magnetic induction, the electric motors in the cars being powered by matching induction coils in their floors. Since this meant a car had essentially limitless range without needing to carry its own fuel in any form the technology had played an important role in the early need for Esperia to compete economically with the vast human resources of Earth. Most vehicles did, in fact, carry a small battery cell kept fully charged by the induction systems and available for short trips from one major road to another.

Taeris and Adrael climbed easily into the car. Adrael had chosen to wear normal civilian clothing, Taeris still hadn't recovered his muscle tone, let alone the bulk of his strength, and elected to go with powered armour even in the relatively light gravity of Esperia. The car was computer controlled, as most were. A useful feature of the induction method was that the road itself could continually adjust power, speed and relative distance of cars and a passenger could simply indicate a destination and the vehicle would be guided safely to it. The drawback of this was that only induction-powered vehicles could be permitted on the roadways, but the system was operated by one of the giant corporates, Transcorp, and it was very comfortable with owning exclusive access to all major routes across Esperia.

The car set off smoothly across the plaza, following a complex route of curves and straights that was unmarked for human eyes. It took just a few minutes to arrive in the vehicle-lobby of the Praetorium, the centre of government for the Republic.

As Taeris and Adrael made their way along the elegant, neo-classical corridors of the building Taeris kept glancing up to take in the sight of the decorative ceilings that he'd really only noticed properly on his last visit. They were fewer and more discreet than the ones in the Praesidium, but no less elegant for it. Adrael paid them no attention but perhaps he was more familiar with the building.

The two climbed a sweeping staircase and arrived at an enormous double door. Adrael opened it without hesitation and Taeris followed him into the outer office of one of the most powerful men in the Republic. There was no question of the position Tribune Stentael held in the hierarchy once his office was seen; the outer office had no fewer than six secretaries and none of those men were youngsters, they each carried themselves with poise. The door through to the inner office was open and Adrael ignored the secretaries as he strode onward and into the Tribune's private office, Taeris following in his wake.

Stentael stood to welcome Adrael into the impressive room, frowned slightly in case his welcoming gesture was taken to include Taeris, and waved his visitors to a lounge area inside the bay of a huge window overlooking the gardens behind the Praetorium.

The Tribune smiled warmly, somehow an impression derived not from his facial expression but from some expansive movement of his entire body, much as a python might show delight on seeing a mouse. "Welcome, Adrael, can I get you something to drink?"

Adrael shook his head slightly. "We're not here for a social visit." His tone made it abundantly clear that if this had been a social visit then Taeris would not have been in the room. "I have received information about the treasonous rebels that requires me to speak with you."

Stentael shrugged. "Surely it can't be that important. The rebellion is essentially over, is it not?"

Taeris expected Adrael to concur and then find a subtle way of implying the truth, but Adrael seemed unwilling to follow the usual protocol.

"You appear to be misinformed, Tribune." As Stentael didn't respond Adrael continued, "I must first tell you that the rebellion is far from contained. It remains as a nuisance on Prosperity, now that the major population centres are cleared. It also remains a severe problem on Citaeron. The Legate there has released plague over the rebel territories on the planet so this is likely to severely impact rebel activities but there will be economic effects."

The Tribune looked horrified. "How severe will this plague be? Any disruption to industry on Citaeron will raise disagreements with the corporations."

Adrael's face was impassive. "How severe is plague usually?"

Stentael thought for a moment. "This plague will end the rebellion quickly?"

Adrael turned to Taeris. "Legate, your opinion?"

Taeris had not expected to be asked a question like this in

177

front of a Tribune. "The plague is likely to end rebellion on Citaeron, at least in the short term. Unfortunately the plague will probably isolate Citaeron completely for a time and once normal traffic resumes the news of the plague might cause other planets to rebel."

Stentael looked confused. "Why?"

Taeris said, "Relatively minor feelings of dissatisfaction might become more animated if people feel the Republic was unreasonable in dealing with rebellion on Citaeron."

The Tribune still hadn't grasped the problem. "Ridiculous. Once people learn that the rebellion tried to use plague on Citaeron they will quickly prevent any further problems from appearing."

Taeris didn't know what to say, but Adrael answered, "I think the Legate's concern is that the people might not believe the official version of events."

"What?" Stentael looked surprised. "There is no such thing as a version of events. The Praetorium will issue the relevant information, as always."

Taeris was emboldened by Adrael's assertiveness. "But if the people start to discuss, illegally, a different version of events. This could lead to further rebellion."

Silently the Tribune looked back and forth between his two visitors. After a moment he said, "Ridiculous. I assume this is not the reason you came here?"

Adrael said, "No, Tribune. Information gathered from the senior captured traitors indicated that the rebels have become concerned that the Republic is crushing them everywhere they appear. While this treason is not yet contained, it is under pressure. Their greatest success has been with their modern and mobile fleet and they have therefore determined on a bold course of action. They intend to strike here, on Esperia, soon. They anticipate a victory in orbit and then a landing of the larger part of their infantry forces. While Esperia is not undefended, this action would make it hard to argue that the rebellion was a local or trivial matter."

Stentael laughed. "Obviously this is false information. A few dirt-covered rebels hold no threat for Esperia. Adrael, I'm surprised at you."

Adrael was trying to formulate an answer when Taeris spoke, "Tribune, with respect, there was a time when it seemed laughable that a few rebels could threaten Citaeron. Now that world is a plague-ridden cautionary tale. What if some of those dirt-covered rebels that land here come from Citaeron and bring the plague with them?"

Stentael shook his head firmly. "In orbit above my head is the First Fleet. Not a single rebel ship will make it to the surface. I thank you, Adrael, for bringing me your opinion as always but this is foolishness. Now if you'll excuse me."

Within moments Adrael and Taeris stood at the top of the grand staircase once again.

Taeris looked over his shoulder. "He wouldn't listen."

Adrael nodded. "You really don't understand how the Republic works, do you?" When Taeris didn't reply Adrael took a breath and adopted a studious expression. "Stentael is very senior within the government. He's so senior, in fact, that he has almost no power or authority to do anything. Our visit here today was to inform him of the situation, not to enlist his aid, because he has none to offer. Had the President been available today I would have briefed him instead, and the President is so senior that he might as well be a woman for all the power he wields."

Taeris looked baffled. "The President is the most powerful..."

"No," Adrael interrupted, "The President is the head of a government that only ever has one policy. His only job is to order that the policy be carried out. If he were to decide on a different policy then he would be, by definition, unrepublican."

"Have you never noticed that the most senior military commanders are given no troops to command? Our most senior naval personnel almost never leave the Admiralty building, it is their juniors who command fleets. In the Republic we pathologically distrust anyone with actual, demonstrable, authority. We suspect they are the weak link, capable of treason and with the infrastructure at their fingertips to make that treason very costly. As Legate, your job is to stay out of trouble until you can be promoted to the Legacy committee full-time. At that point, as long as you keep mouthing the right words, you are safe from denunciation."

Taeris stared in shock at Adrael. "Was that why I was denounced?"

Adrael smiled his thin smile. "No, you were denounced because Caeranion wanted to advance himself above one of the more gifted Legates in the Republic. I suspect he didn't need to bother, you were always a bit of an outlier, never likely to win promotion to the highest levels. In any event it was your ability that led to your denunciation. Presumably Caeranion had been waiting for an appropriate moment but even he must have been surprised that you delivered such an impressive demonstration of public disloyalty in front of the President. It was an opportunity he was never going to miss."

Taeris was open-mouthed. "That's monstrous!"

"That's one way of interpreting it," Adrael nodded, "I prefer to think that you loaded a weapon and handed it to Caeranion before asking him to shoot you. It isn't his fault that he knew how the Republic worked and you didn't."

Adrael walked off, shaking his head sadly.

Taeris called out after his retreating back. "Does it work like that in the Magisterium?" No answer came.

The Legacy

Adrael had immediately left to make his way to the Magisterium, another of the six buildings that formed the centre of the Republic's government. Taeris made his way in the opposite direction deciding to avoid the vehicle-lobby and instead let the powered armour take the strain as he ran in great bounding steps to the Legacy. The Legacy was one of the smaller buildings on the hexagon, though larger than the Admiralty one building over, and it was more functional than attractive. On his way through the gardens Taeris became acutely aware of women walking around in a way that he hadn't seen in a very long time. Of course women held no rank within the Republic, they could neither be employed by government nor corporation, instead they were taken as property by the relevant authority and then offered as inducements to men who had a sufficiently important role. Some men still wanted to have children in the traditional manner, but the vast majority of births made use of the wombs of less valuable women as incubators for fertilised eggs made in combination by a man and a woman whose genetic cross value was high, even if they never actually met. On Earth it was not uncommon for a woman to work as well, but in the more civilised parts of the Republic women were either used as mobile baby-farms or as a reward for eligible men. On Esperia no woman worked, in fact almost all of the birthing mothers would be assigned somewhere of lower importance than the capital planet as well. A woman on Esperia was almost certainly someone's reward for a job well done. As the women were spectacular and the climate was warm Taeris found his attention most pleasurably diverted by their bare legs as they made their way to and from the buildings where their men worked. Inevitably his thoughts turned to Laesa and thinking of her made the few minutes of journey pass very quickly.

His mood lifting, he even chuckled a little as he bounded completely over a hurrying Aedile on his way into the Legacy. Once inside the low, heavy architecture lowered his mood as it always had and he walked stiffly up to the offices reserved for the 6th Infantry Legion on the upper floor. This was a very different office to the immense and imposing home of the Tribunes in the Praetorium; large enough but lacking any grace and with a determinedly functional aspect. The office was empty, as he'd expected, but with typical Republican efficiency there was a room reserved for the Legate of the 6th and his name had been marked upon the door. Marked using decidedly temporary lettering, Taeris noted.

Inside there was little to distract the eye, but he sat at his desk and opened up the computer. He immediately looked up his own file, to find out where his living accommodation was located. The file gave him this information at once and indicated that Laesa had, as promised, been moved there. To his surprise there was also an indication that a second woman had been assigned to him; not in itself unusual for someone of his rank but something he'd always declined in the past. Idly he wondered if he'd failed to respond to some interminable communication from the Legacy and they'd assumed a second woman was his preference.

He quickly checked that his property and conditions had been updated to reflect his status as a Legate and then turned off the computer. On his way out of the office he was startled by a large man coming in.

"Caeranion." Taeris greeted his old friend with as neutral a tone as possible. He replayed in his mind the conversation with Adrael.

"Welcome home, Taeris. Have you had time to visit Laesa yet?"

Taeris knew that the older Legate had to know the answer to this already. "Not yet. I was, in point of fact, going there now."

"Ah," said Caeranion, "I'm sorry but I'll have to delay your trip a little. The Legacy is eager to hear your reports of victory over the traitors."

This was literally true. The Legacy would be eager to hear reports of victory and only of victory. "Of course."

They walked to the large chamber that formed the centre of the Legacy and, by extension, the centre of the infantry forces of the Republic. It was too big for the current number of legates that could attend, spaces in the inner ring reserved for guards legions far from full and the outer ring needing only two of its twelve stations to accommodate the two undersized Infantry Legions that currently served. As was standard practice Taeris went first to his own desk, the one reserved for the man in his position, and waited to be called into the middle of the circle to begin his briefing. The purpose of these briefings was always lost on Taeris, as the official record would always show steady and successful progress on all fronts. At least he could mention the areas where the fighting was still ongoing. He looked intently around the room, remembering the last time he'd stood here. Caeranion had denounced him in this room. It was here that his old life had ended. Over there. Caeranion had stood there, behind the desk reserved for the 2nd Guards

Legion, that desk now deserted.

The round table in the centre of the room was reserved for the legates with no legion of their own to command. Here Caeranion had his chair and it was he who called Taeris forward. Taeris took his time walking into the centre of the round table, hoping that a delay of even a second or two would cause a little frustration among those assembled.

"Fellow Legates," Taeris began, simply to see the others frown at being included in any group with a formerly disgraced man such as he, "I bring an update on the continuing struggle to end the treason that has reared its head on several planets."

Caeranion interrupted immediately. "Continuing struggle? Was it not your responsibility to end it?"

Taeris forced a smile and nod as he continued, Caeranion was clearly not willing to take any responsibility upon himself, "I have to report that the job is not yet done. Rebellion began on Prosperity and it has suffered several small defeats there. Unfortunately I was forced to withdraw my legion from the planet before that work could be finished. I suspect that reality might dictate that the permanent suppression of treason on Prosperity will be a work of many years. On Prosperity we were able to capture Faeral, the leader of the traitors, and I have been able to extract useful information from him. I intervened briefly on Citaeron, where the traitors launched a new front in their campaign. As soon as I was relieved by the Eighth Guards I left that planet to them."

Smoothly the legate commanding the 1st Guards Legion interjected, "And no doubt they have crushed all treason."

"It seems so," Taeris answered, "I must point out that the Eighth has suffered very heavy casualties and that now there is an outbreak of plague on the surface of the planet." The complete absence of surprise at this announcement made it

185

clear to Taeris that the Legacy was already in full possession of the facts about the plague. He wondered briefly why these Legates had already known the facts in hand, but the Tribune seemed to be less informed. "I returned to Esperia because I have information that this world is going to come under rebel attack."

Only smiles greeted this announcement. Caeranion went so far as to laugh. "Oh no. Whatever will we do? A mere two legions of Guards, a huge force of local Guardians and the largest fleet in the Republic is clearly no match for a handful of angry peasants."

Taeris tried to keep his voice level. "These are the angry peasants that destroyed the Second Guards and the Second Fleet. They are the same peasants that have reduced the Eighth Guards to a mere shadow of a legion. These peasants are coming here next."

Halgerin, the short and ruddy faced commander of the 1st Legion, spoke loudly, "What madness is this? The traitors would never dare to come here. Your alleged information is obviously false. How could a rebel force hope to harm us on Esperia?"

Caeranion jumped in, "I find it unbelievable that a man of your already dubious reputation would come here and throw such idiocy at us, Taeris. Fortunately I do not need to deal with you any further. Before you arrived we discussed the options we have available and we have decided to relieve you of your command. For the time being you will remain at your current rank, in view of your recent service, but another will be placed in charge of the Sixth Infantry. Legate Trantier; your command."

Taeris wished he could have been surprised. Obviously he would be relieved of command as soon as it made sense and with Citaeron bathed in the plague and Prosperity subdued for the time being there was no need for the Legacy to deal with a man like Taeris. Only if they had believed that a new rebel attack would take place might he keep his command and clearly they did not. He cast his eyes across the round table to identify Trantier.

Trantier was another who sat at the round table. He had the tall, rangy look of an Esperian native. He waited for a moment before beginning. "The Sixth Infantry will be leaving shortly for Prosperity. Once there it will put down the remaining dregs of treason. I trust I may count on the continuing services of the Third Fleet?"

Before he could receive an answer Legate Driastren said, "My Fifth Guards will soon be battle-ready. Let us take the fight to Prosperity."

Caeranion stared at Taeris as he spoke. "A good plan. The Sixth Infantry will remain here until the Magisterium has had a chance to evaluate its current state of readiness. Once the Fifth is ready we will send both legions to Prosperity."

Taeris fought to control his anger; the term 'state of readiness' was a euphemism for 'loyalty to the Republic'. In fact almost everything was a euphemism for that. He knew no protest could change the outcome of this meeting but he still had to try. "I will remain with the Sixth for long enough to ensure an orderly transition to its new leadership."

Trantier smoothly said, "I don't think that will be necessary."

Caeranion stood, effectively ending the meeting. "It is decided. In the President's name." Before he could take a step from the table, however, two smartly-dressed civilians entered. Both were immaculately groomed and carried with them an aura of power.

"Legates." One of the men spoke and both walked into the middle of the room to stand alongside Taeris. "If we might have a moment of your time? We are legal representatives of Transcorp and Agricorp. I am here to ask for information pertinent to our claim for compensation for our severe losses on Citaeron."

Driastren said, "This is not the time nor place for that. The Praesidium is but a short walk from here."

The more talkative of the company men replied, "And yet the Praesidium claims no knowledge of the blockade of Citaeron, indicating that it remains an ongoing military campaign, and refers us here."

Caeranion looked annoyed. "Well then gentlemen, come with me and I shall explain the situation on Citaeron."

It was the other company man who answered, "We are fully aware of the situation. We require our compensation. In order for the money to be paid we have to present a report on the operation. As this is, it seems, an ongoing operation, this report must be compiled by the Legacy."

The assembled military men seemed baffled. It was unusual for them to deal with a corporation directly. After a moment Caeranion broke the silence. "The rebellion on Citaeron is the underlying cause of the blockade. That rebellion was a mere offshoot of the rebellion on Prosperity. The rebellion on Prosperity was a consequence of the actions of Agricorp on that world. Accordingly the blockade of Citaeron was initiated by the corporations and they, seeing as they are so enthusiastic about compensation, will no doubt arrange to compensate the Legacy and the Admiralty for the losses and expenses of the campaign."

Most of the room smiled. The company men did not. One immediately said, "Please don't forget that you work for us.

We will set the terms of our relationship."

The other had a different question, "I assume you can prove your assertion?"

"Oh yes," said Taeris, finally finding someone he could irritate properly. "I have in custody the leader of the traitors and he is most clear that it was a dispute with Agricorp that led to the rebellion. In fact the first act of the rebellion was to free him from Agricorp's grasp in order to prevent him from being executed. As you know Agricorp is directly responsible for the actions of all of its employees and Faeral, you will find, is on your list of employment."

The two civilians exchanged a glance. "We will examine your claim for veracity. Even if it proves to be true, there is the other matter of the plague being released on Citaeron. This is the cause of the greatest losses and costs for us. I suspect you cannot demonstrate that the plague was an essential strategic weapon and therefore we will demand compensation for those losses at least."

Caeranion was warming to his task. "But the plague was released by the traitors, it too is a consequence of the Agricorp rebellion, not of the Legacy."

"You ask us to believe that the rebels unleashed plague in Aepolia?"

"Not at all," Caeranion smiled, "I ask nothing of you. I merely direct your attention to the official history of the Citaeron campaign; a document which I'm sure will identify the rebels as the direct cause of the plague."

"Can we have a copy of this document, so we might evaluate it."

Caeranion answered, "Naturally. As soon as we have finished writing it."

Helplessly the civilians looked at each other and then

around the room, hoping for some sign of support. They looked in vain. Expressions of real anger were now plastered on their faces. While it was, technically, true that the Legacy reported only to the Praesidium, nobody in the room could have possibly believed that. In fact the Legacy reported to the Praesidium for its orders, to the Magisterium for its internal affairs and, frankly, to the corporations for its budget.

Taeris watched the two corporate men leave without sympathy. The corporates had an immense amount of power, perhaps even enough to make Caeranion regret his arrogance. Not perhaps. If they really wanted Caeranion humbled then they could make that happen. Taeris wondered where the grinning Legate found his confidence, surely it couldn't be from a friend in the Magisterium?

As Taeris left the Legacy building he was followed by Caeranion who spoke only once they were outside, "I enjoyed that."

Taeris turned. "The way you ambushed me? I suspect it would have been more enjoyable for me had I not been the focus of the attack."

Caeranion shrugged. "There is a limit to my influence. That chamber is not full of your supporters and when you arrive with stories of such fanciful nature it is inevitable that you will be ignored."

Taeris fixed his old friend with a stare. "Why didn't you tell me you had commanded the Third Guards? Why didn't you tell me what happened to them? Why didn't you tell me how long this rebellion had been building?"

Caeranion turned away and walked back into the Legacy, speaking as he left. "Because my friend Taeris died when he was denounced. Whoever you are, you're not him."

Taeris glared at Caeranion's retreating back. He wanted

to have the last word but in truth there was nothing to say. He was not the same man who had been in command of the 3rd Guards. Caeranion might mourn the loss of his old friend but it was the stocky legate's denunciation that had killed the old Taeris.

Laesa

The ground car was almost silent as it rolled along the smooth expanse of Admiralty Street. The street was named simply because it ran from Republic Plaza past the Admiralty building and out into the outer regions of the city of Esperia. Each of the main spokes were named for one of the six main government buildings, which was a simple and logical choice, if a little mundane. At first the disappointment of the events at the Legacy weighed heavily on Taeris' mind, but as the journey continued these thoughts were replaced by the anticipation of seeing Laesa again. Seven years was a long time to be apart, Taeris wondered how she'd changed.

The car automatically pulled off the street and crossed a small patch of non-inductive surface before finding another powered street, this time forming part of one of the hexagonal rings around the city centre. After a minute of this new direction the car slowed and turned into a small private courtyard. Legates were generally assigned such residences and Taeris had been automatically placed here when he was promoted. Once he'd climbed from the car he walked up to the elegant front door, which recognised his biometric signature from a distance and opened for him as he approached. The door closed behind him and he looked around the hallway. It was, if anything, slightly more grand than the one he'd been assigned before his denunciation, though it was significantly further out from the centre of the city and so a less prestigious address.

From the outside there could be heard a subtle whine as the car made its way automatically to its next errand. Once that sound faded there was absolute silence in the house. Despite having been assigned it, Taeris didn't feel as if this was his home and his footsteps as he walked through the hall and into the wet-suite at the back seemed uncommonly loud. In order to reach the wet-suite he had to pass the doors into the main front rooms and peering into the one on the left he saw Laesa sitting bolt upright in a chair. He abandoned his initial objective and walked over to her. She wore a short blue dress with sandals and her hair and make-up were immaculate.

"Laesa. You look wonderful." It was undoubtedly true; she had always been beautiful and she remained so. Age had slightly thinned her frame and robbed her of the perfect curves she had in Taeris' memories but those memories themselves were imperfect. She was now a little over thirty years old and retained that elegance she had always had.

She looked at him with almost no expression, as if she was thinking other thoughts. "Taeris. How kind of you to reclaim me."

Her voice lacked warmth. Taeris said, "I thought of little else during my education."

Still expressionless. "Then you must have been a poor student indeed."

Taeris wanted to take her upstairs but something was clearly wrong. "Are you angry with me, Laesa?"

Her eyes hardened. "Angry? No. How could I be angry? You threw away your position, rank, progression, even your loyalty to the President. Did you even consider what that would mean for me?"

Truthfully Taeris hadn't. He had only begun to think of

what would become of Laesa after his denunciation; the risk he was taking with her life and position in society had never entered his mind before it was too late to do anything about it. "I worried about you."

Laesa stood. "I was given to Caeranion. Did you know that?"

"Not until I was redeemed." Taeris didn't know what he could do to get his woman back to the warm and sparkling person of his memories. "Did he treat you with respect?"

She rested her hands on her hips, possibly intended to be a forceful gesture but it reminded Taeris of how desirable she was. "Oh yes. He treated me exactly the way you would expect, given that I became his fourth woman."

Taeris knew little of the things women considered to be important so he guessed. "He paid you no attention at all?"

A short laugh, almost like a bark, was her response. "Oh no. I got plenty of attention. At night he was very attentive indeed. Naturally outside his house he took his first woman with him, it was important that people knew he had won me in your denunciation but it wasn't important that he be seen with me. I never left the house and because I was the youngest and the busiest his other women hated me."

Taeris said, "I'm sorry. I wish things had been different."

Laesa grimaced slightly. "Then, of course, I find a way to live. I survive and I keep going and at least I can console myself with the thought that my man is influential, powerful. And then you come back into my life and instead of being the fourth woman of an important man, I am now the second woman of a disgrace."

"The second?" Taeris did sympathise with her but her last comment was senseless. "What do you mean 'the second'?"

Laesa smiled, but there was no warmth in it. "Your new

woman. I assume she will be treated as your first? After all I'm now third-hand. Perhaps you intend to send me off to Earth or Mozart to become a breeding woman? Will you make me carry the child that the two of you conceive together?"

Taeris held up a hand to stop the flood of questions. "Laesa, please. I have apologised for the effect my disgrace had on you. I did not ask for a second woman and believe me when I tell you that you are the only woman I have thought about or dreamt about for seven years."

Laesa's eyes narrowed shrewdly. "So you will declare me to be your first woman still?"

"First and only," Taeris responded, "I will send this other woman away."

If he expected Laesa to be pleased at that he was sorely mistaken. "You will do no such thing. She did nothing to you and you will not throw her away. Her chances of a good future are almost nothing if she is passed on to another man. Previously owned women hold so little status as to be ignored, except in bed."

Taeris blinked as if in a bright light. "Whatever you say. I shall do whatever you like."

Laesa nodded firmly. "Now that's settled. Tell me of your recent redemption and return to the Legacy."

Laesa could be very efficient when it suited her. Clearly she intended to identify precisely where Taeris appeared in the current social order. He began recounting the details of the recent weeks. She listened intently and without interruption until he finished with the loss of his legion earlier that same day. "So I am now a Legate with no legion."

Laesa sat and waved Taeris to another chair. "It is better than nothing. How confident are you that this rebel attack will take place?"

Taeris had been very confident when he'd first learnt of it, but as more and more people told him it was a ridiculous idea he had started to wonder if he'd been cunningly mislead by Faeral on Prosperity as a way of forcing him to move the 6th Legion away from the rebel heartland. "I am quite sure." He hoped Laesa didn't catch the possible double meaning of the sentence, but his hopes were dashed.

"Do you mean you are certain, or that you are somewhat sure?"

Taeris smiled slightly. Few of the officers in the Legacy would have spotted that so quickly. "Somewhat sure. It remains a possibility that I was fed deliberately false information."

Laesa thought for a moment. "So we need to construct a situation that will ensure that if the attack takes place you are credited with the warning and if it does not then you are credited with preventing it by moving the legion to Esperia."

Taeris laughed. It was easy to forget that women could be as clever and manipulative as men. Laesa was possessed of a good brain and had always been determined to use it. From what she'd said about Caeranion it seemed he'd failed to see that in her and take advantage of it. Well that was his mistake and one that Taeris would not repeat. "How can I make that come about?"

Laesa looked at him with a little bit of pity. "You can't, obviously. The Legacy will always look at you as a suspicious outsider. I can, however. Once I start to be seen about town again I will be questioned by dozens of other influential women about the scandal of my being reassigned back to you."

He was about to offer her some form of flattery when another woman entered the room. She approached, looking down at her feet as she did, and when she got close enough to be sure Taeris had noticed her she bobbed a little curtsy and her posture became even more timid. Both Taeris and Laesa stood to meet her.

Taeris looked down at her, for she was far from tall, and said, "What's your name?"

A small voice emerged from under the fringe of hair that was completely obscuring her downward-tilted face. "Salassa, if it pleases you."

Taeris chuckled slightly. "I'm sure it pleases me more than adequately. Could you look up at me please?"

Salassa did so, her fine, straight, blond hair parting to reveal a startlingly beautiful and very small face. She looked utterly delightful and her nervousness only added to her wan beauty. After a moment holding Taeris' gaze she lost her nerve and dropped her eyes back to the floor again.

Laesa put a gentle hand on the smaller woman's shoulder. "Salassa is only just nineteen and she has come here from a very rural background."

Taeris nodded, "On Citaeron, from her accent. Are you Aepolian, Salassa?"

Salassa nodded at once. "I apologise if my accent is unpleasant."

Taeris smiled indulgently. "You never have to apologise for anything, not to me."

Salassa nodded again, but seemed unconvinced. She turned and fled the room as soon as she was no longer the absolute focus of attention. Taeris turned to Laesa and said, "She's very pretty, if a little quiet."

Laesa said, "Yes, she is. Should I have her stripped and put in your bed tonight?" Her tone of voice and the imitation curtsy she performed while speaking imposed a huge weight of sarcasm on her comment.

Taeris grinned. "I've really missed you."

Laesa nodded in acknowledgement of the compliment. "Now you've told me what you did but not why. What was your strategy?"

Taeris had not been so competently questioned by either his subordinates or his superiors, again he relished the brain inside his woman. "It's simple really. On the land, face to face, the traitors cannot win. They have a mobile, light and modern fleet that can appear and vanish at will and is at least the equal of any Republic fleet, however. Additionally on Prosperity and, seemingly at least, part of Citaeron they can melt away into the local population."

"Is this because they have managed to terrorise the local population into harbouring them?" Laesa's face was a picture on innocence.

"Yes," Taeris replied carefully, "I must assume they have terrorised the local population into a state of full cooperation with them and have been so effective at it that the civilians are driven to affect not merely functional support but even emotional fervour and absolute, unswerving, devotion on the rebels' behalf."

Laesa nodded slowly. "I assumed that must be the case."

Taeris continued with his explanation. "In practice Prosperity is in rebel hands, but they only control that fraction of the planet that is not underneath the armoured boot of a soldier. Obviously, given the size of the planet, that fraction is disturbingly large. We can punish them at will, but inflicting a telling blow will never be possible when they operate in small groups."

"So Prosperity is just a waste of effort, for the time being."

"Yes," Taeris said, "I think it is supplying resources to the rebels but there is little I can do about petty smuggling.

Meanwhile on Citaeron the main rebel thrust comes from the city of Aepolia. It seems that Citaeron as a whole is also undergoing some form of terrorism to convert its people to rebel-sympathisers."

Laesa interrupted, "I hear rumours of plague in Aepolia."

Taeris was about to respond when Salassa came back into the room. "Plague? In Aepolia?" She must have been listening; not that Taeris could blame her.

Taeris nodded with genuine sadness. "I'm afraid so, Salassa. I don't know what the state of the area is now."

Salassa's face was frowning with the effort of keeping her calm. "How did it happen?"

Taeris made the decision, foolish though it might have been, to be as honest as he could. Something about Salassa made him doubt she was an agent of the Magisterium. "The official history will state that the rebels attempted to produce a plague in order to infect the Republic's troops on the planet. It will further state that some accident or internal division led to the release of the plague in Aepolia and across the entire area of the surface under rebel control. It will indicate that by some fortune the areas under Republic control were not immediately affected. It will describe this as the inevitable consequence of treason as the historical record shows how the Republic has always been the only true path forwards for humanity."

Laesa snapped a sharp look at Taeris, warning him about being so open with a virtual stranger, but in fact his words were both accurate and reasonably loyal. An astute operative of the Security Divisions would have easily heard the implied treason, but the words themselves could not condemn Taeris.

Salassa stood before them with tears rolling down her face. Laesa stepped over and put an arm around her shoulders in sympathy. She looked up from the blond's face to Taeris again.

"So, continue, why are you here?"

Taeris said, "I received intelligence that the next major attack for the rebels would be here, on Esperia. I was wasting my time chasing rumours on Prosperity so I came here, hoping to force a decisive fight with the traitors."

Laesa finished the story herself, "Where you were laughed at for suggesting the rebels would dare attack Esperia and your command was taken from you."

Taeris nodded. "Which brings us to here."

Salassa interrupted. "Can I send word to my family on Citaeron?"

Taeris thought for a moment. "No. I will not have communications from this house sent to the Aepolians, especially before the quarantine has been lifted."

Salassa sobbed a little. Laesa said, "It's the right decision." Salassa crept out of the room in silence. Laesa turned back to Taeris. "You say the rebels have a mighty fleet. Where did they get such a thing?"

Taeris shrugged. "It's a fleet of armed merchantmen. A large number of small vessels fitted with powerful weapons. Individually they're nothing, but in large numbers they are formidable."

"More formidable than a battleship?"

Taeris tried to find a way to explain. "A battleship carries immensely powerful weapons, but only a few of them. At any one time it can only engage a few enemy ships, though those it does engage will be obliterated. Most of that vast energy will be wasted, of course, as a much smaller beam could destroy the enemy vessel. In comparison these enemy ships are well armed for their size, but mostly not well protected. They accept their vulnerability as part of a wider strategy. Their numbers, their agility, their determination to press home the attack, these make them very dangerous."

Laesa busied herself making some drinks. "Surely that's no different from dealing with attacks by fighters?" she asked. She seemed genuinely curious, after all she had a fine brain and almost no experience of military technology.

Taeris leaned against the wall beside her. "Most of the tmetics on warships are of three main types. Big beams to fire at big ships, secondary beams to destroy fighters and steerable tmetic panels to engage missiles. Essentially most of our secondary weapons aren't big enough to reliably defeat these enemy vessels. The rebels use ships that are small, by the standards of our warships, but much larger than fighters. Someone, some rebel, has designed a fleet to be deliberately hard for our main fleets to fight. They are willing to launch attacks without heeding their casualties, send scouts into a system to find our ships just moments before an attack and their missile boats are formidable."

Laesa turned back to Taeris and looked him over, then reached out a hand to touch his white hair. "Your hair."

Taeris nodded. "I'm sorry, it happens to everyone who spends long enough in EF-Seven, I don't know why."

Laesa smiled a sad smile. "I loved your hair. Now it's a badge of honour."

Taeris leaned down and kissed her on the lips. "Only you could make me feel better about white hair."

Laesa relaxed in his arms for a moment, then gently pulled away. "Tell me of the missile boats?"

Taeris regained his composure. "It's an old tactic. Essentially a missile makes a small boat capable of delivering a mighty strike, because capacitance shielding is ineffective against missiles."

Laesa frowned. "Why?"

"I'll need to explain a little physics." Taeris saw his woman nod so he continued. "Tmetic energy, basically, is a blast of electromagnetic radiation. On hitting a target the energy pours into the structure of the ship, or vehicle, causing the site of the impact to expand. This expansion makes the impact site explode and split the areas around it, tmesis is simply an old word for splitting. To protect ourselves against this type of weapon we embed superconductive mesh into the outer surface. This mesh can conduct the energy away vastly faster than the normal metals, ceramics and polymers that make up our equipment. The energy is actually slightly mitigated simply by this conduction, but more so by a capacitor connected to the mesh. This capacitor absorbs the energy as fast as it can, then bleeds the energy back out as heat. My armour is protected like this."

Laesa nodded again. "Why not make armour out of this superconductor entirely?"

Taeris grinned. "Physical armour is designed to provide protection against physical threats. A man might wield a knife, for example. None of the superconductors yet discovered are hard enough and tough enough for that task. Essentially the same problem happens with missiles. Ordinary conventional explosives produce very little tmetic energy but they can batter armour and destroy a ship, nuclear weapons are more powerful but a massive amount of their energy is tmetic. Anti-ship missiles, generally, use kinetic energy to achieve their damage. A missile, travelling very fast, hits a ship, smashing through its armour, and ignoring its capacitance mesh entirely. The rebels are using a very old trick, but it still works, and their tactics are set to make best use of it."

Laesa was silent for a moment. "These rebel tactics. How do they work?"

Taeris took a deep breath. "The missile boats jump into system at very high speeds, then launch their missiles at close range in large numbers. They simultaneously launch a large number of decoys. Experience tells us that some of the missiles are too primitive to even have a jump mass and are essentially just unpowered projectiles launched at very high speed. There is evidence that some are tipped with explosives. Broadly this means that their weaponry is extremely cheap, easy to produce and yet powerful when deployed in large numbers."

Laesa sat for a minute. "How will these rebel tactics adjust themselves to forcing a landing on Esperia?"

Taeris shrugged. "I don't know."

Laesa frowned at him. "I don't care that you're unsure. I need to paint a picture of how the rebels will come. In a few days I will have spoken to half the women of the most powerful and influential men on Esperia. What do I tell them?"

Taeris was forced to think for a minute. "Tell them that the rebels will scour Esperia with a bombardment then land suicide units to slaughter everyone they can find. Tell them that the Legacy isn't even considering the threat."

Laesa nodded firmly. "I shall. I shall also tell them that the only man the rebels fear has come here, at the cost of his command, to warn us and to be ready for action."

Taeris blinked at her. "I didn't know you felt that way."

Laesa looked at him, searching for artifice on his face. "Oh shut up, Taeris," she finally said.

Attack

There was no landing that day, or the next. Day after day Taeris waited for the news that didn't come. He went to the Legacy most days and he listened to the interminable updates on the readiness of the 5th Guards. He listened as others laid out the plans for ending the rebellion; others who had yet to face combat and those who had faced it and failed to emerge with victories. In the Republic, of course, these things simply didn't exist as there was no concept of recording a defeat. More than once Taeris was tempted to visit the archive to see how the official record made sense of the loss of the 2nd Legion, or the 3rd.

Laesa had become the absolute centre of attention among the women, as she'd predicted. She was, to hear her describe it, making excellent progress in briefing those women as to the brilliance and loyalty of Taeris' strategy. Taeris thought he could identify the trend himself in the way Caeranion glared at him with pure hostility when they were alone. Caeranion managed to remain cheerful and smiling around others, however, perhaps not wanting to reveal his irritation.

Caeranion was the man who outlined the overall strategy, which was in two main parts. The 4th Fleet, based at Earth, would pick up the 7th Infantry Legion and take it to Citaeron. The 7th was not even close to full strength with just two regiments, but it would provide substantial reinforcement to the 8th Guards. Caeranion's plan called for every attack to be led by a Guards unit, since he felt the leadership of the Infantry forces was lacking in republican enthusiasm. He mentioned this several times and each time threw a glance at Taeris. Once the 5th Guards was ready it would be transported by the 3rd Fleet from Esperia to Prosperity. The fleet would then return to collect the 6th Infantry and transport it also to Prosperity. Taeris thought the plan, in general, had some merit but only if the assumption was made that Citaeron and Prosperity were the only imminent targets of the traitors.

More importantly there was a truly awful series of briefings. Trantier's first task as commander of the 6th was to orchestrate the formation landing on Esperia to free the littorals for their mission of moving the 5th Guards. It was almost physically painful for Taeris to hear the minutiae of the movements, hearing the numbers of 'his' battalions, the names of 'his' officers. It was during one of these that Trantier raised the question of what should be done with Faeral. Caeranion thought for a moment before suggesting that Faeral's biggest contribution to the Republic now would be via a widely broadcast execution.

Taeris was about to speak against that when he found he didn't need to.

"I think he may yet be useful alive," Said Driastren, the commander of the 5th Guards, "As a source of intelligence."

Trantier answered him, "We already know he has effectively lied about rebel plans, how could we trust anything he says?"

Driastren nodded in agreement. "It is not so much what he says, as how he says it. Since being transported to the facility on Esperia he has only spoken in gibberish. I mean to find out how he managed to deceive an experienced legate without even communicating in English. Perhaps he is a sorcerer?"

So this was it. Driastren wanted to use Faeral's linguistic stubbornness to accuse Taeris of unrepublican activity; all he needed to do was to prove that Taeris spoke this 'gibberish'. Taeris spoke up in his defence immediately, "Legates, I can resolve this matter at once. I speak this 'gibberish', though its users refer to it as Aepolian."

Everyone pretended to be shocked, though it was hard to believe that anyone in the room had not known this. Caeranion affected wounded innocence. "Well, Taeris, this is unrepublican activity and I shall have to place you under arrest. We will discuss possible denouncement."

If Taeris was taken from the room then he was doomed, his only remaining chance was to make his defence count in front of those officers that hadn't yet come to despise him. "It was on the orders of the President that I learnt Aepolian."

The chamber was deathly silent. Who would dare to lie about such an order? Even Caeranion, a consummate negotiator, was taken aback and it took him a moment to frame his question. "What do you mean?"

Taeris rolled his last, desperate, roll. "Aepolian is the spoken language of Education Facility Seven."

"That's not an explanation," Caeranion said, "People sent there are likely to be sent for such activities as speaking this bastard dialect. It is a mere coincidence that some there spoke it."

Taeris smiled with confidence that he did not feel. "It is not for me, a simple student, to question the wisdom of those who educate me. I am forced to learn everything placed in front of me. Would you like me to recite the three-hour lecture on the subject of the responsibilities of the Legacy? I had ample time to memorise it. I must assume that it is the intention of the Republic that English is not the language used in EF-Seven.

If it is not the President's intention then why does it continue?"

Caeranion was about to call this suggestion laughable before he checked himself. If he went on record, in front of these people, with the opinion that education was not actually intended to educate, merely to kill slowly, then it might be something they would remember. Definitely they would remember. It would be noted down somewhere, ready to be brought out at his own trial. He also couldn't suggest that the lack of a crackdown on Aepolian in EF7 was a failure of oversight, after all suggesting a failure within the Republic could also be a cause of denunciation. Suddenly he realised that Taeris, because of his lowly social standing, actually had more freedom than he. Unconsciously the officers here tolerated slips and queries from a rehabilitated man that they would be shocked to hear come from the lips of a man who had never faced such disgrace.

Taeris decided to dull Caeranion's pain by allowing him a way out. "Of course we must keep Faeral alive until the completion of any compensation hearings with the corporations, as he might be our only witness to the origins of the treason."

Caeranion jumped on the suggestion like a man grabbing for the last oxygen mask in a damaged ship. "Yes, of course. We must transfer Faeral to Taeris' custody as he is the only man who might be able to communicate with him."

From that day forward Caeranion dropped even the outward show of geniality toward Taeris. He glared, he frowned and he spoke sharply. Taeris assumed this was because of this most recent moment of deflating the senior legate but he couldn't be certain. He had embarrassed the man before his denouncement, embarrassed him further by emerging to resume his duties, been a thorn in his side ever since and stolen Laesa back from him. Of course it was possible that Caeranion didn't see the loss of his fourth woman as a serious matter, but as a trophy she was surely of value, symbolising his victory over a rival.

On the way from the chamber, as was increasingly common, Taeris was briefly stopped by an Aedile, who wanted some information on the worrying power of the rebel fleet. After explaining the details of his concerns Taeris strode off, smiling. Obviously Laesa was quietly getting through to all sorts of people that the Legacy might not be the only informed source in town.

Taeris had been avoiding the quarters of the 6th Infantry on Esperia; he didn't want to see his former troops, but there was no way of avoiding it now he had to collect Faeral. He had arranged for a small but secure facility to be selected close to his assigned home and had a small force of the Guardians of Esperia tasked with securing it. A detachment of those Guardians accompanied him to Faeral's accommodation, increasing his humiliation. Entering the barracks of a fully professional, battle-hardened unit like the 6th in the company of a handful of shabby-looking part-timers coloured his face with embarrassment.

Doloras greeted him and handled the details of the handover. He was, as always, professional and friendly but now his loyalty lay elsewhere; the 6th had a new commander.

Faeral was in reasonable health. His arm had healed, though it was a little twisted, and he looked pale but composed. Taeris didn't try talking to him during their journey or once they arrived, leaving him secured and heading home to brood over the shame of the day.

At least there were compensations at home. Taeris woke each morning tangled in the naked limbs of Laesa, which was even more wonderful than the dreams of such mornings that had sustained him through seven years of imprisonment. He had also hatched a plan to make Faeral more compliant.

Taeris' relationship with Salassa had never really started. She was too timid, too quiet to become a vibrant part of the household and he left her alone at night. He determined to secure her involvement in the questioning of Faeral, partly because she was a native Aepolian and partly because men, in general, became more cheerful in the presence of a pretty girl. He asked Salassa to join himself and Laesa for an evening, over which he would discuss her possible role.

Salassa and Laesa were waiting for him when he got home that evening, Laesa looked pleased to see him; whatever emotions Salassa felt were, as usual, hidden under her fringe. He did feel that something was slightly odd that evening. Salassa seemed as distant and monosyllabic as ever, but something was making Laesa tense. As Laesa went to pour out some drinks for the three he joined her and quietly asked if something was wrong.

"Salassa seems very taut this evening."

Taeris hadn't noticed, but then he'd spent very little time with the tiny Citaeronian so it wasn't surprising if he'd missed it. "I'll ask her about it." He turned and it was this act, perhaps, that saved his life. Salassa was raising a small sidearm to point at him and if he'd turned just a second later she would have had time to fire. Taeris reacted instantly, as experience had taught him, his legs pushed hard at the ground and the muscles, aided by the growth stimulators and the countless hours working against the resistance of his armour, threw him upwards and forwards. As he was unarmoured he couldn't leap very far or very fast but the low gravity and his artificially enhanced strength meant that he easily reached the ceiling with his hands. His arms bent to absorb the impact and then straightened to hurl him down again, this time directly at Salassa. She fired, but his leap had clearly caught her unawares and he landed on her uninjured. He probably weighed twice as much as she and her frame collapsed under the impact, the weapon skittering away across the floor to rest against a wall. For a moment there was silence. It was broken by a loud wail from Laesa. Ignoring the panting figure under his knees, Taeris turned to see if Laesa had been hurt. No, the one shot fired had gone high above her, almost hitting the upper corner of the room, she was shocked but not hurt. The same could not be said of Salassa; as he examined the woman he found that her right collarbone had been broken where his weight had come down on her.

Laesa, shaking and holding her arms wrapped around her belly as if she was cold, stepped forward. "What did she do?"

Taeris seemed to be unaffected by shock, perhaps he was just more used to sudden danger. "She tried to kill me."

Laesa looked at him in confusion and asked, "Why?"

Taeris thought it was a good question and he decided to get an answer. He grabbed Salassa's shoulder and gave it a gentle squeeze. Her small form twisted beneath him and a scream of pain boiled through her clenched teeth. "Why did you attack me?"

She didn't answer for a second so Taeris shifted his thumb slightly, feeling the ends of the broken clavicle scraping together. "Faeral!" Salassa screamed, using the Aepolian pronunciation of his name with the emphasis on the second syllable.

Taeris let go of her shoulder. "Faeral ordered me killed?"

Her eyes shot open at this, obviously she didn't want Faeral to be blamed for her actions. "Ana! No!"

"Then why?" Taeris reached out towards her shoulder again.

She answered before his hand got there. "You're the man who took Faeral."

Taeris nodded. "I am. How did you know?"

"A man told me, a Republic man. He told me I would be given to the man who took Faeral."

Taeris sat back. "Interesting."

Laesa said, "She was sent to kill you by a Republican?"

"It seems so, or at least a Republican put her in my household, gave her a weapon and cause to use it." Taeris answered. "I think it's time we patched up her shoulder and asked her some serious questions."

Gritting her teeth, Salassa said, "Miaegondivogayza anuzdi vidiq!"

Laesa stamped her foot in anger. "Now she won't even speak English!"

Taeris smiled. "If she is to be believed then that is irrelevant."

"Why?"

"She said she wouldn't tell us anything anyway." Taeris enjoyed the look of shock and horror that crossed Salassa's face. "I imagine the man who sent you forgot to mention that I speak Aepolian."

Laesa sat down in a chair as far from Salassa as she could get within the room. "Will you kill her?"

Taeris looked at the small, trembling woman under him. "No. Whoever sent her will try something else if he knows she's failed. Salassa, do you know Faeral, personally?"

She thought for a moment then shook her head. "He's," for a moment she grappled for the right words, settling on a phrase she must have heard a thousand times, "Onash ee zdradanezd viro."

Taeris remembered to translate for Laesa. "He's the first

211

and truest man."

Laesa noticed the small handgun and reached down to pick it up. "It's small."

Taeris looked over to confirm the identification with his own eyes. Small and elegant but packing a deadly shot. "Whoever assigned her to me will have given it to her. That weapon is currently being issued to members of the Magisterium."

Laesa looked at the small weapon in her hand. "Someone in the Magisterium sent her?"

Taeris shrugged. "Not necessarily; these weapons aren't hard to obtain if you're in a relatively senior position. Laesa, I must thank you."

"For my comment? Pure luck."

"No," said Taeris, smiling, "I must thank you for being so utterly charming and desirable that I didn't succumb to the temptation of taking this little traitor to bed. I suspect if I'd been alone with her and sleeping after sex I would have been an absolutely helpless target."

Laesa laughed slightly, the first time she'd relaxes since the weapon had been drawn. "At least I don't have to worry about you falling in love with her now."

Taeris gently moved his weight off the small blond girl, allowing her to cradle her broken shoulder. "I'm not sure about that. I've always liked my women feisty. But I think you're right. I think I have a better plan for her."

"What sort of plan?" Laesa asked.

Taeris looked down at the exquisite girl underneath him. "She seems to have a great deal of affection for Faeral, even though she's never met him. As it happens I want Faeral to become a little more cooperative than he is currently inclined to be. Perhaps if I give him a woman of his own, especially one who worships him, he might be more accommodating."

A wild look of pathetic hope flashed in Salassa's eyes as Taeris stood and dragged her upright by her unharmed arm. Even so, she also yelped in pain.

He towed her to her bedroom, roughly stripped her and then used plastic strip-clips to attach her uninjured wrist and one of her ankles to the posts of her bed. Quickly he injected analgesics, a sedative and an osteogenic drug into the site of her broken bone, then carefully set it in line using a visor, not unlike the sensors in his armour, to guide him. Finally he sprayed the skin with a further anaesthetic and hardening mixture to help immobilise the shoulder. Salassa was fast asleep within minutes and by the time she woke she would essentially be healed. A few more days of discomfort as the bone completed its mending could be ignored with relatively minor pain medication.

Taeris left her and walked out into the corridor, to find Laesa waiting for him.

Laesa looked at him critically. "You can't believe that an addled anarchist like your prisoner will open up to you in exchange for a woman, however beautiful."

Taeris smiled and kissed her on the forehead. "Of course not. I do think it's worth letting them become close for a few weeks and then see what I can get out of him by threatening to dismember her in front of him."

Laesa nodded slightly. "If that threat doesn't work?"

Taeris took her by the hand and gently pulled her towards his bed. "Then, Laesa, I shall dismember her in front of him. I don't make idle threats."

The 5th Guards

Taeris placed Salassa in the same room as Faeral. It was the only secure place he had available that wouldn't be visited or examined by senior officials of the Republic. The leers and smirks that she got from the Guardians on duty confirmed for Taeris that these irregular troops were not close to being as professional as the legions. Faeral said nothing when she was brought in, but Taeris hadn't expected much response.

He left for his one engagement of the day, the formal commissioning and departure of the 5th Guards Legion. A ground car took him to the Legacy building and once inside he changed the pattern on his armour to the solid blue of the Infantry Legions. He could no longer wear the uniform of the 6th Legion, that honour had been taken from him and given to another.

Centre of attention today was Driastren, the man in charge of the new legion, and he seemed perfectly within his element, accepting the praise and congratulations of his peers with a perfectly balanced blend of confidence and modesty. In the plaza below there were the familiar sounds of a legion forming up, but Taeris had seen that sight many times before so he ignored it for the moment.

Eventually the room emptied as the officers went down into the plaza and because of his lack of earlier curiosity Taeris found out only then that the legion had been formed facing the Praesidium, not the Legacy. Only one thing could be meant by this decision; the President himself was to witness the new formation's commissioning.

Taeris allowed his eyes to wander across the assembled 5th Guards. They looked immaculate, flawless. Everything about them was new and it showed in every glint of sunlight from a polished piece of armour. Without warning they all came to attention, precisely in harmony, and seeing this Taeris turned to see the President walking to his position on his balcony overlooking the plaza. Seven years seemed to have affected the man barely at all. He was still tall and elegant, poised and calm.

He waited for a long time before beginning his speech, a sure sign of confidence that this audience would stand at attention for him for as long as he demanded. "Soldiers of the Fifth Guards Legion!" His voice echoed off the slab-sided buildings all around the plaza. He was enough an orator to demand that the artificial amplification for his voice was just turned down enough that he would have to shout to make himself heard. In that shout came the faint impression that his voice might actually carry unaided across the plaza, though in fact even people gathered beneath the balcony would be unable to hear him if the microphone was switched off. "Today you embrace a destiny by renewing a storied name. One hundred years ago there was a Fifth Guards and it was the legion commanded by a man who would go on to be one of my predecessors as President! He was the last President to have served as a Legate, the last of a line of magnificent leaders to have done both. He retired the old 5th as an honourable decision, so no legate could say that they commanded the President's Legion! Here today we establish this legion anew. Men of the Fifth; read the history of the mighty legion that your uniforms now echo. Look at their battles! Look at their victories! Look at yourselves and decide today! Right now!

That you will not live up to their splendid example, for that is not what I ask! I ask that you exceed them in every way! You are the best the Republic can offer. You are stronger, faster and better trained than your forebears. On your mighty backs rests the weight of our Republic and with it human civilisation itself!"

He paused for a moment, for dramatic effect. "I ask you this! Will you carry the standard of the Republic to the enemy and teach them what it means to be a soldier?"

Taeris assumed this was a planned moment, because the entire 5th responded with one voice, thundering across the plaza, "Yes!"

The President smiled fondly down. "On this charge I commission the Fifth Guards Legion into the command of Legate Driastren! I pity those who raise arms against the Fifth Guards!"

Wild roars and cheers filled the plaza and continued almost unabated as the doors on their Tyrant vehicles opened and in a smooth and elegant pattern of take-offs, the 5th lifted to fill the littoral ships above them.

Taeris watched them go in awe. Pity, indeed, those who fought such men. Last of all Driastren climbed into his command Tyrant and flew off to join the fleet, as quiet fell across the huge plaza.

Taeris watched the President step off his balcony back into the Praesidium and then turned to join the other Legates inside the Legacy but he was interrupted by a channel opening from the Spica. "Taeris, Raephus."

He stopped and responded, "Taeris."

In the low orbit there was very little delay in the communications. "I wanted to pass on some information before we depart. Naturally the President and the Legacy will already be aware of this, I'm sure, but there has been an unusual amount of activity at the jump-relay recently and not all of it seems to be the routine exchanges of general communication."

Taeris frowned. "Unusual activity, such as flights into and out of the system to conduct reconnaissance missions?"

Raephus' voice was clipped but clear as he said, "Very much like that, in fact very much the way we have disguised our own missions to Citaeron. But I doubt the results of those missions would be of interest, given that the Eighth Guards will obviously have kept you informed."

"Obviously," Taeris said, "But I would hear anything they might have forgotten from you."

"Rebellion on Citaeron has essentially ceased. The arrival of the Seventh Infantry has bolstered the force there and the plague has destroyed any organisation on the rebel part. Unfortunately the plague does seem to have spread to Tyrenia, as was expected. A number of wealthy and powerful people, especially those that have senior roles in the corporates, have fled the planet."

Taeris took in a deep breath. "Fled the planet despite the quarantine?"

"It appears so, and potentially a grave development."

Not for the first time Taeris wished he understood the additional importance that the word 'grave' gave this pronouncement. "I understand, Admiral, thank you."

The channel dropped and less than a minute later the Spica dropped from the local communications grid as it led the 3rd Fleet to Prosperity. Taeris thought for a moment. There could be plague on some of the ships that had slipped the net at Citaeron. A rebel force might well have sympathetic Citaeronians, even those that might also be corporate officers, and some might be aboard the next fighting force to be launched. Not for the first time Taeris searched the sunny sky for any sign of attack, but the air was clear. If he'd watched for just two minutes longer he would have seen the rebels appear overhead.

Taeris was back inside the Legacy when an alert was opened across all the channels of senior commanders. The 1st Fleet was reporting a large force of enemy ships arriving in the Esperian system. As a man standing on the surface of the planet there was nothing that could really be done, but Taeris automatically looked around the room to find Trantier, the new commander of the 6th. Trantier was quietly talking with Caeranion in one corner and Taeris hurried across to join them. As he arrived they both stopped talking and looked at him with open hostility; clearly the fact that his warning, so readily dismissed by the Legacy, had proved to be accurate wasn't going to earn him any respect from these men. "Legates, tell me how I can help."

Trantier shook his head emphatically. "You can't."

"I know the Sixth better than you," Taeris said, "I can help you get them deployed faster."

Caeranion sniffed in a truly derisory manner. "The Sixth has not yet been approved as battle-ready by the Magisterium, it will not be deployed until that work has completed."

Trantier nodded his agreement. "No ground forces will be needed for this battle anyway. The First Fleet will destroy all enemy forces before they threaten the surface of the planet."

In stunned disbelief Taeris looked at the display on his wrist that was updating him on the situation in orbit. "Your confidence may be misplaced." As soon as he said those words he knew he'd made a mistake. Both faces became as fixed as a death-mask and with about as much humour. After they glared at him for a few seconds he turned and walked out of the room and then out of the Legacy. The lack of urgency was baffling and it wasn't just the senior officers. There seemed to be very little happening in the other areas he passed on his way out of the building and the entire Legacy was indistinguishable from how it would have been on any typical day. He threw himself into a ground car and as it carried him smoothly out of the plaza and along the broad spoke-road he turned his attention back to the information on his wrist. The sheer quantity and speed of the updates was making the flow hard to understand but after a few minutes, as he was dropped off in front of his house, he felt he had a broad understanding of the situation.

In general the Republic seemed to have the upper hand. Several hundred small, modern ships had jumped into the system at extremely close range. They had divided immediately into three formations and the largest of these, both in size of vessel and number, launched an attack on the warships of the Republic fleet. A second group had taken advantage of the distraction caused by the attack to drop into the atmosphere and begin a landing while a third group of small craft broke into the atmosphere and began attacking installations on the ground. Devoting only light craft to the ground-attack role had inevitably limited the amount of damage that could be caused. Had the rebels believed, even for a moment, that the leaders of their enemy's regiments would simply stay in the Legacy waiting for good news from the fleet then they could have spared some heavier craft to destroy the building and, with it, the entire officer corps of Esperia. This was not the first time that the traitors had overestimated the competence of the Republic but it seemed certain to Taeris that they would eventually learn and they would then become much more destructive foes.

Taeris could see a few craft flitting through the atmosphere as he made his way into his house. Laesa was standing in the front hall, her face tense with worry. "Laesa. I'm pleased you're safe."

She looked at him with pleading softness. "Am I? Are you?"

It was more than a fair question. "The rebels have made a mistake. They will be defeated here and the losses they suffer will end the rebellion for good."

Laesa visibly calmed herself. "What should I do?"

"Pack a bag. I'm taking you to the house where I sent Salassa. I trust you to stop trigger-happy Guardians from killing the prisoners."

Laesa stepped into a side room and returned, seconds later, with a bulging bag she'd prepared in case she had to leave the house quickly. "Let's go."

Taeris smiled at her fondly. This was his woman and she was a marvel.

As they left the house, Taeris glanced down at his screen again. A fourth group of Rebels had appeared above Esperia, but not moving into orbit, they were heading towards the planet at tremendous speed. Quickly the computers identified them as missile boats, but the newcomers had already unleashed their vast swarms of unguided projectiles at the Republic fleet, itself silhouetted against the surface of the planet. Many of the missiles were intercepted and destroyed, the ships giving priority to those that were on direct paths to strike them, but in that decision lay one huge problem. The missiles that flashed harmlessly past the fleet would all strike into the atmosphere of Esperia. As Taeris helped Laesa into the car he stood and looked around him at the beautiful, suburban neighbourhood. It wouldn't look like that again for a long time.

rt 3 - Dig two graves

The Fighting 6th

There were supposed to be two Guardians outside the secure building where Faeral and now Salassa were living. As the ground car pulled to a stop and Taeris climbed out he noted that they seemed to have left their posts. A rebel fighter suddenly shot overhead, faster than a bullet, leaving the sound of its passing like thunder being shredded by a machine. Laesa looked up, startled, at the sound.

"Don't worry," Taeris told her, "I think the ones you hear have already left you alone." This thought didn't seem to cheer her up a great deal, perhaps men and women were different that way.

Inside the building there were four Guardians who made a show of trying to come to attention, not very seamlessly. Taeris ignored them and led Laesa towards the back room. The door was not obviously distinct from any other, but it had been fitted with a good lock. He unlocked and opened the door to reveal the two people inside. Faeral looked up slowly, calm and composed, Salassa had jumped at the sound of the door opening and she looked terrified to see Taeris again.

Taeris fixed his gaze on the rebel leader. "This is my woman, Laesa. She is in charge of you while I sort out important things." He made an obvious show of handing the small pistol, taken from Salassa, to Laesa, so the captives would know she was armed.

Faeral stood, accompanied by the sounds of cracking

223

knee-joints. "What's happening outside?"

Taeris smiled. "The traitors have attacked Esperia. Once they have been destroyed here the rebellion will be over."

Faeral looked down at the floor. "I'm sorry it comes to this."

Taeris turned and left them, striding back outside to his ground car. This time he directed it towards the barracks of the 6th Infantry Legion and as he travelled he opened up a channel to Adrael. "Adrael, Taeris."

The delay was long enough that Taeris wondered if he was going to get a response at all, but eventually Adrael's voice came through. "Adrael."

"Adrael," Taeris said, "I want to know if the Sixth Infantry is battle-ready."

Adrael was a security man and his first instinct was suspicion. "Why?"

Taeris fought back a sarcastic answer. "I'm close to their barracks, I can begin the deployment while Trantier gets over to them."

Back came Adrael's voice, "I don't see the need. If the legion is to be deployed then Trantier will deploy it."

"Of course the Sixth must be deployed! Traitors are attacking this very city. Can't you see that from the Magisterium?"

A pause again before Adrael answered, "I'm not in the Magisterium. Republic Plaza and its immediate surroundings have been evacuated for our safety."

Taeris couldn't believe what he was hearing. "So who is now commanding the infantry?"

Adrael responded smoothly. "I don't know, but it is not for me to intervene. This is a matter for the Legacy."

Rage filled Taeris, "I hope you mean the people of the

Legacy rather than the building, just in case that's already in the hands of our enemies!"

Adrael's voice was cold. "Are you asking for my permission to deploy the Sixth Legion?"

"Yes!" Taeris shouted at his wrist.

"Very well," Adrael's voice was still almost robotic, "Do as you see fit. I will make a note of our conversation and describe it to the Legacy when this fighting is over."

It was the best Taeris could expect. He had, at least, flimsy justification for taking his old legion back to war. There would be discussion afterwards about whether or not his actions were unrepublican, but that was after the battle and, he smiled grimly at the thought, he might well be dead by then anyway. His car swept into the open space in front of the barracks building and his heart turned to rock in his chest.

The barracks had taken direct hits from what might be several missiles. The buildings of the complex were mere piles of smoking rubble, surrounded by untouched civilian structures standing tall in tribute to the accuracy of the traitors' attack. Those strikes must have been carried out by atmosphere-capable craft, not the almost random impacts of the unguided missiles from space. He leaped from the car, all speed and determination, even though there was nothing he could actually do. Cruelly, at that second, a flight of atmosphere fighters in Republic markings flew overhead. He looked up at them mentally demanding to know where they were when the missiles came. He was pulled from his reverie by an obvious thought. He had quick-links on his communicator to the channels of most of the officers of the 6th, if any yet lived he could talk to them. In seconds he discovered that every single one of his links to his men was fully operational. Numbly he opened a call to Doloras.

"Doloras, Taeris."

Doloras' voice was as crisp as ever. "Doloras. Do you know if we have any orders yet?"

Taeris laughed out loud for a single second as relief flooded through him. "I thought you were all killed."

Doloras came back to him at once. "We were ordered by our commanding Legate to remain in our barracks. It seems that all four of the regimental commanders in the Sixth misunderstood these orders. I feel greatly ashamed."

Taeris grinned, "Where are you?" A second later his wrist came alive with tracking information. They were close enough that the car would not be needed. Taeris allowed his armour to do the work and he sprinted along the streets to where his former command awaited him. On the way he passed a Sagittarius air-defence vehicle manned by some nervous-looking Guardians. They'd managed to site the vehicle under large amounts of overhead cover, guaranteeing that they had no useful way of hitting enemy aircraft with either the rapid-fire tmetics or the vicious missiles in the vehicle, while also ensuring that any strike landing near them might bury them in masonry. Guardian training might need some attention before this war was over, it seemed. Taeris shouted orders at them as he passed, but he didn't wait to find out if they were obeyed. He sprinted on towards the 6th Legion.

He arrived to find a command Tyrant with the back door open for him and the familiar face of Doloras perched atop the massive armoured torso inside. Scattered around the small roads in all directions were other Tyrants, placed to be far enough apart that a single weapon wouldn't hit more than one or two of them. All of them looked like indistinct and fuzzy-edged shadows because of their complete lack of any electromagnetic emission, they looked like splashes of matte paint against the houses and commercial buildings of the suburb.

Doloras frowned as he approached. "Out of uniform, Legate?"

For a moment Taeris didn't follow, then with a grateful laugh he reset his armour briefly to the tiger stripes of the 6th and then flashed it back to shadow-black. "What's the situation on the ground?"

Doloras gestured grandly across the display screens inside the Tyrant. "As you would expect the indomitable forces of the Republic are sweeping the rebels from the planet with grace and ease."

Taeris threw a grin at Doloras. "It's going that badly?"

Doloras nodded. "Yes, we are being terribly heroic."

He wasn't exaggerating. The rebels had attacked a number of important locations from the air, in particular the hangars of the fighter regiments, the barracks of the legions and several command buildings, including all those surrounding Republic Plaza. While these attacks were generally not by heavy craft they were nonetheless destructive and in the aftermath there didn't seem to be much in the way of effective leadership. Most of the Esperian fighters had managed to get airborne and they were slowly clearing the skies of enemy craft, but they were working as individuals and small groups without much in the way of coherent orders so they were much less effective than normal. Worse, many of them had no working hangars to return to when they needed to re-arm. If there was a second wave of rebel ships then they might face almost no fighters at all. The rebels had also landed a substantial ground force in Republic Plaza, the very centre of the city. Immediately the 1st Guards had encircled it, using the damaged government buildings as shelter, but the rebels seemed to have expected this and the perimeter had been seeded with time-delayed weapons as part of the original bombing. The 1st had taken heavy casualties as all those explosives detonated under and around them and as they reeled from the attack several more rebel contingents were landed outside them in the city, pinning them between enemy forces. The 10th Guards was slowly deploying, but seemed to have no overall orders and this made their counter-attack slow and unfocused.

Doloras gave Taeris the few minutes needed to take in all this before he said, "Sir? What are our orders?"

Taeris looked as him curiously. "What makes you think I'm in charge?"

Doloras shook his head. "You're the ranking officer; until a President shows up, you're in charge." Clearly Trantier had not yet issued any battle-orders.

Taeris tapped his wrist against the console in the Tyrant. It immediately recognised him and began showing him his options. He began by redeploying the fighters. In a few minutes he'd formed all of the craft into large formations and set them to sweeping the skies clear; he was determined that he wouldn't expose his infantry to danger until they could count on air-superiority. That condition was already coming about by default. The enemy fighters were fleeing back above the atmosphere to rejoin their fleet and significant elements of that fleet had already jumped out of system. Taeris swore at the screen. If the Rebel forces left orbit mostly intact then they could be out there, waiting for another assault. At least they must have delivered most, if not all, of their ground forces into Esperia and those forces could be killed.

He then took in the position of the 10th Guards. As a unit they seemed to lack a legate, but more seriously they also had none of their regimental commanders online. In such a situation each battalion commander would have no choice but to command his own troops independently, something that actually suited the dense, urban layout of the city but did not at all suit the mindset of the Guardsman. Taeris was acutely conscious of the fact that the 10th would follow standard Republic doctrine and that this included the instruction to never retreat from the enemy. In an infantry fight through a city this was suicidal, you needed to trade metres for lives in such a battle. He decided to order each of the battalions of the 10th to a single location in the city, with orders to stop any rebel forces from getting past them. His placement of the legion made a large, rough circle around the entire centre of the city, which contained within it all enemy ground forces that he knew of. It would take a while for those orders to bear fruit, but soon there would be a ring of steel around the centre of the city, one simple line of defence to keep the invasion contained. A few seconds later he'd sent orders to all the Guardians he could find online to form a reserve line behind the 10th and delegated their command to the Guards' battalion commanders. Step one. Landings contained. Of course that made a few assumptions, not least that the rebels, now withdrawing much of their fleet, had landed all the troops they could. If that proved untrue then there was a possibility of another landing behind the lines of the 10th, an encirclement, a brutal fight to the death in some obscure suburb of the city, a suburb that would ever more be known by that battle, the battle of, wherever.

With the fighting strength of the 1st Guards a mostly unknown quantity, Taeris ignored them for the moment and started to order the four regiments of the 6th into action, on a front that would see them hit the outer ring of rebels and hopefully smash through them to relieve pressure on the troops

229

inside. The overview map of Esperia City now looked rather like an archery target. Rebels in the middle, with the 1st Guards surrounding them, rebels in a loose ring around the outside of the 1st and with the 10th forming an outer ring around it all. The electronic map casually overlaid the current positions of troops, the positions they were ordered to occupy, their estimated times before those orders would be complete. The information thus displayed was vast, but easy to understand, because each set of data was projected as a layer in three virtual dimensions, just the slightest move of the head would allow the eyes to find and fix on the relevant layer. Another layer was devoted to information about enemy forces, that layer still worryingly blank.

As the 6th Infantry started to roll in formation the picture looked even more convincingly like a target, with a long, thin arrow made of the 6th, slowly creeping in from one side of the map toward the centre.

Taeris' Tyrant lifted and moved with the others, surrounded by infantry moving in rapid jumps and steps in almost random directions, over such a battlefield the infantry would all be out of their vehicles.

Suddenly a piece of the screen flashed red, an enemy fighter automatically detected overhead one of the leading Tyrants. The vehicle's turret raised and swivelled to track the craft but by the time the gunner had authorised the fighter as a legitimate target it had flown across the street and vanished behind a building. That didn't save it. The computers on all the Tyrants beamed a complex network of directional information along the streets, Tyrants on corners received these messages and beamed them down the connecting streets, in a fraction of a second almost every Tyrant in the 6th had the location and track of the enemy fighter and as it crossed over its next street the turrets were already angled to intercept.

To its credit, the craft took more than a dozen hits that were absorbed in its capacitors before it received a killing blow. It kept going, street after street, now tumbling, burning, breaking apart, the vehicles below kept firing as they saw the pieces of the fighter, they would keep firing until someone manually declared the enemy craft destroyed. By the time that command was issued there was a spread of small debris flying along the path that had previously been followed by a deadly combat craft, so much had the size been shredded that the individual pieces of the fighter did almost no damage as they crashed into buildings and roads across a small district of the city. A single missile from a Sagittarius flew up through the track, too late to be involved, and detonated in the air once it found itself without a target. Taeris pulled up the layer showing the disposition of the Guardians and rapidly corrected the air-defence portion of their deployment positions. In the Carmine park, just outside the perimeter defined by the 10th and right behind the 6th, he deployed a dozen of the Sagittarius units, a battery powerful enough to stop anything coming overhead. That should prevent any enemy atmosphere fighters from flying along the line of the 6th's advance, potentially the most damaging approach a fighter could take.

The forward elements of the 23rd Infantry were just reaching the outer ring of the 10th Guards. The troops glanced at each other in passing but no messages were exchanged, once sealed inside armour you needed radio to send messages and, however tight the beam, every signal sent ran a risk of detection. Taeris was concentrating on his command screen in the deathly silence before battle would be joined when his data refreshed to show that the rebel fleet, or its remnants, had jumped out of Esperia. For the remainder of this battle the Republic would have control of the atmosphere.

Once the troops had moved past the 10th Guards they were in territory that the enemy was trying to occupy and it wasn't long before Taeris' infantry units began launching some of their suits' inbuilt reconnaissance drones into the air above them. The drones were capable of independent flight and moved in essentially random patterns, so individually their movements might not cover the area of crucial importance, but they also knew where each other were so they spread out over the battlefield. Of course their very presence could give advanced warning of an infantry unit's presence, but wouldn't give away the positions of individual soldiers. Tyrants also carried such drones and in greater numbers, but in this battle the Tyrants were hanging back a little to provide cover and support where needed. True to their form, the rebels had broken into small units, hiding each in whatever cover presented itself within the city. Several of these positions started to open fire on Taeris' troops and at once Taeris sent out the orders he'd planned for this moment. Tyrants rose up behind his troops, already knowing exactly where to fire their mighty Vikings. At the same instant fighters overhead poured beams into the same positions. The infantry had been told to hold fire and shoot at enemy troops only as they fled the positions under fire; flee they did.

In seconds the first few positions had been smashed and their troops slaughtered as they tried to retreat. Inexorably the 6th Infantry moved forwards, spreading out a little, but maintaining enough proximity to support each other from every side. The first exchanges of fire were against enemy forces that had not had the time necessary to build a proper defence. This haste was now costing them in lives. It was a situation that couldn't last. As the 6th moved further into enemy territory it must encounter opponents with more resources and greater time to dig in.

The Curse of Citaeron

Taeris grimaced in frustration as he watched the battle overview change in front of him. "Too slow!"

Doloras looked at the screens as well. "Legate, our forces are advancing carefully."

Taeris was about to snap back, then relaxed a little. "You're right. We're moving forwards and we're hurting them a lot more than they're hurting us. I just wish the President or the Legacy would get back on the communications grid."

Doloras nodded slowly, it had to be worrying him as well.

Taeris threw his hands up in irritation. "Now the One-thirty-ninth has stopped moving as well!"

Doloras didn't say anything, Taeris could see as easily as he that the battalion was taking fire from four positions and had decided to duck into cover while they waited for Tyrants or fighters to help them shift the rebels. With every step they took closer to the plaza the concentration of enemy forces increased; as did their ability to effectively protect each other. Eliminating them in sequence, without exposing the 6th to powerful attacks from its flanks, was painstaking and slow work. Worse, Taeris was convinced that the rebels had hidden some positions and allowed the legion to pass them unnoticed; to stop these forces from creeping out of the centre of the city and into undefended areas was the job of the 10th Guards, so they couldn't be called forwards to aid in the attack.

Suddenly a region of the screen flashed red. Doloras

called out, "One-eleventh under attack. Taking casualties fast."

Taeris pulled up all the information he could. "Enemy forces are mobile, this isn't a fixed position it's a counter-attack."

It was certainly a well-timed manoeuvre, as well. The 111th had divided its forces down each side of an enormous housing block, moving down two parallel streets. The distance between them was almost negligible but they couldn't provide complementary support with the massive building in the way. Normally the solution would be to climb the building, taking the top of it and joining the 111th back together that way, but enemy forces appeared to be in the block, also in the blocks to each side and were attacking from the front as well, trying to push the 111th back down the streets, hoping to concentrate them, confuse them. Doctrine called for a mass strike forwards, attacking the oncoming enemy, but doing so across broken ground, exposing the flanks of the troops, could be very costly indeed. The 111th was one of Doloras' battalions so he started to give orders to pull back to the near side of the block, so the two halves of the battalion could offer each other support. Taeris was intently studying the screen as well. "Wait!"

Doloras stopped and stared at Taeris. "What's wrong?"

Taeris didn't answer, instead opening up a channel to the Major commanding the 112th. "I'm sending you an attack order, Major."

Doloras looked at the order as it was sent. Taeris was ordering a massive strike by the Tyrants of the 112th into the empty street behind the 111th's position. "Legate, that will demolish several buildings there, The 111th will have rubble to its rear." His concern was logical. Rubble meant that the retreating 111th would have to climb out of the streets and the higher you stood on a battlefield the more exposed you were.

Taeris didn't answer, but nodded. The enemy attack was

beginning to cause escalating casualties in the front ranks of the 111th and Doloras was desperate to withdraw them so an air attack could be mounted. Until his troops were clear of those two streets the weapons on the fighters would pull down the massive blocks on top of the battalion. The 111th was holding position as best it could, losing men quickly, communications from its officers were now a continual stream of requests to withdraw, something Taeris was extremely proud of as, before his tenure at the helm of the legion, these officers would have regarded retreat as unthinkable. Taeris watched them facing fire from all sides, cover almost impossible to find in this trap. Agonisingly slowly the 112th moved into position and began its attack. Now the junctions the 111th needed for its retreat were being torn to pieces by Viking cannon. At least that brought a pause in the retreat requests, no officer willingly moved into that hail of random fire. In the midst of the blasts, perfectly displayed in the command Tyrant by the many cameras pointing into the crossfire, a number of secondary explosions started to appear. Some seemed to be in the middle of the street, others on the corners of the buildings. For a moment the buildings stood, just sliced and scarred by the powerful beams, but then the entire circle of buildings surrounding the junction began to fall, all at once, filling the entire junction with massive destroyed masonry and reducing the surrounding structures to vague skeletal outlines poking through a sea of devastation. One or two stunned enemies climbed from their destroyed positions, Taeris saw one torn to atoms by infantry weapons, his arms held aloft in an attempt to surrender. Taeris didn't wait. "Now! Retreat the One-eleventh!"

Doloras gave the order and watched as the battalion moved jerkily back over the pile of new rubble, slowing its progress a little, but providing plenty of cover for its infantry.

Those explosions, those sudden collapses; a trap had been laid there for the 111th and if they'd retreated when Doloras wanted them to the entire battalion would be a memory. The enemy was much more tactical than expected. This trap didn't merely function if Republic doctrine was followed, it functioned as well, or even better, if doctrine was ignored. It was as if the unknown, unseen enemy had planned this trap specifically for a unit commanded by Doloras. He stared in wonder at Taeris, imagining the carnage if his Legate hadn't been here. He was so engrossed that he failed to notice what Taeris was doing with the rest of the regiment.

Led by the 112th, the bulk of the 23rd Infantry Regiment was pouring forwards, heedless of casualties. Losses were mounting, but the sudden leap forwards seemed to have caught the rebels unawares. Ignoring the two streets that formed the trap for the 111th, the Republic surged forwards in a huge envelopment, a dozen blocks wide. Given the speed a Tyrant could move this was achieved in less than two minutes and following the path Taeris had planned the two arms of the attack folded inward and met beyond the traitors' position. Inevitably the enemy had left traps and troops to slow the attack but these were small and easily dealt with. Doloras had begun to understand the plan and he ordered the 111th to fortify their positions as best they could. They didn't have long. Leading elements of the envelopment forces, almost the entire 23rd, were now charging back towards the 111th in exactly the opposite direction to the line of attack that the enemy had predicted the legions would use. Most of the rebel positions were horribly exposed from the rear and the enemy abandoned them with scarcely a fight. Fleeing rebels routed down the streets they'd so carefully prepared as a death-trap for the Republic; at the end of those streets the 111th waited for its revenge, dug into the piles of rubble that the enemy had intended to be their mass grave. The tmetics opened fire, sweeping across the enemy troops, tearing them apart. The mobile forces were flying down the streets at 150m altitude, so they could pour fire into the helpless rebels without risking any of their fire reaching the 111th. The 111th, low and dug in, kept their fire level, below the altitude of their allies. As the targets thinned and eventually disappeared the remaining infantry of the 23rd bounced across the scene, hunting hidden enemies, clearing the buildings. Bayonet fighting. Butchery.

Doloras turned his head from the graphic slaughter and looked to Taeris. "Thank you."

Taeris smiled. "It's easy with these troops. I'd have no luck at all making a Guards Legion fight like this." As if that acted as a prompt he flicked his screen across to show the current status of the 1st Guards. It made for dismal viewing.

It seemed that each battalion had simply thrown itself towards the nearest enemy it could see; not an elegant strategy at the best of times. Worse, the enemy most of them could see was a concentration of heavy armour right in the middle of Republic Plaza. Something about that armour looked familiar, but Taeris couldn't place it, exactly. While they'd still had fighter cover, the rebels had poured air-dropped mines into the periphery of the plaza and fully half of the entire complement of Tyrants in the 1st Guards had been damaged or destroyed by them. Worse still, the open nature of the terrain had dictated the infantry remain in their vehicles until they got close enough to receive effective enemy fire from the ground. As far as Taeris could tell the legion had never reached that point, so what infantry was visible was crawling, crippled and disoriented from the wrecks of their Tyrants. Some units seemed to have got to the plaza well after the others and each was following precisely the standard Republic doctrine, one after another. As Taeris watched a fresh company of 25 vehicles threw itself across the open ground, Vikings firing, and one after another they were slowed, stopped, broken and silenced by the implacable mines they crossed.

Doloras looked across in horror. "Can't they fly higher?"

Taeris shook his head sadly. "Doctrine states to remain as low as possible to avoid direct fire."

"But they're not taking direct fire!"

"I know," Taeris answered, "Republic doctrine is inflexible. They aren't thinking of the reason behind the rules, just following the rules."

Doloras understood, of course. "So they'll all die."

Taeris reached a hand across to rest it on his Colonel's shoulder. "They will. Gloriously. In the finest traditions of the Republic. Songs will be sung."

Doloras nodded, he was as republican as anyone. "We should all be proud of their loyalty."

Taeris turned back to the screens. He checked on the progress of the fighters overhead. Some had managed to retain some weaponry and though he wanted to keep those back for close support of the 6th, he sighed and redirected them to smash the heavy armour in the middle of the Plaza. Hopefully once the armour was destroyed the 1st Guards would stop throwing themselves at minefields.

Increasingly the streets were filling with civilians; the centre of the city was densely populated. In the first few minutes of the assault, perhaps, these people had simply hidden in their lodgings, but as the sounds of war became more and more violent many decided to brave the streets and flee for the suburbs. It was horribly dangerous for them but staying in a building that might at any second be destroyed by explosions or cut in half by heavy beams offered no safer alternative. At least if they were outside the soldiers could see them and try to avoid hitting them; hidden from view they would be gone from the minds of the armed troops.

In some ways this choice was fundamentally similar to the one faced by thousands of different civilian populations over thousands of years of conflicts, but in one way the modern war had made their flight much more risky. The same computer system that tracked the locations and information gathered by every combat unit also included a device to automatically warn off or even interdict the firing of a weapon that would directly strike a friendly soldier. If a soldier's arc of fire swung across the position occupied by one of his fellows then the system could be made to flash a warning, to both soldiers. Most soldiers turned that off in battle because the frequency with which your weapon's aim would intersect another friendly soldier was simply too high, adding to the information load unnecessarily. Taeris was unusual in that he always left the warnings on. As a commander he wanted to ensure that as he approached a position his alert troops did sweep him with their weapons, before they were assured he was a friendly. Instead soldiers usually chose not to be kept informed, neither when their weapon was pointed at a friendly nor when a friendly's was pointed at them, but for the suit to simply interdict any of their own shots that were aimed directly at a friendly soldier. As a system it was imperfect. Only shots fired at a soldier would be stopped, not those that landed near him and sometimes these could still kill or injure. Even so the infantry came to rely on this system to reduce the risk on the battlefield. In that reliance there was a danger. The modern infantry weapon could fire until it overheated or became unserviceable. Unless a plasma slug was inserted into the barrel, an occasional choice, there was no way of wasting ammunition. The modern infantryman therefore fired a lot. When at the front of an advance he fired even more than that. While it was possible to manually set the system to identify a specific person as a friendly, there was little time in warfare for such niceties. Soldiers shot at things that moved, hoping the computer would stop them from hurting allies. In such a place the unarmoured civilian was taking a severe risk indeed.

Despite this, the numbers of civilians steadily increased. Many, perhaps most, were emerging from their buildings behind the 6th Infantry, but increasing numbers were becoming casualties-in-waiting in front of the unit's weapons. Taeris noticed that a small group had clustered around the back of his Tyrant, perhaps disoriented by the noise, the fear and the simple fact that the main street they walked or drove every day was now buried under thousands of tonnes of rubble, decorated like a macabre cake with the corpses of the dead.

Opening the back door of the Tyrant, Taeris stepped out. Several infantrymen were trying to organise the civilians and direct them away from danger, towards whatever help the 10th Guards might be able to supply. Taeris had come to offer his own voice, or weight of rank, to the discussion, but one look at the confused, stunned and injured group told him that mere words wouldn't reach them. He turned back to his vehicle. If he couldn't help then he would ignore them and get on with his own job. As he did, something on his arm caught his eye and he froze.

Resting, pointlessly, on the matte black forearm of his armour was a single, tiny flea.

He used his other hand to crush it, but his mind was racing. He jumped back into the Tyrant and grabbed Doloras' shoulder.

"Sir?"

"I just killed a flea out there."

For a second, just a second, Doloras' face started to twist into a grin, before the possibilities swept his calm away. He snapped the helmet on his suit closed, as Taeris did the same. "I don't know what to do."

Taeris leapt to the communications channel in the Tyrant and opened it wide. Everyone would hear this. "Soldiers, this is Taeris. Seal armour at once." Most of the infantry outside their vehicles would already have their suits sealed, but a reminder to the others couldn't hurt. "Evacuate Tyrants at once and make room in there for as many civilians as you can find. We have fleas on the battlefield, unarmoured people are in huge danger."

He turned, at once, to the console in the vehicle. Most of the troops of the 6th had started following his instructions. No movement from the 10th Guards, their infantry seemed content to sit in their Tyrants. Now he was reviewing the overall status once more, Taeris noticed something unexpected in the way the 1st Guards had deployed. Only three of the five regiments that comprised the legion had thrown themselves so wastefully against the rebels. The other two had deployed behind the Praesidium, between it and the massive Corporate buildings. To protect the President, perhaps? If so, why had they left the Praesidium building between themselves and the enemy troops? Could they be hiding behind the President? Did that even make sense?

Taeris tried to focus on them in more detail, to see what they were doing, but the computer would only show the most essential of details; he couldn't pick up the feeds from the units' own cameras or sensors, he couldn't listen in to their chatter. He actually had exactly enough information to avoid shooting them by accident and not a single datum more. Why had they hidden their main reports from the grid? What was going on?

The Second Casualty

For the next hour, Taeris and Doloras offered what help they could to their troops. A good commander can see a wide and deep view that his soldiers cannot while they have to concentrate on staying alive. Good soldiers learn to listen and obey, because sometimes the orders are for the purpose of the objective, sometimes they are intended to keep the soldier alive and well. Nothing in the way those orders are issued ever reveals this intent to the soldier and in this way obedience is assured and the soldier acts in the best interests of the Republic. Soldiers of the 6th had greater reason to obey their commanders than most as they had followed orders in the past that turned out to be for their benefit.

Taeris tried not to look too hard at the automated reports flowing in from the 10th Guards. Their commander had clearly decided that, for the safety of the city, there could be no civilian allowed past the cordon maintained by his legion. Any terrified people who tried were being ruthlessly killed. Taeris wished he could order the man to stop, but it wasn't the fact that they were of the same rank that prevented him. He couldn't order an end to the slaughter because he would have issued the same orders and he hated himself in that moment for his choice, pragmatic beyond compassion. So he didn't look. He tried to pretend that he might have done things differently, better. He lied to himself while he oversaw the collection of the civilians he could save. Those Sagittarius vehicles had been drawn up to join the 10th, they were fitted with powerful, very rapid-fire tmetics. Designed to bring down aircraft and missiles these weapons could also tear through massed groups of infantry with spectacular ease. Infantry, or civilians.

Doloras had been trying to raise the Legacy. Surely they now had plenty of time to find a new and secure location? Where were they? Had they all been killed in the landings? The fleet was manoeuvring overhead with purpose, but it had stopped responding to Taeris. Presumably it had to be following someone's orders, but increasingly Doloras got the feeling that the strategy was being decided and carried out without involving the 6th at all.

Taeris was trying to raise a response from anyone he could in a senior position, but he was getting nowhere. The only significant change on the screens was that the 1st Guards, at least the two regiments that still had their full strength, was now moving rapidly away from the centre and out through relatively minor resistance and towards the outer encirclement of the 10th Guards. One of the reasons for the trivial nature of their opposition was obvious. The fighters of the 1st Fleet had been exclusively engaged in smashing them a clear path out of the centre of the city. Not a single fighter was doing anything else, not even flying reconnaissance over the wider city. Something important had to be going on here but, like the familiarity of those armoured vehicles in the plaza, understanding escaped Taeris. Eventually there was little point to his being in a command vehicle, so he and Doloras opened the door and stepped out, waving a number of civilians in to find some hope of shelter inside. A Tyrant's infantry compartment could carry eight troops in full armour, and though the command variant had a smaller compartment it could still easily fit 20 unarmoured people. The door shut and Taeris stared glumly at his wrist and the display projected from his helmet that appeared to hover before his eyes, layered over the image of the real world, itself enhanced by a computer view that made the darkest night and thickest fog seem like perfect daylight.

There was still no response, no information. The only occasional flashes on his screen were the momentary warnings as a Republic beam weapon's bore swept, unfiring, across the location of his armour. Taeris and Doloras fell silent, looking at each other with resignation. If something was to be done then it would take people far more senior than they. Taeris tried again to raise a sensible response. He was the only man who had warned of the rebel attack, and he'd been mocked for it, still nobody would listen.

As they waited, the remnants of the 1st Guards reached and passed through the lines of the 10th, not stopping to add their numbers to the defence, but moving onward into the suburbs.

When the communications silence was broken it was so sudden that Taeris jumped a little in his armour. "Republic ground forces, Admiral Kreltaen, First Fleet."

Taeris immediately started to respond, but then he noticed that the channel had been opened for broadcast only; something quite sensible if the entire ground forces on Esperia were being included.

Kreltaen waited for just a second. "All Republic ground forces must immediately return to their armoured vehicles. Massive strikes from the sky will be beginning shortly and the intensity of the strikes will be above the tolerance of infantry armour. Once again, all Republic ground forces must seal themselves inside armoured vehicles at once, attack will begin in five minutes."

Doloras pulled open the rear door of the command

Tyrant. He shouted for the civilians to get out, but they were too afraid to move. It was likely that the message from the fleet had been played through the internal speakers of the Tyrants. Doloras did not need the cooperation of the civilians to carry out his orders. One after another he grabbed the terrified people and threw them out of the back of the Tyrant onto the rubble-strewn street. Taeris wanted to say something, wanted to stop the Colonel, but he had no words that could make sense. His mouth was dry and, as the last wretched man landed on the street in a heap, Taeris walked numbly into the Tyrant and shut the door.

The screens at the front of the command vehicle were a vision of hell far beyond that imagined by the most extreme religion. Men, women and children were hurled, broken, bleeding and screaming into piles of human refuse. Their places in the safety of the vehicles was taken by grim, wet-eyed men. As each door slammed shut the sensors around the Tyrants showed more horrors. Helpless, unarmoured people tearing each other away from the sealed doors of the vehicles so they could take their place, beating their fists pitifully against the armour. The superb sensors on the Tyrants picked up every cry, every oath, every plea, every offer of money, of sex, of anything they had.

Then came the fighters. Flying in perfect formation, line abreast, at a fixed height above the city. A pattern that only a computer flight control system could maintain so flawlessly. As they crossed over the lines of the 10th Guards they began to spray a thick, white vapour. For a moment the cries subsided a little. Perhaps the sight of the fighters made some of the desperate people believe a new plan had been conceived. Perhaps they thought this slowly sinking mist was a poison that could kill the fleas, leave them alive.

If that was their hope, it was dashed as soon as they could smell the thick, oily scent of the vapour. It was fuel. Some of the people outside may have been chemists, possibly they could have even told you the composition of the mist, but it availed them nothing. There was an agonising delay as the mist settled. It stretched longer and longer.

Doloras's voice croaked. "Have they failed to detonate?"

Taeris responded, at least he assumed it was him, there was no emotion in the voice. "No. They're waiting. It's got to get everywhere."

Doloras closed his eyes, wished he could do the same with his ears. The mist had to penetrate every crevice in the rubble, every hiding place. It had to penetrate the lungs of its victims. The waiting was torture. The end was quick.

A vast wall of roiling orange fire swept down the street. It passed with a howling gush of air that rattled the Tyrant and after it, for a moment, there was total silence. Then the wind came again. It rocked the Tyrant gently, almost soothingly, but Taeris knew that to achieve such an effect it must have been very powerful. Slowly the wind died, the smoke blew clear and Taeris turned back to the sensors, hoping the fire would leave nothing behind. It didn't.

Everywhere he looked the terrain was dark grey, dark brown and black. It had that deep matte look of a charred piece of wood. It took a second before he started to register shapes in the strange landscape. Then he saw an arm, bent at the elbow, wrapped around a rock. A head, mouth open in a final scream, eye-sockets empty and black as space. A small child, no, not all of a small child, resting on a, what was that? Oh yes. Resting on a body, maybe a parent. Suddenly he could see them everywhere. Even if he found a pile of rock that was free of horror his mind would fill in the gap, forming skulls, bones, flesh and torment out of charred stone. Tears flowed down his face and he sat in silence.

Doloras broke his reverie. "It had to be done."

Taeris knew what he meant. Doloras needed to believe that, as did he. "Yes."

A long pause before Doloras spoke again. "If the plague had got out of the city. It..."

"Yes."

Again that long pause. "The President had no choice, none at all."

Taeris tried to keep the vicious sarcasm from his voice, but failed. "His mercy inspires us all."

Doloras made no comment, but turned to his command screens and began checking that his troops were all coming back online.

Once he'd satisfied himself he relaxed again. "They were casualties of war. Not even the first casualties."

Taeris closed his eyes. "No. The second casualty. The second casualty of war is honour. First Citaeron, now here. No honour."

Doloras asked, "I don't know that saying. What's the first casualty of war?"

Taeris spat out an answer. "Look it up."

Before Doloras could respond a stream of orders came through the computer. The 6th was to re-group and move to Republic Plaza, confirming that all rebel forces had been destroyed. Doloras obeyed automatically. Taeris watched him, angrily.

Slowly, the 6th Infantry moved forwards. The city was now uniform in colour, at least. Some buildings had partly survived the blast, but only their main structures. There wasn't a window, a roof anywhere in the centre of the city. In places the heat had melted pools of glass and they'd flowed, cooling, like a cascade down piles of rubble. Now solid again they were oddly beautiful but bore testimony to the heat of the purging fire. No resistance was encountered, none, and soon the legion was formed up on the edge of the plaza. Here the elegant, pale surface was torn and charred, but the broken ruins proved that there was not going to be any need to worry about mines anymore.

In the middle there were still those heavy, squat, armoured vehicles. Impossible to tell if their matte black colouring was a consequence of the fire, or intentional as camouflage. Either way it worked, they blended perfectly, only their silhouettes gave their position away. Past the broken and crushed Tyrants from the 1st Guards' assault, past the torn and twisted remains of the troops they'd carried, the 6th crawled forwards in silence. Taeris looked across at the Legacy building. It still stood, too massive for a fuel bomb to raze, but it looked like a mere skeleton of its former glory.

Slowly, from several different angles, the 6th approached the formation of armoured vehicles. Large, ugly machines and quite a large number of them, but dwarfed by the sheer scale of the plaza. Taeris' own Tyrant was not near the front of the unit, but he could make out the scene very clearly using the sensor screens in front of him. It took him longer than it should to recognise the vehicles for what they were; Emperor tanks. Initially he didn't believe his own eyes, but as the forward elements of the 6th came closer and closer it couldn't be denied any more. "Emperors."

Doloras looked over in surprise. "The tanks?"

"Yes," Taeris said, "I remember them from before. We used to use them as practice targets. It was mostly all they were good for."

"Where did they get them?"

Taeris thought for a moment. "The scrap-yards of Citaeron."

Doloras nodded. The Emperor was the last model of full-scale tank the Republic had used. He'd seen them, of course, their imposing size meant they were often placed on display in front of military buildings or facilities, but they hadn't been current military hardware for many, many decades. Scrap-yards must be full of the things, slowly decaying, weapons removed or spiked. Silently Doloras issued orders to stop the advance, the only danger from those old battle-waggons was any mines or other traps placed in them to catch the unwary. Even those must have been destroyed or detonated by the pressure wave and fireball of that mighty blast.

For a heavy tank, the Emperor was still relatively modern equipment. Its exterior was a fracture-pattern of flat panels made of absorbent armour, garlanded with the superconducting fibres of capacitance shielding against tmetics. The armoured panels were each mounted on an inertia generator, so they could be made relatively light in practice, or made so dense as to be almost impenetrable. Such a system was heavily trumpeted during the early years of adoption, but rapidly fell out of favour, partly because these types of field worked relatively poorly in atmosphere, causing fast, vicious winds to flow down the armour, kicking up dust and debris from around the tank. Even at its lightest the vehicle massed around 70 tonnes, with the armour panels toughened it would exceed 300. The cost of providing lift engines to such a beast at its full load was prohibitive so it sat on modest units and, in practice, these proved insufficient to stop the vehicle sinking into the ground when at its heaviest. Lightened, it could move swiftly but was horribly vulnerable. Made weighty it was almost immobile.

Republic doctrine had little time for a vehicle that had such grave problems when moving to attack. After a mere decade of service the Emperor was retired and, with it, the concept of the battle tank.

Taeris closed his eyes in horror. The rebels hadn't had any armoured vehicles, so they'd landed some old wrecks for the Republic to attack. The 1st Guards had thrown away countless lives foolishly crossing a minefield to attack something no more dangerous than a piece of recycled metal. No, he corrected himself, not all of them had. Two whole regiments had been spared, presumably because they were tasked with shepherding the President and his senior staff out of the centre of the city. He opened a channel to Laesa. "Laesa from Taeris."

"Laesa here. Is it over?"

Taeris melted at the sound of her voice. "Yes, Laesa, it's over. The rebels have been crushed here."

Laesa's voice was full of emotion when, finally, she responded, "I'm so glad. The traitors must have taken huge losses, maybe this is the end of the rebellion."

Taeris, privately, agreed. Even the disproportionate damage that the rebels had caused here couldn't disguise the fact that their forces had been badly hurt. It wasn't that thought that filled his mind, though. It was the civilian dead.

In Harm's Way

Taeris had no orders to follow. No commander contacted him and there was no longer an enemy to fight. He led the 6th back through the positions that were still held by the elements of the 10th Guards. The Guardsmen would have been fairly obvious anyway, given their large vehicles and their decision to occupy elevated positions, but the first obvious sign of the ring was the piles of civilian corpses torn apart by heavy beams as they tried to flee past the soldiers. Taeris was thinking of those two regiments that left the centre and passed the cordon. Was someone checking those survivors for signs of disease? It was not his problem. He left the 6th back at their barracks with instructions to carefully clear the interiors of their Tyrants of any potential fleas that might have slipped inside before the fire.

He summoned a ground car but the destruction around the barracks made it impossible for it to get to him, so he jumped over a couple of buildings' remains until he found himself on a broad, undamaged street. The car found him quickly and he set it rolling towards the small, secured house. As he moved further from the centre the damage became much less frequent. Occasionally a building had been smashed or collapsed, but it might be a fair distance between such incidents. It was a far cry from the scene of universally burned destruction in the centre of the city. The house was untouched, presumably because it was completely unremarkable externally, but the Guardians had abandoned it either to follow other orders or to run as far from plague and fire as they could get. Taeris wasn't surprised.

After walking inside he immediately saw Laesa, sitting on a chair in the large front room. The floor showed the signs of mud and damage caused by careless soldiery. She leapt up as he entered and ran over to embrace him. "Taeris, I'm so glad you're alive."

He fondly stroked her hair back from her face. "You were in more danger than I."

Letting go of her he opened the door into the quiet, windowless room where the two rebels were waiting. They looked up as he entered but not with the same look of pleasure that Laesa had worn. He surveyed them for a moment, then said, "The traitors attacked this city and they were destroyed. I haven't seen the full reports yet but they lost a large number of fighting ships in the attack and their entire landing force has been annihilated. They brought plague to Esperia, but that has been destroyed as well. Your treason ended today."

Salassa looked at the floor and started to quietly cry.

Faeral's face hardened. "They were annihilated? How?"

Taeris felt slightly sick as he answered, "The centre of the city was destroyed by fire."

A little gasp from behind him indicated the shock that this news had caused Laesa. It would be very difficult for her, she had lived in this city for most of her life, amongst the charred remains of civilians would be some she had counted friends.

Faeral looked resigned to the bad news as he said, "I think the Republic will take little credit for this act."

Taeris agreed, but said, "I think it will emerge that there was no choice, given the plague."

Faeral nodded sadly. If he caught the subtle sarcasm in Taeris' voice he didn't make anything of it.

Laesa, tears on her cheeks, shouted at Faeral, "How could you do this? Plague on Esperia?"

Her outburst seemed to shock the room into silence for a moment before Faeral responded, "I did nothing. Plague was a weapon turned upon us, not one we wielded."

Laesa snorted. "Liar." The plague on Citaeron hadn't been described extensively by the media on Esperia but the reports on the quarantine had made it completely clear that the rebels were responsible.

Taeris decided to press on. "Faeral. This treason is over. Fighting has ended on Citaeron, what forces made it to Esperia are dead. Only Prosperity remains as a world in revolt and, you must see, that will be quickly brought to heel. I want you to make a transmission to tell your forces on Prosperity to surrender."

Faeral seemed to give no thought at all to this. "I assumed that was why you'd kept me alive. I'm supposed to tell my allies to throw themselves on the mercy of the Republic?"

"Not all of them need to die," Taeris answered, "I can offer them a choice."

"You can? Most of them are employees of the corporations. What can you offer them?"

Taeris had expected this. "If they are employees then they will face the corporations for their justice."

Faeral laughed, a harsh sound. "Justice. I would rather tell them to fight to their last breath than experience the justice of the corporations."

Taeris grimaced. "Then there is nothing I need from you." He turned and left, securing the door behind him. He led Laesa back to the front room. "Laesa, keep an eye on them for me."

She looked surprised. "You aren't going to execute them?"

"No," Taeris answered, "I think killing them would be wasteful. I might yet be able to prevail upon him to do the right thing. Once he has had time to become close with the Aepolian girl he may be willing to help the Republic rather than see her slowly pulled apart."

Whatever Laesa thought of the plan was interrupted by a channel opening to Taeris' communications hub. He glanced down to see it was the President calling him directly. "Taeris here, Sir."

"Legate, I'm sending you a location. Come here at once."

"Yes Sir." Taeris leaned down to kiss Laesa. "I don't know when I will return. Keep them fed and well. Do not make threats or do them harm."

"I understand."

He smiled at her and then left the house, climbing into the first ground car that passed. The location he had been sent was unfamiliar to him, but the car's systems knew exactly how to get there. The route was not back towards the centre of the city, something for which Taeris was grateful, but along one of the circular roads, crossing two of the spokes on the way. Most of the properties out here were independent, detached houses, standing in small plots of green land. Some were of a substantial size, clearly indicating that they were the homes of prominent corporate men, or possibly very senior government officers. No, even the most senior men in government wouldn't have such grandeur in their homes. Just off one of the main roads the ground car came to a stop in front of a large gate. The pause was just long enough for the systems to identify that Taeris was aboard and to scan the car for any other people or, presumably, explosives. The gates sank down into the ground to permit the car to pass and the vehicle made its silent way up a curving driveway to stop in front of a huge house. It was easily the largest private dwelling that Taeris had ever seen. The building itself must have been twenty times the size of his own spacious quarters and the land could have held fifty more houses suitable for a senior officer.

The door silently opened as he approached and, inside, Taeris looked around a large and imposing hallway. The house had three different stair-cases in the hall, each going in different directions and to different floors of the building. They were joined by small, hanging, mezzanines with an assortment of connecting platforms and stairs. The effect was somehow haphazard, but also rather attractive, drawing attention to the sheer size and complexity of the building.

A woman stepped out to greet him; a strange anachronism if this was serving as the President's quarters. "Legate, please follow me."

Taeris followed the woman along the hall until she turned to the left, entering a large dining room where the table appeared to be covered in computer screens and communications devices. The compact but functional electronics seemed oddly out of place in the dining room with its painted walls, accented columns and hardwood furniture.

Inside the room were three men, all seated, none paying attention to the computers. Caeranion was one of them, the others were unknown to Taeris. Caeranion didn't stand as he spoke, "Taeris. Welcome to the Praesidium."

Taeris looked at the other two in turn. "Thank you. And you gentlemen are?"

One laughed immediately. "I keep forgetting where you've been for the last seven years. I'm Viandrael, Chief Executive of Agricorp. This man is Farastrael, my deputy. This place is his house."

Such a house could belong to a Deputy? "Thank you, Sir.

257

I was called here by the President."

Viandrael smiled easily. "Yes, because I asked him to."

Taeris thought the corporate man might enjoy being someone who could issue instructions to the President. "I see. Perhaps I should see him to find out what is needed of me."

Viandrael waved Taeris into an empty chair but Taeris shook his head. He had no idea whether the furniture could take the weight of an armoured man but he was sure that the expense if a chair were destroyed would be eye-watering. Viandrael shrugged. "As you are aware the Legacy has been destroyed. With it died most of the senior commanders of the military."

Taeris was shocked. "What? Why weren't they evacuated?"

Farastrael gave a careless wave of the hand. "Essential personnel were evacuated, of course. Only Caeranion was essential to the operation of the Legacy."

Two regiments. Ten battalions of Guards. That was the evacuation force, Taeris remembered. They could have evacuated the Legacy ten times over. Surely such a force wouldn't have been deployed purely for the President and Caeranion? "Just the President and Caeranion were essential?"

"Oh no," Farastrael said, "I was essential, so were a large number of the senior corporate officers. I'm sure you understand."

Taeris frowned with concentration. "I don't see why only your employees were essential."

Viandrael leaned forward in his chair. "The military has a responsibility to stand between the civilians and the enemy, of course. We could not, in all conscience, evacuate the military and leave our staff behind."

In that moment, finally, certainty flooded through Taeris.

He finally understood the horror he'd seen. "Of course, Sir. I think I misunderstood for a moment. The Republic's military will always lay down their lives to protect the people from their enemies."

The other three smiled with satisfaction. Caeranion picked up a small computer and looked at it for reference. "Taeris, you will take the Sixth Legion to Citaeron. There you will collect the Seventh Legion and move on to Prosperity. I expect you to finish the rebellion very quickly."

Taeris' face was expressionless. "I shall do as ordered. Putting down the entire rebellion quickly may require the use of extreme force."

Viandrael nodded. "Approved. Kill everyone on the planet if needed. We are training up new staff already so our profits won't be significantly harmed. I do appreciate your concern, though."

Taeris felt faintly dizzy. "Thank you, Sir."

Caeranion put his computer down. "Do you have any further questions?"

"Just one, Sir." Taeris gathered his thoughts. "Should I be concerned at the possibility that any of the civilians brought outside the cordon before the burn could carry the plague?"

Farastrael frowned at this. "Why is that of your concern?"

Taeris looked him in the eye, hoping his real motives weren't obvious. "The Sixth Legion has protected itself during the battle and its return to barracks, but if there is a chance that the plague could have infected some of my troops since then I need to institute procedures to ensure it isn't spread accidentally."

Farastrael stared at him, perhaps trying to detect if this was a false justification. "No, you need have no fears on that score. I can't be more specific but the plague will not spread on

Esperia. Anything else?"

"No, Sir," Taeris answered, "I understand the mission."

Less than a minute later he had climbed back into the ground car and was speeding towards the ruined barracks where the 6th Infantry was waiting. On the way he passed a number of buildings that were marked with warning signs, implying that the occupants were potentially diseased. Given what he'd just been told, that had to be a precaution only. By the time he reached the barracks the streets around it had been cleared of rubble and the barracks itself cleared enough to permit its use by the legion. The buildings were no less destroyed, but by sweeping their remains aside the large square could, once more, be used for assembling the troops. Everywhere Taeris looked, the streets were deserted. Civilians, perhaps, had walked further out of the city, fearing that the battle might not yet have ended, fearing the fuel bomb could come again.

In the parade square the convenient balcony, made available for addressing the formation, was rubble along with the building it had adorned, so Taeris chose to jump onto the top of the nearest Tyrant to make his presence obvious to the troops. In seconds they had all stopped their activities and turned to watch him. He had thought about what to say to them on the ride over, so his pause before he spoke was purely for dramatic effect.

"Soldiers. We are soldiers. I was just reminded of this as I was given my orders. As soldiers, we stand between the civilian and the fire, between the loyal and the treacherous, between the Republic and its enemies, even if those enemies rise within the Republic itself." Taeris looked down to his right, where Doloras stood, he seemed to be happy so far.

"I have been ordered to take back Prosperity. We will join with the Seventh Infantry for this task. We will destroy the enemies of the Republic wherever we find them and by any means that we see fit. There are those who would harm our Republic. From this day and until our enemies are no more, we stand in harm's way!"

The Infantry

The Legacy was a smoking ruin, not just the building but its lauded officers. No man took the time to compose a paean for them; the heroes of Esperia were the soldiers of the 1st Guards Legion. Caeranion was all that remained of the senior staff, nobody had yet counted how many Aediles had been killed, probably the vast majority. The corporations solemnly broadcast the scale of their own loss, leading to the clear perception that the majority of casualties had been their employees. The fact that it was a wildly misleading impression was beside the point, or, more accurately, the misleading impression was entirely the point.

It took three days to marshal the 6th Infantry and effect such repairs as could be managed before the lift. In truth it simply took all the time that was available before the 3rd Fleet could pick them up from Esperia. Taeris' first indication that the fleet had arrived was when Raephus opened up a channel.

"Taeris, Raephus."

Taeris couldn't help but smile at the sound of the voice. "Taeris. How's the weather up there?"

Raephus laughed, "Chilly. Are you ready to lift?"

"Yes, Admiral, we can load into Tyrants on your command."

This was an operation that the infantry had now carried out many times and the 3rd Fleet was, if anything, even more experienced. Taeris watched the complex loading procedure take place without a hitch, feeling a sense of pride in the professionalism of the men. No, wait. Pride in the Republic, that's right. Pride in the Republic is allowed because it leads to motivated troops that are inevitably victorious.

As he took his turn in the lift process, in his case a shuttle that would deliver him to the Spica, Taeris looked down over the destroyed centre of Esperia City. Somehow seeing it with his own eyes was a powerful experience, even though he'd had access to countless images taken from the air already. Something about the matte black smudge, like a giant inky fingerprint, was haunting. He tore his gaze from it and looked out into the suburbs, using the computer systems in his helm to find and magnify the house where Laesa waited with the prisoners. Unremarkable. Perfect.

Docking was as smooth as ever, but there was a slight traffic delay due to the sheer number of ships moving in intricate patterns to dock with each other and then separate again to collect the next tranche of troops. Once the lock opened Taeris flew through into the battlecruiser, handling weightlessness as few could. It was a minute to the bridge and Raephus was waiting for him, Adrael alongside. Interesting. Had Adrael been fortunate and been absent from the centre of the city? Had he had advance warning? Had he been evacuated by the Guards?

"Adrael? I thought you might still be on Esperia."

Adrael's subtle smile gave nothing away. "I felt I could be of more service to the Republic here."

Raephus smiled broadly. "Welcome, Legate. I must say, I'm delighted to find you in good health."

Taeris nodded an acknowledgement, "No more so than I, Admiral." He wanted desperately to have a private word with Raephus, but there was no way of dismissing Adrael; however the problem resolved itself as Adrael excused himself to open a channel privately to the Magisterium. As soon as he was gone Raephus turned, expectantly. "Admiral," Taeris began, "I am really pleased that you are to be our escort for this trip."

Raephus nodded modestly. "We all serve where we can. It also appears that the Legate in charge of the Eighth Guards was becoming somewhat irritated with me."

Taeris feigned surprise. "Really? Whatever could have caused that?"

"It seems," Raephus answered, "I wasn't providing him with the reconnaissance reports that he wanted."

Taeris was about to ask why not, but his mind caught up before he spoke. Of course, Raephus would be providing perfectly accurate reports but if they didn't show what Graelen wanted them to then obviously he would shout and scream about how inaccurate they were. Instead Taeris decided to take advantage of the Admiral's experience. "How are things on Citaeron?"

Raephus clenched his teeth. "Such resistance as remains is limited to painting rebel slogans on buildings. Graelen rules with a titanium gauntlet, randomly killing anyone who is a beat slow when singing the new songs about the glorious Republic victory over Aepolia. That city has essentially been destroyed. The rebels are now known as Aepolians, the loyal as Citaeronians."

Taeris was familiar with the process of vilification that the Republic used. Intimately familiar. "What about innocent Aepolians?"

Raephus shook his head. "No such thing. On Citaeron you can be executed for having the wrong accent."

Taeris allowed the sarcasm to fill his tone. "Truly the mercy of the Republic inspires us all."

Raephus frowned. "Graelen is not the Republic and the Republic is not Graelen. I know I lost your trust when Justinian took to the skies, but there may yet be those who are able to rise to your standards."

Taeris suddenly heard the screaming, begging and hollow pounding of desperate civilians outside his Tyrant. "Admiral, I don't know how you recognised my disappointment in us all over Justinian but I owe you an apology for that. I set a standard that none could meet. I, to my shame, fell woefully short of it."

Raephus studied him carefully. "If the glory and honour is due only to the Republic then surely so is the shame."

Taeris stared, open-mouthed. "You seem to have slipped further from the republican way than I had believed possible."

In response, Raephus nodded. "And I think you have managed to simulate republican conduct more efficiently than I had believed possible. Given that you may be the most treasonous man in the entire Republic."

Automatically, Taeris looked around in alarm. He was expecting armed men to have quietly slipped in behind him to arrest and denounce him on the Admiral's word.

Raephus laughed out loud. "See how a brave man such as yourself might come to be alarmed at the thought of the Republic's mercy? So gentle and benevolent a state can never have enemies, no doubt."

Taeris nodded and chose his words carefully. "Oh I think the Republic has many enemies."

Raephus was choosing his words just as carefully. "I think you may be right."

Taeris finally took the leap of faith. This was the moment where, if Raephus was loyal to the Republic regime, his existence would end. "I find that they are not the same people as those we currently name 'traitor'."

Raephus smiled, the tension of the moment fading. "I find that also. Perhaps you could come to my cabin once we have started the jump. There may be matters of gravity to discuss."

At that moment their conversation was effectively ended by the reappearance of Adrael, who drifted into the bridge and awkwardly grabbed one of the hand-holds. "Are we ready to jump, Admiral?" Adrael asked quietly.

Raephus nodded abruptly. "On your command, Sir."

Adrael smiled broadly. "Then by all means let us jump to Citaeron."

In fact there was no time during the jump for Taeris to privately talk with Raephus, the transit was only a handful of hours in length and most of that time Adrael seemed to want to spend with Taeris. Could he be suspicious of the Legate's activities? If so he didn't show it, but maybe the losses the Legacy had suffered on Esperia meant that he wasn't willing to denounce one of the few remaining Legates in the Republic.

Once the fleet had dropped below light-speed there were too many other things for Taeris to handle. He immediately opened a channel to Graelen, the Legate commanding the Republic forces on Citaeron.

"Graelen, Taeris."

There was a long pause; insultingly long. "Graelen. What do you want?"

"Thank you for responding," Taeris knew that comment would infuriate Graelen, "I am to take command of the Seventh Infantry Legion and lift them from Citaeron at the earliest possible opportunity. I want to ensure that this doesn't interfere with your ongoing operations."

Graelen growled, "Take them. They're useless to me.

Not even half a legion and definitely not like the Guards."

Taeris rolled his eyes slightly. "Thank you Legate. As you won't miss them I'll contact their Legate directly."

This time there was some humour in the growl. "You'll be lucky, they haven't got one. A couple of Colonels and two regiments of cowards."

Taeris privately saw this as good news as he didn't want to struggle for leadership with another Legate but he said, "I'm sure they'll prove to be useful to me."

"No doubt," Graelen responded spitefully, "I saw the action reports from Esperia. I noticed you let the Guards do most of the dying."

Taeris couldn't defend himself, not to a man like Graelen. "The First Guards were very brave."

Graelen grunted approval. "You got that right." The channel dropped immediately.

Taeris took a deep breath and opened another channel. "Colonels commanding the Twenty-fifth and Twenty-sixth Infantry Regiments, from Legate Taeris, commanding Sixth Infantry Legion." Seconds later Colonel Thaeton of the 25th and Latonis, of the 26th, had both responded so Taeris began. "Gentlemen, I understand there is no Legate commanding the Seventh?"

"That's correct, Sir," Thaeton answered, "I have been operating in temporary command of the legion since our Legate became unavailable."

Unavailable. So he was denounced, probably by Graelen. The Republic was rapidly running out of Legates and good Legates had always been a scarce commodity to begin with. "Thank you Colonel. I need an estimate of how long it will take to ready both regiments for lift."

Latonis let out a sharp laugh. "We can be ready in a few

hours, Sir. We've been doing almost nothing here."

Thaeton cut in, "I think Latonis means that we've been eager to prove our usefulness to the Republic and that's been hard here because of the leading role taken by the courageous Eighth Guards."

Latonis immediately added, "I think that is exactly what I meant Sir."

Taeris maintained a dignified tone. "I was fairly certain it was. Both of you report to me on Spica as soon as your troops are lifted." He dropped the channel and turned to Raephus. "Admiral, if you need me for anything I shall be in my cabin."

Raephus responded, "I imagine there may be a few administrative details, but nothing we can't solve."

Taeris smiled and nodded to Adrael as he floated out of the bridge hoping Raephus had understood him. In fact it was over an hour later when his cabin door opened to admit the tall figure of Raephus. "Admiral. How can I help?"

The door closed before Raephus spoke. "You've seen that Graelen is simply terrorising the Citaeronians into submission?"

Taeris nodded and said, "I have. He seems to enjoy killing people to prove that he can. Presumably the corporations were knocked back by their losses on Esperia so nobody's telling him to leave their employees alone."

Raephus studied Taeris for a moment. "What losses on Esperia?"

"When the city was bombed, a great many of the senior corporates lived and worked in the hot zone. While the Guards were sent to rescue their top leadership the remaining corporate elite was devastated. The media has been reporting lists of many corporate dead."

Another moment of pause. "I see. It appears I have news for you. All of the senior corporates were evacuated before the

268

bombing."

Taeris looked surprised. "What? But the risk of the plague spreading?" Even as he spoke he understood. Two regiments of guards hadn't gone to pull out the President and Caeranion and a handful of executives, of course not, they'd evacuated thousands of corporate people. The quarantined houses he'd seen made sense as well; in case any of them had brought the plague with them. "Wait, even if they made it out alive, many of them would be dying of plague, or quarantined and unable to work. That's got to be a big hit to their operations."

Raephus shook his head. "Supplying the quarantined areas has been left to the First Fleet, as they can drop supplies without risking spreading infection. Their reports are very complete. There are barely any dying of plague. Maybe ten, at most."

Taeris frowned and said, "No, that doesn't make sense. If plague got into them, into their buildings, then hundreds would be dying at least, maybe thousands."

The admiral paused before answering, "I think you may have overlooked another possibility. What if the corporates have a cure for plague?"

If that were true, Taeris thought, then the Republic was more corrupt than he'd ever known. Only during the time of the antibiotics had plague been controllable; as the diseases became immune to each in turn and the supply of new medicines ended the bacteria had won the fight and returned to their traditional slaughter. "Antibiotic?" Taeris asked weakly.

Raephus nodded. "I assume as much. Presumably they found a new one and decided to keep it for when it was most needed. Anyway the tone of the news broadcasts has already begun to shift. Many of those named as casualties have miraculously been found alive in the rubble. Their courageous stories of survival and fortitude are filling the media. Many of the most senior people, it seems, worked under enormous pressure to save as many civilians as they could, even at great risk to their own lives."

Taeris shook his head in horror. "None of that's true. Nobody could have survived that fire. If they had medicine..." Taeris was crushed. Graelen had been happy to massacre the civilians of Citaeron. The corporates had calmly extracted their people from the cauldron of Esperia. All the time there had been a cure. There had never been a need to burn the city, they could have fought for it, won it. What possible reason did the corporations have for wanting the centre of the Republic burned. At the back of his mind Taeris remembered the two men who'd visited the Legacy and how they'd been sent away. Was that the moment when the Legacy was doomed, almost to a man? Graelen must be the pawn of the corporates, his every move now seemed to be perfectly suited to the corporate agenda. Caeranion? Why had he been saved? What deal had he struck with those manipulative organisations?

Raephus looked intently at the Legate. "I think you have a decision to make."

Taeris felt as if an enormous weight rested upon his shoulders. "I wouldn't say this to anyone else, but it seems to me that this fleet and its troops would be better used on Esperia."

Raephus nodded. "I agree. Of course it's impossible, there will be security men seeded throughout my command and yours. Any attempt to take this fleet to Esperia would lead to our pointless execution."

"We should be waging war on the corporations," Taeris said, "but I agree, we cannot."

Raephus studied him. "A course of inactivity seems unlikely to result in any real change."

Taeris nodded, placing his trust in the Admiral. "But history has a way of allowing certain individuals, those perceived as heroes, to have a disproportionate effect on public opinion. Such a victorious commander might be able to interdict even the most senior of the Republic's leaders, and its corporations."

Raephus spoke very softly. "Their stories of courage and fortitude are filling the media." Raephus saw the pain on Taeris' face and left him alone, but only minutes later the officer corps of the infantry legions arrived for their meeting. Adrael took his unobtrusive place in the corner of the room. Taeris looked at the only civilian present. Would Adrael be shocked if he learnt the truth of Esperia? Taeris couldn't risk speaking of it with him. Instead he turned to his officers. "Gentlemen. We are going to Prosperity to end the rebellion." If the rebellion could be stopped quickly enough then maybe he could lead his troops back to Esperia and begin fighting the war he was now sure needed fighting. If Raephus was wrong.

The Plan

Driastren looked at Taeris much as he might have peered at a particularly unsightly insect. Taeris looked back with an expressionless face. The guardsman licked his lips slowly and said, "The Sixth and the Seventh are with you? The Sixth has been cleared battle-ready?"

Taeris kept his expression neutral. "The Magisterium is now an irregularly shaped pile of charred rubble. It's possible that in the aftermath of the bombing it had more important things to do. However Adrael, whom you may know, is a senior member of the security divisions and he is with us."

Driastren grimaced at the sound of Adrael's name. Did anyone actually like the security man? "Well, there is work here on Prosperity for your troops. I shall issue the relevant orders after they are landed and ready for deployment."

Taeris smiled slightly. "I think you can discuss the deployment of my troops with me and I shall issue their orders."

Driastren stiffened. "Or alternatively I can remove you from command and add the individual regiments that you've brought directly under my own command."

"You could do that," Taeris said, "I'm sure it's a very tempting thought. Bear in mind, however, that the Republic seems to be seriously depleted of senior leadership and that my appointment was approved by the President, Caeranion and presumably Adrael. As far as I know they may be the most senior representatives of government, military and Magisterium left alive. Of course you are within your rights to assert your seniority over me. All you'll have to do is explain to your superiors why you feel your judgement is so much better than all of theirs."

Driastren looked like he'd tasted something unexpectedly sour. "It seems to me that taking on another six regiments myself would probably be a worrying workload. I shall leave you in place for the moment, but you report to me."

Taeris nodded calmly. "I am in awe of the wisdom of your decision. Now would this be a good moment to explain your strategy and discover how we can help?"

Driastren still looked unhappy, but he pulled up a map on the largest screen in the room. "Essentially I have divided Prosperity into sectors. I have set patrol forces to ensure that there is no civilian movement between the sectors. I have then been clearing each sector in turn."

Though the manual was, among other things, rather more detailed, this was a perfectly good description of exactly how every Republic officer was taught to clear an area.

Taeris looked at the map but the details were not important to his opinion. "Well organised but this will take a long time."

Driastren nodded, "I estimate about three years, probably closer to two years with your regiments."

"Yes," Taeris continued, "I see. Would you be willing to consider a plan that offers less rigour but could effectively end the rebellion here within weeks?"

The guardsman looked shrewdly at Taeris. "I will hear it, at least."

"In that case," Taeris said, "I propose we construct a trap. Essentially a target that is hard, but not impossible, to attack. We make it something that the traitors cannot ignore but something that will require they deploy as much of their capability as they can. When the trap springs we will destroy them. Ultimately this is about making the rebels group together into a single large force and then making them fight on a field of our choosing. This is playing much more effectively to our own abilities, rather than scouring the planet for every rebel hiding in a hole."

Driastren laughed contemptuously. "Only you could suggest such a thing. The Guards Legions do not hide and wait for the enemy to attack. We attack with main force."

Taeris tried again. "It may not be the way we have fought in the past, but it offers the opportunity for a swift victory. The rebellion is finished on Esperia, all but ended on Citaeron. In a few months we could consign the entire treason to the refuse-pile."

"By surrendering the things that make us soldiers of the Republic? That is just another form of defeat." Driastren made a firm cutting motion with his armoured hand. "We fight as we always have and we win, as we always have."

Taeris nodded, "I understand. I shall begin dispersing my troops to join with yours. I will set aside one regiment to construct a new base of operations in a suitable place to support your mission, perhaps here." Taeris pointed at an area of the map still not cleared by the 5th Guards. "We can use that as a starting point for extending your grid."

"Yes," Driastren said, "I approve." He turned and stalked off, leaving Taeris alone.

As soon as he was alone Taeris opened up a channel to Doloras. "Doloras, Taeris."

The officer's voice came back immediately. "Doloras, Sir."

"I'm sending you a map reference," Taeris said, "I want you to land the Twenty-third Infantry Regiment on that spot and begin constructing a base of operations. I'll be back in orbit soon to oversee the remainder of the landings and make sure we line up with the Fifth Guards."

Doloras sounded a little weary as he replied, "Yes Sir. I assume that means your plan wasn't approved by the Legate?"

Taeris smiled at the communicator. "I'm not responsible for the assumptions you make."

In fact Adrael was the first person Taeris saw when he arrived back on the Spica. He hung in the corridor immediately outside the docking port where Taeris' shuttle had touched. He glared at Taeris for a second before speaking. "Legate. Tell me the purpose of this forward base on Prosperity."

Taeris drifted out of the port into the companionway before he responded. "If I'm going to be an effective ally to Driastren then I will need a base of operations for my troops."

"Why?" Adrael asked with a faintly sour expression on his face.

"It's a large number of troops. They need a base for their quarters and their major equipment. We can also protect a medical facility there to treat the wounded, it can become a base for the operations of our intelligence teams and a fire-support and maintenance location for our field-operations."

Adrael nodded after a second. "And it will in no way be set up as a potential target for the rebels to attack?"

"Well," Taeris answered with a broad smile , "I have not been included in the rebels' plans for their forces, however it is clearly something they might consider to be a threat."

"Legate, if you care at all for your troops, do not attempt to go against Driastren's legitimate orders."

Spreading his arms wide in a gesture of peace and assuming a faintly offended expression Taeris said, "I would never disobey legitimate orders." He threw himself down the companionway towards his cabin.

Adrael watched him go, a grimace on his face. The commander of the 6th had a way of saying what you expected to hear without actually telling you anything.

In fact it was Doloras who asked the question that really mattered, a few hours later. "How do you intend to get the rebels to attack us?"

Taeris had given the matter some thought and the more he considered the problem the more obvious the solution became. The two other main areas of rebel activity had been threatened and ultimately destroyed by plague one way or another. This was the threat that the rebels would fear; this was the one thing they could not ignore. "We will construct a facility for breeding fleas."

Doloras nodded. "I thought that might be it." The colonel then left to prepare for the landing with his troops.

Taeris didn't land with the front lines of his troops. His first sight of the piece of land that had, until that moment, been simply a point on a map to him was after a large number of the 6th and some of the 7th had already touched down. The area was marked on the maps as still being under the control of the rebels but no active resistance had been encountered during either the landing or the establishment of a secure perimeter on the shore of one of the large crater-lakes that covered the planet. Nobody was in any doubt that the rebels would be watching, especially since a number of civilians had been seen in the area, but whatever forces they had in place were clearly not interested in engaging the almost 40,000 troops that were landing in waves. Taeris stepped out of the back of his Tyrant after it landed in the area designated, near the centre of the plan, for command facilities and looked around him in awe. Thousands of Tyrants were moving, taking off, returning from patrol. It looked like the complex movements of bees around a hive and shared that sense of underlying order, that if you could understand it then it would all make sense. The edges of the site were the most advanced in construction, surrounded by a fence made of twisted strands of carbon-fibre. This fibre was very tough, but very fine, and could carry a current that would detect any break in the fence. The same basic material had been used by the 5th Guards to divide the surface of the planet into sectors and it had the tremendous benefit of being created by a machine called a fibre-gun that span the fibres out from raw-materials like silk from a spider's spinnerets. At intervals along the fence they installed small generators to maintain a slight current throughout, each also had a large additional capacitance capability, triggered automatically if the resistance of the fence were to be suddenly altered. Anyone cutting through might suddenly find hundreds of amps of current flowing through that section of fence. Even running into the fence with significant force could end up triggering this, potentially fatal, reaction.

Out towards the shore of the crater the troops had begun digging a deep pit that would later accept a laboratory building. Taeris walked over to inspect it. The ubiquity of powered armour had rendered most engineering machines irrelevant and in the pit a few hundred soldiers were digging with their massive, armoured hands at such a rate they they'd almost finished the pit in less than two hours. Taeris watched as they leapt from the pit and returned with fibre-guns to spray a layer of stiffening carbon around the sides and floor of the pit. Interesting though this was he had to ensure the command centre was being set up correctly so he turned and strode back to the middle of the compound.

In the short time since his landing, the major

prefabricated rooms of the centre had been installed. They were made of metre-squares of plastic that could be attached in countless combinations to form walls, floors and roofs and which stiffened when a current was briefly applied. They had that matte black look of military hardware and their strength was considerable despite being barely thicker than an eggshell and as light as a piece of paper of the same dimensions. They certainly couldn't be considered armoured, or even protective, in a firefight but they were tough enough to resist powerful wind and other natural challenges.

Inside there was the faint sound of the remainder of the complex under construction, but in the large central space Taeris found his Tyrant acting as the command centre, exactly as he planned. He climbed in and sat in the chair to survey all the information flowing in from his thousands of soldiers. Most of the troops were still assembling the base but Doloras' 23rd Infantry was scouring the surrounding geography for potential threats. They found plenty of people but none that shot at them, which was the only sure way to separate rebels from the civilians who held no hatred for the Republic. Assuming there was such a thing as a civilian who didn't hate the Republic.

A quick look at the progress of the base. The prefabricated barracks for the infantry were going up all over the area, so fast that Taeris couldn't keep an eye on all the work. The large laboratory pit was now covered and its internals braced with poured concrete. A light-weight building would be placed on top, but the real work could be conducted safely below in the armoured vault of the pit.

Sure it was all going well, Taeris closed his eyes and let the armour inject a sedative with instructions to let him sleep for two hours.

When he was awakened the base was all but complete. He opened a channel to Driastren. "Driastren, Taeris."

After a few seconds he heard the response, "Driastren."

Taeris grimaced at the sound of the man's voice. "Reporting that all facilities are now complete and my forces are now at your disposal."

If Driastren was impressed by the speed shown by his fellow legate, he didn't let it interfere with the scorn in his voice. "I'll pass the message on to my officers. Maybe they can find something for your people to do." He signed off immediately.

Taeris didn't waste any time before contacting Doloras. "Colonel, I've been reviewing the readiness reports for the Twenty-third Infantry, they are significantly worse than for the other units under my command."

Doloras was clearly surprised. "Sir? We have been on active patrol without return to base. Perhaps our reactions are a little slow."

Taeris snorted. "Colonel, I do not accept excuses for unsatisfactory performance. I expect it to be resolved immediately. Recall your regiment to base and I'll task the Seventh Infantry Legion with your patrol mission."

Doloras' voice was clearly unhappy as he responded, "I will do as you order, Sir."

The Calm

Kitelya gripped his arm where the carbon fibre had burned him. He knew he had burns on his torso too, but it was his arm that hurt badly. The arc of electricity that had torn through his clothing and seared his flesh should have been avoided by his careful attachment of additional conducting wires around the breach he cut in the fence but obviously something had still triggered the current. Idly he wondered if the other burns were so deep that they'd destroyed the nerves in the skin and that was an explanation for the lack of pain.

He'd left the infantry base behind him three hours before so he was still in the same sector as when he'd breached the wire, but he was now extremely close to the border. The fine black fibres were hard to see in the fading light so it was as much luck as skill that he was able to stop himself before plunging headfirst into them. He caught his breath for a few minutes, desperate to get through and under cover before night fell; the night that would strip him of his most useful sense but fail to seriously inconvenience anyone wearing the sensor-filled helm of an armoured suit.

The night was febrile and his fingers dripped onto his little bundle of clips and cables as he quickly worked to build a bridge for the electricity across the gap he would soon cut. In theory this would make his passage undetected, but this was the same theory that had burned him once before, literally.

After a few minutes he was finished and he took out his

improvised cutters. He had made them from two pieces of metal joined by a bolt and while they were far from elegant, they were functional. One by one the fine fibres were cut with a gentle click sound and in a few minutes Kitelya rolled onto his back and used his heels to slide himself, headfirst, through the small hole. He seemed to have managed it this time. No sudden pain as the fence hurled amps at him, no sound of approaching Republic troops. He had barely caught his breath on the other side of the fence when he heard a female voice, quite close, say, "Republic?"

Kitelya froze. "Ana, Aepoliach."

A quiet rustle revealed a woman of middle years cradling an old but well-maintained longarm. "Aeboliash yezda?" She was not convinced he was Aepolian as he claimed.

"Aya, Mipeya Kitelya Aepoliach." He introduced himself by name, hoping that might make the woman relax a little, she still stared at him with deep suspicion.

After a second she nodded abruptly. "Viladayza Migone." She might not be convinced, but if she was asking him to come with her then she might have at least decided to give him some benefit of the doubt.

Kitelya followed her. Initially he thought that the burn on his arm was slowing him down, but soon he realised that his difficulties were more accurately ascribed to her astonishing facility in the terrain of Prosperity. She was fast and quiet, perhaps skills she'd needed for hunting or simply for efficiency but they were nonetheless skills a soldier should envy. He eventually asked her, "Sipeya lankan yesta?" Is it far?

"Ana," she answered, but what she thought of as being not far was starting to strain Kitelya's muscles. When the journey came to an end it was an absolute surprise, there had been no indication of any change in the terrain. The woman led Kitelya

281

down a gentle slope and it ended with a tunnel entrance. Thick foliage grew around the tunnel, disguising it from the air and making it hard to spot even from the ground.

The tunnel was smooth and tall enough for Kitelya to stand, if he stooped his shoulders and bent his head. The woman was shorter and could walk erect, occasionally ducking her head to avoid a tree-root or the edge of a large stone embedded in the tunnel roof. The way was far from straight, having several deliberate turns in it, possibly to protect from direct assault by rocket or beam, more likely to prevent accidental radiation leaks from sneaking out into the outside world where they could be detected. The torch the woman carried threw a competent light but hardly dispelled the somewhat close atmosphere of the tunnel. Kitelya thought the sides showed evidence of being excavated by hand, if so this was a major feat of engineering. Eventually the tunnel came to an end, opening into a large chamber, roughly circular in shape, with curving walls and enough height for Kitelya to stand fully upright. There were two other tunnels leading from the room and several large twisted roots ran from ceiling to floor, presumably providing support for the soil above and ensuring that this large space didn't bury its occupants.

Occupants. There were at least thirty people in the room, not crowded together as the space was more than sufficient. They looked up as Kitelya entered then, as if it had been planned in advance, they all frowned in disapproval. For a long moment, nobody moved or spoke, then one man, leaning against the nearest massive root, said, "Sipeya yesta?" He was asking who Kitelya was, as he clearly recognised the woman.

Kitelya decided not to let the woman speak for him. "Mipeya Kitelya Aepoliach. Milatayka Prosperitiq Republic Infantry tisikone." His hope was that telling them his name, his

282

place of origin and the fact that he'd been brought to Prosperity by the Republic Infantry might make these people accept him. It also crossed his mind that simply speaking in Aepolian might do much of the work for him.

The man stared at him in the dim light of the room for a long moment but then said, "Why did they bring you?"

Kitelya smiled and began to explain, "I'm a geologist. They needed someone to help them with a big excavation."

"I see." The man cast a glance at another, back in the shadows against the wall. "I'm Tifalta. Tell me about this excavation."

"They wanted a large underground space to be cut into rock. They wanted it to be close to a crater-lake but to make sure there was no danger of anything leaking into the water."

Tifalta nodded. "Did they tell you why?"

"No," Kitelya shook his head, "I thought it might be a bunker, but I don't know why they had to have it sealed so carefully. They seemed almost frightened of it."

Tifalta waved Kitelya forward into the middle of the room, where there had been left some step-like ridges to act as ad hoc furniture. Kitelya took a seat, wincing slightly as his arm reminded him of his journey here. The man in the shadows stepped forwards and as he came into the light Kitelya had a shock. The person was a woman, and her features were so similar to Faeral's that she could only be a very close relative. Kitelya took a risk, to see if that might pay off. "Vaeral?"

She stopped in her tracks for a moment, then nodded. "I am. You know my brother?"

Kitelya nodded, forcing a warm smile onto his face. "I have had the privilege. He didn't tell me of a sister, even though we have talked a great deal."

"That is Faeral," Vaeral laughed, "I no longer need his

protection but it's habit to a big brother."

Tifalta had visibly relaxed, and the mood in the chamber as a whole was much more friendly. Someone pressed a drink into Kitelya's hand and Vaeral joined them on the steps.

Tifalta turned to his guest. "You must have an idea about the purpose of the giant hole."

Kitelya slurped his drink. "At first I assumed they'd want me to oversee a number of these bunkers to act as the defence hard-points for bases. When I learnt that my work was finished with the first bunker, my mind turned to darker thoughts."

"As would mine," Vaeral added, "I assume we're all thinking about laboratories?"

"Yes," Tifalta said, "A place to breed plague."

Kitelya nodded sadly. "I slowly became more and more certain as I saw equipment being lowered into the hole. Eventually I had to escape, to try to find you."

A slight eyebrow-raise of suspicion seemed to flicker on Tifalta's face as he said, "I would be interested to hear how you managed that."

"I'm an engineer. I know how their fences work. I stole a few wires and pieces of scrap, here," He pulled out his improvised cutters, "I made this. Also I may have been over-confident." Carefully putting down the drink, he pulled his close-fitting shirt off his body. The sweeping, curving arcs of seared black flesh that scored a pattern in split skin across his chest were easily visible even in the low light.

Vaeral reached out a hand to carefully touch the damaged flesh. He recoiled from her touch. "I'm sorry, it must hurt."

"No," Kitelya answered, "I have no pain from it, but it's open to the air, I need antiseptic."

At once Vaeral stood and retrieved a battered satchel from a small alcove in the wall. In a few seconds she'd taken out a spray-bottle of antiseptic wound sealant. This compound was a familiar sight across the Republic, used to form a barrier across a wound, infuse it with antiseptic, numb the pain, promote rapid healing and eventually bond with the new skin to leave almost nothing visible of even the most severe abrasions. Once Vaeral had carefully sprayed the sealant across every mark, burn and scratch on his ravaged body she replaced the precious bottle in the satchel and returned it to its alcove.

As she did so, Tifalta asked, "I need to know more about this laboratory. Can you make maps for us?"

Kitelya nodded thoughtfully. "I can. I can also describe the daily operations of the troops. Sometimes the base seemed to be packed, other times almost empty."

Tifalta laughed. "Oh yes, that sounds like the Republic. They fail to take us seriously. We might have to teach them better manners."

At this there were echoing laughs from a number of the others in the chamber.

Making the maps, on the backs of large sheets of poster-paper, took a few hours. Kitelya made sure each was accurate before turning his attention to the conduct of the attack. "I assume you have some experience of planning these sorts of thing?"

Tifalta didn't look up from his master copy of the map as he replied, "I have some. Not on this scale."

Vaeral's soft voice spoke up. "Destroying the laboratory is critical, even if we all die in the attempt."

Tifalta seemed to slowly nod his agreement but Kitelya said, "I'm sorry, but no. If we kill the laboratory they'll build another. If we kill the troops they'll send more. Whatever we do, it has to be the end of the battle here."

Silence fell for a long time. Finally Tifalta said, "I agree.

285

What can we destroy that's irreplaceable?"

Vaeral finally answered, "The scientists. We have to kill them in their pit."

Tifalta thought for a minute. "Yes. That means we have to hold from attack until the laboratory is built and operational. How do we then stop the disease from escaping?"

"Fire." Vaeral's answer was definitive. "It's good that we have time, because we're going to need to pull together every soldier we can for the attack."

Tifalta stood, effectively ending the discussion. "Let's start sending messages immediately."

Runners were dispatched to nearby concentrations of rebels, groups that were further afield were sent messages by pigeon. Kitelya admired this immensely; those pigeons would be ignored completely by the Republic's troops. All the messages were carried by people unaware of the details of the plan or its target. Additionally they were encoded using a sophisticated paper-based cipher that had to be constructed in tables each time a message was sent and could then be destroyed completely, resurrected as needed for future messages.

Despite the manual process and the distances involved, rebels started to filter into the area around Tifalta's stronghold within a few days and after a week it had become a flood. Kitelya's engineering skills were tested again and again as he found ways of protecting their growing numbers from being spotted from the air, even though this sector was not currently being cleared and so almost all the Tyrants in their area stayed close to the sector-fence.

If hiding thousands of people was a challenge, moving them silently through the electrified fibre with the equipment they would need to launch the attack seemed an insurmountable difficulty. Kitelya began constructing kits that could be carried by each team of rebels as they breached the wire, dozens of kits as each team would need at least one. Individuals were selected to act as leaders for each team and they were set practice tasks, breaching mocked-up sections of wire and moving stealthily through the gaps. Some groups of soldiers had a very long way to travel and so they would not have enough time to train. These were assigned leaders from other groups that had completed their preparations.

For an army without much in the way of central leadership the rebels proved remarkably cohesive, something that would have been much less likely without Vaeral. She was forged from the same steel as her brother, calm and resolute, and was clearly held in high regard by the soldiers, so much so that almost all of them would visit her to pay their respects at their very first opportunity.

As for the timing of the attack, that had to be left up to the experienced local scouts who were adept at movement through the difficult terrain. Each night there would be a meeting underground of the most senior rebels, a description Kitelya was surprised to find included himself, and the latest reports would be relayed. It seemed that the deployment of individual formations, numbering a full five regiments in strength, was indeed on a lazy routine cycle, indicating that the Republic underestimated the nature of the rebellion. Regiment insignia were counted and the units identified. The 23rd Regiment was an odd absentee from a base occupied by the rest of its legion and for a while it caused some consternation, until word leaked out that it had been withdrawn due to efficiency failings. Periodically there were times when, for a few hours, there would be no significant military presence at the base. More interesting were the reports on the progress of the underground facility. For weeks large containers had been landed and carefully taken into the above-ground buildings over the pit, presumably delivering equipment, but in the last few days those deliveries had slowed to almost nothing. Now the movement around the facility was mostly people, likely scientists and their assistants. They mostly wore the powered but unarmoured suits of naval personnel; incapable of resisting much damage but more than sufficient to protect the wearer from toxins, diseases, even complete vacuum. For the rebels this was a clear sign that the attack had to be soon, or not at all. One warm, humid, quiet night, Vaeral spoke to her senior commanders.

"It is time." Her warm soft tones carrying the voiced consonants of the Aepolian female dialect easily through the dim chamber. "Tomorrow we will attack. The Republic is not evil, it is beastly. It is worse than evil, it doesn't hate us, it simply ignores us. We die by the thousand, by the million, brutalised by unfeeling and uncaring overlords. Not because they despise us but because we are nothing to them. We are allowed to die when we are useless like a cow grown too old to produce milk. The farmer doesn't hate the cow, he just doesn't care enough to keep feeding it. In such a position we have already won an important victory. We have raised a standard and beneath it we have fought. The friends we have lost have not been neglected until they died, they have been killed by force and they have exacted a toll on their killers. Tonight we exact another such toll, tonight we fight because the alternative is to fade from the pages of history. Every act we undertake is like a drop of ink in a bucket of water. At first it is sharp, distinct, easily visible. Over time it fades until it can no longer be seen; but while it may not be obvious it still darkens the water, just a little. Enough drops of ink, acts of rebellion, and the water now is so dark that a drop of ink becomes invisible, acts of rebellion are the routine. We won't know which act of rebellion will finally turn the bucket dark until after it is over, but the cause we defend will ultimately triumph and tonight could be the moment that becomes inevitable. If not, then may it be the next act, or the next."

She paused for a dramatic moment. "My brother once said that the Republic is ignorant of its heritage and so it couldn't see the way this fight had taken place across all of history, over and over again. More, he told me, that the victors had always been those fighting for their freedom. Not without cost, sometimes great cost. He once said that the motto of the Republic should be 'Viri equos non portant.', but for whatever reason it is not, it is 'Vox populi vox deo.' The Soldiers we fight tonight may mouth the second, but they believe the first. We will correct them of this opinion."

Kitelya wondered what the first phrase meant, though he could guess it was probably the same long-dead language as the motto that had emblazoned the front of the Praesidium. Glancing around him he noticed that he was the only person to seem baffled. He mustn't draw attention to himself.

Vaeral drew in a deep breath to finish. "Tonight we have but one target. The underground laboratory at the wetside of the base. If it costs us every one of our soldiers we must get to it and then deliver our fire into it. Any scientists we find are engaged in military work and they are military targets. Teams will assemble at their planned start-points and will move out on schedule twenty minutes before dawn. Simply by marching to the fight we score a victory. Let us score a second victory and remind the Republic and its President that we are people, as much people as the corporate overlords and military officers. Tonight we strike for Prosperity, for the rebellion, for my brother and for freedom!"

289

The Storm

Vaeral was not joining any of the teams striking towards the base, her importance to the rebellion was such that she couldn't be risked. She quietly offered Kitelya the chance to stay with her, but he refused. He might be able to offer help if any of the teams encountered unexpected traps or additional fibre-wire, he said.

He joined the nearest large team, the one that fell under Tifalta's direct command, a team of some forty soldiers. They moved out in early morning, on schedule, a time intended to minimise any advantage that the impressive sensors in the helm of each Republic soldier gave him. In darkness an unaugmented human was almost helpless while the legionary would be able to perceive the battlefield with little difficulty. The same logic had been used to hide the rebels as they gathered for the assault. It's all too easy for an armoured trooper, looking at a full-colour display, to forget that it's a computer simulation and visible light is not forming part of the image. It was a strange departure from most of human history, when night would be used by light forces to hide their progress, on the modern battlefield it was daylight that offered the chance to make the fight more even.

If their timing was correct then there should be no scheduled flights over the heads of any team during the advance but the silent, careful progress gave testament to the tension stuffed like a cannonball into the gullet of each man. A noise in the lightening dawn. A Tyrant's screaming engine, the sudden crack of tmetic energy expanding one tiny part of a person or a tree or a stone as if it had become explosive; the sound of death by beam. Someone had been spotted. Perhaps it was inevitable, the plan assumed that if one or two teams were intercepted then that would never provide enough information for the Republic to gauge the scale of the assault and react in force, but it was a chilling moment. Onward went the team, quiet, shaking, terror gripping their very joints like vices.

The first obstacle they had to traverse was the sector fence. Their route took them to a prepared gap, opened with precision and disguised by geography. The gap was there, it hadn't been repaired. No threats visible around, no reason for fear. Two by two the team crawled through the gap, silently spreading out on the far side, slowly and carefully towing their heavy equipment behind them. The brightening day made everyone feel intensely vulnerable and there wasn't a smile to be seen on the dapple-painted faces. This was war done the old way. Battledress of cloth, dyed to blend, the sweat of the brow irritating the eyes as it flowed. Strips of torn green hessian tied to shoulders to break up the outline of the man. The team froze at every sound, looked to their fellows to see if they had frozen too. Hour after hour, joints aching, jaw muscles screaming in pain from the clench. Every insect felt like a hornet, every rustle sounded like a battalion.

Six hours of hell before the team could stop. Close to the base now, just outside the fence, they carefully assembled their equipment and then waited for the moment of attack. Precisely on schedule the Republic 25th regiment took off to begin its work clearing a sector, off to the East. Even the knowledge that this left the base largely undefended and the certainty that, with all the rebels clustered along this lakeshore, there would be nothing for the Tyrants to find and kill was not enough to lift the atmosphere. The minutes ticked by. Had all the teams made their progress as smoothly? Was this team the only one left? There was no way of knowing, the attack would be executed on schedule and hopefully all the rebels would attack together. Tifalta nodded theatrically to Kitelya and the two of them crept on their bellies up to the perimeter fence for the base. They had practised this a thousand times. Connect the wires to each side of the mess of fibre strands, hang the middle of the new wires high up on the fence, carefully cut each fibre strand in between the clips, fold it away to each side so the needle-sharp ends wouldn't hurt the troops. All so simple, all so routine, all so much harder with shaking hands, adrenaline coursing through the body. Kitelya swallowed, but the hollow sound, from a dry throat, seemed deafening. Tifalta crawled through the gap, his team following behind. They spread out, the fence to their backs, readying their weapons. The rockets had been left outside the fence, indirect weapons wouldn't be hampered by it, but everything else was with them. Now the waiting seemed stupid in the extreme. Sitting in the open, waiting to be discovered, who could endure this? Wait they did. They had to give enough time for every team to breach the fence and slide into position. Tifalta was now staring at his wrist, watching the seconds. Ten seconds. He raised his arm slightly and made a fist. Five seconds. He held the arm straight out sideways. Without a tremor he suddenly pulled his fist back in and grabbed his longarm with it. There was no battle cry but the rebels stood, ran. Looking for targets, looking for the reassuring sights of their comrades. To the left, to the right, across the base, figures were running. Rebels charged silently towards the centre of the base from everywhere, thousands of volunteer soldiers. A sudden sonic crack as a weapon fired and then, as if that was the starting gun, a crackle of fire, a yelling of orders, a screaming of wounded.

The battle had begun.

Kitelya ran with his fellows towards their first target. A large accommodation block near their breach in the perimeter. A few shots at the building and it began to bleed people, flooding from it and running towards the laboratory complex, seeking shelter underground exactly as Vaeral had planned. The rebels weren't slaughtering these people, they were herding them. Hundreds of people fled the buildings in which they lived and ran into the laboratory. Once inside they could hide in the pit, seal the doors, hope that a rescue could come before the rebels forced their way underground. It seemed a desperate hope, but a hope nonetheless. Almost no rebel casualties. It was astonishing. Tifalta must have been stunned at how smoothly the plan was working. If so, he wasn't experienced enough to understand what that presaged.

As the rebels closed their ring around the laboratory building they held their positions and dropped to the ground. Now was the time for the rockets. Tifalta pressed his remote trigger and all around the base the savage hiss of propellant ignition was suddenly the only sound to be heard. An almost perfect ring of emplaced fixed rockets all launched at the same instant. Their white trails curled up and inward so, for a moment, the whole base looked like a giant crown. Then, all at once, they fell into the laboratory. One spiralled off and landed out in the lake. Another fell short, landing dangerously close to some rebels. The remainder, dozens of them, struck home.

In a rippling, tearing, burning roar the main building was turned to flying debris. A vast pall of smoke obscured the site. Breathless, the rebels waited to see if the pit had been breached. The smoke began to clear. Just the concussion-ringing in

Kitelya's ears could be heard. Then one, then another, shouts of joy. Kitelya couldn't see, the smoke was too thick, then suddenly he could. The roof of the pit was buckled and twisted, flames licked across its surface, holes had been torn in its carbon protection. Many holes. Enough holes that the few armed defenders couldn't possibly protect them all. The butchery hadn't begun yet but victory was now assured. Surely.

Forward surged the rebels. Many were readying the small incendiary bombs they'd been issued. Thrown into a laboratory they would kill the people, but also destroy the plague. Tifalta turned as they ran and grinned at Kitelya. Kitelya, not a young man, was falling behind.

The leading elements of the rebel force had just reached the edges of the pit when it, with no warning, exploded upwards.

Kitelya had been quietly moving sideways, rather than forwards, and he was nowhere near the pit, but a few eager and fast rebels were torn to shreds by the burst of flying shrapnel. Towards the centre of the base, Kitelya ran, looking for a special place, a marking on the ground. He found it quickly, despite the chaos surrounding him, near the middle of the central landing area and he threw himself to the ground on top of it.

Behind him the battle was changing decisively. From the pit, pouring out vertically, were Tyrants. The entire 23rd Regiment had been carefully hidden down there waiting for this moment. There were no labs, no scientists, no special equipment, just a huge underground lager for armoured vehicles. The hand-picked men who had dressed in civilian suits and fled to the pit when the attack started were infantry like any other. They had now joined their fellows in their vehicles and were flying out in a huge formation. Some rebels simply stopped where they were, their hopes so thoroughly dashed that they couldn't even react as the cannon tore them apart. Others vainly tried to fight, or run, but no weapon they could carry would hurt a Tyrant and no sprinter's legs could outrun one. Worse, the leading Tyrants quickly landed at the perimeter breaches, so the vicious fibre fence was now preventing any rebels from fleeing to the forest. Some ran blindly into the thin fibres and were sliced to ribbons. Some tried cutting them and were burned by the electricity. One by one, hundred by hundred, the rebels died.

Kitelya watched from his spot on the ground. This exact spot had been marked electronically as a no-fire zone for the legion. As long as he stayed here there would be no danger, except from random fire from the rebels. Then, impossibly, he saw Tifalta. A burst of smoke had obscured him and he'd found shelter between two buildings. He turned and saw Kitelya and, seeing how exposed the engineer looked, he waved for him to come to the building's corner. How little he yet understood. Eventually Tifalta seemed to change his mind and ran to Kitelya's side. "Are you hurt?"

Kitelya shook his head slowly and shot Tifalta through the head.

By any standards this was a slaughter. When the final tally was counted there had been two killed and six wounded amongst the Republic troops. Of the rebels, none had escaped. More than seven-hundred bodies were recovered, but that would not be close to the whole tally, some of their deaths had been violent enough to leave little but a smear of blood, lost in countless other smears of blood.

Striding across the smoke-blackened base, Doloras held out his armoured hand to help Taeris rise. "Well done, Sir. I think that's it for the rebellion."

Taeris smiled back. "A perfectly executed mission,

Colonel. Now I want you to send some troops out to an underground rebel base and round up any captives they can find. In particular I'm interested in a woman called Vaeral. She's Faeral's sister and is held in great esteem by the rebels. Her death, or better still her capture, would be a powerful victory. While you're doing that, I'm going to put my armour back on, I've felt naked without it."

Quick though the Tyrants were, accurate though their directions proved, Vaeral was not at the underground base. The massed forces of the infantry scoured the area and every nearby sector, but she could not be found.

Aepolia

In the swelling floor of the canyon in front of the city of Aepolia there was an impressive sight. The 3rd Fleet, in orbit, had sent most of its shuttles and landing craft and a huge formation of fighters to carry out a dramatic flypast of the city that had once rebelled. On the floor of the canyon, in perfect formation, were the infantry. Those citizens who had survived the plague and the harrowing that followed had been ordered from their homes and formed into a ragged group before the city walls. They were here to witness.

Adrael stood, a helm amplifying his voice, next to Taeris. He glared at the civilians with distaste. "Citaeronians. You are here to witness the end of the rebellion. Days ago the traitors on Prosperity were crushed in one decisive battle. These soldiers before you struck that blow, this man beside me commanded them. We paraded on Prosperity to celebrate this great day for the Republic. We now parade here to permit you to share in the joy of this day."

Based purely upon the expressions of the mass of civilians it would have been a very extreme interpretation of their bearing to ascribe the term 'joy'.

On and on Adrael droned. At the beginning he was full of praise for the troops and for Taeris. By the end he was extending his fulsome generosity to the guards, the government and, subtly, himself. At each pause there was a round of applause that seemed mechanical to Taeris but if Adrael thought the same then he didn't show it.

Finally the speech ended, the applause came one more time, the civilians trudged back into their city. Taeris, curious, decided to follow.

Aepolia had never been a beautiful city, but now it was hideous. Many houses were splashed with painted warnings about disease. Countless doors had been smashed and splintered, whether by desperate residents seeking food or medicine or by the armoured boots of Graelen's men. Graelen and his troops had been too busy to attend a ceremony honouring Taeris, naturally, so they were nowhere near but for a frightened Aepolian the sight of Taeris in his armour was enough to drain what little colour remained in their cheeks.

Towards the centre of town was a large forum square. In the middle was a public fountain and a number of children were scooping water from it to carry back to their families. Not all children, no. Some were older. Some were adults but skinny, wretched adults. One stepped over to him. She must have been sixteen, but had so little fat on her that she could have passed for twelve. She was pretty, and if she was pretty today she must have been ravishing before the privations of war and occupation. "Sir, you're a Legate?"

Taeris nodded but remained silent.

She smiled as best she could. "Do you want a girl? I can wife for you, or just serve you. I can't stay here."

For a moment Taeris looked her up and down. She misinterpreted his look and began to strip so he could get a better look at her, right in the middle of the street. How desperate had this girl become? "Stop." She froze in stunned incomprehension. Taeris was a soldier. He'd never owned money, nor had he any method of getting any. He couldn't take this girl with him, could he? If he did, would a thousand more follow him out of the city begging for his help? "What's your name?"

"Zala," she answered, "If that pleases you."

Taeris nodded. "I have need of a guide to Aepolia, Zala. If you show me what I wish to see then I will take you with me when I leave."

The look of gratitude that crossed her face was desperate and pathetic.

Over the next two hours Zala showed Taeris the visible face of hell. He had no money, no food, nothing to give, but his fixed expression betrayed nothing of the anger he felt for the way these people had been treated. He spoke to a few people but they were nervous about opening up to an officer of the Republic, even if they had recognised the pattern on his armour and understood that it declared him as being different from the guardsmen that they referred to as 'Thaetroskiste', the murderers. In this regard Zala proved to be the only way to get any coherent information from the terrorised Aepolians at all. The plague had struck the city hard and deep. Almost no families had been unaffected by the disease despite their best precautions and plenty of districts had been almost completely annihilated. The real horrors, though, were the decisions that the disease forced upon the Aepolians. Districts sealed off and allowed to die, doors barricaded against close friends and family. Every survivor had such a memory, every survivor had something that shamed them and kept them awake at night. Then, as the disease waned, the thaetroskiste came. Murdering and brutalising as they came, killing mercilessly and forcing terrified citizens to flee into the canyons or breach their carefully defended quarantines. A second outbreak of plague spread, the gruesome sight of the heads of fellow Aepolians stuck on stakes outside the main gates by the soldiers became commonplace, starvation in the canyons seemed a better death for many.

Despite it all the Aepolians survived. Their population was less than a tenth of their former numbers and the remainder were sick, starving, traumatised. Yet they lived, if this existence counted as living.

In the midst of it all there were one or two people who recognised Taeris from his description. These people didn't despise him for the actions of the violent guardsmen, but honestly, for his own actions, his infiltration of the rebellion and his underhanded trick of speaking Aepolian. Taeris realised that word of his work on Prosperity had now spread so far that never again would the simple mastery of a forbidden language be enough to make a spy welcome in the enemy camp. Not that it mattered, the rebellion was almost a memory now.

On he walked. Around a corner there were two dead women on the street. No obvious signs of the cause of death could be seen. Starvation? Neglect? A brutal beating? How many remained unburied in the city? Even though the plague had abated there was little enthusiasm for dealing with the dead. Wildly sprayed markings showed which streets were unsafe for movement, if the buzz of flies didn't provide enough warning. Suddenly, from a turning ahead, two young boys chased each other into view, laughing. They saw Taeris and stopped in terror. Nothing Taeris could say would help them, but there was something he could do. He opened a channel.

"Thaeton and Latonis, Taeris." It was mere seconds before both officers were answering. "I have a task for your units. Bring them to Aepolia and take over the administration of the city."

Thaeton responded at once, "Yes Legate. Are you concerned there might be a new uprising?"

Taeris picked his words carefully, "I am concerned that citizens of the Republic are in danger of being caught up in a violent situation over which they have no control."

Latonis' tone was equally careful. "We should perhaps bring supplies, with which to assure the cooperation of the city?"

Taeris was very pleased his men had caught on so quickly. "Yes, good idea. If we make sure their basic needs are met then they won't fall to temptation. Bring food, medical supplies, building materials, the usual things."

Thaeton's answer was everything Taeris could have wished. "As you say Legate. We will bribe the city with basic supplies to keep it compliant and we will defend it against external influences that might cause trouble."

Zala had not been privy to this conversation as it had been by radio, but she was looking at Taeris with worry, not knowing what orders he'd given.

Taeris smiled at her. "Is Zala your real name?"

"Yes," she answered, "I am Zala. It's not my full name but it's what everyone calls me."

Taeris beckoned her to follow him and began to walk back to the main gate of the city. Sitting outside was the squat, ugly shape of his Tyrant and he led her into the compartment at the rear. He pulled down a ration-pack and handed it to the girl, smiling as she tore into it and began gulping down calories as fast as she could. "Slowly, Zala, you'll make yourself sick." Despite his warning she did indeed make herself sick, but after returning to the compartment she immediately resumed eating. She was finishing her first substantial meal in weeks when she suddenly stiffened and ran outside. Overhead, hundreds of Tyrants flew towards Aepolia. Her horror took her to her knees.

Taeris touched her shoulder, ignoring the way she flinched from him. "My troops. They are bringing food and medicine."

Zala trembled in fear. Perhaps she couldn't believe what she heard. As the vehicles settled into their landing fields inside the city she listened. She listened for the sounds she knew so well. No screaming. No tmetic cracks and rips. No explosion, no fire. Silence. After a few minutes she believed. She stood and turned to throw her arms around Taeris. He held her tiny frame for a moment before carrying her back into the Tyrant.

Zala was all sorts of entertainment aboard the Spica. She'd never experienced freefall before and though there was a tiny gravitational tug on the battlecruiser it was almost impossible to detect as you floated through its corridors. She was deeply impressed by the ship's cat, an animal that had spent most of its life weightless and which moved in impossibly elegant twisting leaps from wall to wall. Zala tried to emulate it, without any notable success, and even tried to catch it to administer a cuddling, again fruitlessly. The cat didn't want to be caught and even the most experienced of the crew aboard would have fallen short of the speed and agility required to over-rule that decision.

Taeris reported to Raephus' cabin as soon as he had installed Zala into his own quarters, to find Adrael waiting there for him as well.

Adrael actually smiled on seeing the Legate. A seemingly genuine, warm, smile; giving lie to the widely-held belief that the muscles required for such an expression had atrophied in the security man's face. "That was a remarkably entertaining sight, the ship's pet playing with your own. I assume she's travelling with you?"

Taeris nodded. "With the Admiral's permission, yes."

Raephus laughed. "I think we can find room for one tiny girl aboard a battlecruiser."

Adrael stopped smiling and returned to business. "It is

time we returned to Esperia. We must report back to the government."

Taeris mildly said, "I assume there still is a government then?"

Raephus allowed a grimace to cross his face but Adrael answered the question with his normal severity, "There is always government. The rebellion is finally ended, Legate. You can take no small measure of credit for that achievement, but you still answer to your superiors, do not forget that."

Taeris nodded quickly. "Forgive me, Adrael. I was attempting to continue the light-hearted nature of the discussion. I meant no offence."

Adrael's face was now completely expressionless. "Then I shall assume none. You assigned the Seventh Infantry to the protection of Aepolia?"

"Not exactly," Taeris answered, "I sent them to ensure no further rebellion there, and to begin the process of getting the city back into operational state."

"No," Adrael shook his head firmly, "I think you sent the troops there to secure the area and let the civilians pick up their lives again, to protect them from the depredations of Graelen." Taeris waited for Adrael to order the troops back out of the city again, but instead the security man went on, "I think the time is right for Aepolia to begin recovery, something that might be difficult while the Eighth Guards keep beheading them. Do you have any other orders to assign or can we leave for Esperia?"

Taeris was a little surprised by Adrael's position but he said, "I have nothing else."

In fact Taeris was eager to reach Esperia as quickly as possible. His entire plan hinged on arriving at the centre of the Republic, to a warm reception, at the head of a victorious army. That, and only that, would bring him the required leverage.

Maybe not even that, in fact, but it was the one and only chance he would get.

On the way back to his quarters, Taeris passed the cat again. Automatically he looked to see if it was still being chased by Zala, but the girl was nowhere to be seen this time. Once he had closed the door to his cabin behind him, the reason for her absence became clear. Zala had stripped her clothes off and tucked them into some of the elasticated straps that covered the walls; she floated, naked, against the far wall of the cabin, one hand gripping a strap behind her to keep her position. She was nervous, unable to meet his eyes. Taeris thought for just a moment before saying, "Not yet, Zala."

She looked confused, but seemed to have relaxed a little. "I thought this is what you wanted."

Taeris smiled as comfortingly as he could and said, "Not yet. I'll tell you when."

Zala quickly grabbed her clothing and began pulling it on, jerkily, spinning herself around in the cabin. Taeris suppressed a laugh, it would have embarrassed her.

She was really severely starved, her skeleton looked to have been shrink-wrapped in skin. The thighs were much narrower than the knee joints, her shoulders and hips seemed to be trying to force their way through the skin entirely, her fingernails and hair were damaged by lack of essential vitamins. For a citizen of the republic to be starved almost to death while, on the same planet, a Legate could cheerfully go on and on, inflicting his will unfettered was something Taeris found sickening.

Once she was dressed she rested against the cabin wall, not looking at Taeris. He let her calm a little before speaking, "Don't worry, Zala. First we get you healthy, then we find a place for you. You are safe now." Even as he said it he wondered if that were true. Was she safe? Was he?

He put her from his mind. He had a speech to prepare, the most important of his life. Possibly the last of his life.

The Magisterium

Taeris had returned to the fleet with a determination that he must act now or lose his opportunity forever. If Adrael had noticed this resolution then it didn't seem to affect him, but for the entire journey it had been impossible to get Raephus alone. Without that moment of privacy Taeris couldn't tell Raephus of his plan, couldn't enlist his aid. Eventually Taeris just accepted that he would first visit Esperia without the plan in place, he could always find an excuse to visit Raephus later, but still before the Republic had found time to return matters to normality. Worse, Adrael had made no mention of a parade, a public reception, even the normal traditions accorded a returning victor. Taeris barely had time to make arrangements for Zala before he was shuttled down to Esperia with only the silent Adrael for company.

Republic Square was just as blackened as the last time Taeris had seen it. Large cracks marred the surface and, as the local information system made clear, had destroyed the delicate induction coils. For the moment vehicles moving across the vast expanse would need to bring their own power. The rubble from the main buildings around the square had been removed, as had the vehicles and corpses that had littered the space. The Legacy, once disinterred from its own remains, proved to have most of the structure still intact, and on the lower two floors there was now glass in the windows, lights in the offices. This time, however, Taeris was being taken to the Magisterium, the highest court in the Republic and the headquarters for its security apparatus. From the square the building appeared relatively intact, but once inside there was ample evidence of the coruscation that had vapourised anything weaker than stone. Every now and then there would be a corner, an angle, even a wall that had escaped the worst. Taeris followed Adrael downstairs into the cellar. Here the building looked much less affected, but nothing could disguise that charred smell.

Adrael asked, "Have you been down here before?"

Taeris said, "No, I've only been..." He stopped. Adrael was grinning at him. The security man had made a joke. Of course it was only funny if you understood the former reputation of the cells under this building; funny if you found torture and murder funny. Seven years ago Taeris would have laughed.

They made their way down a wide corridor and turned into a small office. Taeris reminded himself that, in such straightened circumstances, even a small office might be a rare commodity. This one claimed to be the office of a Magister, the most senior of the lawmen in the Republic, then he stopped. This was the office of Magister Adrael. Taeris looked at his companion. "You're a Magister?"

Adrael smiled modestly, "As it happens I'm now the only Magister." He waved Taeris into a seat and sat facing him. There was no ostentation in the room, it was almost bare. Perhaps Adrael needed or wanted no show of power. "Now, that brings me to the matter at hand. In all the confusion of the rebel attack here, we seem to have lost track of the terrorist, Faeral, I assume you know where he can be found?"

Taeris nodded. "I do. I'm afraid I had him quartered in an area that fell within the fuel-bomb blast. He, and the traitor-girl Salassa were destroyed."

The Magister nodded, he showed no sign of recognition at the name 'Salassa', which was useful information, but the fact that he also showed no curiosity was more so. "It's not a matter of concern. Now, onto more important things. Where do you see yourself going next?"

Taeris hadn't thought about it. "I suppose I will firstly return to Laesa and find my feet again. Of course I shall be ready for deployment at the President's command."

"Will you indeed," Adrael said, "I think that's a very wise position to take, in this room."

Taeris was suddenly alert. "I don't understand."

Adrael's face hardened. "Do not underestimate me, Legate, I'm not some mindless fool who parrots back the words of the Republic unthinking. I am a Magister and I have weighed, just as you have, doctrinal obedience against the flexibility of initiative. Where we differ is that I know what the worst is, and despite your formidable experience, you do not."

Taeris thought back to the plague, the starving civilians, the mindless violence he'd witnessed. "I don't know what you mean."

Adrael said, "I assume you don't know any history." Taeris began to speak but Adrael waved him quiet. "I don't mean dates and battles. The Republic teaches events, it doesn't teach history. I am unusual in that I have had access to historical texts and a genuine interest in them. History used to mean looking at the causes of the past, finding out what the people thought of them at the time, and in hindsight. You have studied the Terran Second World War?" Taeris nodded silently. "What do you know of it?"

"It was the war where the old colonial powers were defeated by the forerunner of the Republic." Taeris frowned. "I think it also was the time humanity began using atomic power."

Adrael nodded. "This is what passes for history in every school in the Republic. It is, at the same time, so simplistic as to be unarguable and also completely misleading. I'm not going to correct your education, it would take longer than either of us will live, but I am going to tell you something I learnt from the totality of my learning. Empires, Republics, Commonwealths, they come and go. This Republic has already lasted longer than any before it. As they go they are replaced by others and these new nations always promise that things will be better. For the people running the new nation, in fact, things are better. In a trivial amount of time the situation changes. Whichever group of people now feel weak start to resist, then rebel. Some rebellions succeed and when they do there may be a great moment of equality. It may last a few months or years but eventually the poor, the weak, the downtrodden will begin to blame the government for their lot. No government has ever been perfect for everyone, no government has ever been loved by everyone. Do you understand?"

Taeris nodded, doubtfully. "I do. But isn't that healthy, ultimately?"

Adrael smiled broadly. "It is. It truly is and an astute point if I may say so. It offers new ideas and with each new government there is a chance that they will learn from the past and be just a little bit better. The problem is at the point of rebellion. In a purely intellectual sense the good ideas that the old regime might have had are automatically discredited because of the regime that espoused them. The lean is thrown out along with the fat. If there is true progress I have yet to see it, but that's not the real danger. At the change of government there is chaos and anarchy; the people suffer and die in vast numbers. Sadly it is always the weakest that suffer the most, because the rich and powerful protect themselves at the expense of the common man. A wise man once described it thus, 'Men don't carry horses, horses carry men.', the powerful will always rise and will do so on the backs of the weak, do you understand?"

Taeris took his time answering, he knew what a horse was, at least in theory. "You think that, despite its faults, the Republic is better than the upheaval caused by its overthrow."

Adrael smiled. "I do, I also think that the worst of the 'upheaval' will always fall on the weak, those who wanted it the most. Anarchy is always worse than government, even where the government has flaws, as all do."

Taeris nodded slowly. "Why tell me all this?"

Adrael stepped over to a small cabinet on the wall and poured out two drinks. He brought them back and handed one to Taeris. "You are an exceptional commander, Taeris. You're intelligent and responsible, but you are wise enough to understand the truth when you hear it. The Republic must continue as always, the alternative is anarchy, but I am in a position to make sure your position is ahead of all others in the military. I have also mentioned the idea to Admiral Raephus. You would run the troops, he the fleet, I the Magisterium. We are clever men, we could do a great deal of good work."

"And," said Taeris, "I wonder what happens to the 'horses'."

Adrael had the decency to look down as he answered. "There are always horses. What do you say, Legate? Will you take Caeranion's place and make the military a better, finer thing?"

Taeris thought for a moment. "I don't even know where to begin. You've opened my eyes to things I knew nothing of, nothing at all."

Adrael sat back and finished his drink, his eyes were

narrowed, Taeris wondered if that was simple shrewdness or if the Magister was suspicious. Ridiculous thing to think, the Magister was always suspicious of everything. "Of course. Go to your woman. Give it some thought. Give me your answer tomorrow." Nothing about the man's demeanour now indicated he was worried about Taeris' answer, in fact he was smiling slightly.

Taeris drained his own glass and stood. "Thank you Magister. I will do just that. I will return tomorrow with your answer, if I may take my leave."

The Magister nodded, still smiling, "I imagine you'll also want to consider the potential future you and your woman might enjoy. Depending on your decision, naturally."

Taeris kept his own smile fixed, but he didn't miss the meaning. Adrael was a man who might be able to use him, if that worked out for everyone then that was just fine, if it didn't then the Magister would dispose of him and Laesa without a thought. Caeranion could just as easily fulfil the role of military commander. He stepped to the door and stopped as a thought crossed his mind. "Magister, I was wondering if you knew the origin of that quote about men and horses, I'm sure I've heard it once before."

Adrael nodded, he enjoyed showing off his learning, "Indeed. It's not English originally, in the original it is 'Viri equos non portant', have you heard that before?"

Taeris shook his head, though his mind raced. "No, perhaps the English version was something I heard or read years ago, perhaps I'm simply mis-remembering." He walked out and closed the door.

Alone, Taeris was shaking with fear and anger as he strode back upstairs and out onto the ruined square. He stood for a moment, before noticing the ground-car that waited for him. It was a hasty conversion, a large fuel-cell strapped into the back seat to allow it to function on the roads of the shattered centre of the city, he climbed in and instructed it to take him to his house. Once underway he checked behind him to see if he was being followed. Nothing visible. Of course that didn't mean he wasn't being followed, it just meant he wasn't being followed by idiots. How many idiots did Adrael tolerate?

All his bold plans seemed fantasies now. He had imagined returning to Esperia at the head of a loyal army but reality, as always, fell far short. He knew nobody at all that he could truly trust in his own legion, nobody he could treat as a confidant. In fact his legion would follow the orders of Adrael before his own, naturally, he should have foreseen this. He had assumed that the return to Esperia, like the triumph on Citaeron, would include a mass parade of the 6th Legion, but Adrael seemed determined that in the capital the credit should be left with the most senior commanders. The few snatches of reports Taeris had seen on the Mediacorp channel mentioned his name only in passing. He had planned to speak at the victory parade, announce the rotten core of the Republic and trust that his troops would be frightened enough of the retribution of the Magisterium that they would join him in its overthrow. That had seemed possible. The legion would remember what happened to the last legion that tolerated his unorthodoxy. In hindsight it was a terrible plan, but the only one he had. Adrael, seemingly without even making a conscious decision, had stifled that one forlorn hope of freedom.

While the journey was underway he opened a channel to Laesa.

"Taeris! You're back on Esperia!"

"Yes, Laesa," he couldn't help but smile at her excitement, "I am back. Has it been a long time since you visited Sharla?"

There was a baffled pause at the change of conversation, but Laesa was nobody's fool. "A long time, yes, but you know that."

Taeris swallowed his fear before saying, "I want to see you. Perhaps we could combine the moment, meet at Sharla's place."

Laesa took a long moment before responding. "But I've still got..."

"The house-guests? Bring them too."

"They may not cooperate," Laesa said.

Taeris thought for a moment. "Tell them this, exactly, you'll need to write it down."

After a second Laesa said, "Ready."

Taeris spoke slowly. "Fitilatay mikone Vaeralq. Viri equos non portant."

Laesa read it back to him twice until he was satisfied she had it right, or close enough at least. "What does it mean?"

Taeris answered, "It means I'm taking him to his sister. It also explains why." He dropped the channel and quickly changed the programmed destination of the ground car to the assigned barracks-building of the 6th Infantry. Only the 23rd Regiment had so far landed, in the short time since the fleet had reached Esperia, but that was easily enough. The car turned at the next junction, unerringly finding its way through a city where every building now looked like a ruin of its former self and any road markings or signs had been obliterated. Occasionally Taeris thought he recognised something, but he couldn't be sure. Eventually the car passed through the strange transition to the outskirts of the city, where everything looked just as it always had, and minutes later it stopped outside the barracks building. Taeris climbed out, made sure his armour matched the colour scheme of an officer in the 23rd and sealed his helm to protect his identity.

The automated security systems knew him for who he was and opened doors for him as he approached. He made his way into the command centre, but found it empty. The building was in the process of being reconstructed, the main structure in place, but none of the comfortable amenities. Of course wearing his armour he had no need for windows, chairs, or any of the other accoutrements of civilisation. The computers in the base were powered up and working correctly so he quickly looked for the information he required. Yes, a number of fully prepared Tyrants were in the parade ground. He rapidly used his personal code to assign one of them to himself and then walked confidently outside to collect his new vehicle.

There it was, sitting idly, doors closed, fully fuelled and ready to go. Taeris walked over to the cockpit hatch and pulled it open. He was about to step in when he heard a voice behind him say, "Legate?"

Taeris turned and saw Doloras standing before him with a puzzled expression on his face. "Doloras, good to see you."

"What are you doing here, Sir?"

"It's been a long time since I flew one of these. I thought I might take it for a spin. You don't mind, do you?"

Doloras shook his head, smiling. "Of course not. I just wondered why you wouldn't head home to see your woman at once." There was something about Doloras' smile. Taeris immediately didn't trust it.

Taeris thought about it for a moment. "I think I might fly this beast to the house, now that you mention it." Something momentarily flickered on the Colonel's face. At once Taeris knew that Doloras was one of Adrael's men. The thought of it upset him more than he cared to believe, Doloras had been a friend and a brother in arms. If Taeris was to escape the Magister's clutches then he had to move quickly, before

Doloras could report his movements.

"You've always been a bit eccentric, I suspect she'll find it charming," Doloras said, "Enjoy your reunion, Legate."

Taeris smiled and turned back to the Tyrant but as he did so, a little red alarm showed in his helm. Every soldier had seen it many times. It was the identifier that a fellow soldier had pointed his weapon in your direction. Taeris reacted on instinct alone. He leapt as high and as fast as he could. There was a strange hum as the tmetic beam fired by Doloras missed him and was absorbed by the armour of the Tyrant. Still rising, Taeris looked back. Doloras was raising his weapon, tracking his target, ready to fire again, fire the shot that would kill Taeris.

Doloras was an excellent soldier but he hadn't had to live his life on the razor's edge the way Taeris had. Without giving it conscious thought, Taeris fired his beam downward, not even aiming. His shot slammed into the stone of the parade ground and its energy immediately caused a crater of heat and concussion in the stone. Fragments of stone flew out in all directions, some fast enough to embed themselves in Doloras' armour. In the sudden flurry of heat, dust and impact Doloras wasted a second in closing his helm, blinking tiny specks of dust from his eyes. It was the last mistake he would make.

As the beam recharged, Taeris touched the control that loaded a plasma slug into the barrel of his weapon. Now he took his time aiming, maybe almost a second. An eternity. As Doloras recovered and looked up Taeris fired, the tmetic beam burning through the slug in almost immeasurably short time. The formed solid was now a plasma and expanded with such ferocity that it flew out of the barrel of the weapon at many times the speed of sound. Its signature 'crack' sounded nothing like that of an unaugmented beam, the atmosphere carried its pressure in a solid shock-wave. Ahead of the wave, the plasma struck Doloras on his helm and armoured shoulders. Powered armour could resist impressive temperatures, but nothing like the fierce heat it now bore, hotter than a star. The outer layers burned away, with them the capacitance mesh that provided the principal defence against beams, and the sensors automatically shut down to protect their delicate electronics for long enough to reset. The ceramic layers in the armour did as they were designed, absorbing temperatures that hadn't existed in the natural universe since a fraction of a second after the big bang. Doloras was alive, but temporarily blind and stunned.

Taeris was climbing again, the recoil throwing him upwards. He gritted his teeth and kept his aim on Doloras, firing as soon as the weapon was ready. Taeris missed the head, but the shot struck the right shoulder and this time, with the mesh damaged, the armour parted and broke. Doloras fell to his knees, his armour trying to keep him upright, then fell onto his back. Taeris landed nearby and ran across to see if the commanding officer of the 23rd needed to be killed.

Doloras was alive, but horribly wounded. His right shoulder had been burned away, leaving a charred remnant of his right arm, clearly visible where the armour had cracked around it. His chest was ruined and, despite the suit's best efforts at automated medicine, he wouldn't be alive much longer.

Taeris looked at the wreck of a man before him. He couldn't think of anything to say.

Doloras, his voice thick with pain, said, "You are under arrest by order of the Magisterium. Stop... Stop..." He suddenly stopped speaking and his muscles relaxed for the last time.

Taeris turned and climbed into the Tyrant as dozens of soldiers ran across the square to see what had happened. He launched quickly and turned towards his house, diving low enough to fly between the buildings and along the streets.

Vestiges

Taeris had no intention of going home, nothing waited for him there, but he had to pick a direction and this one had the benefit that it might convince any pursuers that they knew his destination. In battle any electromagnetic signal could give away your position fatally so Tyrants were designed not to leak any such signals. Taeris couldn't say the same for civilian ground cars and that was why he'd wanted to change vehicle. In his mind, though, he could only think about Doloras. He had known the man was a good republican, of course, but had he entirely imagined the feelings of friendship between them? Had Doloras been planted in his command to keep an eye on him? If so, who had made that decision? Adrael? Caeranion? The President himself? Perhaps it was some other man, someone Taeris didn't even know.

Staying low, almost ground level, Taeris flew an erratic path from junction to junction. He periodically flew several blocks in a straight line to see if he could observe any pursuit, but he could see none. He flew on through the city, moving outward until the carefully ordered structure of the central districts were replaced by a relatively random and irregular arrangement. Here could be found the power-stations, engineering and manufacturing facilities, chemical plants, refineries and the cheap housing that the corporations provided for their workers.

Taeris knew little of the lives of those employed by the

mighty corporations and that which he had learnt was mostly from Laesa's recollections of her youth, as she had come from a corporate family. As far as Taeris could recall there was only one truly significant difference: Employees of the corporations were paid in money, servants of the Republic were unpaid but had their needs provided for depending on their rank and time of service. Taeris had never actually owned anything, as far as he could remember, but he had been provided with housing, food, medical care and, if this could be included, a cell in an education facility, all for free.

Almost at the very edge of the city, where the buildings eventually ended and the roads became the only sign of human presence, Taeris brought his Tyrant down into a tight circle and landed smoothly on the flat expanse of a prepared landing pad next to a line of huge buildings. He keyed a few settings and then jumped out of the Tyrant even as the engine was spinning down and ran his power-assisted sprint to the building marked with a large blue sign reading 'Hangar 6'. Speed was important, he was not merely a criminal but might even be the most wanted man in the entire Republic right now. Probably the alerts were being sent across the planet, but hopefully his pursuers hadn't yet understood that he had prepared a way off the surface. The hangar had one massive door spanning most of its frontage and next to it was a pedestrian entrance that looked comically small in comparison. In fact it proved easily large enough for Taeris in armour to bound through and find himself inside the enormous hangar building. Perhaps thirty vehicles of one kind or another were silently waiting in the hangar. The height of the building was enough to permit them to fly over each other to enter and leave the hangar, so their individual spaces on the ground were packed together as efficiently as possible. Naturally no government craft were kept here, this was a private facility for private vessels that the wealthy corporate officers could own and cherish.

Near the middle of the hangar there was a space reserved for a very expensive corporate spaceship. It massed 112 tonnes and could manoeuvre like a fighter while maintaining its occupants in a level of luxury that no government craft could match, save perhaps the Presidential Yacht. Based on an old corvette hull, the craft was ideal for Taeris' plan, even though it was unarmed and had almost no capacitance armour, that having been deleted in favour of comfort and performance. Taeris ran to it, pleased to find its entry ramp already extended and the electric lighting inside lighted and welcoming. As soon as he entered he shouted, "Laesa!"

"Here!" A female voice responded, but it didn't sound like Laesa's.

Taeris slowed his walk, entering the command deck cautiously. Laesa was sitting in a chair, but clearly it hadn't been her voice after all, she was tied and gagged. Faeral was crouching beside her, pointing the small handgun at her head, and Salassa was hiding behind Laesa. At the far side of the bridge, in a chair vastly too large for her, Zala was curled up with an expression of terror on her face. Obviously Raephus had delivered her to Esperia as promised. In purely tactical terms there was little the rebels could do to harm Taeris in his armour, and they knew it, but Laesa's life was in very real danger. Taeris stopped and said, "I really don't have time for this foolishness. We need to get off Esperia right now." Zala jumped up and ran across to Taeris, throwing her skinny arms around him in desperation, Taeris resisted the temptation to push her away.

Whatever Faeral had expected Taeris to say, it clearly wasn't that, because he looked very startled. "We?"

Taeris became intensely frustrated. "Yes, we. I'm a fugitive from the Republic and they might well be a few minutes behind us." There was the distinctive sound of more than one Tyrant landing nearby. "Or less than that."

Faeral shifted his grip on the pistol. "Tell me how to launch this thing and get out, we'll leave Laesa somewhere safe. Alternatively take off your armour, I'll kill you and leave Laesa here."

Taeris couldn't help but laugh, "Laesa isn't safe anywhere; the Republic is going to kill us all. I'm leaving, you're coming along." Faeral looked uncertain so Taeris walked over to the console, dragging Zala behind him, and touched the control that closed the entry-ramp. He sat down and began starting the engines of the small craft. The Sharla was designed to be operated by a single pilot when needed and in seconds the ship was ready to leave.

Faeral might have been overtaken by events, but he knew Taeris as an enemy. "Get away from those controls or I'll kill her."

Taeris turned to him. "I understand. You have no reason to trust me. Now listen, those Tyrants aren't here for you, they think you're already dead. They're here for me."

Faeral glared at him, unmoved. "Everything you have ever told me is a lie."

Taeris looked at him, helplessly. Finally he remembered something. In desperation he tried the only thing he had left. "Listen, Faeral. This is a very grave situation."

The expression on Faeral's face changed instantly to one of utter surprise. "Who told you that? No wait. I don't want to know." He lowered the weapon.

Taeris nodded. "Time to leave."

Faeral seemed to have made up his mind about which side

he was on, as he sat down next to Taeris. "How do we get past the Tyrants?"

Taeris grinned. "I know a few tricks." He rapidly began issuing commands via his communicator. After a few seconds a countdown appeared on the screen. "Five seconds."

Faeral frowned, "Until what?"

As the count reached zero there was the sudden sound of tmetic energy outside. In the same instant Taeris launched the ship upwards and out of the hangar doors, its inertial compensator allowing that manoeuvre to be immensely fast. As they flashed out over the landing pad Faeral looked in wonder at the scene below. Two Tyrants were exchanging fire as fast as their main beams would recharge, a third was smoking through a vicious-looking split in its side armour.

Faeral barely had time to shout, "We can't leave an ally!" before the scene was vanishing beneath them.

"No ally," Taeris said calmly, "I just remotely commanded my Tyrant to engage the Republic troops. Looks like they didn't expect that, the first plasma slug seems to have knocked one of them out."

Faeral looked at the Legate in wonder. "You don't think like most Republicans."

Salassa was hauling herself into a seat behind them as she said, "That's why we should kill him." She looked baffled at the sudden change of direction the confrontation had taken. Whatever the jargon-code 'grave' meant to Faeral it clearly meant nothing to her.

Unhurriedly the rebel commander turned to the young woman behind him. "I think, if it's all the same to you, I'll decide who we kill." Salassa turned red and looked at the floor. Zala looked uncertainly back and forth at the people on the bridge.

The Sharla flew up through the atmosphere with a speed that even a fighter would have found hard to match, but fighters didn't need to, of course, as there were already fighters in orbit ready and waiting to intercept. Taeris scanned the screens as the Sharla broke free of the last tendrils of atmosphere to see where the fighters were. It wasn't going to be easy, but with this ship's agility and speed it was definitely possible to outrun a few of them. Possible. The screens updated and to Taeris' shock there were no fighters closing on his position.

Rapidly the data updated. The fleet was there, the mighty battlecruiser Spica glowing as a highlighted panel of information. Zala seemed transfixed by the screens, she finally let go of Taeris and stared into the instrument panel, slowly moving her head from side to side to experience the layering effect. It seemed she'd never seen a modern display before, presumably the corporations didn't feel the need to equip a mining community with anything so expensive.

Taeris kept checking the screens, looking for the inevitable rush of fighters, but none seemed to come. It was as if his yacht wasn't deemed a target out here, something that was almost impossible to believe. Unless. Could Raephus have stepped in? Would the patrician naval officer truly risk everything for him like that? Was it even a risk? It must have taken a few moments for the forces on the ground to report the successful escape of the Sharla, in fact if they were damaged by the programmed Tyrant they might not yet have had the opportunity. Possibly only Raephus even guessed what was happening, as his scanners would have cheerfully informed him that the speeding yacht was registered to Laesa's family. At moments like this Taeris felt very good about the lack of initiative held by Republic troops. Unless the Sharla was explicitly identified as a threat then she, being a corporate ship, would be treated with absolute respect. Troops on the ground probably couldn't even have identified the escaping yacht with enough confidence to allow the fleet to fire on a luxury craft that might be carrying someone important. The thought made Taeris grin, in a way the Sharla was carrying the most 'important' person in the Republic. In a way.

Zala had taken firm hold of a hand grip and she looked around her new surroundings with a lost expression. Taeris wasn't going to wait longer than necessary before making a jump away from the orbit of Esperia in case his luck was about to run out so he picked a piece of space, randomly, and programmed the Sharla to make best speed to it. Sharla's best speed was extremely impressive and the jump, countless light-years into empty space, would take less than a minute, including the pre-jump calculations. Once the ship was moving faster than light Taeris turned his command chair and surveyed the deck.

"Welcome, Zala," he said with a smile, "I should introduce you to everyone. This is Faeral, leader of the rebellion, the nervous woman behind him is the spy and assassin Salassa, the woman rolling her eyes at me over the gag is my woman, Laesa. Everyone, this is Zala, a stray I found in Aepolia, assuming you haven't already worked that out. May I take this opportunity to thank you for not murdering her on sight? Now before we go any further, Salassa, would you mind releasing Laesa?"

Salassa looked to Faeral for guidance but he nodded firmly. She floated across to Laesa and in a few moments had freed her of her restraints. The screens showed the Sharla slowing back into recognisable space. Laesa pulled the gag off herself before glaring sullenly at Taeris.

The Legate looked around the mixture of anger, confusion, doubt and fear on the faces arranged before him. "Everybody happy?"

Laesa ran her tongue around inside her lips, her mouth must have become dry while gagged. "Do we have a plan, Taeris, or is running away as far as we can for as long as we can the whole idea?"

Faeral chuckled at this but turned a raised eyebrow to Taeris, "Yes, Taeris, a plan?"

Taeris looked slightly hurt as he responded, "In my defence I have just smuggled the lot of us out of the capital of the Republic while being hunted by the Magisterium. Don't I get some credit for that?"

There was a short pause before Faeral said, "No plan, then. Excellent."

Laesa was very even-handed when it came to the distribution of her scorn, "Faeral, you're the rebel leader, you come up with something useful for a change, where's the safest place for us to go?"

Faeral thought for a second. "Ultimately, Earth, so crowded that we can get lost there and never be found again. Of course..."

Taeris interrupted, "Earth is almost impossible for a landing. I doubt my credentials will work there now." It was true. While Earth wasn't protected in any special way, the sheer numbers of craft traversing the atmosphere meant that traffic control was intensely important. It was unlikely the Sharla would get permission to reach the planet itself, and would be directed to an orbiting station where the passengers could use a scheduled shuttle service instead. Doing so, without forged credentials, would be suicide.

Salassa said, "Aepolia. We can blend in there among friends."

"No," a quiet voice said. Everyone turned to see Zala

shaking her head. "Aepolia is..."

Taeris helped her out. "It's not the way you remember it, Salassa. I'm sorry. Prosperity is possible, or one of the other new worlds."

Laesa said, "Prosperity? I thought that was now firmly back in Republic control."

Taeris nodded in agreement. "It is, but it's a big world with a lot of places to hide. Small farms, spread out."

Laesa snorted, "So that's it, is it? We run and hide?"

Taeris had no answer for her, but Faeral did. "Hiding is certainly the first part of the plan. Is there a second part? Taeris, what are we now?"

Taeris frowned. "I don't understand."

Faeral made a sweeping gesture with his arms. "Are we, in this ship, for the rebellion now? What other ships still fight? I'm out of contact with the freedom fleet so your information is likely to be more current."

Taeris stared at him. "Your 'freedom fleet' has suffered a few casualties recently. The last time I saw numbers it was a few dozen craft in number, most of them simple missile boats. As for whether or not we are effectively part of the rebellion? Maybe we are, but not unless we sign on for that. Everyone here gets a choice. I'll try to find a safe place for anyone who wants to leave."

Faeral smiled warmly. "I am for the rebellion. Who's with me?"

Salassa and Zala both cried out, "Me!" Zala had a look of determination on her face that was new to Taeris. He could understand it, she'd been helpless and directionless for so long it must appeal to her to find a purpose.

Taeris wrapped an armoured arm around Laesa. "We will make our own decisions, for that we need time. For now let's drop these traitors somewhere safe and then work out what we're doing next."

Laesa glared at him. "No, Taeris. The Republic will kill us, so will the rebels, except perhaps for those in this ship. What other options remain, piracy?"

Taeris shrugged and nodded. "You're right. We have no future at all. For the record I love you. What do you want to do?"

Laesa and Taeris exchanged a long look. Finally Laesa said, "Just for the record I hate everyone in this ship. However, I now seem to be for the rebellion, whatever that means. It seems the Republic has left me little choice." Taeris smiled at her, perhaps the reality of her new life had yet to sink in. In fleeing the Magisterium Laesa had become not merely a traitor but a priority. If Adrael realised that Taeris had lied to him about Faeral's death then that importance might climb to unimaginable levels. Entire regiments might be sent to pursue them. Perhaps Raephus would subtly be as incompetent as possible in the hunt for the little band, but nobody else would offer even that slender assistance.

Everyone turned to Taeris. After a moment he nodded to Laesa. "Good, Laesa, if you're a rebel then so am I. So now I'm a rebel, what do I do? I don't even know who's in charge!" Everyone levelled a blank look at him. "Oh, no, tell me it's not me!"

Loyalty

Taeris listened attentively to the animated discussion between Faeral and Laesa. Laesa was extremely clever when it came to understanding the way the Republic worked and Faeral had led a rebellion for years. The other people on deck could offer little to the discussion.

"If we restart the rebellion then it has to be from the ground up." Faeral's volume had steadily increased but he was clearly making an effort to remain level of tone.

Laesa dismissed this with a gesture. "Restart it? I think you may have forgotten what happened to it!"

Faeral responded, "I don't see any other way."

Laesa smiled like a cat as she said, "That is why you lost."

The rebel leader grimaced slightly. "Fine. So if we can't go and rally support from the employees and the workers, where do we get a rebellion?"

Laesa paused long enough to gather her thoughts. "What is a rebellion, Faeral? Is it battles and marches? Songs and pamphlets? Is it politics?" Everyone stared at her, waiting to see what she meant. "No, Faeral. A rebellion is what happens when politics doesn't work. The popular movement, the names and the songs and the rest of it, those are the lies that rebellion wears, just as government wears lies by the name of 'democracy' or 'freedom'. Rebellion is war. It is nothing short of the overthrow of everything. It cannot be run like a political campaign, because the game of politics is rigged. The house always wins, always. No matter who you vote for, the government always gets elected."

Faeral nodded. "Beautifully said, Laesa, but aren't those words just the lies that your rebellion would wear?"

Laesa nodded. "So we forget the lies. We tell the absolute, unvarnished truth."

Salassa spoke up, "Faeral has never lied to us."

"Really?" Laesa said mildly. "He never said the rebellion would be successful?"

Faeral nodded soberly. "I did say that."

Zala added, "I think he actually said success was inevitable, an historical certainty."

Faeral nodded to her sadly. "I did say that. I lied, of course, to get an army together. I fell into the same trap as the Republic. But without giving people hope we have no army."

Laesa said, "I think you're wrong. I think we can tell the complete truth and we can still get an army. A better army."

Faeral looked unsure but said, "If you can do that, you can work miracles."

Laesa smiled around the room. "If I may say so, I don't think that's a miracle. I just happen to believe that if you want to climb over an obstacle then it's better to stand on people's shoulders than their throats. Obviously we can work on the details, but imagine if this is your rallying cry: We offer true freedom, for you and for the generations that follow. We offer an end to the corporations and their tyranny. We cannot promise victory but we can promise that failure in this cause is a better thing than the long life of a slave. We can also point out that the foremost strategist in the entire Republic, brought out of prison as he was the only way the enemy could win, has joined us. We can go and see what happens when we have the best commander on the field, the wisest leadership in the galaxy and the best interests of everyone at heart. Is that a cause you could follow, even if it meant your own death?"

Zala broke the silence, "I would follow that cause. With these men to lead me I would do whatever it takes." In her eyes was some shadow of the horrors she'd seen. Suddenly everyone else understood that if this teenager could stand and fight then there was no excuse for anyone else.

Faeral nodded emphatically. "It's the right thing to do. Any who follow us will do so with eyes open."

Taeris asked, "So where do we start? Are we looking for the rebel fleet?"

The rebel leader was his assured self again as he answered, "No, Prosperity. I have no idea where to find the freedom fleet."

Taeris frowned at him. "You do know how to find some rebels though? I mean the entire rebellion isn't currently on board this ship?"

Faeral shrugged. "A substantial portion of it might be," he said, "I don't find myself able to share any more with you yet for obvious reasons."

"After what's just happened!" Laesa shouted at Faeral. "I would think you could trust us now."

Faeral looked at her. "In the spirit of perfect honesty, no, I don't trust you. I barely know you. However, that aside, it's not the reason I'm hiding things from you. Everyone will only be told the minimum they need to know, just the minimum. Whether I trust you or not it will never change that basic rule of war."

Laesa snorted. "I promise you there's no way I'd ever talk to the Magisterium."

Taeris rested a fond hand on her arm. "Did I tell you about the economy of Educational Facility Seven?"

Laesa seemed momentarily baffled at the change of topic.

"What economy?"

Taeris looked into the distance. "I mean the economy in the broadest sense, how it functions. Periodically a ship comes by with new prisoners, and it brings a few packets of vitamins and minerals to throw into the recycling system, but most of the time the basic needs of the prisoners are met by the recycling unit itself. Everything that is excreted is poured back into the system, chemically altered and then used as food and water."

Laesa nodded, not understanding, but Faeral did. "That can't work," he said, "I know enough chemistry to know that, the amount of nutrition left in the human waste wouldn't sustain the system, too much of it is retained by the prisoners."

Taeris, in a monotone, said, "Yes. But the solution, obviously, is to use the same recycling system to get rid of the bodies of dead prisoners. That's where the nutrition is put back in."

After a moment everyone understood. Taeris squeezed Laesa's arm. "Until you know what the Republic may do, you can't begin to understand how it will affect you. Within weeks of my denunciation I would have done anything, said anything, just to be freed. Within months I was babbling my every thought just in the faint hope that someone might hear me. After years I barely remembered what life had been before. Faeral must keep his secrets, nobody else can do it for him." Nobody spoke for a long time.

Taeris turned his attention back to the screens and began working out the route to Prosperity. This was the truth of EF7. Whatever else the Republic had wanted to impart through the education process there was one, unintended, lesson that had been received more profoundly than any other. The Republic, like EF7, fed on itself, fed on its citizens. It was through that prism of understanding that Taeris had seen everything since his redemption. It was that undeniable lesson that had taken a bright, unorthodox, imaginative, fundamentally loyal soldier and turned him into an enemy of the Republic and its very existence. Nobody had even known enough to ask the question and as nobody had, previously, ever been released from EF7 there was no way to know how that place might affect an inmate. It was this secret that had driven every decision Taeris made, every disloyal thought he harboured. Yes, Taeris was willing to devote himself to bringing order to the Republic, but the extremes of conduct inherent to the Republic's lack of humane morality would never again be something he could accept. Now, having seen it for himself, he couldn't even stomach the regular military operations for this cannibal regime. He wondered how he'd ever been able to. Of course that was ridiculous. Before he'd accepted the official reports, understood only the good that firm, orderly government could bring. Now things were very different. He looked at Laesa. How had she accepted this change so easily? Then she turned and smiled at him. Oh yes. Trust. She had placed her trust in him. Silently, as he smiled back, he vowed not to let her down.

Any sign of active rebellion on Prosperity had ceased when Taeris crushed the main enemy force and, for the moment, the 5th Guards Legion was still stationed on the planet to ensure there was no resurgence of such behaviour. The Sharla flicked into orbit close to the planet to find that there was a great deal of activity around Prosperity. The Corporations had begun reconstructing the damaged or destroyed infrastructure and ships were arriving, departing and transferring cargo from shuttles to long-range transports in a vast cloud of engine flares and electronic communications. In such an environment the Sharla was barely even noticed as she dipped her streamlined nose into the fringes of the atmosphere and began braking for a place to land. Faeral knew the planet very well and he had selected a shared landing-field between several agricultural facilities, the sort of place a corporate ship might come and go fairly frequently but also a popular landing site for cargo shuttles and smaller engineering craft. All these were good reasons for selecting this landing site but none of them were the key reason. The decision was made because this region was where Vaeral, Faeral's sister, had planned to flee if she came under threat of capture. At the back of his mind, unworthy though it was, Taeris was irritated that this place, just forty kilometres from the base he'd constructed for his infantry and the scene of the decisive battle on Prosperity, had escaped his notice during the battle. Now that was a good thing, for their collective future, but back then it was a lapse in leadership that permitted a senior rebel commander to escape his clutches.

The landing was quiet and uneventful. Only two possibilities presented themselves to explain this easy arrival; either the Republic had failed to identify the Sharla with sufficient accuracy to spread its description around the worlds or they had been permitted a landing to lead Driastren to their rebellion contacts on Prosperity. Taeris knew that if he were in Driastren's place the latter would be much the more likely but it wasn't in the nature of the Legacy, or those it promoted, to think tactically.

Nothing, not rejecting the Republic, not fleeing like a criminal, not finding himself without troops to command, drove home to Taeris his altered condition like the removal of his armour. On Prosperity the bulky protective shell would make it almost impossible to blend in. He hated removing it but that was the only reasonable choice. In its place he dressed in the powered suit of a ship's crewman, taken from the locker on the Sharla, which still offered many of the same safety features but lacked the integrated weapons, battlefield helm-sensors and reassuring armoured surface of the infantryman's suit.

Faeral wore a similar suit, as did Laesa, but the two Aepolian women dressed in fabric clothing, a thoroughly practical choice for a civilian on the planet's surface. Taeris slipped a small pistol into one of the belt-slots on his suit and nodded approval when Laesa did the same. As they left the ship Taeris found himself staring at the Aepolian women, Salassa in a short and flowing dress, Zala in a figure-hugging cat-suit. There were definitely compensations for not being part of a legion any more. The air was warm and moist and it smelled of life. If this was the only place to find the rebellion then it was also a lovely place to visit. Laesa almost trembled with excitement, having never visited Prosperity before. Taeris idly wondered when she'd last been away from Esperia. Not recently, as far as he knew.

The group walked to the only building on the landing pad and, finding it empty, walked on to the main road leading to the nearest farm. Perhaps, walking at a pace dictated by those wearing ordinary clothing, it would have taken as much as half an hour to reach their destination but just minutes into the walk a ground car approached and pulled alongside them. This wasn't the automated vehicle of Esperian use, but a car driven by a man. He opened the door and leaned slightly in their direction. "Are you looking for Herrat?"

It was Faeral who answered, "If Herrat is where the folisa fertenest can be found."

There was briefly a look of shock on the driver's face but he quickly said, "Get in."

The group climbed in, the large working-vehicle easily

held them all. The drive was silent for a moment before Laesa, her manners intact, said, "Thank you."

The man grunted, "I'm Graeder, the farmer up here."

Laesa asked, "Are you taking us to your farm?"

"No," he said, "nothing for you there. I'll take you to the tree."

Laesa broke the tense silence in the car, quietly saying to Taeris, "I see you're back where you started, dishonoured in the Republic, only this time I'm with you. I'm not sure that's an improvement."

Taeris grinned at her. "Not quite back where I started. They haven't caught us yet, and that's definitely an improvement."

The car sped past the farm, then another and another, before turning left onto a narrow track. Another left saw them approaching a dilapidated farmhouse, with almost no roof left. To the experienced eye the damage was suspiciously reminiscent of the tmetic shattering of a Tyrant's cannon. The car made a slow loop around the farmhouse and came to a stop behind it. "The path over there," Grader waved a hand to show them. "Into the forest then a few hundred metres to the lake. No idea what's there, don't want to know either."

The passengers got out of the car and as soon as the last door was shut Graeder took off back towards the main road. Taeris shrugged and started to walk down the path, the trees crowding more densely with every step. After only a minute the path was more a theoretical route than anything properly distinguishable from the forest either side. The lake was further than Graeder had indicated, maybe closer to a kilometre, but they made good time in the pleasant afternoon air and soon could make out the glint of water through the trees.

At the lake there was nothing to indicate this was a place

different from any other forested lake-shore on the planet. They stood, looking around, for a minute or two in case they had overlooked something.

There was suddenly a creak, from the forest to the left, and a carefully camouflaged wooden hatch opened up, just off the path. A woman jumped out at speed, holding a longarm firmly against her shoulder as she approached, the weapon trained steadily on Taeris. She looked calm and composed, not taking her eyes from Taeris.

"Hello brother, the Republic has been broadcasting news of your death, so I assumed you were well," she said, "I'm afraid I have to tell you that this man beside you is Legate Taeris of the Republic."

Faeral laughed out loud. "I know, Vaeral mich. Lower the rifle and I'll tell you everything."

"He is a liar. He speaks Aepolian as well as I do." No sign that the rifle was going to be lowered.

Taeris actually laughed. "I am a liar. I'm also a traitor and a murderer so I think liar's quite a way down my list of crimes."

Faeral became more serious. "Put the gun down, Vaeral. He is an enemy of the Republic now, just as much as you or I."

Slowly, very slowly, as if she thought that the moment her weapon was lowered Taeris would leap on her, Vaeral swung the barrel of the rifle down to point at the ground. "I'm taking a lot on trust here, Faeral."

Faeral stepped forward and threw his arms around his sister in a great hug. "I've missed you."

Vaeral returned the embrace, but kept her eyes firmly on Taeris. Even as she stepped aside and indicated that the group should go into the secret underground hide she didn't let him slip from her sight and she waved him ahead of her into the passage.

Compared with the underground complex where Taeris and Vaeral had first met, this was a small and stale hole. Vaeral had done her best to keep things orderly but it seemed airless and damp, her supplies were piled in one corner, her bedding in another. She sat on a ledge that ran around the walls, carved directly into the earth itself, the only thing that looked remotely comfortable in the dark chamber. One by one everyone found seats along the same ledge. Laesa, in particular, had an unhappy expression on her face as this was not the level of comfort to which she was usually accustomed. As far as Taeris could tell Vaeral was alone here, but that didn't necessarily imply she had no allies at all.

Laesa wanted to start speaking, but Taeris shook his head at her. He was much more familiar with the traditions of the Aepolians and it was impolite to speak before the host had a chance to welcome the visitors.

Welcoming visitors didn't seem to be the foremost thought on Vaeral's mind, however. She asked Faeral, "What is this drozgizze doing here?"

Taeris nodded. "I deserve that."

Vaeral turned to him. "They call you 'Ze zizmidaya thaedrozgarde', did you know that?"

Laesa looked lost, not speaking Aepolian. Taeris translated for her. "The corpsemaker. Well maybe I am nothing but a troskisse, a murder-weapon, but I'm a weapon in your brother's hand now."

Vaeral's every instinct must have been telling her to kill the Legate while she could, but she looked to Faeral instead.

"He's with us, now. He will be very useful." Faeral spoke with a level, final tone.

Vaeral eventually nodded. "So your pet izze will fight for

us. We have no army, thanks to him."

Faeral nodded agreement. "And, it seems, not much of a fleet either. One thing at a time, however. First we have to make a move to more suitable surroundings. Somewhere larger, safer and with power, communications and supplies."

Vaeral scowled, presumably she hated the idea of showing these potential enemies to a location the rebels considered important. Taeris, again, had to consider her with respect. She was hiding in a damp hole rather than risk her presence in more comfortable surroundings revealing anything about the rebellion.

Laesa sat up much straighter at that, since the description implied a level of comfort far above a hole in the ground, and asked, "Where are we going?"

Faeral threw his arms wide and grinned at her. "Catwater Castle."

Acknowledgements

This book would have been possible without the assistance of other people but it wouldn't have been the same book and it would have been far less enjoyable to write...

Firstly I must thank my parents for their unending support, my friends for their enthusiastic encouragement and James for his notes.

Secondly I must thank Dagmar, Abby and James at The Java House in Faversham for keeping me sane and caffeinated while working.

Thirdly I must thank the people at Faversham Library and all the pubs and restaurants in Faversham who let me work quietly without the faintest hint of complaint.

Finally I must thank Graham Guy for his extraordinary efforts. His part in making the book is notable, his part in making the author is incalculable.

Thank you.